MATTHEW FLINDERS' CAT

BRYCE COURTENAY

MATTHEW FLINDERS' CAT

VIKING
an imprint of
PENGUIN BOOKS

Further information about the author can be found at www.brycecourtenay.com

Viking

Published by the Penguin Group
Penguin Books Australia Ltd
250 Camberwell Road, Camberwell, Victoria 3124, Australia
Penguin Books Ltd
80 Strand, London WC2R 0RL, England
Penguin Putnam Inc.
375 Hudson Street, New York, New York 10014, USA
Penguin Books, a division of Pearson Canada
10 Alcorn Avenue, Toronto, Ontario, Canada M4V 3B2
Penguin Books (NZ) Ltd
Cnr Rosedale and Airborne Roads, Albany, Auckland, New Zealand
Penguin Books (South Africa) (Pty) Ltd
24 Sturdee Avenue, Rosebank, Johannesburg 2196, South Africa
Penguin Books India (P) Ltd
11, Community Centre, Panchsheel Park, New Delhi 110 017, India

First published by Penguin Books Australia Ltd 2002

1 3 5 7 9 10 8 6 4 2

Cover design by Cathy Larsen, Penguin Design Studio
Text design by Tony Palmer, Penguin Design Studio
Cover photograph by Tim de Neefe
Ship illustration by Craig McGill
Author photograph by Graham McCarter
Detail of General Chart of Terra Australis 1814 from Mitchell Library,
State Library of New South Wales
Strange Fruit (Lewis Allan) © Lyrics reproduced with kind permission by J Albert & Son Pty Ltd
Typeset in 12/17 pt Sabon by Post Pre-press Group, Brisbane, Queensland
Printed and bound in Australia by McPherson's Printing Group, Maryborough, Victoria

National Library of Australia
Cataloguing-in-Publication data:

Courtenay, Bryce, 1933– .
Matthew Flinders' cat.

ISBN 0 670 91061 9.

I. Title.

A823.3

WRITERS' BLOC

THE READER IS ALWAYS RIGHT

www.penguin.com.au

For Dorothy Gliksman

*

Also
The Salvation Army

&

Jeff and Alina Gambin
of the Just Enough Faith Food Van

ACKNOWLEDGEMENTS

Authors such as me wouldn't get very far without the generous help others afford them. Readers sometimes ask me where I learn all the stuff in my books and the answer, of course, is that I borrow material from minds far better than my own. Those of us who write are literary magpies gathering bright objects for later use in our work.

For all the bright objects in this book I thank the names that follow. Firstly, my partner Dorothy Gliksman on two counts: she gave me the space to write uninterrupted, and she was my first proofreader. Her suggestions were always considered and wise.

Then my thanks to Celia Jarvis, who was again the principal researcher on this book and, as always, did more than I could possibly have asked from her, often working through the night to keep up with my not always reasonable demands. I cannot thank you enough.

There were the others who gave unstintingly of their knowledge and offered help. From the Salvation Army, Gerard Byrne, Major Cliff Randall, Christine Garvan, Major Kevin McGrath, Vincent Byrne, Captain Paul Moulds and Annie Winn, I thank you all.

At St Vincent's Hospital, Associate Professor Gordian Fulde and his staff in the Emergency Department.

Senior mental health worker at The Station, Danny Gibson. The Just Enough Faith food van, Jeff and Alina Gambin, who feed the destitute, the homeless and the hungry every night of the week. Alcoholics Anonymous, Mission Australia, the Royal Botanic Gardens, and the NSW Department of Health. Steve Despea, my bodyguard, who accompanied me into dark corners where this book often took me. Ian Faulks from the Committee on Children and Young People, Mrs Nerida Murray, Principal of Plunkett Street Public School, Senior Constable Paul Hunter from Brisbane Central Police Station, Rick Osborne from the Albion Street Centre, Jeff Fenech from Team Fenech, Martin Mulhall, Kings Cross Police Station, William MacKenzie, Drug and Alcohol counsellor, Alan Jacobs, Consensus Market Research Analyst, Dr Michael Gliksman, Dr Irwin Light, Alex Hamill, Owen Denmeade, George Christou and any others I may have missed and who gave me advice and help.

My sincere thanks for the help I received from the following web sites: Australian Child Protection Alliance, Australian Institute of Criminology, Parliament of New South Wales, Matthew Flinders Electronic Archive, State Library of New South Wales, NSW Commission for Children and Young People, Australian Bureau of Statistics, Interpol International, The Law Society of New South Wales, Parliament of Australia, Justice for Juveniles, Department of Community Services, NIDA, and the hundreds of other sites we dipped into. Whatever the pros and cons of the Internet, it is an author's very best friend.

Dozens of books were consulted for a work such as this one and I thank all the authors who gave me of their knowledge. My special thanks to Tim Flannery for his *Terra Australis*, and to Paul Brunton for his *Matthew Flinders – personal letters from an extraordinary life*, published by the State Library of New South Wales. Their scholarship and writing on the subject of the great navigator made my task easy. Also to Sue Williams for her book *Peter Ryan: The Inside Story* and to Dr W. F. Glaser for his paper, 'Paedophilia: The Public Health Problem of the Decade', Australian Institute of Criminology Conference, University of Sydney, 14–15 April 1997.

Finally, my heartfelt thanks to my publishing family at Penguin who help so very much. My publisher Clare Forster, Peter Field, Bob Sessions, Julie Gibbs, Gabrielle Coyne, Peter Blake, Ali

ACKNOWLEDGEMENTS

Watts, Anne Rogan, Cathy Larsen, Tony Palmer, Leah Maarse, Mark Evans, Katie Purvis, Elizabeth Hardy, Danielle Roller, Louise O'Leary, Stephanie Rhodes, Leonie Stott and Beverley Waldron.

But always, last and most, Kay Ronai, my editor, who saw me through the bad times in a book that wasn't always easy to write. Without your help, the task would have proved beyond me.

BOOK
ONE

CHAPTER ONE

Billy O'Shannessy woke to the raucous laughter of two
kookaburras seated on top of adjacent telegraph poles.
The birds, whom he had christened Arthur and Martha,
were like a married couple who could only communicate
by insulting each other and stayed together out of sheer
spite. Much as he resented Arthur and Martha's intrusion
into his hangover, they served as his regular alarm clock.

Billy lay still for a few moments longer, staring through
the canopy of leaves directly above him. The bench he lay
on was within a small public garden sandwiched between
the side wall of the State Library and Macquarie Street. At
this time of the morning the flow of traffic had almost
ceased and, with only an occasional early jogger passing on
the way to the Royal Botanic Gardens, the city had an
empty feel. It was as if the towering architecture set so
close to the magnificent gardens was a mirage imposed on

a native landscape where the birds assumed, as always, the responsibility of opening the day.

Despite his usual condition upon waking, Billy always felt as if he alone was the human component to the coming of dawn in the city. Now he waited for the correct opening sequence to occur. The new day was always prematurely announced by the two kookaburras quarrelling in the dark. In between the raucous cackle of Arthur and Martha, Billy listened for the high-pitched screeching of flying foxes returning to their roosts in the Royal Botanic Gardens directly across the road from the library. Their dark tent-like shapes filled the pre-dawn sky and he imagined them as sky-sweepers, sent up to capture the darkness and to fold down the night. In a few minutes, with the coming of first light, he would begin to hear the persistent cries of the currawongs and, shortly after, the carolling of magpies. This was the correct order nature employed to open a bright new summer's day in Sydney, the city of burnished light.

Billy gripped the handle of the briefcase that lay on his chest and was handcuffed to his left wrist. He lifted the briefcase and sat up slowly, placing it beside him on the bench. His head ached from last night's booze, though not too badly. He'd known it to be a lot worse. Then he became aware that his right leg was painful and that the blood supply below the knee seemed to have been cut off. It was the knee that constantly gave him trouble and would sometimes collapse without warning. He started to massage it gently with his right hand, feeling the slight indentation where the last slat at the edge of the bench had pressed against the side of his knee. His leg must have slipped over the edge during the night. After a while, the pins and needles ceased and his knee settled down to its usual dull, early morning ache.

Still a little bleary-eyed and with his hand trembling, he reached for a solid-looking brass key that hung from a chain about his neck. He removed the chain and, with some difficulty, positioned the key into the lock of the handcuff clasped about his left wrist and unlocked the cuff. Bending, he clipped it to the leg of the bench, slipping the chain back over his head.

Billy stood up, testing his gammy leg with a tentative first step. The need to empty his bladder made him ignore the pain and he moved unsteadily towards a clump of palm trees and tree ferns at the extreme perimeter of his sleeping quarters. The foliage was sufficiently dense to conceal him from the early traffic just beginning to flow in to Macquarie Street. Normally he would have been loath to soil the environs of his arboreal bedchamber but the added pain to his knee would delay his progress to the toilets at Martin Place railway station.

He had no sooner done the deed, zipped himself back to respectability and moved out of the foliage than he saw a boy standing beside the bench where he'd left his briefcase. Billy panicked. 'Hey, you!' he shouted out.

The boy turned slowly towards him, then looked away again. He carried a skateboard under his arm and did not appear in the least disturbed by Billy's warning shout.

Billy hobbled over, his heart pounding. If the boy was a street kid he could be in for real trouble, though the need to protect his briefcase overcame his fear. As he drew closer he shouted, 'What do you want? That's my property!'

The boy faced him and it was as if he was seeing Billy clearly for the first time. Ignoring Billy's outburst, he pointed to the wall of the library. 'That your cat?' he asked.

'You leave my briefcase alone!' Billy warned, wagging his finger. With a sweep of his arm, he shouted, 'Go on, get going!'

The boy, unfazed, glanced down at the briefcase handcuffed to the leg of the bench. 'That yours? What's innit?'

'None of your business!'

'Yiz a derro, it'll just be junk,' the boy said dismissively. 'Like them bag ladies pushin' old prams with plastic bags in 'em.' Then, losing interest in the briefcase, he looked back at the library wall. 'Don't suppose derros have cats, dogs sometimes, but not cats, eh?'

Billy saw that the boy was no more than ten or eleven and therefore less of a threat than he'd at first supposed. 'Cat? What cat?' he asked.

'That one, on the winda ledge over there.'

'Oh, you mean Trim?' Billy glanced at the windowsill where the statue of Trim stood with his paw in the air and his head slightly raised as if looking at something. At first glance it would be quite possible to mistake the life-sized bronze for a real cat.

'Yeah? That its name?'

'*Was* his name, he's long dead.'

The boy squinted, attempting to look more closely. 'It stuffed? What's it doin' up there?'

Billy realised that the boy must be short-sighted. 'It's a memorial to a dead cat whose name was Trim.'

'That like a gravestone?'

'No, it's a bronze figure.' Billy, who had reached the bench, now sank slowly onto his good knee and proceeded to unlock the handcuff from the leg of the bench. He stood up painfully, holding the briefcase in his left hand, while his right hand gripped and pushed up hard from the edge of the bench.

The boy stood watching, then asked, 'Why'd they make a statue of a cat?'

Billy sighed. It wasn't going to be easy to get rid of the brat. 'Trim was a very famous cat in history.' He pointed to the large bronze figure on a granite plinth that stood four or five metres in front of Trim and helped to conceal Billy's bench from the street. 'He belonged to that man, Matthew Flinders, a famous navigator and explorer.'

The boy looked up at the statue and cast a doubtful look at Billy. 'Cats don't get famous, only people.'

'Well, as a matter of fact, you're wrong, this one did.'

'That's bull, explorers don't take cats with them, dogs maybe for huntin'!'

It was an unexpected reply and told Billy the boy was intelligent and thought he was being patronised.

'He was a seagoing cat.' Billy looked about him as if trying to decide the easiest way to escape. 'Look here, boy, I have to be going now.'

The kid ignored him. Pointing at the statue of Flinders again, he said, 'You just said he was an explorer.'

'Well, yes, a navigator and an explorer, he took his cat with him when he went exploring the Australian coastline.'

'You mean the cat stayed on the ship?'

'Hmm, not always, but you're right, Trim was a ship's cat, the most famous ship's cat that ever was.'

The boy looked up at Billy. 'How come you don't talk like no derro?'

Billy sighed, 'I'm a derelict by choice. As for my grammar, it was my misfortune to be born into the wrong family.'

The boy suddenly paused. 'Cops,' he said in a low voice. He quickly crossed the small courtyard on his skateboard and, instead of taking the pathway, he did an ollie, jumping high over a bed of native iris and landing on the other side, his skateboard wheels hitting hard onto the pavement. Moments later, Billy heard the skateboard jump the kerb and rumble across Macquarie Street. Billy knew the boy couldn't have seen the policeman, that is, if there was one approaching.

Billy followed him. If the boy was correct, he'd better be on his way. There was no time to shackle the briefcase to his wrist and, with handcuffs dangling, he made his way onto the pavement via a small pathway, reaching the pavement at almost the same time as the police officer reached him. Abruptly he walked away, increasing his pace, though his knee hurt like hell.

'Hey, not so fast!' the police officer called after him.

Billy turned, 'Who? Me?' he asked, trying to look unconcerned.

'It's Billy O'Shannessy, ain't it?' Without waiting for a reply, the policeman continued, 'Yeah, I recognise the face. Bit late this mornin', ain'tcha?'

Billy attempted a smile, 'Yes, a little, must have slept in, officer.'

'Know the feeling, hard to get out of a nice warm bed, eh?'

Billy glanced up at the big cop for the first time, trying to see if the joke was intentional. The policeman had a grin on his face and Billy felt momentarily reassured.

The policeman, a three-striper, smiled, then jerked his head to one side, 'Better get going, mate, you know the rules, no loitering around the library.'

'Thank you, officer.' He now recognised the man as Orr, Sergeant Phillip Orr, the sergeant-at-arms at Parliament House, the building next door to the library. He'd once cross-examined him in the late eighties when Orr had been a witness in a case involving a Liberal politician and a television reporter who'd had an altercation leading to a fist fight on the steps of the State Parliament. He now remembered the reason for the fight. It had something to do with the reporter asking the politician if he'd known about a prominent judge who'd been arrested for child molestation and whose case had simply been removed from the police files. The point, if he remembered correctly, and Billy usually remembered correctly, was because the politician had been the shadow minister for the Department of Community Services (DOCS).

Orr had appeared on behalf of the politician. Billy had

lost the case for the television station on the evidence of the police sergeant, who stated that the reporter had provoked the politician well beyond reasonable limits, but he couldn't remember if there'd been any particular incident involving himself and Orr at the time.

However, he now recalled that although the Liberal–National coalition won the 1991 election, replacing Labor, the publicity surrounding the case was said to have cost the politician his seat. The new government had promptly appointed him to a senior position in DOCS in lieu of the ministry he'd been promised. There had been the usual five-minute 'perks for ex-pollies' outcry where the premier had pointed out that New South Wales couldn't afford to lose a man of such outstanding ability, integrity and blah, blah, blah, and it had all gone away.

Billy's massive fall from grace was, of course, well known among legal circles as well as to many of the older policemen and that's how he guessed Orr would have recognised him. 'Just on my way now, sergeant,' Billy said meekly.

'Be good then,' Sergeant Orr called, 'Never you worry, Billy, the bench'll still be there when you get back tonight.' He grinned, 'I'll attend to it, personal.'

Billy didn't reply, the policeman calling him Billy he knew was a deliberate insult. Orr would regard the familiarity as some sort of natural justice. Billy told himself he was long past caring about such things. He had no status to preserve and the past was gone. He spent most of his waking hours trying to forget it. He recalled a fellow derelict who'd once said to him, in a particularly sanguine piece of advice, 'They can call me dogshit if they want, as long as the bastards leave me alone.' He'd already said too much to Orr. One of the few principles the homeless try to maintain is to avoid talking to the police. There was even a name for it, you were 'a dog' if you were seen talking to the law.

Turning his back on the policeman, he commenced to walk down Macquarie Street towards the Quay as quickly as his leg permitted, the handcuffs banging against the worn leather of his ancient briefcase.

However, it seemed the policeman wasn't quite through with him. 'Hey, Billy, them handcuffs, where'd you get 'em?'

Billy stopped but didn't turn around.

'Handcuffs! Where'd you get 'em?' Sergeant Orr repeated, this time in a slightly sterner voice.

Billy was forced to turn around. 'They're American, Confederate Army issue, 1875.'

'Yeah? Lemme take a look.'

Billy now had to wait while Orr approached. 'I have every right to own them,' he said defensively.

'Not so sure about that, Billy. Can't have every Tom, Dick and Harry walking around with a pair of handcuffs now, can we?' The police sergeant winked at Billy, 'Unless of course you're into S & M?'

Orr was playing the Billy card for all it was worth. 'They're to keep my things safe, officer.' Billy pointed to the open handcuff that hung from the handle of his briefcase. 'I usually wear that one around my left wrist.'

The policeman raised one eyebrow, 'Come now, Billy, you know better than that? Only police officers are allowed to own handcuffs and only crims are authorised to wear them. That is, them and prison officers, not even the private security blokes. No one else, it's against the law.' Billy could see that Orr was beginning to enjoy himself. That he'd decided not to let him go on his way.

Billy knew that no such law existed. 'They're not standard issue, sergeant, not regulation, they qualify as genuine antiques, a collector's item.'

'Oh, is that so? Antiques, is it? Valuable then, eh?' The policeman reached down and examined the handcuffs, which were plainly quite different in their configuration from the ones he carried on his belt. 'What's so important that it needs to be handcuffed around your wrist?' He looked at Billy sternly, 'Maybe I'd better take a look, eh?'

Billy drew back, unable to conceal his anxiety from the policeman. There was nothing in the briefcase that could be thought of as contraband or even valuable, except perhaps the handcuffs themselves, but his briefcase contained all that remained of his private life. The thought of Orr's big paws rummaging through his personal possessions was more than Billy could bear. He could demand that Orr produce a search warrant, but he knew how provocative that would seem. The cop had been mocking him all along, but he'd nevertheless been pleasant enough. He accepted that policemen hate defence lawyers, particularly the ones who regularly got their clients acquitted. 'Please, sergeant, it's just, you know, my personal things, bits 'n' pieces.' He recalled what the boy had said earlier about his briefcase. Attempting a grin, he added, 'I'm afraid I'm a bit of a bag lady.'

'Nothing stolen, eh? Drugs? Block of hash? Some pot?' Billy knew Orr was having him on, playing a game when he knew Billy couldn't come back with a clever rebuttal. This wasn't the courtroom, where a suitably acerbic comment could put an officer of the law in his place. Again he wondered what he might have said when Orr had been in the witness box.

'No, sir, please, sir, you know me. I'm a derelict, there's nothing else!' Billy knew precisely the tone of voice the police sergeant required of him, though he hated himself for his sycophancy.

The big policeman looked at Billy and grinned, he had achieved his purpose. By thoroughly humiliating Billy, he could now afford to be magnanimous. He glanced at his watch, possibly remembering that he had a train to catch, then looked back at Billy, 'Righto, on yer bicycle, son, 'ave a nice day.'

'Yes, thank you, officer,' Billy said softly, accepting this final insult. He turned quickly to where he intended to cross at Shakespeare Place, but the sudden movement caused his bad knee to give and he toppled to the pavement.

The policeman stepped toward him, grabbed him by the back of his shirt collar and hefted him onto his feet. 'You orright?' he asked.

'Yes, thank you, it's . . . it's my leg,' Billy stammered, shaken by the fall. 'I . . . I . . . woke up this morning with a gammy leg. Bad knee, you see.' He could sense how pathetic he sounded.

The policeman nodded in the direction of Sydney Hospital, the next building on from Parliament House, 'Have the hospital take a look, tell them I sent you. Sergeant Phillip Orr, they know me there.'

Billy smiled weakly, 'Yes, thank you, sergeant, I'll tell them.' By supplying his name, it was obvious Orr thought Billy would not have recalled their previous encounter.

The policeman looked to see what traffic was approaching up Macquarie Street and then raced across the road, dodging between an oncoming white laundry van and a taxi approaching from the opposite side of the road. Billy watched as Orr turned down Bent Street, half running. He waited until the light changed to green and crossed Shakespeare Place, keeping to the Gardens side of Macquarie Street. For some strange reason, probably the adrenaline pumping into his system as a result of the fall, his knee felt considerably better.

It occurred to Billy, who, like most drunks, was somewhat paranoid, that Orr might have so enjoyed the banter that it would become a regular morning occurrence. In his experience bullies were like that, returning day after day to repeat their intimidation and to enjoy the fear and humiliation it brought about in their victims. Orr was the archetypal beer-gut sergeant whose time had passed and, as further promotion was unlikely, he possessed a highly developed sense of injustice against his calling. Billy was simply someone to humiliate, a way of venting his frustration.

Billy had experienced the same thing with several older cops, who were apt to show more interest in him than any of the other drunks in the area. They would bail him up on a fairly regular basis, curious to see if the grog had destroyed his once famous legal brain.

The standard routine employed by the homeless drunk was to shout and hurl abuse when a police officer pulled him up. Most younger officers simply couldn't be bothered going through the routine of an arrest and the subsequent paperwork involved and so moved on. But creating a fuss when cornered wasn't something Billy knew how to do. Moreover, he'd long since given up trying to behave like a gentleman, which policemen such as Orr simply saw as an attempt to appear superior and took great pleasure in disabusing him of this notion. Now, when confronted, Billy made a point of showing how his brain had become addled by alcohol and that he was a pathetic, harmless creature. Criminal lawyers are, after all, good actors and playing the role of a gormless drunk wasn't difficult. It was what a certain class of older police officer required, the satisfaction of confirming how far the mighty have fallen. For the most part the police would ask a few questions, cluck their tongues, shake their heads and move on. It was unusual for such a confrontation to go as long as it had with Orr, and Billy was annoyed that he hadn't adopted his role of brain-dead drunk immediately.

Billy again tried to recall whether he had given Sergeant Orr a hard time when he'd had him in the witness box, but nothing came readily to mind. Policemen have long memories and it doesn't take much for them to feel slighted by defence counsel. There was an old saying among the constabulary: *If the Law is an ass, then the lawyers do the braying and the police do the donkey work.* Most older police officers who appeared for the prosecution deeply resented seeing months of painstakingly gathered evidence swept away by what they regarded as smooth-talking, pettifogging criminal lawyers.

Billy contemplated finding another place to sleep. He'd been sprung twice there in one morning. First by the kid, who on the face of it seemed harmless enough, then by the big cop. Was this a warning? You never could tell with street kids. What if the boy belonged to a gang? They'd come back on pension day to rob him.

Billy loved this part of the city, it was where he had practised as a barrister. The Botanic Gardens had been his private joy since he'd been a junior in a law firm when, each lunch break, he would take his cheese and pickle sandwiches and a bottle of milk to sit on a particular bench beside a small pond. The thought of moving from his summer residence, located as it was in this, the most beautiful part of the inner city, filled him with a terrible anxiety. The bench under the ficus tree beside the library wall and within spitting distance of the Gardens was now as much a home to him as the Eastern Suburbs mansion he'd once occupied.

He knew that he was taking a risk by staying; street kids depended on pension and dole days almost as much as the recipients themselves, and there could scarcely have been a drunk in the Woolloomooloo, Kings Cross, Darlinghurst or Surry Hills area who hadn't been robbed by a bunch of feral kids. The dispossessed children roving the area lived without the luxury of conscience, they were ruthless and unfeeling and, like all predators, they looked for the already wounded, the easy victims. In a perverse sort of way, the feral kids were a part of the street culture, many already dependent on hard drugs, and while they were to be greatly feared, they were part of the environment in which the alcoholic learns to survive. There were worse around.

Like most homeless people, Billy feared the thrill-seekers the most. They were the young hoons who came from a background of so-called respectable parents with homes in the outer suburbs. While the street kids robbed you, they usually left you unharmed. If you resisted, they'd give you a bit of a kicking, then leave you to sleep it off. It wasn't nice, but then it wasn't life-threatening. The feral kids weren't silly enough to kill their major source of income. The rampaging youths who came into the inner city mostly on the weekends were quite a different matter. They liked to kick and maim, and if they found a drunk unconscious in an alley, they would soak him with the remains of the metho he'd been drinking and set him alight. They were more interested in persecution and gratuitous violence than the few dollars they might take from a drunk.

Now, on his own again, Billy began to feel somewhat calmer. The boy had seemed uninterested in his briefcase, dismissing it as commonplace, he also seemed quite intelligent so Billy argued with himself that there was a good chance he'd leave him alone. In the case of Sergeant Phillip Orr, had it not been for Billy's sore knee, his need to urinate and his conversation with the boy, he would have been well gone before the policeman came off duty at six.

Billy sat himself down in a bus shelter and locked the handcuff back around his left wrist. Only when the briefcase was shackled to his person did he ever feel truly secure. His greatest fears were that the briefcase would be taken from him in a bashing or he'd forget where he'd left it during a drinking bout.

The scuffed briefcase carried an odd assortment of bits and pieces, each of which represented some small, sane purpose in his life, a reminder that he was still in contact with some aspects of reality. Some of it was essentially practical, such as a bottle-opener and corkscrew combination, a tin-opener, his spectacles, a pair of nail clippers, his knife, fork and spoon, a box of matches, as well as several short pieces of string and three corks of various sizes, to be used when he lost the top to a bottle of scotch or, for that matter, a bottle of anything else he might be drinking if he couldn't afford his favourite tipple.

More unexpected was a bundle of press-clippings, all of them of single-column width and the longest no more than twenty centimetres. Some appeared yellowed with age while others were of more recent origin, all held together by a large black bulldog clip. Also in the briefcase was a plastic raincoat, a packet of rat-poison pellets and a box of disposable surgical gloves and, next to this, a battered barrister's wig.

In a tiny leather pouch, greasy from being handled, were three small polished pebbles, one of them rose granite, the second a tiger's eye and the last a clear green chrysoprase. Each pebble was approximately the size of a ten-cent piece and had a distinct function, depending on the calibre of the hangover Billy might possess on any given morning. He would often wake up with his mouth so dry that his tongue was stuck to its roof. If his hangover came from the luxury of drinking scotch the previous night, he would pop the tiger's eye into his mouth and suck on it until he had produced sufficient saliva to allow him to clear his throat without gagging. If his tipple had been moselle or port, known as monkey's blood, he'd choose the green chrysoprase, or if rum or brandy, the rose granite. While he couldn't remember how he'd first acquired the habit of sucking the appropriate stone, he was convinced that the stones had magical properties, so using the wrong stone would mean his headache would last all day.

The next item in the briefcase was a photo album, about twenty-three centimetres high and twelve centimetres wide. It held two dozen clear cellophane envelopes though not all of them contained a photograph. To the casual observer, there seemed to be the usual random selection of family pictures. The first page started with a black-and-white snap of a very attractive, slender young woman in a bridal gown, though closer examination of the album revealed that the following seven pages showed the same woman, each print taken a few years apart, moving from the early black and white snaps to colour photos. In each photo, the woman had become increasingly plump until, on the final page, she was hardly recognisable, a huge, obese woman in a shapeless blue cotton tent. Her hair was untidy and she squinted at the camera, her expression decidedly grumpy, as if she greatly resented the intrusion of the lens.

The next set of seven pictures appeared to be the usual melange of childhood snaps, all in colour, starting with a baby in a richly decorated and enamelled Victorian cot. The photos also seemed to progress in periods of about three years, the second photograph showing a little girl standing behind a doll's pram. She was wearing white socks, nearly up to her knees, and a pink organza dress with a matching ribbon in her hair. In the next photo the girl seemed to be about six years old and in her first school uniform, her Panama hat throwing a dark shadow over the top half of her pretty face. Then there was the same girl, around nine or ten, wearing riding breeches, jacket and cap, seated on the back of a palomino pony. Next followed an image of her as a nicely tanned teenager in a white bikini, holding a cone containing an extravagant whirl of green ice-cream, which she observed with a cross-eyed and comical expression, her pink tongue about to wind itself about the icy swirl. After this there seemed to be a somewhat larger division in time, perhaps five or six years. The next picture was a close-up of a very pretty young woman in her early twenties wearing a cap and gown. It was obviously taken at a graduation ceremony as two out-of-focus images of students, also in cap and gown, were in the background, against the cloisters in the main quad of

Sydney University. The final photograph, closer in time to the graduation shot, showed the girl wearing the same wedding gown as the woman on the first page of the album. Both her pose and her physical resemblance to the original woman were uncanny, as if the film in the camera had somehow been wound back to the first exposure thirty or so years earlier.

The two women in the album were obviously mother and daughter, and if they were also Billy's wife and child then it had to be said the girl had inherited none of her looks from her father. The O'Shannessy lineage had clearly been subjected to a severe case of gene swamp by his wife's side of the family.

After the daughter's wedding picture, the next seven pages in the album were vacant, although more careful scrutiny of the cellophane envelopes would have shown that they'd been disturbed and several of them had minute tears at the top corners where a photograph had been removed. It was curious that not a single picture of Billy existed.

If the person viewing the album had continued turning the seven blank leaves until they reached the eighth page, they would have come across one final photograph showing a large tabby cat sitting on the polished, grey-granite apron of a gravesite.

The cat was seated on its haunches, obscuring most of the inscription on the headstone behind it, although above its head the name 'Charlie' was carved and etched in white into the grey granite. It was as if the cat was posing rather grandly under its own name, but the camera shutter had captured the cat in the process of licking its chops, its pink tongue obscuring its nose.

The last items to be found in the briefcase were a dozen spiral-bound reporter's notepads of the kind you can purchase at any newsagency as well as two biros, one blue, the other red. They, more than anything, served to keep Billy anchored to the world outside his life on the street. Billy had become an inveterate correspondent to the letters column of the *Sydney Morning Herald*, where under the pseudonym 'Billy Goat' he had become a regular and popular contributor.

Billy told himself that alcoholism and writing enjoyed a long history together. While he had never had anything outside of an occasional legal opinion published in the *Law Society Journal*, he nevertheless cherished the thought of becoming an essayist. He was convinced that, given his interest in the botanical differences that made Australia's flora unique in the world, he had a subject waiting to be exploited. The average person knew nothing about Australia's ecosystem and it led to the land being constantly raped. Eighty-five per cent of the world's plant species were indigenous to Australia and most of its citizens couldn't tell a dahlia from a chrysanthemum, let alone identify any of the native species. We had conned ourselves into believing that the European floral impostors that filled our parks and suburban gardens in spring and summer gave us our sense of truth, yet these intruders had turned our seasons upside-down and were preferred to the glory of our winter-flowering indigenous plants. Even the neatly clipped lawns we so cherished were constructed from imported grasses that had no right in gobbling up the precious water resources of the driest land on earth.

Billy's big problem was getting the essays he wrote in his head onto paper. His obsessive personality allowed him to write the essays in his imagination with a white-hot intensity, so that they were all-persuasive, wondrously original and solidly wrought in argument. But when it came to writing the essays in the notepads, his information appeared insubstantial and contrived or, worse still, the ravings of an ecology nut.

The truth was that he seldom remained sober long enough to write an outline and do the required research in the library. His spiral notepads were filled with jottings and promising beginnings, most of which ended abruptly, his neat handwriting slipping into illegibility. Billy set himself high standards and was his harshest critic, so that his red biro, used for crossing out errant sentences, dominated every page.

Billy's brief and often blistering missives sent to the *Sydney Morning Herald* and, as often as not, accepted for publication, were his only reassurance that somewhere deep down inside him there was a writer trying to get out, an essayist with a profound message.

With the briefcase securely handcuffed to his wrist, Billy continued on his way towards the Quay. He cast his mind back to the moments before the police sergeant had interrupted his conversation with the boy. The lad had thought the cat real and, possibly, that it belonged to Billy. In a funny way he'd been right. Billy would sometimes, usually when he was half-cut, look up at the statue of Trim and wish him good evening and even have a bit of a chat. On other occasions, as the night continued and he became more and more pissed, the conversation with Trim would get quite animated. There were even times, usually when he was reduced to drinking monkey's blood, that Billy would think he was Baby Grand, the cat in the last photograph in his album, and then he'd happily chat, cat to cat, for several hours. Billy was an unabashed cat lover and, when sober, liked to think that any nation who would honour a cat meant all was not lost. The statue of Trim on the window ledge above his bench was yet another reason why he had no wish to relocate.

Billy now asked himself what he would have told the boy about Trim had they been able to talk a little longer. How would a young lad such as this one ever come to possess a sense of history and some understanding of who he was and where he had come from? Billy had no illusions about himself, he accepted that his drinking was a choice he'd made himself. He also accepted that he was weak and gutless. Having been given every opportunity to succeed, he had failed miserably. Blaming the dreaded grog he knew was pointless, the reason he was a drunk had little or nothing to do with a genetic weakness. His more or less constant state of inebriation allowed him to pull a curtain over the past and, except for rare moments, he'd managed to build a successful screen.

But what of the boy? He knew nothing about the kid, though his expression, the look in his eyes, told him enough. Was the lad already among the doomed, destined to serve his time on the streets until he inevitably experimented with his first drugs? He seemed bright enough, alert to what was happening around him. Billy knew that the progression from what is euphemistically known as a 'recreational' drug, usually marijuana or ecstasy, to heroin was a fairly short one. Once addicted, a street kid would need to pay for his habit. Being under-age, he would become the perfect bait for paedophiles, which would inevitably lead him to 'The Wall' at Darlinghurst, the high outer stone wall that formed part of the old Darlinghurst prison, where young male prostitutes plied their trade. Any kind of rescue after this would be extremely rare.

What happened to the boy with the skateboard was none of Billy's business, he couldn't do anything for him anyway and if he did meet him again, it would probably be to cop the toe of the kid's runner in his face. Nevertheless, the image of the boy persisted in his mind.

Billy smiled to himself at the boy mistaking the statue of Trim for a real cat. If Orr hadn't arrived, the least he could have done was tell the boy to go to the Eye Hospital in Woolloomooloo and have his eyes tested. Then he recalled that the Eye Hospital had moved and the building it had occupied was in the process of being converted into apartments. Its close proximity to the city, the Harbour and the Gardens made it one of the projects favoured by a nationwide developer attempting to gentrify the essentially working-class suburb. The famous Finger Wharf, with its warehouses near the same location, was another project designated as luxury accommodation for wealthy bankers, brokers and media folk. In the end the rich got everything worthwhile while the poor were moved along. With the Olympic Games coming to Sydney in four years, the state government would want the poor tucked away out of sight.

Instead, he would have had to take the lad to Sydney Hospital in Macquarie Street where the police sergeant had suggested he go for his leg. It wasn't more than a hundred and fifty metres from the library. For a moment Billy imagined himself turning up with the boy, but now doubted that he would have gone. In his day, kids didn't like being called 'four eyes' and it would still be the same. Glasses weren't tough and such a boy would need to think of himself as tough.

One thing led to another and Billy began to think how he might have told the story of Trim if the boy hadn't left. Would the boy enjoy a history lesson? Probably not. He'd have to keep things light. How light? He stopped, looking skywards, and watched as the latecomers among the fruit bats continued coming in, wheeling above him, their wings shaped like nomad tents flapping lazily, dark silhouettes against the pale-blue sky.

Perhaps he could start by telling the boy the story of the fruit bats, how they were the only remaining colony of a rare species now threatened with extinction. He would tell him how they had found refuge in the Botanic Gardens slap-bang in the middle of a large city when tree-felling on the north coast had destroyed their natural habitat. But now the fruit bats were damaging the trees they chose to roost in and it had become a matter of nature versus nature, with the authorities scratching their heads for a solution where both the trees and the fruit bats might be saved. Billy loved trees, but he also cared about the fruit bats and he thought how typically the dilemma was of our own making. Would the boy be interested in or care about the fruit bats or the trees? Probably not.

Billy continued on his way down to the Quay, thinking now how it was that humans seemed to destroy almost everything they touched in nature. He knew this wasn't an original thought and whoever had first come up with it, probably Charles Darwin, would soon enough have realised that it was one that had little or no power to change things. Humans, like all creatures, put themselves first. The only difference was that, unlike other species, they had the power to alter the balance of nature, and it was this that made them so dangerous. History was all about greed. Enough is never quite enough.

Billy had momentarily forgotten about the boy but soon found himself thinking about him again. He told himself that his mind was like a sieve and if he couldn't get the street brat out of his head, he'd have to *think* him out of the way. He'd get on with the story about Matthew Flinders and his cat and try to make it sound like a story and not a history lesson. It would have to entertain or, at the very least, amuse the boy. Having told him the story, if only in his head, the child would become less of a distraction.

He accepted the challenge that this was the age of television, where pictures were the true language and the spoken word was merely the frame that gave them focus. In the cartoon world in which Billy assumed the boy's vocabulary largely existed, the cat would take on a far more important role than the great navigator himself. The lad had ignored the statue of Matthew Flinders, only glancing at it briefly. His sole interest was in the cat. Trim would tell his story in a way natural to a cat without wanting to alter everything to suit himself the way humans do. It would be history seen from a cat's point of view.

Billy started to imagine . . .

As it turned out, one of the world's most famous loners, Matthew Flinders, the great navigator who first mapped the coastline of a large and mysterious landmass he would eventually name Australia, was never quite alone, because, you see, he had as his constant companion and fellow explorer a tomcat named Trim.

Matthew Flinders was a ship's captain, by nature stubborn, impatient and self-righteous, much preferring his own intelligent company to that of his boorish shipmates. Trim Flinders, his cat, was quite the opposite. He was a ship's cat and, while capable of being 'quite the proper gentleman', he possessed in him the spirit of a larrikin and was given to the company of rough men and always happy in boisterous and even drunken company.

While Matthew Flinders earned their admiration and respect, he was never much liked by the men who sailed under him, but Trim received their unequivocal love. His periods of indifference, common among all cats, were always short and the seamen would hear no ill spoken of him even if sometimes he appeared to take their abounding affection for granted.

Billy was aware that he was using words that might be too complex for the boy but as this was only an early draft he would correct it later. The thing was to get the sequence down correctly. And so he continued . . .

The fact that, like most cats, Trim dozed roughly eighteen hours a day seemed to bother none of his admirers. 'Aye, he does his share o' graft does that one, never shrinks from a task given,' the bos'n might remark, pointing to Trim asleep in a patch of warm sunlight atop a water cask. 'I'll vouch there's naught of his kind on the seven seas that could take our Trim on at the ratting trade.' It was a sentiment they all shared. Trim Flinders was fireproof and could do no wrong.

Despite being constantly indulged, Trim remained a working cat and it was this work ethic that earned the crew's constant admiration. He was an intrepid hunter and more than earned his reputation as the scourge of the mice and rats which had the temerity to sneak on board at a foreign port of call or, alternatively, the extreme misfortune of being born at sea. Trim saw to it that they had a very short life expectancy.

While some mice did manage to remain safely hidden in the deepest, darkest holes and crevices the ship could provide, the rats were seldom fortunate enough to find a safe place to live. Trim was a patient and merciless hunter of the genus *Rattus*, his otherwise generous nature showing them no mercy. Should he come upon a rat's droppings or sniff its urine, he would remain concealed in the area for as long as two days and nights without taking food or water until the miscreant rodent was driven by hunger from its hiding place and straight into the deadly claws and mighty jaws of the great seagoing hunter.

Trim didn't always keep his prey and was known to be very generous on occasions. Matthew Flinders could count on finding a dead rat laid neatly on the decking beside his bunk after one of Trim's prolonged stake-outs. He was reminding his master that he always delivered and was prepared to do his share of the work while at the same time contributing to the ship's larder.

Although Trim was prepared to accept the occasional handout from the cook, he would seldom partake of a seaman's vittles. Trim ate at the officers' table, always being the first to meals. He neither meowed nor made a fuss but expected to partake of the fare on an equal footing with the other officers. Nor did he hang around the chair legs, brushing against the officers' boots and begging for scraps as might any other cat. Instead, he began each meal with his paws together and his tail neatly curled, sitting upright upon the table directly to the left of his master.

By tradition, though no one could remember when it had originally come about, the first forkful off the master's plate belonged to Trim. Matthew Flinders would solemnly cut a morsel of meat to the required size and hold it out on the end of his fork. Trim, with a great delicacy of technique and good manners, would then remove it from the tines, never touching the fork. He would remain seated and proceed to masticate, cleaning his paws and licking his chops. Moving left, in imitation of the port decanter, which would make the same journey at the conclusion of the meal, he would then seat himself to the left of the first officer and wait to receive a similar offering at the end of his fork. This process was repeated around the table until Trim found himself once again seated beside the ship's captain, though this time to the right. Nor was he a glutton. Having completed the round and in the process received a square meal, Trim would never embark on a second helping, no matter how tasty the mutton or salted beef. Trim thought himself an equal in any man's company and felt no need to be grateful for this repast. He was sufficiently arrogant to know that he could fend for himself and catch his own grub. He refused to be under an obligation to anyone for his vittles.

Billy was again conscious that a word like 'vittles' was probably beyond the boy but he was beginning to enjoy the story he was telling and was loath to stop for corrections.

A larrikin among the seamen and a gentleman among the officers was Trim Flinders, a cat admired and respected by all and about whom the opinion was often enough expressed by both officers and crew that he would have made an ideal ship's captain had he not had the misfortune of being born a cat.

In any case, Trim did not perceive his feline nature as a misfortune, nor was it likely to prohibit the vocation of ship's master, which he regarded as his right, and he behaved accordingly. He ran the ship with an iron paw, and many an errant seagull, thinking it might perch on the ship's rail or stroll along the deck on the lookout for a free feed, soon departed with a loud flapping and shrill squawking in a cloud of floating pin feathers.

It was Trim's custom to inspect the ship thrice each day. In the morning after breakfast, at precisely seven bells, he would inspect the hammocks to see that they were piped up and the between decks washed and swept. He kept to his master's instructions that the *Investigator* was consecrated to science, where slovenly methods and careless observation were the great enemy. At noon and again after the evening meal, he would patrol the main deck to ensure that the ropes were belayed and coiled fair and the sails trimmed to perfection with no possible afterthought of lifts, braces and backstays.

It was Trim's custom to perform a small concert to benefit the men after the evening inspection. For this entertainment he would choose a cockroach. There was always some fool cockroach which neglected to look twice over its varnished shoulders before venturing from its dark cracks and crannies onto a moonlit deck. Trim would pounce upon it and play with it in much the same way a boy might perform tricks with a football on the front lawn. He would juggle the cockroach with his paws while standing upright, throw it high into the air and catch it in his mouth, flick it left or right a dozen times in a blur of pawmanship or send it skating several yards across the deck. Whereupon the dazed and disoriented cockroach, thinking it had made good its escape, would attempt to scurry away. Watching it out of the corner of his eye, apparently bored with the cat-and-roach game, Trim would allow it to think it had escaped his beady eye. Then, with a sudden electrifying burst of speed, he would perform a series of paw springs and somersaults and come to land with his front paw neatly pinning the hapless insect to the deck.

The seamen, taking the evening breeze while smoking a tobacco pipe, would applaud loudly and consider themselves greatly privileged to be members of the audience in this one-cat show. Later, swinging in their hammocks in the darkness of the fo'c'sle, they would regale their shipmates with a blow-by-blow description of the evening's performance where the mighty Trim Flinders got the better of Speedy Gonzales, the dastardly Mexican cockroach.

While cockroaches and seagulls might be considered amusing to Trim, not so rats and mice. Trim ran a strictly rodent-free regime, retaining only a few rats and a handful of mice for purposes which will be explained at a later time. Those small whiskered creatures who formed the vermin community and, by virtue of cunning and good luck, managed to survive, lived for the day the ship would reach dry land. It was an accepted part of the ship's lore that when the vessel commanded by Captain Trim Flinders came into port, any rats and mice that had somehow survived the voyage would pack their bags in the dead of night and tiptoe across the deck down the gangplank to seek a berth on another ship under the command of a less ferocious cat.

If Trim was in a playful mood, which was quite often, he'd jump over a sailor's extended arm or perform all manner of tricks taught to him as a kitten. He could do somersaults and backflips, fly through a small hoop held high above a sailor's head, climb up anything, cling to a fiercely flapping sail in a breeze that would rip the canvas from a seaman's grasp, and balance majestically on a most precarious perch or atop a mast that swung through thirty degrees in a stiff ocean breeze.

There was one trick in which every man on board hoped he might at some time participate. Perhaps not really a trick, for in Trim's mind it was clearly not intended to amuse or entertain. It was a manoeuvre entirely of Trim's own invention and it only ever took place if the ship was entering a harbour preparatory to docking or putting down anchor.

With not so much as a by your leave, Trim would leap onto the back of a sailor's neck. His front paws, claws sheathed, would grip about the seaman's forehead while his rear end placed itself squarely at the base of the sailor's neck, which was flanked on either side by the hind legs to form a furry black collar, with their white tips forming a snowy clasp over the sailor's Adam's apple.

With his ears fully foxed, and his head held well above that of his human perch, Trim would observe the approaching landfall or quay and immediately commence to issue a series of meowing instructions. With his tail flicking to indicate port or starboard, Trim Flinders guided the ship to a safe berthing or anchorage.

The crew agreed among themselves that Trim Flinders was a very practical seaman. They would point out that he could as easily have found a sufficiently convenient lookout amongst the rigging but that this would have prohibited them from hearing his instructions or observing his tail. Like any good ship's master, he preferred to remain among the men. This, they insisted, was an indication that he thought of himself as one of the crew, albeit always their superior.

Bringing the ship alongside was clearly a procedure Trim was convinced could not be achieved without his personal supervision. His frequent meowing and tailed instructions would persist until the vessel was safely moored and the gangplank about to be lowered. At this point, with a rope secured to a bollard on shore, he would leap from the shoulders of his moving platform and make a dash for the foredeck where he would hop onto the ship's rail and immediately place a front paw on one of the ship's hawsers. With the grace and confidence of a seasoned tightrope-walker, he'd run along the rope spanning the gap between ship and shore so as to be the first to put a foot on dry land.

It may be that all cats, given the opportunity, could be taught to do all these things, although the most seasoned seamen aboard would swear that they had never witnessed the likes of Trim Flinders among all the ships' cats with whom they'd had the pleasure or otherwise to sail.

Seamen are experts at the business of a seagoing cat's behaviour. Unlike the average household tabby, which leads a secretive life its owners may only guess at, a ship's cat has nowhere to hide. A domestic tomcat is fortunate enough to possess his own backyard as well as any other vacant neighbourhood territory he chooses to stake out and fight to maintain. A ship's cat only has a small area above and below decks to patrol and is almost always in the process of being observed by someone. Trim Flinders, like all ships' cats, had no secrets from the humans with whom he shared his cloistered life.

On long tedious voyages, Trim's feats of derring-do often formed the prime subject of conversation among the crew, his daily exploits invariably recounted with a fair dollop of exaggeration, most of it concerning his hunting skills, his mastery of the art of acrobatics and his extraordinary sagacity. In the minds of Trim's admirers, this level of practical intelligence was placed well above that of many an admiral of the fleet.

Billy thought a moment about cats. He had always been passionate about them, and Baby Grand, the cat of his own and later Charlie's affections, had lived to be almost twenty when he'd died. In the last years of his life, Baby Grand had been in and out of the vet's so often that Billy had learned a great deal about the anatomy of a cat. In his mind he now explained to the boy why the average domestic cat is remarkable in several respects.

A cat's body contains two hundred and thirty bones, twenty-four more than a human skeleton. Its pelvis and shoulders are more loosely attached to its spine than most other four-legged beasts, which gives it extreme flexibility. Its capacity for great speed over short distances is founded in muscles that seem larger than necessary for so small a frame. Like a monkey, a cat is also equipped with a tail that provides the necessary balance when jumping or landing on a narrow branch or ledge, surface or wall.

Cats can leap from considerable heights and they do so with their backs arched and all four legs extended, which allows the shock of landing to be spread evenly and so cushion their fall. Their forelegs can turn in almost any direction so they almost never fall awkwardly or sprain a wrist or jar a heel. Their heads can turn nearly 180 degrees so that they can look to the rear without employing their shoulders. They can see well enough during the day, narrowing their pupils against the brightness, as well as exceptionally at night when their pupils expand to utilise all of the available light. Their hearing is acute and a cat can distinguish its master's footsteps on the pavement several minutes before he arrives home. Unlike most animals, they walk on their toes with the back part of their paw raised. Their paws not only hold things down but may be used to scoop, lift, grip, pat, pummel and punch.

Trim and his feline family are remarkable athletes, although they are sprinters rather than endurance runners, stalking their prey and then accelerating at high speed to make a kill, like the larger cats in the wild, particularly a cheetah stalking an antelope, which is a picture you see often enough on television.

The cat's chest cavity is small and equipped with a compact heart and lungs that tire easily, and after short bursts of high activity require long periods of rest. This narrow chest cavity allows more room for their digestive organs, which are comparatively large, suggesting that before cats discovered the comfort of humans with their meals provided on tap, they didn't always have things their own way. Large digestive organs allowed the cat to gorge on a kill and then engage in a fairly prolonged period of fasting. Which turned out to be a very useful characteristic for Trim Flinders to possess, as in the course of his ardent and adventurous life, he would endure good times and bad, and had he been born a dog, he might not have survived.

Billy was approaching Circular Quay and the New Hellas Cafe owned by Con the Greek. Constantine Poleondakis was a fifty-five-year-old widower with two unmarried adult daughters of his own and another three nieces, only one of them married and the youngest in her late teens. Con had assumed responsibility for his sister's kids when she and her husband had been buried in their bed after a mudslide hit the outskirts of their mountainside village. The mudslide took the half of the farmhouse occupied by her, her husband and the family donkey, while missing the other half where the three girls lay asleep.

Surrounded by females at home, Con's first real contact with a male his own age each day was when Billy appeared at half-past six every morning, just as Con had completed cleaning and testing his precious cappuccino machine. It was a task he would never willingly leave to one of the girls, as the New Hellas Cafe enjoyed a city-wide reputation for the quality of its coffee. By seven o'clock in the morning, the queue of commuters looking for their first caffeine fix would be twenty metres long. Con greeted each one in turn with the same words, 'In the world, the best, no questions, put down your glass, fair dinkums, myte!' Con was convinced that it was his peculiar downward pressure on the cappuccino handle that made the entire difference to the taste of his coffee. It had become a ritual, perhaps even a superstition, that the first coffee he pulled each morning to test the machine would be set aside for his good friend Billy O'Shannessy.

'Good morning, Con,' Billy called, approaching the counter at the entrance of Wharf Two. He was feeling considerably better for having composed a good part of the essay on Trim, promising himself that this time he'd get it down successfully on paper.

'Gidday, myte!' Con called back, 'How's tricks?' Con spoke with a strong Greek accent but was desperate to sound like an Australian. He also added an unnecessary *s* to most of the slang he used, for example, 'fair dinkum' became 'fair dinkums'. He now pointed to the styrofoam cup fitted with a plastic lid that sat at one end of the counter. 'The coffee I got it ready already, myte. Perfect, best in the worlds.' Billy saw that half a loaf of bread in a plastic bag rested to one side of the coffee container, and on the other side, on a paper napkin, Con had placed a finger bun with pink-iced topping. 'Today, you eat something, hey, Billy. It's no good not to eat for the stomach, myte.'

'Did you send off those migrant papers to Canberra?' Billy asked.

'For sure, myte.' Con grinned happily, 'Soon I be having a new young wife, eh? Very sexy, young Greek girl. Very lovely, I think. Not like Arse-stri-lian lazy bitch.'

Billy laughed, 'Con, the photograph your cousin sent wasn't all that clear, it was in black and white and looked as though it might have been taken a fair while back. You sure she's only twenty-seven?'

'No worries, myte. No colour photograph on that island. She's a name Sophia, beautiful, I'm tellin' you. That's for sure, fair dinkums, cross me heart, myte, spit on the devil.'

Billy grinned, 'I hope you're right.' The slightly out-of-focus photo of the young woman, Sophia, looked as if it had been taken on a box-brownie camera and the dress she was wearing appeared very much like one his first date had worn back in the early sixties. Still, Con's people were peasants. He supposed things didn't change all that much on an outlying Greek island.

Billy couldn't help wondering to himself why, with his

five women, all of them working in the cafe, Con could possibly want another woman around to look after him. Con was of an age where paying a visit to a lady happy to accommodate him for a small return would have been more sensible than sharing his cot with a randy peasant girl who might prove much too much for him. But Billy kept this opinion to himself. Greeks, on the whole, seemed to enjoy being married. A client once explained to him that marriage allowed them to misbehave in safety as Greek couples almost never divorced. The client, a Greek himself, went on to say that a Greek male was far more likely to make an accommodation with a lady once he was married than he ever would while single.

Con couldn't write in English so Billy had helped him complete the forms to sponsor a migrant girl as well as acted as his referee, signing himself 'W. D'Arcy O'Shannessy, LLB, QC'.

Did the street boy even have a female in his life who cared about him? Probably not. If he was a street kid, he'd have left home because of domestic violence from both parents. Where there was a mother present who wasn't an addict, the kids usually stayed on. It was different with a father, where drunkenness often led to violence and sexual abuse.

Billy had barely completed the thought when he felt a sharp, agonising pain behind his eyes, so much so that he visibly winced and was forced to his knees, his eyes tightly closed. The last time he'd had a boy to worry about he'd . . .

The pain in his head increased in intensity until it blocked his thought. Holding his thumb and forefinger to the bridge of his nose, Billy squeezed hard until the pain in his head started to go.

'You orright, myte? Maybe to eat somethings, eh?' Con asked, peering over the edge of the counter, looking concerned.

'Yeah, fine, right as rain,' Billy replied, taking a deep breath while slowly straightening up, 'Touch of the collywobbles.'

'I make you sanwitch, eggs, bacons, lettuce, beetroots, pineapples, what-a-ever-you-wants, my fren.'

'No thanks, Con, this bun'll do me nicely.'

Billy took the pink bun, placed it in the plastic bag with the yesterday-bread and then into his briefcase. Taking up his coffee, he turned to Con. 'Thanks, mate, as always I'm truly grateful.'

Con smiled, his head to one side, 'It's a my pleasures, myte.'

Billy smiled back and added as an afterthought, 'For the bun as well.'

Con nodded. 'Hey, Billy, what's a mean this words collywobbles?'

'It means you're a bit dizzy, a bit crook, but then you quickly come good again.'

'Right as rains?'

'Yeah, right as rains.' Billy turned away from his friend and walked along the Quay to his usual spot in the sun. It was the first time since he'd wakened to the sound of Arthur and Martha quarrelling that he'd been able to pursue his normal routine.

Chapter Two

Billy made himself comfortable on a bench alongside the Quay and prepared himself for the day to come. He sipped slowly on the container of coffee, still hot and strong, and immediately felt a little better. Coffee was the civilised side of his addictive personality, one of the things that kept him anchored. Well, if not anchored, it allowed him not to drift too far from his mooring. He had discovered that with a caffeine fix laced with six sachets of sugar, he could stave off the need to be waiting for the doors to open at the early-opening pub in Woolloomooloo.

The story of Trim had succeeded in driving the boy from his head. He absent-mindedly peeled the bright-pink icing off the finger bun, set the bun aside for ammunition, and ate the sticky mess, further satisfying his sugar craving.

Gulls gathered expectantly at his feet, their beady eyes fixed on the bread. Billy removed several slices from the plastic wrapper and set them beside the bun. He placed his coffee down and waited a few moments until a dozen more gulls had landed before he rose from the bench. The birds scattered anxiously on either side of him as he stepped towards the water's edge. Removing the remainder of the bread from the wrapper, he hurled it into the air. A frantic squawking was followed by an eruption of spray as birds and bread met the surface of the Harbour together. In less than a minute, not a morsel remained and the small polite waves had returned to slap against the granite wall of the Quay.

Billy rather liked seagulls. They were the coastal garbage collectors, cleaning up the waterfront and the beaches. The silver gull was Australia's most ubiquitous seabird and a natural part of the environment. He saw them in every way as true Australians, loud, aggressive, lacking in subtlety, highly competitive and devoted to cricket, even turning up at the SCG for Sheffield Shield games.

However, Billy's love of birds was by no means all-encompassing. There was one avian species he considered his mortal enemy. This was the presence, in ever-increasing numbers, of Indian mynah birds, *Acridotheres tristis*, which had replaced the sparrows, pigeons and gulls as the city's most potent pavement polluters.

He regarded the mynah bird as a foreign invader which had infiltrated the country and multiplied while nobody was looking. The black and tan, beady-eyed, sharp-pointed, yellow-beaked birds strutted about on spindly curry-coloured legs wherever there was a chance of a free feed, and drove him to distraction. They would gather, in what he preferred to think of as street gangs, on the steps of the State Library where lunchtime workers sitting in the sun would throw them crusts from their sandwiches. Billy's pleas to all and sundry not to feed 'the bloody pestilence' went unheeded. Most of Sydney's urban population could scarcely tell a kookaburra from a sparrow. These airborne shit factories were simply more of the same to them.

While Billy was aware that the European sparrows were also interlopers, they'd come out with the First Fleet and had earned their migrant status. Pigeons, as an early source of food to both convict and free settler, had also earned their tenure. Not so the mynahs. They were, pound for pound, the greatest defecators on the planet, producing more shit than a gannet four times their size. The grey-tinged-with-white splat they left everywhere clung like superglue to the caps of the Corinthian and Doric columns of several notable buildings. It could be seen on the moulded ledges and decorative stonework of the State Library, the Art Gallery, the Queen Victoria Building, the old Commonwealth Bank building and the GPO in Martin Place, to name but a few.

Moreover, unlike the sparrows and the pigeons, the Indian mynahs had systematically eliminated all of the smaller species of native bird life which were attracted to the grevillea nectar and the wildflower seeds found in the Botanic Gardens. As an amateur naturalist, this was of major concern to Billy. The smaller birds, the Bluetit, Rose Robin, Red-capped Robin, White-winged Triller, Rufous

Whistler and Willie Wagtail, as well as several other smaller species common to the Gardens, had disappeared, the mynah birds having destroyed their eggs or taken their fledglings while still in the nest.

To Billy this was an act of war, a foreign invader systematically murdering the indigenous population as the first white settlers had done. This time somebody had to fight back. He accepted single-handedly the task of exterminating the tyranny from the steps and pavement outside the State Library, the part of the city he cherished the most.

When Billy had finished his coffee, he rinsed out the container and set to work. He removed the packet of rat poison and a pair of transparent latex gloves from the cardboard dispenser and carefully pulled them on. Then he commenced to mould a single poison pellet into a tiny ball of well-kneaded dough and dropped it into the container. He continued until he had fifty or so tiny rounded morsels, the required number for the day's Operation Mynah Bird. He replaced the plastic top of the coffee container and put it in his briefcase along with the rat poison, peeled off the gloves and deposited them in a nearby rubbish bin. It was time for a pleasant morning stroll through the Botanic Gardens he so dearly loved and then on to his assignation with the Flag Hotel in Woolloomooloo.

The Flag was already busy by the time he arrived around nine-thirty. The patrons at this time of the day were mostly shift workers from the Garden Island dry dock, retired waterside workers who lived in housing-commission homes in the immediate neighbourhood, or the homeless drunks who lived in the Domain, the open parkland surrounding the Botanic Gardens.

The proprietor of the Flag Hotel was a large, beefy man in his early fifties named Samuel Snatchall who, before he retired prematurely and bought the pub, had been a notorious standover man for the Painters & Dockers Union. Known by one and all as Sam Snatch, his union career had involved several well-publicised court appearances, all of them involving the charge of causing grievous bodily harm. Sam's greatest claim to fame was that he had never been convicted, which was in itself, a great many people felt, a serious indictment of the legal system of New South Wales.

Sam Snatch didn't much care for his description as a one-time standover man, but he happily described his previous occupation as 'an attitude adjuster in the union cause'. It was his way of reminding his customers that he wouldn't stand for any nonsense.

The Flag had always been a hotel for dock workers and, prior to being owned by Sam Snatch, its proprietor for a short period had been George Smiggins, the undefeated welterweight champion of the world. Smiggins soon grew weary of the drunks who wanted to brag to their mates on the docks that they'd taken a poke at the ex-world champion and he retaliated by banning dock workers from the pub. This proved to be a fatal mistake as they constituted the major part of his clientele. Sam Snatch came along and made Smiggins an offer, an amount just about sufficient to cover George's outstanding debts to the brewery. Even so, the price of the pub would have been well outside the range of a minor union official like Sam Snatch.

Claiming he'd won $250,000 in the NSW State Lottery, Snatch came up with the scratch. With this, taken together with his superannuation payout and, he claimed, a second mortgage on his home, Snatch raised the money to buy the pub. Nobody believed him, nor could anyone recall any such windfall in the Snatch family, unless he had found a way of borrowing money on government-owned property. Until fairly recently, he'd lived in a three-bedroom housing-commission flat in South Sydney with a rent of sixty dollars a week. All of this was said well out of earshot, even at fifty metres, since Sam wasn't the sort of bloke you questioned too closely if you wished to remain with the sum of your working parts intact.

However, Billy received the red-carpet treatment at the Flag. If he'd been the state premier and called in for a drink, he couldn't have been greeted more cordially. Billy had defended Sam Snatch in all five of his appearances in court, getting him an acquittal each time. On Sam's fifth appearance, the bookmakers among the nation's waterside workers offered odds of twenty to one on an acquittal and were scarcely able to attract a punter, the general consensus being that Snatch was almost certainly going down this time. Had Snatch been smart enough to put his pension on Billy winning once again, he would have been able to pay for the pub twice over.

'Gidday, Billy!' Sam Snatch yelled out from behind the

polished counter of the small private bar known as
Marion's Bar, 'One Black Label comin' up, old mate.'

Billy limped up to the bar, the walk through the gardens
had set off the pain in his knee again, 'Thanks very much,
Sam, but I'd prefer to pay for it myself.'

Sam Snatch, not known for his generosity, feigned a
look of astonishment, 'You'll do no such thing, my son! Not
in my pub.'

Billy sighed, 'Well, just the one then, Sam. Hair of the
dog.'

Grinning, Sam Snatch planted a scotch glass on the bar
and poured him a shot of Johnnie Walker. The proprietor
of the Flag was also not known for his subtlety, yet this was
a ritual which took place every morning and was designed
so that Billy could maintain his dignity while accepting the
handout.

Marion, who usually ran the bar, placed a small jug of
water beside his drink. 'Mornin', Billy,' she said, smiling.
'Leg hurtin', is it?'

'Morning, Marion, woke up with it. Getting old.'

'Nah, never, not you,' Snatch interjected, 'Yiz strong as
a mallee bull.'

'Couple of blokes here to see you,' Marion said, 'Come
in early. Been drinking steadily, could be they're too far
gone by now for a meaningful conversation.'

Billy laughed, 'Meaningful conversations are not
common among the brotherhood of inebriates, my dear.'

In her early forties, Marion packaged herself into an
image that met the wishful thinking of most of the working-

class patrons of the Flag. In fashion terms she was over-enhanced in the front, a generous C-cup perfectly contoured under a tight-fitting pink sweater. Blonde curls cascaded to her shoulders à la Dolly Parton. She always wore black satin miniskirts that showed a well-rounded derrière and good legs that ended in a pair of six-inch stiletto heels.

Marion dressed like a tart because it was good for her business. The only thing about her that wasn't deliberately contrived was her voice, which, activated by three packs of Kent a day, had the resonance of blue metal in a cement mixer. If she possessed the heart of gold usually attributed to barmaids, it hadn't been noticed by the patrons. She was tough and she was sexy, but Billy always suspected she was something else as well.

Despite her *Australasian Post* magazine looks, Marion occasionally displayed a vocabulary that caught Billy by surprise. She'd once told him that the only thing she'd usefully acquired from the unending misery of attending boarding school at Santa Maria Convent in Orange was a love of the written word, though he doubted that this alone accounted for her lapses into correct grammar.

It was generally agreed by the morning patrons that Snatch and Marion were on together. Why else, the argument went, would a great-looking sort like her work for a fat bastard like him? It was a good question, but as much as the proprietor of the Flag may have fantasised about a roll in the cot with his overendowed barmaid, it wasn't true. What occurred between the two of them was strictly a business arrangement. Snatch allowed Marion to use the three rooms and bathroom above the pub, paying her well below her worth as a cocktail hostess, the difference being calculated as the rent for the rooms.

The Inn Keepers Act required city hotels to offer overnight accommodation of at least three bedrooms and a communal bathroom, which in strictly drinking pubs such as the Flag were never utilised. In this way, Snatch didn't have to show the rental income he'd deducted from Marion's wages on his books, allowing the rooms to seem available to comply with the law. In fact, Marion used them for her business, one as a reception with a comfortable lounge and a TV set where videos were shown of models wearing the lingerie, the other as display, fitted with wall-to-wall mirrors with a small curtained-off area used as a customer change room. The third was a private office for Marion and her assistant and was always locked because it also contained stock. There was a bathroom and toilet next door and, because some of the customers liked to nip into the bathroom wearing something they'd picked out for themselves, there was a sign on the inside of the bathroom door which read:

CUSTOMERS WEARING
NEW LINGERIE IN THE BATHROOM
MAY CONSIDER IT SOLD.

The rooms upstairs were known to Marion's regular customers as 'The Boys' Boutique' although her business cards, many of which were carried in the innermost recesses of the wallets of some very unexpected people, read ambiguously enough:

KINGS CROSS-DRESSERS
Men's Outfitters
FLAG HOTEL
WOOLLOOMOOLOO

Marion's business was a lingerie boutique for cross-dressers, transvestites and drag queens, and was reported to be making her a small fortune.

Marion was a triple-certificate bartender who had won the Suntory Cup twice as well as three International Bartenders Association (IBA) Australian trophies. She had represented Australia in the IBA International awards in Rome in 1987 and was runner-up to the winner, Anacleto Jose Abreu of Portugal, with her cocktail 'Moonlight in Kakadu'. She could easily have doubled or tripled her salary in any of the fashionable bars catering to the new IT elite in town, but the Flag was the ideal location for her lingerie business. It was next to Kings Cross, the centre of Sydney's various deviant communities, close to the CBD and also on the waterfront. Sailors from all over the world stopped off at the Flag and they, along with blokes in from the bush at Easter Show time, provided the cream on top. Her bread and butter came from the local transvestites and the legions of cross-dressers in the community.

Cross-dressing has no social demographic and adherents ranged from panel beaters to barristers, men working on garbage trucks to others from the big end of town. They would drop in during the course of the day ostensibly for a quiet drink at Marion's Bar, and at the same time do their business with complete discretion. After a drink, all it took was a nod and a wink and they'd be directed upstairs, where they could try on a range of beautiful local and imported French lingerie, attended to by an outrageous transvestite known as Gorgeous Gordon, who also doubled as a fashion adviser. Although most transvestites are extroverts and usually gay and mostly happy to be named and talked about, Marion's more discreet clientele, the strictly heterosexual cross-dressers, knew that she would keep their identities secret to her grave.

Sam Snatch appeared to have it, coming and going. Marion's cross-dressing customers were always singularly serviced upstairs and so waited patiently downstairs with an overpriced cocktail in front of them. Once they made their purchases, they could leave by a set of back stairs leading directly onto the street from the pub.

Billy didn't feel up to meeting the two men waiting for him in the beer garden. 'Don't think I want to meet anyone today, love,' he said to Marion. 'Do I know them?'

'Yeah, one, Casper Friendly. He's with a new bloke, blackfella, haven't seen him around here before.'

Snatch turned, suddenly agitated, 'Aboriginal? From Redfern? We don't want none of them bastards in here.'

Marion sighed, 'How would I bloody know where he

came from, Sam? And, by the way, it's Aborigine *not* Aboriginal.'

'He's a bloody boong as far as I'm concerned. How'd yer see them anyway? It's not your job to serve out there. Come in for a pair of pantyhose, did they?'

Marion looked scornfully at Snatch and took a drag from her cigarette, allowing the smoke to escape through her nostrils. 'Yeah, right on, two blacks, one a derro, the other from the boonies. How many pairs of French knickers do you reckon they gunna buy between them?'

'Yeah well, you know how I feel about Abos, nothing but trouble.'

Marion shrugged, 'What am I supposed to do, ask for his bloody passport? Shirley was late in so I served them in the beer garden. Casper's a regular early drinker and he brought a mate.' She commenced polishing the surface of the already immaculate bar, 'Tell you what, though, the new bloke's carrying a stash of fifties you could choke a horse on. They's drinking scotch as well.'

'Drugs! He's a fuckin' pusher!' Snatch was paranoid about drugs. There were plenty of cops and judges out in get-even-land with old scores to settle with him. In his new vocation as a publican he was determined to keep his nose clean, aware that the next time he appeared in court he might not be fortunate enough to find another Billy O'Shannessy to defend him.

Marion rolled her eyes. 'Drugs? Now why didn't I think of that? He's a black Lebanese who wears moleskins, an Akubra and badly worn riding boots. As a disguise, it beats the hell out of a Hugo Boss suit, hair gel, gold necklace and a diamond-encrusted Rolex.'

Snatch ignored her sarcasm, suddenly excited. 'From the bush? D'ya say this bloke was from the bush?'

'Can't say for sure. Anyway, that's what his clobber suggested. Maybe you're right, he's a pusher disguised as an Aborigine disguised as a stockman.'

Billy knew what Snatch was thinking. It was unusual, though not unheard of, for an Aborigine to come to the big smoke after working on a contract for several months in the mines or as a stockman or fencer, his accumulated salary paid in a lump sum. Many of them would virtually hand their pay over to a publican, agreeing to drink it out, living and eating at the pub. These men, who also had their equivalent in merchant seamen paying off and waiting between ships, were a bonanza no publican could resist. They were usually loners who worked hard for a living and then went on a 'booze and bird' holiday for a month before returning to work. It was a tradition started by itinerant shearers way back in the middle of the nineteenth century and such men didn't consider themselves alcoholics or layabouts.

Snatch now turned to Billy. 'Do us a favour, will ya, mate?'

Billy knew what was coming, 'What is it?'

'The Abo bloke and Casper, them two, they come to see you. You know the drill, check the boong out for me, will ya? Bring him over after?' He winked, 'Could be a quid or two in it for you?'

Billy looked up at the proprietor of the Flag Hotel, then back at the glass of scotch on the counter, and cleared his throat.

Snatch got the message. 'Scotch for Billy and yid better keep an eye on them two, Marion. Don't let them scarper before Billy gets to them.'

'Yeah, righto,' Marion said, then looked at Billy, one eyebrow slightly arched, 'Black Label, wasn't it, Billy?'

'Christ no! Red!' Snatch yelled out. 'Red Label! Bloody hell!! Think I'm made of money, do yer?'

Billy smiled at the barmaid, happy enough at the prospect of getting a second scotch out of Snatch.

'Jesus, you ain't even touched the first! Drink up, mate,' Snatch instructed, impatient to get Billy out the back.

Marion gave a snort, 'Take yer time, mate, them two aren't goin' nowhere. Casper was more than anxious that you should be informed of their presence the moment you came in.' There it was again, two sentences, one coarse, the other well structured.

Business among the homeless was usually conducted in the mornings when most of the derelicts were still sober. It invariably took place in the beer garden at the rear of the Flag Hotel, which, until the staff turned on the smokeless barbecue, Sam Snatch allowed to be used by the alkies. In this way he kept them out of the pub itself while ensuring that most of their dole or disability pensions would be spent at his bar or on supplies purchased from his bottle shop.

At noon the beer garden entered another dimension when

it catered to patrons drawn from the various small businesses in the area. They came in for a couple of lunchtime middies and one of Snatch's famous aged Aberdeen Angus T-bones. At half-past ten, a barmaid would take the last orders from the morning drinkers and, precisely at eleven, Snatch's huge frame would appear at the doorway leading into the pub, from where he'd shout out, 'Righto, piss off, the lot of yiz! Out of the garden! I'll be waitin' for yiz in the bottle shop! Sorry, no credit, gennelmen, unless you bring yer bank manager to guarantee yer financial status!'

Billy was usually called in by the brotherhood of inebriates when there was a problem with someone's pension or the dole. More often it was the need to open a bank account. Welfare payments were now being paid into bank accounts and many of the alcoholics had never operated one. They usually fell far short of the mandatory requirements known as the Hundred Points, the criteria set by the banks to qualify for a cheque account. For many of the homeless it was a catch-22, the Department of Social Security insisted that all dole and disability pensions be paid into a personal bank account while the intended recipient often had no chance of qualifying for one. Billy would be called in to straighten things out with a bit of what he referred to as 'creative paperwork'.

Occasionally it was a more complex issue, with a wife or kids involved, where a letter was needed to one of the many authorities that control the lives of the poor. Often a legal document would be sent to a man who, at best, was semi-literate. It would need to be translated and replied to in kind. There was scarcely a drunk in the inner-city area who hadn't at one time or another enjoyed Billy's services.

Billy now assumed that Casper's new mate would have some sort of problem along the usual lines. But today, with his routine disrupted by the kid and the cop, he didn't feel up to the hassle of dealing with someone else's problems. However, Sam Snatch had forced his hand and he knew he lacked the internal fortitude to stand up to the aggressive publican.

Billy took the first fragrant sip of neat scotch. Every morning he faced the same battle, forcing himself to drink his gratuitous first nip slowly. Billy told himself that while he maintained this go-slow ritual, he remained in some sort of control, a problem drinker rather than a confirmed alcoholic. Drinking branded scotch was an example of maintaining one's standards.

He knew he must avoid, at all costs, the way many alcoholics approached the first glass of the day. That is to say, holding the glass in both hands, its base resting firmly on the counter, then bringing the mouth down to the lip of the glass, tipping it very slightly and feeding the precious liquid down the gullet so as not to spill a drop. Billy would always drink his like a gentleman, lifting it to his mouth in one hand while seated on a bar stool, his back straight. Drinking his first of the day in this way was one of the many benchmarks he set for his self-image. It was undoubtedly one of the hardest for him to observe as, once the scotch was placed in front of him, every nerve in his body screamed out to him to swallow the lot in one gulp.

Lifting the scotch glass carefully, he took a tiny sip and brought it back down to the counter. With his briefcase resting on his lap and his left hand still shackled to it, he was forced to keep his right hand steady. There had been times in the past when his hand had trembled so badly that he couldn't lift the scotch glass for the first twenty minutes. But today, thank God, his hand was behaving itself and he reached over to the small glass jug Marion had placed on the counter beside him and added to the scotch an amount of water roughly equivalent to the sip he'd taken from the glass. The end of the first drink would eventually arrive when his final sip contained only a vague tincture of the beautiful malted whisky.

He would never be seen drinking anything but scotch in public, and Sam Snatch's free tipple meant that Billy could maintain his affectation no matter what the state of his finances. After this, Billy would make his way to the bottle shop and purchase whatever type of booze his current finances would allow before leaving the pub and returning to the Botanic Gardens. It was only when there was business to attend to, such as today, that Billy remained at the Flag. Business meant two further glasses of scotch, the price for his services.

Billy had done business with Casper Friendly before, but always with reluctance. The quarter-caste Aborigine was a notorious wheeler-dealer invariably operating some sort of scam involving the ignorant and the desperate. Even though Billy was always willing to help for a very modest cost in kind, many of the men were too ashamed to approach him directly. They may have been drunks but they still had their pride and they'd been concealing their inability to read and write all their lives. Billy, despite his status as a homeless drunk, represented some sort of educated authority they couldn't bring themselves to face.

On the other hand, Casper Friendly was illiterate. 'Whitefella don't give Abos no teachin' in my time,' he'd laugh. Knowing that some of the blokes in need of help would come to him rather than go directly to Billy, Casper's illiteracy had become his calling card.

Casper had an easy laugh and appeared generous with his money when he was working a client, so that it wasn't difficult for a mark to confess that he had trouble 'readin' and writin''. He often enough became the acceptable conduit for the help the homeless needed. The final thing in his favour was that he was perceived to be an Aborigine and therefore carried a status on the street even lower than the white alcoholic needing help, so there was no need to 'eat crow' by coming to him.

Billy had no problem with any of this, it was Casper's charges as an introduction agency he objected to. If he brought Billy a customer who needed to open a bank account, he would charge the customer ten dollars a fortnight from his pension for the first year and five dollars forever after. The commission Casper earned helped to keep a gang of freeloaders faithful to him. They served as his standover men in the event that one of his clients failed to pay up on pension day.

Billy found himself caught between a rock and a hard

place. While he would have preferred not to work with Casper, an outright refusal would have been unthinkable. Besides, he wasn't at all sure that Casper's henchmen wouldn't come after him if he proved refractory.

Casper Friendly was a man in his sixties, almost ten years older than Billy, which made him old for a street alcoholic. Thin as a twig, he had been a fringe identity around Darlinghurst as long as anyone could remember. The pension office records had him registered as Casper Friendly, though neither of these names was correct. Someone, way back when the cartoon had first featured in Saturday afternoon matinee shorts, had named him after Casper the Friendly Ghost. This had been modified over time to his present name.

The original nickname, it seemed, was arrived at because he was an albino as well as a quarter-caste Aborigine and he resembled someone with bleached eyebrows and hair suffering from a severe dose of sunburn. To add to his overall paleness, he only ever wore white cricket gear. In moments of sobriety he would explain that his grand-daddy had been a member of the first Aboriginal cricket team to tour England in 1868, and wearing cricket gear was an honour bestowed upon his family by the elders of his tribe and had something to do with their secret men's business. Like Sam Snatch buying the pub with his windfall and savings, it was generally accepted that this wasn't true, but veracity has no priority among the homeless and nobody cared, so Casper was free to claim anything he liked.

Billy finally completed drinking the second scotch and

made his way through to the beer garden, where Casper sat with the black man. The Aboriginal albino waved over to him. 'Hey, Billy, where's you fuckin' bin, man?' Casper indicated the man beside him, 'We bin waitin' here since fuckin' openin' time!'

Billy ignored the question, drunks don't keep time and it was pointless telling Casper that he never arrived before nine-thirty. 'Good morning,' he said formally, looking at a point somewhere between both men, the accepted etiquette among the homeless.

'Yeah, gidday,' Casper said absently, pointing at the black man beside him, 'This is me good mate, Trevor.'

The Aborigine nodded, but didn't offer his hand or look directly at Billy, 'Ow ya goin?'

'He come from out Wilcannia way,' Casper volunteered, 'From me own tribe.' Casper turned to the Aborigine beside him, 'What's your last name again, mate?'

'Williams,' the man replied. He was dressed the way Marion had described, though she hadn't mentioned his red woollen tartan shirt with the short sleeves rolled country-style well above his biceps. The Akubra he wore had seen all the drought and rain there'd been over the past twenty years and Billy could see where the stirrup iron had worn a mark on the side of the Cuban boot closest to him.

'Yeah, that's right, the Williams mob, real big in them parts of the Darling River. I had an auntie was a Williams. Bloody good woman.' Casper laughed, 'Real cranky, had a backhand send you across the fuckin' room, no worries, mate!'

'Nice to meet you, Trevor. Long way from home. Stockman, are you?' Billy asked, knowing that Casper had probably invented his tribal connections to the bloke from the bush.

'Yeah, mostly, done a fair bit of fencin', some railway fettlin', worked in the mines up Broken Hill way . . .' His voice trailed off.

'What brings you to Sydney?' Billy now asked.

'He's had a spot of bother, needs your help,' Casper cut in, not letting Williams explain.

Billy nodded, it was more of the same. He hoped it was something straightforward he could deal with quickly.

'Yeah, mate, legal,' Casper continued. 'I told him about you being a big-time lawyer, you know, how you got Sam Snatch off five times, lotsa others, like that hood in the Cross, the bloke who worked for Abe Saffron that topped that stripper with a cleaver and fed her through one o' them restaurant meat mincers to hide the evidence!' Casper laughed. 'No fuckin' body, yiz got him off extra quick.'

'The law doesn't always get it right, it was a technicality,' Billy replied.

'Yeah, well, never you mind, you got the bastard off, didn't ya?' Casper turned to Williams, 'If Billy O'Shannessy took the case, you knew the bloke was fuckin' guilty, no risk!' Casper roared with laughter, 'That right, ain't it, Billy?' He leaned back slightly and, grinning, pointed at Billy's chest, 'But yiz always got them off, didn't ya? Every time.'

'Steady on, Casper, I lost a good few over the years.'

Casper Friendly ignored Billy's protest, 'You lookin' at the best in the biz, mate. They don't come no better.'

Williams glanced at Casper and then at Billy, but remained silent. Like many blokes from the bush, he seemed naturally taciturn and talked only when it was absolutely necessary.

Billy grew suddenly concerned. Casper was half-cut but his elaborate build-up and the mention of one of the more squalid cases in his legal career didn't suggest this was routine business. 'Did you say you had a legal problem? Broken Hill would be a whole lot nearer to Wilcannia than Sydney, I dare say there are good lawyers available there.'

'Nah, fuckin' trouble's down here, mate.' Casper turned to Williams. 'That's right, hey, Trevor?'

'Yeah, me daughter.'

At that point Marion came into the beer garden. Billy remembered Snatch had asked her to stay interested in the blackfella. 'Watch your language, Casper, or Mr Snatchall will be out,' she warned.

'Language! What I fuckin' say?' Casper looked mystified. 'All I said was Billy here is an ace fuckin' barrister.'

Despite herself Marion laughed, then smiled winningly at Williams, 'Sorry I didn't introduce myself to you before, busy time. Shirley, who usually serves out here, was late coming in. Welcome to the Flag Hotel, from out of town, are you?'

Williams, taken by surprise, didn't know how to respond. Averting his eyes, he said, 'Yeah, miss, Wilcannia.'

'That's nice,' Marion said, not listening, or perhaps not

knowing where Wilcannia was. 'Hope we'll see more of you, Mr . . . ?'

'Williams, miss.' The black man had still not looked up.

'You must visit me at Marion's Bar, Mr Williams. People from out of town are always welcome.'

Billy knew that Marion would no more welcome a type like Williams to her cocktail bar than she would Casper Friendly. Or, for that matter, had it not been for his special relationship with Sam Snatch, Billy himself. And if the Aborigine had approached her bar on his own and without her knowledge of the fortune he carried in the pocket of his moleskins, she'd have soon enough sent him packing with a flea in his ear. Aboriginal stockmen were not, in her experience, either cross-dressers or transvestites. The big come-on clearly indicated to Billy that Sam Snatch had cut her in on the deal.

Marion, of course, was well aware of the effect she was having on the black man and now she glanced down at the two empty glasses resting on the metal table and smiled. 'You boys havin' a drink or just here for the fresh air?' she growled in her gravelly voice. She didn't wait for an answer, 'What's it to be, same again and one for Billy? Whose shout?' Marion knew the drill. With derelicts, you collected the money first or a newly arrived drink could be down the hatch before the recipient admitted to being unable to pay for it.

Casper dug into his filthy cricket longs and appeared to be fumbling for change, the top half of his over-large cricket trousers a sudden whirl of activity. Then, with his hands still in his pockets, he shrugged his shoulders. This surprised Billy, Casper always had money and, if he was with a potential client, he would spend liberally. This must be one of the rare occasions Casper was skint.

'I'll get it, miss,' Williams offered politely and produced the notorious stash. Peeling off a fifty, he handed it to Marion. Billy had to admit, from the look of it, there must have been three or four grand in the roll, maybe more. Surely no one in today's world could be sufficiently naïve to keep it all together like that. It said something about the values still existing in the bush.

Marion waved the fifty-dollar note, 'You boys gunna drink this out?'

Casper nodded, not asking Williams, 'Can't think of nothing better to do with it.'

Billy glanced over at the stockman, who nodded, 'Yeah, righto, miss, scotch again.'

'Well then,' Billy said, looking up at Marion, 'it's sufficient to buy a bottle. Why don't you bring us the bottle, Marion?'

Marion turned her shoulder slightly to emphasise the curve of her breasts, 'Nah, sorry can't do that, Billy, house rules, more than me job's worth. It's drinks by the tot out here. You can have a bottle but I'd have to charge the bar price per nip, thirty nips to the bottle.'

Billy remained silent long enough for Marion to say, 'Well, scotch all round then?'

Billy looked up, meeting her eyes with his own, 'Considering the special circumstances, perhaps the bottle-shop price for a bottle of scotch can be made to prevail for our guest, whom you have so very cordially welcomed and who has shown himself to be a serious drinking man. One who might like to return to this hostelry frequently while visiting the metropolis.'

Marion smiled, understanding that Billy wasn't going to help her do Snatch's dirty work, unless she did the right thing. 'Very well, on this one occasion *I shall be prevailed upon*,' she mocked back at him.

Billy smiled sweetly, 'Very kind of you, Marion, and Casper apologises, he simply doesn't recognise he's using explicit language, no offence meant.'

'None taken,' Marion shot back. 'However, *under the circumstances* my *explicit* advice to him is to stop or he will be *prevailed upon* to leave the premises.' She removed the two empty scotch glasses, 'I'll bring you fresh glasses with the bottle. You've got an hour before Shirley lights the barbecue.' She left, and Billy observed Williams looking at her hungrily as the cheeks of her satin-covered bottom responded to the clip-clip-clip cadence of her stiletto heels on the paving bricks. It was a cheap thrill and nobody did it better than Marion.

Casper waited until Marion had entered the pub. 'See what I mean? Bloody silver tongue, best in the fuckin' business!' He grinned, showing three stumpy yellow teeth in an otherwise empty set of gums, 'You done good getting us the bottle, mate.'

Marion returned shortly afterwards with a bottle of Red Label and three glasses. She handed the change to Williams and pointed out to him that the bottle was sealed. She broke the seal, poured a nip for each and set the bottle down on the table.

'Righto, enjoy yourselves. Like I said, you've got one hour.' She turned towards the stockman and, arching her right eyebrow slightly, said, 'You're most welcome to visit me at Marion's Bar, Mr Williams.'

Billy had difficulty controlling his mirth. Marion was being about as subtle as a blow on the head with a sledgehammer, but she knew her business and Williams looked up at last. 'Yeah, thanks, miss,' he mumbled.

Marion turned to go. 'Be good, gennelmen,' she said. Williams couldn't take his eyes off her, following her progress until the last glint of black satin disappeared into the darkness of the pub.

Billy picked up his glass, anxious to cover the embarrassment he felt at being a part of the scam. Surely Williams must realise that he was being conned, that the Marions of this world were well beyond his reach. On the other hand, he might think she was a prostitute and he certainly possessed the kind of money to turn any whore colourblind.

Billy raised his glass, 'Cheers and thank you, Trevor, whatever your problems, may they soon be resolved.'

'Bloody oath! Billy here fix yiz up quick smart,' Casper exclaimed.

The three men sat silently drinking for some moments. Then Williams put down his glass and looked directly at Billy, 'You don't look like no top barrister to me, mate.' He turned to Casper and back to Billy, his eyes steady. 'What's the game, eh? What you two mongrels up to?'

Casper looked at Billy, then at Williams, his yellow eyelashes blinking furiously. 'Hey, wait on, Trevor,' he chuckled, 'we're yer mates!'

'Bullshit,' Williams replied, taking a sip from his glass. 'Yiz no mates of mine.'

'Hey! Hey! Don't be like that,' Casper called out, 'What we done to you?'

Billy looked up, surprised. Both men were well on their way to being drunk and obviously Williams had been slowly building up a head of steam. Casper had probably latched on to him as he got off the train at Central, seeing him as a bushie ripe for the plucking. Now the stockman thought he was about to be the victim in some sort of prearranged scam between the albino and this other drunk who was being passed off to him as a lawyer. He was right, one way or another, he was being conned. Billy didn't entertain the slightest doubt that Casper's agenda, like that of Sam Snatch, was to facilitate the departure of a generous portion of the stockman's earnings either into his own pocket or down his gullet.

'Exactly right, Mr Williams,' Billy said quietly. 'It's been years since I took a case and, as a matter of fact, I lost the last three by being drunk and incompetent.' He shrugged, 'I'm on skid row same as Casper here, one of the ever multiplying fringe dwellers with a bottomless thirst. Whatever your problem, unless it is a spot of simple legal paperwork, you may be quite sure there is nothing I can usefully do to help you.'

'Jesus, Billy, the poor bloke's fuckin' desperate! It's his

little daughter!' Casper exclaimed, still trying to rescue the situation.

Billy gave a small, rueful laugh, 'Casper, with me as his lawyer, our friend's situation would only get progressively worse.'

Williams rose suddenly from the table, kicking back the metal chair with the heel of his riding boot. 'Righto, then, I'm off!' He turned to Billy, 'Maybe you're a fair dinkum lawyer, maybe not, but yer mate's a fuckin' dingo!'

'No, mate, we both are,' Billy said, ashamed.

'Hey, wait on, brother!' Casper protested, grabbing at Williams' arm. 'Don't lissen to him! We're mates, same tribe, man! Darling River! Me auntie!'

Williams pulled his arm away and Billy thought he was going to punch Casper. 'Fuck off, I ain't no brother of yours, you half-peeled bludger!' He marched off, the sound of his Cuban heels echoing across the brick-lined courtyard quite differently from Marion's stilettos. They both watched as Williams disappeared into the darkness of the pub's interior. From the rear, with his straight back and slightly bandy legs, Billy thought he looked like a bad guy about to enter the pub for a shoot-out in one of those old black-and-white Western movies they used to film in Spain.

Billy hoped like hell Williams would leave the Flag Hotel. He might be tempted to accept Marion's invitation to stop off at her bar. If he did, then Sam Snatch would have his stash in the pub safe before nightfall, volunteering to keep it for Williams until the last dollar, with the help of every barfly in the Woolloomooloo area and a bit of dodgy accounting, had supposedly disappeared down the stockman's throat.

'Casper, he's right, you're an unprincipled bastard!' Billy said, moving his chair backwards and reaching for the handle of his briefcase.

Casper seemed unabashed by the insult, 'Wait on, Billy! Have another drink, mate, bloody near full bottle t'go. Jesus, did you see that fuckin' stash? Why'd yer spoil things by tellin' him yiz was no fuckin' good no more? We could've took some of that loot offa him, no fuckin' risk.'

Billy shook his head, 'Even pissed, which he wasn't by local standards, the black bloke would have beaten the living crap out of both of us.' He rose, knowing he was already getting the taste for the scotch. He must leave, it was now or never.

'C'mon, siddown, yer haven't finished yer fuckin' drink!' Casper persisted. In the parlance of a drunk, this was the worst possible indictment.

Billy was sorely tempted, but knew if he finished the glass in front of him he'd follow with another and yet another. Casper may have been unsuccessful with his scam but the scotch bottle was still two-thirds full, a reward in itself. He winced inwardly, desperately reminding himself that an urgent part of his daily routine was still to be kept. He needed to remain relatively sober for Operation Mynah Bird and he knew if he allowed the day to get any further out of hand he'd find himself in the drunk tank tonight. He reminded himself of the terrible humiliation he always felt when he woke up in the company of twenty-six drunks sleeping it off in a windowless dormitory. The drunk tank always meant that once again he'd failed and was one step closer to disaster.

'Casper, I don't want your booze and I don't want your business, you're an embarrassment.'

Casper spread his arms wide and pointed to the bottle of scotch, 'Hey, brother, it ain't my grog, the blackfella paid for it! I'm a fuckin' drunk, you're a fuckin' drunk. You're talking shit, we're already all the embarrassment there is, man!'

Billy had to admit Casper might have a point. He watched as the albino swallowed his scotch in one gulp. Banging the empty glass down on the table in front of him, he smacked his lips and reached out for the scotch bottle, filled Billy's glass and held it out to him. 'Garn, win some, lose some, no offence, mate.'

Billy didn't bother to reply. Holding firmly onto his briefcase, he crossed the beer garden and, to avoid meeting Sam Snatch, took the exit that led directly onto the street through a one-way revolving iron mechanism known locally as the 'Grate Escape'. This was because it was traditionally used by waterside workers to make a hasty exit when news arrived that a cranky wife armed with a rolling pin was on her way before her husband's entire weekly wage packet disappeared into the publican's pocket.

'Ah, fuck off, yer barrister bastard!' Casper yelled out, 'Yer think yer too good for us, that yer shit smells of eudie colognie, but yer not, yer just another fuckin' drunk, mate.'

Billy felt strangely happy that his part of the scam hadn't

succeeded. He reminded himself, though, that Marion still lurked in the darkness beyond the door leading from the beer garden. If Williams had escaped without calling in at Marion's Bar, Sam Snatch would conclude that Casper had somehow screwed up the deal, forcing Billy to leave and the bushie to walk out on him. He wondered how long it would take into the bottle of scotch Casper now had to himself before a thoroughly pissed-off Sam Snatch proceeded to adjust his attitude.

Billy dodged the traffic, crossed the road to the waterfront and then made his way up the Art Gallery steps towards the Botanic Gardens. He was halfway up when he realised that, in all the agitation, he hadn't stopped off at the bottle shop. Briefly he considered retracing his steps, but the possibility of running into an angry Sam Snatch made him decide against doing so. He'd had enough aggro for one day. He told himself he'd pick up a bottle elsewhere a little later on in the day.

As Billy entered the gates of the Botanic Gardens, almost immediately his demeanour changed. Even though he crossed the Gardens to the pub of a morning, his return was an entirely different kind of excursion. It was now his custom to walk every path every day, rain or shine, checking on the trees and the plants, making sure that the gardeners were aware of a shrub or tree or flowering hedge or ground cover that might be in need of care. He noted that the azalea hedge along the Macquarie Wall continued to look sick, he'd have to take that up with the head gardener again.

Whilst he usually had a bottle tucked away in his briefcase, he wouldn't touch a drop until his inspection was completed. It was his habit to sit quietly on the various benches, his eyes closed, listening to the birds and the insects to determine if there had been any changes in the immediate environment. Billy knew what time of the year it was from most of the tiny flying insects that would feed or collect pollen around plants. He deeply missed the cries of the smaller birds that had once been so much a part of the Gardens but which the rapacious mynah birds had systematically eliminated.

Billy had come to regard the Botanic Gardens as his own and assumed a proprietary attitude to all he surveyed. His inspection usually ended around twelve-thirty, when he arrived back at the entrance gates opposite the State Library. It was not until he passed through the gates and crossed the road to the steps of the library on the opposite side that he felt free to take another drink.

Billy was now back where his day had begun but this time he sat himself in the sun on one of the library steps and waited among the early lunchtime crowd for the Indian mynah birds, which would only begin to gather in real numbers around the library steps around a quarter to one. Intelligent birds, they seemed to know the various feeding times and sites. Billy made a habit of sitting in a different spot every day so that the cunning shit-spreaders wouldn't associate one part of the steps with danger. He watched as they started to fly in and waited until they presented themselves in sufficient numbers before he opened his briefcase.

Quietly he slipped a single surgical glove over his right hand, withdrew the coffee container and placed it beside him. Selecting a single pellet of bread, he rolled it down the steps in front of him and watched as a flurry of mynahs made for the prize which was quickly snapped up by one of the bigger birds. Past experience showed that the bigger ones got more than their fair share, which Billy regarded as a waste of precious ammunition. So, observing the whereabouts of the bird who'd won the first morsel, he threw the next pellet as far from it as possible, thus bagging a second victim. Billy patiently repeated the procedure for an hour, until virtually every bread pellet had been nabbed by a different mynah bird. There only remained the denunciation.

Billy peeled off the glove, stuffed it into the empty coffee container, walked over to a nearby rubbish bin and disposed of it. Then he shackled his briefcase about his wrist, walked to the top step of the library entrance and commenced to recite a piece of doggerel of his own composition, causing the people seated on the steps to look at him in bemusement.

No Mynah Matter

All the birds of the air are
a'crying and a'sobbing.
They've heard of the death
of the wren and the robin.

Of the Wagtail triplets
killed asleep in their nest

And poor Jacky Winter,
twice stabbed in the breast.

The birds are all asking
They're all in a twitter.
Is it someone among us
who's Jacky the Ripper?

These are our Gardens
where we've lived all our lives.
Who's the terror among us
with beak sharp as knives?

Hey, beady-eyed stranger
with the long yellow legs!
You've been seen prowling around
where the robin lays eggs.

Ha! Caught you red-handed!
Now it's your turn to pay.
Judge Billy O'Shannessy
has been called to the fray.

The long arm of the law
has reached out at last.
Operation Mynah Bird
is now come to pass.

This promise I make you
as a bird-loving man.
Their mob is in trouble,
the shit's hit the fan!

Small birds will return to
where the kookas laugh.
The wrens seen once more
along the bush-lined path.

The Gardens made safe
for your dear little nests.
There'll be birdsong again
from small feathered breasts.

I swear this before you
on the currawong's cry.
These unwelcome strangers
are all going to die.

So ladies and gentlemen
out enjoying your lunch
You've just seen the last
of this murdering bunch.

My decision is final
my judgement must rest.
The Indian mynah
has robbed its last nest.

It's death by rat poison
because one of us cared.
The invasion is over
the small birds are spared.

Billy completed reciting the poem, which he was the first to admit wasn't very good, and told himself that he had every intention of working it up to scan correctly. Nevertheless, it served his purpose of publicly announcing his personal crusade.

After this, Billy would usually take a sip from his bottle and smile benignly at the sandwich munchers. Then, bowing slightly, he'd wish them all a splendid day and take his leave. One of the very few advantages of being a derelict was that people concluded that you were either drunk or mentally retarded.

He now made his way down the steps and across the road back into the Botanic Gardens. At this time of the day the giant Moreton Bay fig he loved would cast its shadow across a bench beside a small rock pool situated along a little-used path. He'd been coming to this bench all his adult life, first to eat his lunch and later to study for his entrance to the Bar. Later still, he'd come during a recess from a case he was conducting. Now he liked to sit quietly and write while he worked his way through half a bottle of scotch. The day's writing would be concluded when the words slipped off the paper into his lap and he found himself too inebriated to continue.

Today's task was to put down the story of Trim just as he'd imagined it in his head. He told himself that without the half-bottle of scotch, the words had a good chance of remaining firmly anchored to the page. If he could manage to accomplish this, it would more than make up for the day's disruption and give him the perfect excuse to celebrate a little later.

To his dismay, as he reached the small pool and walked

around it to his bench, he saw that it was occupied. And not only occupied, but a body lay stretched out on it. In all the years Billy had been coming to the bench, it had never once been occupied. Billy could barely contain his anger. This was *his* bench and nobody was going to take it away from him. He wasn't a violent man, but things had simply gone too far and he was going to have to do something quite drastic. He cast about for a stone big enough to threaten the intruder and found one at the edge of the pool, a smooth river boulder about the size of a cricket ball. He wasn't quite sure how he'd use it, but this didn't seem to matter, the rock in his hand gave him courage. He'd swear and threaten and hold the rock up in a belligerent manner, and hope this would be sufficient to send the bench thief packing.

Approaching closer, Billy recognised the pair of scuffed Cubans, then the moleskins and the tartan shirt, although the black man's Akubra appeared to be missing. All the steam went out of him. He dropped the rock and stood quite still, waiting for his heartbeat to slow down to normal. He couldn't possibly threaten Williams. If the Aborigine wasn't exactly a mate, he owed him some sort of respect. Besides, his hat was missing and Billy guessed that the ancient Akubra was part of the stockman's very being, that he must have been extremely drunk to have lost it. The least he could do for the poor bastard was find it again. Billy told himself that this might square things up and assuage his guilt for the incident at the Flag.

There was only one way to the bench since the path ended at the pond, so Billy retraced his steps. On a small patch of lawn to the left of the gravel path and some twenty metres down from where Williams was lying, he saw an empty scotch bottle and, half hidden in a patch of pampas grass, the hat.

Williams had obviously selected the lawn as a place to rest but when the sun had moved directly overhead and become too hot, he had decided to move on, falling arse over tit into the tall clump of ornamental grass and losing his hat in the process. Billy could clearly see where the grass had been flattened by his fall. Williams would have regained his feet and staggered along the pathway to the bench, leaving his hat behind.

Billy retrieved the stockman's precious Akubra and approached the sleeping man. Standing over him, Billy inquired, 'You all right, mate?'

Williams didn't move. After a few moments, Billy put the hat down on the gravel pathway and shook him tentatively, then a little more roughly, but still he didn't respond. Finally he shook Williams vigorously, his free hand gripping his shoulder tightly, 'Wake up, damn you!' Billy shouted in frustration, but he knew the black man had slipped into a drunken coma.

Suddenly furious again, Billy kicked out at the bench and felt a stab of pain shoot through his knee. The Aborigine lay face-down, his mouth pushed hard against a wooden slat. It was not unusual for a drunk to throw up while in a coma and if this happened, Williams could possibly drown in his own vomit. Billy knew he'd have to move him so that he lay on his side with his mouth free to breathe. He told himself the bastard could die for all he cared, but knew this wasn't true.

Billy sighed. 'Why me?' he exclaimed, appealing to the sky, then unlocked the handcuff about his wrist and rested the briefcase against the leg of the bench. Williams lay with one arm folded under his stomach while his other hung loosely over the side of the bench, his fingers slightly bent and his knuckles touching the pathway. Billy attempted to roll him over onto his side but the bench proved too narrow and its backrest prevented the black man's body from turning. Billy pulled Williams forward so that half of his body rested over the lip of the bench. Bending his knees to take the man's weight, he gave a great heave and managed to roll Williams on to his side, his head now turned outwards towards the path, his mouth and nose free to breathe. The effort caused Billy to breathe heavily and his nostrils picked up the sour smell mixed with stale alcohol fumes on the black man's breath. He pulled back involuntarily and it was then that he saw it. Clutched in the Aborigine's fist was the wad of fifty-dollar notes he'd seen in the pub.

Billy could scarcely believe his eyes. He'd temporarily forgotten about the money, but now with Williams lying there, he couldn't leave him on his own. He reached down, expecting to have to pry the notes from the stockman's fist, but the moment he touched the blackfella's fingers they relaxed and the stash of pale-yellow plastic notes rolled free and rested on the bench against the stockman's stomach. Billy's heart started to pound and, despite himself, he glanced down the pathway to make sure nobody was coming before he reached for the stash. Bending down, he clicked open his briefcase and quickly dropped the money into its interior, snapping it shut, as if by his action he could make the money disappear from his mind.

Billy had no intention of stealing the blackfella's money. Nor did he want to have the responsibility of keeping it for him. If he was robbed, something that could happen easily enough, or stopped by a policeman, just as Phillip Orr had done this morning, how would he explain himself? He felt both vulnerable and guilty.

Billy tried to think what he should do, but the money confused him, it was too great a responsibility and he simply couldn't cope. He told himself that he wasn't supposed to be responsible for anything or anyone. That was why he was among the homeless. As a derelict, he didn't have to feel guilty any longer. He'd paid the price, he was free of obligation to his fellow man. Why should he care about the black bloke? He was a drunk and drunks get rolled, it was what happened in the big smoke. He thought about putting the money back, shoving it into the pocket of the stockman's moleskins. Maybe Williams would get lucky and wake up and still have it. Even if it was stolen, it was none of Billy's business anyway.

But Billy couldn't do that. He knew that even if the cops found Williams first, the likelihood of him getting his money back was zero. A couple of grand found in the possession of a derelict was a bonus no police officer was going to pass up. He imagined the scene. 'Here, mate, here's your fags and lighter and we found this,' and the cop handing him back his cash. What a joke. It would be a first for the boys in blue all right and, shortly after, the cop who'd returned the money would be officially certified as mentally deficient and dismissed from the Force.

Billy thought about writing a note and stuffing it in the blackfella's shirt pocket, telling Williams he'd meet him at Foster House, a hostel known as a 'Proclaimed Place', run by the Salvation Army and available to drug addicts and alcoholics who would be brought in to sleep it off. Foster House, among other such places, was referred to among derelicts as the drunk tank. Billy hated the drunk tank the God-botherers offered him in the name of charity and a government subsidy. A night spent in the dormitory at any one of the drunk tanks depressed him for days afterwards. Even though he would be too drunk to protect himself when admitted, the twenty-six men in the windowless dormitory who cried out in their sleep, vomited and defecated upset him more than he liked to admit. While the charities made every effort to keep the dormitory safe and clean, waking up in a drunk tank was not an experience anyone would voluntarily submit to. Though sometimes it was necessary, as instanced by Williams, who was unable to protect or care for himself.

Billy knew the routine well enough. He'd call Mission Beat and tell them of the stockman's whereabouts. They'd come in their van to fetch Williams and put him in the drunk tank for the night, where Billy would meet him in the morning after he'd sobered up.

There was only one thing wrong with this idea, he had to

hang onto the money in the meantime, a responsibility he wasn't prepared to accept. In his present state, Billy was convinced the presence of the money in his briefcase placed him in terrible danger. His paranoia was not entirely without reason. If Casper Friendly blamed him for the scam going wrong, he might decide to teach him a lesson and come looking for him with some of his henchmen. Casper believed in intimidation and he and his men would proceed to kick the living daylights out of Billy. Then they might search his briefcase and when they found the money, there was a good chance they'd do him in. Casper wasn't stupid and Billy wasn't just another derelict whose word couldn't be trusted. They'd tell themselves that left alive he'd be a reliable plaintiff, dead he would become just another unfortunate statistic among the homeless. Billy's hope was that the bottle of scotch Williams had paid for had left Casper legless and that he'd wake up having forgotten the entire incident.

Billy couldn't help feeling sorry for himself. From the moment he'd been quarrelled awake by Arthur and Martha, things had started going wrong. First the boy, then the cop, then Sam Snatch putting undue pressure on him, and after that Casper Friendly, and now the blackfella passed out on his own private writing bench. It was little comfort to Billy to think that somewhere in the vicinity there were fifty or so mynah birds wishing their forefathers had remained in India.

Billy tried to think coherently. The only way he could be rid of the responsibility of holding onto the money was to accompany Williams in the Mission Beat van to Foster House, where he'd hand the cash over to Major Pollard.

Pollard was a man of God and Billy would make him swear not to tell anyone that he'd returned the money, though this plan also had its problems. God-botherers were consumed by the duty of honesty and Pollard would be forced to ask himself how Billy or, for that matter, Williams had acquired the money. Pollard would then be compelled for the sake of his own protection to tell someone else or he could be indicted for possessing stolen goods. Billy was a lawyer and he knew that secrets are only kept when the incentive to keep them leads to a greater gain than may be had by revealing them. God's people may not have judged the poor souls they cared for, but they were under no illusions about their charges and weren't silly enough to place themselves in jeopardy by accepting the word of an alcoholic.

Secrets always come out. He could hear it now: 'Did you hear about Billy O'Shannessy? He found this stash, enough to stay drunk for six months, and returned it to its rightful owner, an Abo bloke who'd come in from the bush.' He'd be regarded as the ultimate fool, a laughing stock among the city derelicts who equated honesty with a characteristic most often found among the mentally retarded.

Billy made his way back to the nearest telephone booth in Macquarie Street and put a call through to Mission Beat, instructing them that he'd wait for them at the Botanic Gardens gate across the road from the State Library. Williams, he told the operator, was completely out of it, probably in a coma, and they'd need an extra person to help carry the stretcher.

The woman on the switch at Mission Beat had a high-pitched and whingeing quality to her voice and Billy heard her sigh heavily on the other end of the phone. 'We're short-staffed, the volunteers only come on after five, you'll have to help with the stretcher.'

'Nah, I've got a crook leg,' Billy said, in a coarser accent than his own. He'd done enough for Williams without having to hobble along holding on to one end of a stretcher.

The woman at the other end of the phone gave an audible sigh, 'Hang on a moment,' she said. A couple of minutes later her voice came back on the line, 'It will be about half an hour, wait at the gate.' The phone went dead.

To Billy's surprise, the van did arrive half an hour later and Billy explained that the bench on which Williams lay was a hundred metres or so inside the park. The driver, a fit young Maori in a red and black Canterbury Crusaders' rugby jersey, nodded and then turned to a skinny bloke beside him who looked as if he might be on drugs. 'You git the stretcher out the back, hey.' The young bloke started to get out of the van. 'Nah, wait on, lemme park first, hey.' The Maori indicated to Billy to step aside and pulled the van up onto the pavement before reversing to get as close to the gate entrance as he could.

The young bloke got out and approached the back of the van. 'Gidday, mate,' he said, smiling at Billy and offering his hand. Long strands of dirty, sandy-coloured hair fell to his shoulders and his small goatee was decorated with several pimples on the right side of his mouth. Heroin usually brought out pimples so he was probably on a methadone program and attempting to stay clean. His yellow cap was turned the wrong way round in the current fashion. Billy ignored his outstretched hand, which the kid didn't seem to mind. 'Helpin' yer mate out, that's good,' he said, nodding his head several times. 'No worries, we'll take care of him.'

Billy grunted, resenting the kid's cheerful outlook. He was supposed to be a miserable prick, wasn't he? He noticed that he wore long sleeves, buttoned at the wrist, another sign that he was concealing needle scars. Alcoholics hated heroin addicts and he'd been robbed on more than one occasion by dead ringers for this bloke. Billy thought about the money in his briefcase and what this bloke might do to him if he knew about it.

The young guy threw open the back of the van, which contained no surprises for Billy, who'd been a passenger in it on more than one occasion. A brown padded vinyl bench ran down either side with a stretcher hooked onto the inside roof by means of several brackets. The interior was designed to be hosed clean with a minimum of fuss and Billy's nostrils were immediately assailed by a strong smell of disinfectant.

The bloke on detox, for that's how Billy now regarded him, started to pull at the stretcher, which refused to budge. Then the Maori came around, 'Nah, it's clupped at the back, you got to git in an' unclup it.' Not waiting for his helper, he jumped into the back of the van and unclipped the stretcher, pushing it from his end so that it protruded out of the back of the van for the youngster to pull it free.

'You new to this work?' Billy asked.

'Yeah, doing three months' community service.' He laughed, 'Could be worse, a mate of mine's digging out blackberry bushes for Woollahra Council on South Head, bloody hard yakka.'

He'd been right, the young bloke was a junkie.

The driver jumped from the back of the van. 'Righto, let's go fetch your brother.' He turned to Billy, 'My name's Hopi.' He indicated his assistant with a nod of the head, 'This is Jimmy. You show us where to go, hey.'

Billy led them into the Botanic Gardens, down the main path and then they branched off on to a smaller path leading to the giant Moreton Bay fig. Billy was conscious of the magpies carolling in the big dark tree silhouetted against a washed and clear summer sky.

They reached the rock pool and Billy led them around the back. 'He's round here,' he said, pointing. Then he saw that Williams was missing.

'You sure that's the bench?' Hopi asked.

'Yeah, yeah, quite certain.'

'Lotsa benches in this place, hey?'

'No, not around here. He was out to it, comatose. I shook him, shouted at him, he didn't move. He can't have gone far.'

Hopi shook his head. 'Mate, I can't leave the van on the pavement, I'll get a ticket.' He removed a slip of paper from his shirt pocket and unfolded it. 'Says here the client is reported as being unconscious.'

'That's right, he was.'

'It's the rules.' The big New Zealander shrugged. 'It's the rules. We're allowed to take him in without his permission if he's unconscious. If he ain't, he's got to agree to come.' He spread his hands and smiled, 'Which he can't if he ain't here. Sorry about that.' He nodded to the young bloke, then jerked his head, indicating they should leave.

'Wait on!' Billy cried, 'He could be lying somewhere close by, in the bushes.'

The Maori looked back and said, not unkindly, 'You find him, call us again, we'll come for sure.'

Billy walked over to the bench and sat down, panic-stricken. He had the best part of five thousand dollars in his briefcase and its rightful owner had disappeared. Technically he'd stolen the money. His leg hurt and he needed a drink badly, he couldn't remember when he'd been this sober this late in the day. Somehow he had to find Williams, track him down and give him back his money. It wasn't his responsibility what happened after that, he'd done his best, even called the drunk wagon on his behalf.

Billy rose wearily from the bench and made for the Moreton Bay. Its dark-green foliage reached almost to the ground, and if you didn't mind the bat shit, its semi-dark interior was an ideal place to sleep it off. Williams would have come around, seen the tree and had the nous to crawl into its safety. He was from the bush, he'd have a strong sense of survival.

Billy made his way over to the big old tree and dipped in under the low-hanging foliage to stand in the dark, moist-smelling shade. He waited until his eyes had adjusted before looking for Williams. The giant tree had enormous surface roots that acted as buttresses and could easily hide a man from view. Billy could hear the fruit bats squeaking in the branches overhead as he walked slowly around the tree, looking between the buttresses, certain that at any moment he would find the stockman. But there was no sign of Williams.

Billy searched the Gardens for another hour. He asked several gardeners but only one of them could remember seeing a black man in a red tartan shirt and that was earlier when Williams had first entered the Gardens. Billy crossed over to the Domain and asked a group of derelicts who had settled in to the late-afternoon's drinking session under the trees. They all knew Billy and extended an invitation for him to join them. Alcoholics pride themselves on being social, almost a brotherhood, it is what separates them from the heroin addicts and they'll happily share a bottle with a mate who happens to be skint. Most of them had been helped at one time or another by Billy. Then Billy saw Casper Friendly was among the group, but much to his relief he'd passed out on the grass. He lay on his stomach, his head cradled in his arms. Williams' bottle of scotch had caught up with him.

Billy described Williams and several of them laughed and shook their heads. 'Yer lookin' for a fuckin' boong, mate!' called out one of them, a man named Lofty Mayne. 'Whafuckinfor?' This provoked more drunken laughter.

'He needs a spot of help,' Billy replied.

'Ah, forget the bastard,' Lofty said, 'Here, Billy, have a drink, no good helpin' them black bastards!'

Billy pointed to the unconscious Casper Friendly, 'He's an Aborigine.'

The men in the group all looked at the albino. 'Who, Casper?' Lofty said, turning back to Billy.

Billy nodded.

'Nah, he got hisself scrubbed white, that's different.' This provoked a howl of laughter among the group, several of them reaching out and patting Lofty on the back.

'Garn, 'ave a drink,' Lofty said, pleased with himself.

'No thanks, some other time,' Billy began to walk away.

'Hey, Billy, c'mere,' Lofty shouted, beckoning Billy with a wave of his arm.

Billy stopped, 'What?' he said, turning.

'That fuckin' Abo yiz looking for,' Lofty grinned, 'I reckon he's fell down some steps, them black bastards can't hold their grog! Always fallin' down steps. No fuckin' steps in the desert when they go walkabout, see!' Lofty's attempt at a joke set off another gale of laughter among the drunks. 'C'mere, siddown, 'ave a drink, whazzamatter?' he repeated.

Billy was sorely tempted, but the presence of Casper Friendly and the possibility of him waking up and being curious as to why Billy was looking for Trevor Williams decided him against it. 'Another time. Got to go, mate.'

'Ah, fuck yiz!' Lofty called after him. 'Too good fer us, is yer? Fuck off then!'

As the day wore on, Billy's paranoia increased and while he told himself that apart from the almost three glasses of scotch he'd consumed in the morning, his head was clear as a bell, the only problem was that he couldn't get it to ring, to make any reasonable decisions.

He sat down on a bench outside the Art Gallery, both elbows resting on the briefcase on his lap, his hands cupped under his chin. He watched as several late-afternoon runners passed by on their way to Mrs Macquarie's Chair, doing the loop around the Gardens. A group of middle-aged Japanese tourists was coming out of the gallery in a neat formation, giggling and chatting loudly. Billy thought how nice it would be if he didn't have to think any more and could simply follow the little Jap bloke holding the flag. He'd have a nice hotel to go to, with tucker laid on, a soft bed with clean sheets, and the bill paid in advance. He was exhausted, feeling a little dizzy, and realised that he couldn't remember when last he'd eaten.

For the umpteenth time, he reviewed his options. Now it occurred to him that Williams himself might report the stolen money to the police when he sobered up in the morning, citing Casper or Billy as two people who'd seen the stash in his possession. The police would have no trouble picking Billy up and, of course, they'd find the money in his briefcase.

The more Billy thought of the pickle he'd put himself in, the more he became convinced that unless he got to Williams first, the case against him was open and shut. No magistrate or judge would believe that he'd acted in good faith. If he'd had to handle a case like this when he'd been a practising barrister, he wouldn't have given his client any chance of winning. He'd make him plead mitigating circumstances, an act committed while under the influence, citing the fact that his client had no previous record. The best he would have hoped for was a shorter sentence. Sitting on the bench outside the Art Gallery, the afternoon drawing to a close, Billy could hear the cell door at Long Bay clanging shut behind him.

He'd already thought about giving the money to Con for safekeeping but decided against doing so. Con was his friend, though it was a friendship that had never been truly tested. The cafe owner might well baulk at the idea and Billy wouldn't blame him if he did. Even if he agreed to keep the money in safekeeping while Billy tried to find Williams, if things went wrong, and the lawyer in Billy told him that they invariably do, Con would be an accessory to the crime too. Furthermore, Billy would be totally discredited and no longer eligible as Con's sponsor and character referee, a fact which might well prevent the owner of the New Hellas Cafe from bringing out his wife-to-be from Greece.

Billy had been among the homeless for four years and he'd always told himself that the decision to cut all his previous ties was in the interest of all concerned, that by leaving his wife and the daughter he loved he'd made it easier for them to get on with their lives without the daily reminder of the past that his presence brought them. He was not to be trusted and he was best being on his own, well away from anyone he could hurt. The loneliness that had followed had been of his own making, a punishment he repeatedly told himself he deserved. But now, for the first time, he realised that there wasn't anyone whom he could trust and no one who would trust him. He had gone beyond aloneness and severed even the most tenuous connections of his life.

It was growing dark when Billy finally rose from the bench. Despite his state of anxiety he was hungry, which was probably the cause of his dizziness so he decided to make his way to the food van in Martin Place.

It was only an eight-minute walk from the Art Gallery to Martin Place and Billy arrived before the van had drawn up for the evening meal. A number of people had already gathered and were waiting in the fronts of shops and banks, most of them male. He recognised one or two faces but, apart from a brief nod, there was no contact, which was the accepted convention. The young blokes who came in for a free feed were usually pretty aggro and it wasn't a good idea to look them in the eyes. Anonymity was the unspoken code among the homeless.

Billy found a seat and, placing his briefcase on his lap, kept his eyes on the ground. A young bloke came up to him and asked for a light.

'Don't smoke,' Billy said, not looking up.

'What's with the handcuffs?' the teenager asked, pointing to the briefcase.

Billy put his finger up to his lips. 'Shush!' He looked left, then right, and in a loud whisper said, 'Blueprints, mate. Atomic bomb.' Tucking his head into his shoulder, he repeated the look to each side. 'You haven't seen any Chinese, have you?' He lowered his voice even further, 'They want them urgent, they're going to blow up the White House.' Billy pulled the briefcase tightly to his chest, a look of alarm on his face. 'You won't tell them, will ya?'

The young bloke turned his head to one side and,

pursing his lips, made as if to spit at the ground near his feet. 'Fuckin' schizo!' he said, moving away.

The food van had arrived and people were starting to walk up towards it. The Just Enough Faith van was one of several around the city, most of which were run by religious organisations, although not this one.

Just Enough Faith was run personally by Jeff Gambin and his wife Alina, who came about as close to being modern-day saints as was possible in today's iconoclastic world. They financed the van and bought and prepared its daily fare from their own resources and, in addition, worked to rehabilitate and help the homeless and the destitute. No one needing food or help was ever turned away and they would feed around six hundred people a night. When asked what sort of people came to the van they would tell how their youngest client was just four months old and their oldest ninety-five. The food dispensed free from the van was well prepared with a wide choice and was generally regarded as better than that placed on most tables at home. Not all homeless people were alcoholics and food was an important factor in their lives and so the vans, just like restaurants, were given a rating: Just Enough Faith being the best and the so-called restaurant for the homeless, Our Lady of Snows, near Central Station, regularly voted the worst.

Billy not only used Just Enough Faith because of its convenience and the quality of its food, but because Martin Place was well lit and therefore less dangerous.

After the incident with the teenager, Billy's knees were shaking so violently that he dared not rise. He sat a while longer until his beating heart had slowed and most of the street people had been served. The ruse he'd used with the young bloke always worked, because, apart from the drunks, the addicts, pensioners and street kids, the square on any given evening would contain its fair share of schizophrenics and mentally disturbed who'd been freed from government institutions and allowed to re-enter the community to swell the ranks of the hopeless and homeless.

People moved quietly up to the queue, where the unspoken aggression in the air seemed to dissipate. There was no pecking order as might be expected, with young blokes asserting themselves and pushing to the front. It was first come, first served, everyone acting decorously, choosing their meal in an undertone and then finding a quiet place to eat it. Food remained the only sacred factor in their lives.

'Good evening,' Jeff Gambin called to Billy. 'How are you tonight, Billy? Nice of you to drop by.' Gambin, a Tibetan, was educated in India and later at Cambridge and, recognising Billy for a cultured man, always treated him like a gentleman.

'Good evening, Mr Gambin,' Billy answered, for although Jeff Gambin regarded him as a familiar, he was careful not to take the compliment for granted.

'Nice pot of Irish stew going. You always seem to enjoy it?'

'Yes, thank you, that will do nicely,' Billy replied, not really fussed about what to eat.

'We're moving, Billy, been kicked out of Martin Place,' Jeff Gambin said, handing Billy a brimming plate.

'Oh, kicked out, why is that?'

'The Olympics, can't have people like us messing up the centre of the city.'

'But the Olympics are in four years!' Billy exclaimed.

'Get us used to going elsewhere,' Jeff Gambin shrugged. 'Get us all accustomed to going elsewhere, somewhere out of sight.' He always included himself and his wife when he referred to the homeless.

'Have they told you where?'

'St Mary's Cathedral,' Gambin grinned. 'In the shadow of the mother church, overseas visitors will now see us as God's benign hand at work, not a bad piece of art direction, eh?'

Billy, shaking his head, thanked him and took a small serving of stew and a couple of slices of bread over to a bench where he ate in a distracted manner, hardly tasting the dish. Then he completed the first meal he'd eaten in two days with a cup of hot, sweet, milky tea laced with the usual six sachets of sugar. Considerably strengthened in both body and mind, he told himself that a glass of scotch had been well and truly earned. Just the one glass, mind, to calm his nerves. There was a pub at the bottom of William Street he sometimes used and he set off in that direction, crossing the lights at the museum.

At ten o'clock closing time, the publican threw him out. As he made his way haltingly up College Street and into Macquarie Street towards his arboreal sleeping quarters, he talked aloud to himself, stopping frequently and looking about him, his eyes clearly not focused. 'Done my best, looked for the bugger everywhere, didn't I? Best intentions. Done all I could. Bastard wandered off, wasn't my fault. Done my best.'

He stopped unsteadily in front of Parliament House, head back and to one side, squinting at the policeman standing at the gate. 'Even-ing, offica.'

'Better get your head down, mate,' the policeman replied in a friendly enough voice. 'Want me to call Mission Beat?'

'No, saulright!' Billy called, moving away. 'Nearly there! Thank you. Thank you very . . . much oblige, offica.'

Billy soon forgot the policeman and continued mumbling on about Williams. 'He had no right. Disappear. Do this to me. Make me responsible. Not fair, not bloody fair. Can't help his girlie, can I? Oops! Wash your step, Billy! Abo bastard! Bugger all of 'em. Pestilence on all of you bastards! Shit, I'm pissed! Billy O'Shan . . . nessy, you're drunk as a skunk. Pissed as a newt. In . . . in . . . e . . . briated. Oh shit, I . . . I wanna go home!'

He reached the side of the library. Too drunk to think, he decided to take a shortcut to his bench through a bed of wild iris lining the pavement. The plants fell over the edge, concealing the low wall that edged the flower bed and Billy, failing to allow for it, went flying through the air to land most fortuitously in the centre of a large stand of the irises, missing the edge of the paving by centimetres.

He sat up slowly and examined himself, but, as is so often the case with drunks, seemed none the worse for wear. The automatic sprinkler must have come on at some time during the evening because his arm felt wet. Billy was also vaguely aware that his left wrist hurt where the shackled briefcase had pulled away from his body as he fell forward, but the drink anaesthetised him against any major pain. He tried to rise to his feet, lost his balance and fell backwards onto his bum. 'Oops!' he said to himself, 'Careful, Billy-boy!' His second attempt to rise was more successful. Wobbling somewhat, he looked carefully about and launched his body in the direction of the bench, his hand stretched out towards it in anticipation of his arrival. He reached the bench without further mishap and stood for a moment swaying and holding tightly onto the back rest. Billy glanced up at the statue of Trim on the window ledge of the library. 'Ow yer goin', Trim, old son . . . I'm drunk sa Lord! Drunk sa skunk . . . Who's afraid a drunken sailor, eh? Seenit all, haven't you, son.'

Then he sat down, his bony bum bumping down hard onto the wooden slats. He attempted to lift his briefcase up to the bench, but it was too heavy and again he became aware that his wrist was painful. Gripping the leather handle with both hands, Billy hauled the case onto his lap, allowing it to lie on its side. He lifted his legs up onto the bench and fell back, bumping the back of his head hard against the wooden slats. The briefcase now sat on his chest and he rested his palms on the worn leather.

He watched as the moon shone through the canopy of ficus leaves, moving, dipping and dancing among the whirling branches as he tried, without success, to focus on it. He was drunk and sad, then he began to weep softly.

CHAPTER THREE

Arthur and Martha yelling at each other from adjacent lampposts brought Billy slowly back to consciousness. He lay on his bench, his eyes closed, trying to gauge the extent of his hangover. His head throbbed and he didn't dare lift it or sit up for fear of the additional pain that he knew would follow. Too drunk last night to place the briefcase against the leg of the bench, it now rested partially on his chest, its weight further restricting his breathing. His wrist was painful but he thought of it as only another component of his overall condition. He knew from experience that a hangover of this dimension should be treated with the utmost care. By approaching it slowly and without careless movement, its severity could be somewhat contained.

He was badly dehydrated and his tongue stuck to the roof of his mouth, forcing him to breathe through his nose. With his eyes still shut, Billy located the latch to his briefcase and clicked it open. He was unaware of how badly his hand shook as he rummaged through its contents until he located the small leather pouch containing his hangover pebbles. Fortuitously, the drawstring to the pouch hadn't been drawn and tied so he managed to insert his forefinger and thumb to locate the pebble he needed. He knew by its shape which was the tiger's eye, the preferred pebble when he'd been drinking scotch. Attempting to open his mouth, he discovered that his lips were paper-dry and stuck together. He could feel the sting of the tissue tearing and the salty taste of blood as he forced the pebble between his lips. Then he waited for the spittle to gather around the tiger's eye so he could salivate to the point where his tongue could move freely.

Sooner or later he'd have to stagger over to the drinking fountain in Martin Place, then down into the station to relieve his bladder, but for the moment he was content to lie perfectly still. Billy's head pounded so fiercely he could hear it, clear as a drumbeat, reverberating in his cranium. He was only vaguely aware of the sound of a skateboard on the pavement and the sudden silence as it stopped.

'You've got a hard-on,' a young voice announced.

Billy groaned, 'Not the boy! Please not the boy!' he thought desperately.

A giggle followed, 'Don't worry, I've seen it lotsa times. When blokes come home and it stands up like that in their pants, me mum calls it "the circus tent". You know why?' The voice, bubbling with mirth, didn't wait for an answer. 'Because some clown is about to perform an act!'

Groaning, Billy opened his eyes and pushed himself up

into a sitting position, dropping his legs over the bench. A sharp, almost unbearable pain jolted through his cranium and down his spine and he thought for a moment his head might explode as the blood drained from his brain. His movement caused the briefcase to slip off his lap and fall over the edge of the bench, its weight jerking the manacle about his wrist. 'Jesus!' Billy screamed as the briefcase hung over the edge.

The boy moved forward quickly and, grabbing the briefcase's handle, placed it back on the bench beside Billy. Billy, panting from the sudden rush of adrenaline, waited for the pain to subside a little before reaching for the key around his neck. He attempted to open the handcuff, but his hands shook so badly that it became impossible for him to insert the key into the locking device.

'Here, give's a go,' the boy said, holding his hand out for the key. He unlocked the handcuff and gently eased it away from the wrist. 'It's real bad. Yiz'll have to go to the 'ospital.'

Billy, still too confused to thank the child, tried instead to bring his hands up to cover his face, but the act of moving his left arm sent a fresh stab of pain through his wrist. He raised his head slowly and looked at the boy for the first time, unable to speak.

'Want some water? I'll get you some water if you like?' the boy offered.

Billy nodded.

With the boy gone, Billy looked down at his crotch. He knew he didn't have an erection, or if he did, then the area around his appendage must have suffered some sort of paralysis. Yet an erection was there all right, bigger than anything he'd ever been able to boast about. Slowly it dawned on him. The stash! The blackfella's money! In his drunken stupor he'd stuck the roll of banknotes down the front of his trousers. He put the money into the briefcase and rummaged about for the pebble pouch, but when he tried to put the pebble back, it fell from his grasp and into the bottom of the case. Now he lacked the energy to search for it.

Billy closed the briefcase and looked up to see the boy holding a paper coffee cup out in front of his body the way kids do when they've overfilled a cup, concentrating on every step, careful not to spill a drop. The kid was bright enough, he'd obviously scavenged the cup from a nearby street bin. 'There you go,' he said, smiling and holding out the water.

Billy reached for it, but his hand shook so violently it was obvious he'd spill the contents before he could drink it. 'Here's a go,' the boy said, bringing the cup to Billy's lips and allowing him to take a sip. After Billy had swallowed most of the water, he placed the cup on the bench.

'Thank you, lad,' Billy croaked, his first words to the boy. 'I am most grateful to you.'

'No worries, me mum's same as you sometimes and me nana also, now she's crook.'

Billy was too preoccupied with his own condition to think what this might mean.

'I come about the cat,' the boy said suddenly.

'The cat?'

'Yeah, that one,' the boy pointed behind Billy. 'On the

winda over there. You told me about it, remember? Yesterday mornin'.'

Billy was silent for a moment, his befuddled brain searching for a suitable reply, though in the end all he could manage was 'Trim?'

'Yeah, him.'

Billy appeared to be thinking. In fact, he was stalling for time. He knew he would be quite incapable of any sort of conversation in his present condition, let alone tell the story he'd conjured up in his imagination. He could always tell the boy to bugger off. But that was potentially dangerous. Young as he was, he'd probably know a street gang or even be in one. Besides, it would be lacking in manners, the lad had been kind to him and there was no point in alienating him.

'It's not that easy,' he said at last. 'I'll have to ask him, he may not feel like talking.'

'Ask him? He's already dead. That's a statue.'

'Well, that's true and then again it isn't.'

'What's that supposed t'mean?'

'Well . . . it's why I sleep on this bench.' Billy was becoming exhausted and his head hurt with the extra effort it took to think.

'Eh?' The boy looked confused.

Billy sighed. 'Look, lad, you really must excuse me, I'm just not up to it today.'

The boy ignored his plea. 'What about sleeping on the bench?'

Billy wiped his hand across his face in a gesture of

weariness. 'The cat, I mean, Trim, he sometimes talks to me when I lie on the bench.'

'Dead-set? He talks to you and you talk back?'

'Only in my head, in my imagination.'

The boy, suddenly scornful, drew back. 'You one of them schizos?'

Despite his condition Billy smiled, only a street kid his age would know about schizophrenia.

'No, no I'm not, I'm a . . .'

'Yiz an alky,' the boy said firmly. 'I didn't know alkies also hear stuff in their head.'

'No, they don't usually, not unless they're also schizo-phrenics, the two sometimes go together,' Billy explained. 'It seems schizophrenics use alcohol to stop the talking going on, as you said, in their head.'

The boy pointed over Billy's shoulder, 'But you just said that cat . . .'

'Trim, his name is Trim.'

'Trim then. You said he talks to yiz.'

Billy realised that the boy didn't understand that his conversation with Trim was imaginary and so he changed tack. 'Only in my sleep.'

'Like when you're having a dream?'

'Yes, precisely.'

'Can you ask him stuff?'

'You can do anything in a dream.'

The boy seemed to be thinking for a moment. 'Will yer talk to him ternight?'

'I'll try, he's not always there.'

'Statues don't move!'

'His spirit does, Trim's spirit. Cats like to go walkabout.'

The boy seemed to accept this explanation. 'Termorra. I'll come back termorra mornin'. Promise you'll try?'

Billy grabbed the opportunity to end their conversation and see the boy on his way. 'I promise. Now I really must go.' He made as if to rise.

The boy shrugged. 'I got to take you to St Vinnie's.'

'I beg your pardon?' Billy wasn't sure he'd heard him correctly.

The boy pointed down to Billy's wrist. 'It's swollen somethin' terrible.'

Something terrible. It was a quaint old-fashioned expression a nanny he'd had as a child used to use and Billy wondered where the boy had picked it up. The boy, despite his background, had a confidence about him that belied his age.

Billy straightened up and tried to assert himself. 'You'll do no such thing! I can take myself.'

'Nah, derros won't. They hate the 'ospital.'

'Oh, you're an authority on our medical habits, are you?'

The boy ignored the question. 'St Vinnie's don't mind derros, they're Catlick, see.'

'There's a hospital in this block, not fifty metres away,' Billy protested. 'I can go there,' though he had no intention of doing anything of the sort.

The boy drew his lips into a pout and shook his head, 'Nah, no good.' He didn't explain further.

'You seem to know a great deal about hospitals, young man?'

The boy nodded his head. 'Yup!' Now he squinted at Billy, 'If you'll come to St Vinnie's I'll buy you a coffee at the Cesco Bar.' The boy pulled at the dog-collar chain that fell in a loop from his belt to disappear into one of the many pockets in his trousers and pulled out a small leather purse attached to the end. Opening the purse, he produced a fifty-dollar note. 'See, I got money.'

Billy tried to sound decisive despite the headache that pounded through his temple. 'Thank you, that's very kind, but I don't think so. Despite what you have to say, if I need a hospital, the one next door is perfectly adequate.' He looked momentarily at the boy. 'Besides, I have a great deal to do.' It worried him that a child so young could produce a fifty-dollar note with such equanimity, but then Billy told himself he didn't want to get involved.

'They ain't Catlicks.' The boy returned the money to his purse and pushed it back into his pocket. 'Yiz'll need a needle,' he said.

'Needle? Why will I need a needle?'

'Tetanus.'

Billy glanced at the boy in surprise. 'Tetanus? I have a sprained wrist.'

'Yeah and it's cut, germs'll get in. Pus and stuff. There's probably some there already.' The boy looked serious. 'You can get lockjaw, you know.'

'No, not at all. Tetanus is a bacterium that lives in soil, it can enter when you fall and graze yourself or step on a rusty nail.'

The boy thought for a moment. 'Derros get drunk and

fall over and stuff gets in,' he indicated Billy's wrist, 'Yiz already got some dirt on yer arm, how'd you get that?'

Billy glanced at his arm to see the boy was right, the inner part of his arm, including the wrist area, was caked in dried mud. He vaguely remembered the fall he'd taken the previous night. 'It's only a superficial wound, I'll get something from the chemist later.' Then he added, 'Please, I need to go to the toilet in Martin Place.' He rose and it appeared for a moment as though he was going to lose his balance. Grabbing onto the back of the seat, he steadied himself.

'See! Yiz crook.'

Billy looked down at the child in front of him. The boy was being inordinately stubborn and much too self-assured for his age. 'How old are you?' he asked.

'Eleven, nearly . . . more eleven than ten.'

He'd mentioned a mother so obviously he wasn't a street kid although he appeared neglected, somewhat scruffy and in need of a good feed. He wore a black T-shirt with the word 'Independent' in white letters across the front and, in smaller letters under it, the two words 'Truck Company', a pair of baggy army-disposal shorts that reached halfway down his shins and a pair of Vans. While his clothing was up-to-the-moment skateboard gear, its condition indicated that the adult in his life had a careless regard for his personal hygiene.

'Could you help me with my briefcase, please?' Billy asked, extending his right arm.

'I'll carry it for yiz.'

'No, please! Just shackle it to my good wrist.'

'They know me at St Vinnie's, you won't have to wait, yer know.'

'No, thank you, I'm quite capable of going to hospital on my own.'

'It's swollen real bad,' the boy persisted stubbornly, 'Don't look good, could be broke.'

'Thank you, doctor,' Billy said in a feeble attempt to make a joke. 'Men don't easily break their wrists.' It was something he remembered from a case he'd once conducted. 'The handcuff, would you help me, please?'

The boy sighed dramatically, picked up the briefcase, placed it adjacent to Billy's right wrist and attached the handcuff. 'How you gunna take a shit?' he said.

The question took Billy by surprise. 'The usual way, I imagine.'

'Oh yeah? Don't see how. Who's gunna wipe yer bum?'

Billy finally lost his patience. 'Look, bugger off, will you!'

To his surprise, the boy merely smiled and made no move to leave, cocking his head to one side. 'What's yer name then?'

'Billy! Now get packing.'

'At school when they ask, you're supposed to say yer full name. Want to know what mine is?'

Billy sighed. 'Not particularly, but I don't suppose I have a choice.'

'It's Ryan Sanfrancesco, like the place in America, only with an *e*.'

Billy nodded, his face deadpan. 'How do you do?'

'Can I call yiz Billy? Or do I have ter say Mister . . . and then your other name?'

'O'Shannessy without the *u*. You may call me Billy, but only if you leave right now.'

Ryan grinned, 'Termorra. You won't forget, will ya? You promised yiz'll talk ter the cat. Ter Trim.'

'Yes, yes, tomorrow. I promise.' Anything to get rid of the brat. Then Billy had a sudden stab of conscience. It had been a long time since he'd talked to a child and made a promise for the sake of a bit of peace. He wondered how often he'd done the same thing to Charlie and then failed to keep his word. Later, when his hangover had cleared a little, he'd realise that he hadn't asked the kid what it was he wished him to ask Trim. 'Tomorrow morning will be fine, Ryan.'

The boy named Ryan Sanfrancesco placed his foot down on the end of his skateboard so that the opposite end flipped upwards, allowing him to grab hold of it and swing it under his arm in a single neat movement. He walked the eighteen or so steps to the pavement and turned, 'See yiz!' he called cheerfully. Billy heard the clatter of the wheels on the cement, then a thump as the skateboard jumped the pavement, and later the softer sound of the wheels on bitumen as the kid crossed the road and took off in the direction of Hyde Park.

Billy sat for a while, trying to gather the energy to get going. The boy had exhausted him. After five minutes or so, he rose from the bench and started to walk down Macquarie Street on his way to Martin Place. He felt dreadful and the lad may have been right, his wrist was becoming increasingly painful and beginning to take priority over his hangover. He decided he'd do his ablutions first, then wait until the shops opened and get a sling from the pharmacy across the road, or maybe he'd do his ablutions and go down to the Quay for his usual assignation with Con. There was a pharmacy just across from Con's cafe, maybe he should take a couple of aspirin as well.

'Well, well, what have we got here?'

Billy looked up to see Sergeant Phillip Orr almost upon him. He panicked and turned to run but the policeman grabbed at his elbow and slid his hand down to Billy's wrist, gripping hard. Billy stopped and his legs buckled as he howled in sudden anguish, his knees hitting the pavement.

Orr released his grip and observed Billy's torn and swollen wrist. 'Jesus, what you done to yerself, mate?' But Billy, crouched on the pavement, could only whimper. The cop reached down and grabbed him by the belt and pulled him to his feet. 'Steady on, I'm not going to hurt you. Here, lemme take a look.'

Despite the shame, Billy felt sudden tears run down his cheeks as he held out his left arm for the policeman to examine. 'What yer do, get pissed and fall down?' Sergeant Orr took a step backwards and examined Billy. 'You've done a bloody good job on yerself, haven't you, mate.'

'I fell,' Billy whimpered. He wanted to wipe the tears from his cheeks but he couldn't, his left hand was extended for the cop to examine and his briefcase was shackled to his right.

'Yeah, I can see that.' He glanced at his watch and sighed. 'Better come along with me.' He indicated the hospital next door to Parliament House with a jerk of his head. 'Wrist could be sprained, needs a dressing anyway, looks a bloody mess.'

'No, please, sergeant! I'm . . . I'm just on my way to St Vincent's, they know me there,' Billy said, repeating Ryan's words.

'You a tyke?' Orr asked.

'No, but my wife was . . . er, is.'

'Suit yourself, but there's a perfectly good emergency right here. Take you half an hour to walk to St Vincent's.'

Billy tried to grin, 'Family's always gone there,' he lied.

The police sergeant glanced down at his watch again.

'Please, sergeant, I'll be fine, you must catch your train.'

The policeman hesitated a moment longer. 'Okay, Billy, I'll trust you.' He looked stern. 'But if I see you tomorrow morning and you haven't had it treated,' he paused and pointed to the briefcase, 'I'll find something inside that case to charge you with. Bloke who walks around with a briefcase handcuffed to his wrist is either silly in the head or he's got something to hide. You ain't silly in the head. Get my drift?'

Billy, unable to speak, nodded. The legs of his trousers started to shake as his knees trembled violently.

Orr was quick to see the effect of his threat. 'Got something to hide, have we?' His voice took on a threatening tone, 'Get your wrist attended to or I'm going through your shit like a pig snuffing for windfall apples.

Okay?' Then he turned and crossed the street hurriedly, heading for Martin Place station.

Billy's mouth had gone completely dry again. He felt quite sure he was going to pass out. The shock of the policeman's threat, the pain in his head and his injured wrist were rapidly becoming too much for him to bear and he knew his wobbly legs were unable to take him a step further. The thought of the policeman finding the blackfella's stash made him tremble afresh and he sank slowly to the pavement and sat with his back against the iron-railing fence of Parliament House. He closed his eyes, trying to concentrate in an attempt to bring his pounding heart under control.

'Here, give's the key,' a voice beside him said. He opened his eyes to see Ryan seated beside him, holding out his hand.

Billy hadn't heard Ryan approach and was suddenly unsure of how long he'd been sitting with his eyes closed. He knew that he was beyond protesting but the effort to raise his left arm proved impossible. Orr's fierce grip around his wrist had greatly exacerbated the pain and the slightest movement of his fingers sent an agonising stab, as if a long shard of broken glass was being forced up the inside of his arm and into his shoulder.

'I'll get it,' Ryan said, and leaping to his feet, reached down the back of Billy's neck and pulled the key chain over his head. He grinned, 'See, ya couldn't have wiped yer bum, could ya?' He removed the handcuff from around Billy's right wrist, leaving it dangling against the side of the briefcase. Billy's right hand immediately returned to the handle, gripping it protectively.

'Don't worry, I won't look inside it. I ain't the fuzz,' Ryan said calmly, replacing the key around Billy's neck.

'You heard the policeman?'

'Yeah, some stuff. I was across the road.' Ryan looked at Billy's hand clasped about the case. 'If we're gunna go to St Vinnie's like you told the cop, I'm gunna have to carry it. Yiz buggered, mate.'

Billy released his fingers from the handle of the briefcase. Ryan stooped down and snapped the handcuff around his own wrist.

'You don't have to do that!' Billy exclaimed.

'Yes I do, me mum says I can't trust no bugger and mustn't ever, it's the same for you. I could run off.' He extended his free hand to help Billy to his feet. 'C'mon, grab a hold, let's kick the dust.'

There it was again, an expression from the past. 'I'll be fine,' Billy said, trying to rise. He placed the palm of his right hand on the pavement at his rear and pushed, trying to rise. Reluctantly he took the boy's hand and struggled to his feet. 'Right,' Billy said, looking about, though at nothing in particular. He was trying to regain his composure, ashamed that he had become so dependent on the lad's help. It was just that there seemed to be too many fears invading him at the same time. He was a weak bastard.

Ryan flipped his skateboard up and under his arm and they began to walk up William Street to Kings Cross, turning right along Victoria Street towards St Vincent's. True to his word, Ryan called a halt outside Cesco's. A group of cyclists in their mid-forties and -fifties sat around the pavement tables posing in their skin-tight, multi-coloured riding gear, some of them clearly overweight. They'd removed their moulded plastic protective helmets since they thought they detracted from their image. A dozen or more five-thousand-dollar racing machines were arranged carelessly against the pavement edge in a bright tangle of spokes and neon colours. It was only just seven o'clock yet the place was full of people looking for a coffee fix or simply wanting to be seen.

Cesco, the owner, enjoyed a reputation for the best coffee in town and the shortest fuse. He had reputedly been a cruiserweight boxer in Italy, though nobody could recall if he'd ever been a champion. A pair of red boxing gloves hung from the lip of a giant cappuccino cup and saucer set on a special shelf built high up on the wall behind the espresso machine. Across the face of the cup were the words *Il Campione!* It wasn't clear whether this appellation referred to Cesco's boxing career or to the superior brand of Italian coffee he used. But it nevertheless succeeded in reminding patrons that Mr Cesco was not to be trifled with.

It was one of those curious anomalies that the more aggressive Cesco became, the greater the reputation of his coffee. Although his regular clients included dozens of celebrities and business high-fliers, Cesco was nobody's toady. He played early-morning host to a cross-section of

Sydney society, ranging from prostitutes to real-estate barons, stock-exchange millionaires to nightclub bouncers, lawyers as well as crims, drug addicts, doctors, media tycoons and building workers. All were equally welcome, provided they weren't drunk or off their heads from substance abuse, kept the peace and had the price of a cup of coffee in their pockets.

There was one exception. Children weren't allowed on the premises. Cesco sold only coffee, biscotti and Florentines. He considered caffeine bad for a child under sixteen and the Italian biscuits too good to waste on some yuppie's precocious little bastard.

Ryan placed his skateboard at Billy's feet, walked into the coffee bar and stood at the takeaway counter. When his turn came, he asked for a large cappuccino and held out his fifty-dollar note. The young woman doing takeaway shook her head, 'No kids,' she said, jerking her head towards a sign on the back wall.

'It's not for me,' Ryan protested. He pointed at Billy, who stood to one side in the gutter. 'It's for me friend.'

'Sorry, I'm not allowed,' the waitress said, not changing her expression, clearly not believing Ryan. She lifted her chin slightly and, with her eyes, indicated the next person in line.

Ryan put two fingers to his lips and let out a piercing whistle that brought the entire coffee bar to a standstill. 'A large cappuccino to take away, please, miss,' he said politely, though loud enough for his voice to carry to Mr Cesco as well as to the patrons seated inside.

Mr Cesco, busy at the second espresso machine at the far end of the counter, shouted, 'Whazzamatta?' Then he saw Ryan. 'Oh itsa you!' He nodded at the waitress, making a dismissive gesture with his hand. 'Give him!'

'But, Mr Cesco, you said –' the young woman protested.

'Nevermind I said, you give!' Cesco shouted impatiently, then looked out over the counter at the silent patrons. 'Everybody talk!' It was more an order than a request.

The young woman shrugged and made the takeaway coffee, which she handed to Ryan without saying a word. Ryan held out the fifty-dollar note and she took it with a resigned sigh. Mr Cesco must have been watching out of the corner of his eye because now he shouted, 'Florentine! No money!'

The waitress sighed, handed Ryan back the money and removed the fruity Italian biscuit from a glass jar and dropped it into a small white paper bag, handing it to the boy.

'Thanks, miss,' Ryan said, without having once looked at Mr Cesco.

Several of the patrons laughed as they watched Ryan carrying the coffee in one hand while Billy's briefcase was handcuffed to his wrist. Someone shouted, 'Hey, Cesco, that the bagman doing his rounds!'

Cesco banged his fist on the counter. 'Shutta up!' he shouted, bringing the coffee bar once more to silence. 'You watcha your mouth!' he said to the joker who'd made the quip, and pointed a fat, gold-ringed finger first at him, then at the pavement. 'You drink your coffee, bugger off!'

Billy watched as Ryan approached. His wrist was growing increasingly painful and he was sweating from the walk. He suspected he had a slight fever. 'I seem to create nothing but trouble,' he said, wiping his hand across his face.

'Nah, no worries,' Ryan said reassuringly, handing him the coffee and gripping the paper bag containing the Florentine between his teeth. He brought his skateboard up under his arm, impervious to Cesco's outburst. 'He's our rello, see. Me grandpa was Eyetalian.' He indicated Cesco with a nod of his head in the direction of the coffee bar, 'His name's same as us, but he's changed it since he come here.'

Billy stopped and took a sip, the coffee was still too hot and he drew back suddenly.

'Shit, I forgot the sugar!' Ryan said.

'No, it's quite all right, not today,' Billy fibbed. 'It's very hot, that's all.' Billy couldn't bear the thought of Ryan returning to the coffee bar.

The boy looked momentarily doubtful. 'Really and truly, you don't take sugar?'

'Hangover,' Billy explained. Then, changing the subject, he said, 'Sanfrancesco? Is that Italian? It sounds rather more like Spanish.'

'Hey, how come you know that?' Ryan appeared genuinely impressed. ''Cause it's true. Me nana says me grandpa come from Spain to Australia to work on the Snowy River where he built this big dam we learned about at school and his brother went to Italy where Mr Cesco was born and was a great boxer, then he come out here, not me grandpa's brother, Mr Cesco. He was sponsored by me grandpa when he become a wharfie after building the dam, only now we don't see him no more 'cause me grandpa's carked it, and me nana's real crook and says she'll soon be dead and he can go to buggery, he's not worth the bother and only wanted ter know us when we was useful and he's a flamin' wog, so what can ya expect.'

'Oh, I'm sorry to hear that,' Billy said, confused at the battery of words issuing from Ryan, who was proving to be a regular chatterbox. The coffee was still too hot to calm his nerves and his wrist was now extremely painful, so that he was having trouble concentrating.

'Anyway, that's why he gives me coffee when he won't nobody else who's a kid.'

They'd reached the lights at the corner opposite the hospital when an ambulance, its siren blaring, turned into St Vincent's Casualty. They watched as the ambulance stopped, the siren died and its back door was flung open from the inside. Two men came out of casualty to help remove the patient strapped to the stretcher.

'Artitak,' Ryan said casually, 'that's a priority one,' though Billy couldn't imagine how he could possibly know it was a heart attack. Ryan pointed to the park opposite the hospital. 'No use goin' in jus' yet, best wait ten minutes, yiz a priority four. Chance to get yer coffee down the gurgler.'

They sat in the park and Billy sipped gratefully at the coffee, the caffeine steadying his nerves. Ryan removed the Florentine biscuit from the paper bag and took a bite before offering it to Billy. Billy declined but Ryan persisted. 'It's yours, I only took a little bit. Garn then, you'll like it.'

'No thanks, Ryan, this coffee'll do me nicely.'

Ryan held up the biscuit and grinned. 'Me nana says it's all the bugger's good for, biscotti and Florentines, and the one's too bloody hard and the other's too sticky for her choppers.' He took another bite and, with his mouth full, he explained, 'See, me nana, she don't wear her false teeth no more, don't eat nuffing 'cept it's mashed up before.' Ryan laughed, 'She goes real crook if there's lumps in her potatoes.'

Ryan pointed across the road to the gate leading into casualty where the ambulance was leaving. 'Give it a bit longer, always tell an artitak 'cause the ambulance blokes don't run like an overdose, they already done the stuff they need on the way. You want some good advice, Billy?'

'Always use a bit of that, Ryan.'

'Well, if yer havin' a artitak don't call the doctor, yer call the ambulance, them paramedics know what to do better'n any doctor. Drugs too, overdose, they've got the goods in the back.'

'Well, thank you, next time I'm having a heart attack I'll remember that. You seem to know a lot about hospitals. Is it your grandmother, has she had a heart attack?'

'Nah, me mum, asthma, she's . . .' Ryan stopped short and Billy glanced over at him, waiting, but the boy didn't continue. 'Let's go,' he said instead.

At the entrance to St Vincent's, Ryan halted. 'Inside they've got these chairs like in two levels. Sit on the bench in the front closest to reception and, don't forget, yiz real crook.'

'Don't you think I should do this myself?' Billy asked.

'Nah, best leave it to me, they know me here,' Ryan said confidently, then repeated, 'Remember, you're real crook, practically dying, lotsa pain. Don't say nuffink until I tell yiz, you hear?'

'It's only a sprained wrist, Ryan!' Billy protested.

'It's broken and you could be getting lockjaw from the tetanus, remember?'

Billy sighed, 'I'm not at all sure about this, lad. Besides they don't call it lockjaw any longer, tetanus causes severe muscular contraction and I haven't got that or I wouldn't be able to talk. Perhaps we should just go to the nearest chemist and buy a roll of elastoplast to strap it?'

Ryan looked disgusted, 'What about the needle? Can't take no chances. Pretend yiz can't talk.' He smiled. 'C'mon, Billy, they know me here, it won't take long, I promise.'

He held the door open and Billy, clasping his arm against his stomach, entered reluctantly. They climbed down a short set of stairs, passing two levels of chairs, a bit like the seating for a tiny amphitheatre. There was a door into the emergency area proper that was electronically locked and controlled from the reception window, which was made of bulletproof glass with a slot for pushing stuff to a client onto an outside ledge. There were a series of holes in the glass at voice level for communication to take place.

A very obese woman sat on one of the chairs smoking even though a sign on the wall read 'No Smoking'. She was using a small paper cup from the water dispenser as her ashtray. Two small girls, still dressed in their pyjamas, sat with her. The smaller one appeared to be about three and was sucking on a dummy, while her sister was swinging her legs and singing softly to a rather beaten-up doll. On another chair, his legs extended and his chin on his chest, was a man in his late seventies. He was wearing a white shirt and brown flannels hoicked up to his chest and held up with braces. None of them looked up when Billy and Ryan entered.

Billy sat on the chair in the front row clutching his arm while Ryan removed the handcuff from his wrist and placed the case on the floor. 'Yiz real crook, remember,' he whispered before he walked over to the reception window, behind which stood a thin unremarkable-looking woman in her fifties with iron-grey, closely cropped hair. Her breasts were the only exceptional thing about her. Too large for her slender frame, they stuck out in sharp points under a blue angora sweater. It was as if she'd borrowed someone else's tits before coming to work.

'Mornin', miss, I got a 'mergency,' Ryan called out rather too loudly when he was still two steps away from the window. The receptionist clerk looked up, surprised to see someone so young standing in front of her. 'It's me friend, he's real crook, got a broken wrist and suspected lockjaw.'

The woman tapped the blue and white plastic name tag pinned to her breast with her forefinger, 'It's *Mrs*. Mrs Willoughby!'

'Sorry,' Ryan said, smiling.

'Well, broken wrist or not,' she glanced over at Billy and

then back at Ryan, 'we have to complete the admission form first.' She raised her chin and this time took a longer look at Billy, her expression indicating that she was not too pleased at what she saw. 'Over here, please!' she called out, ignoring Ryan.

Billy started to rise but Ryan signalled with his hand behind his back for him to remain seated. 'Nah, he can't, Missus.'

'Can't what?'

'Do paperwork, I told ya, his wrist is broke.'

The receptionist sighed, impatient. 'Well, if he'll come over and give me his personal details, I'll fill them in for him.'

'Nah, can't do that neiva, I told you already, he's got lockjaw.'

'You said suspected, *suspected* lockjaw!'

It was Ryan's turn to sigh. 'That's why I said "suspected" because he can't say nuffink!'

The woman and the boy locked eyes and Ryan, holding her gaze, spread his hands and shrugged. 'He needs a tetanus shot real bad, Missus.' Sudden tears welled in his eyes and his voice grew small, 'It'll be your fault if he dies.'

'Don't be ridiculous!' the receptionist said, raising her voice.

Ryan took a deep breath, 'I want to make a complaint!' he said loudly. 'I'm not getting no co-operation! I want to see the triage sister!'

'Not until I have the particulars. Besides you'll have to wait, this is a fracture, that's a priority four, she's busy with a cardiac arrest.'

'HELP!' Ryan suddenly yelled at the top of his voice. 'HELP! HELP!'

Billy damn near jumped out of his skin. The receptionist had had enough and pressed a buzzer under the lip of her desk. In a matter of moments two security men appeared, coming down a passage on the other side of the electronically locked door. The receptionist pressed the buzzer and the door opened and the two men stormed through.

Billy jumped to his feet, looking at the entrance and back at them, ready to make a run for it.

The two security men converged on him, one grabbing his arm, the other his bad wrist. Billy screamed as the security man who was holding Billy's wrist twisted his arm behind his back.

'Not him!' the woman shouted, 'The boy!'

The two men released Billy, who fell to his knees whimpering.

'Sorry, mate,' one of them said, bending over him and offering his hand.

'Leave me alone! Please leave me alone!' Billy sobbed as he lay doubled over on the floor, his stomach protecting his wrist.

Ryan turned back to the receptionist, 'Now look what yiz done!' he said accusingly.

The receptionist arched her eyebrow slightly, 'Well, that's one good thing, we seem to have cured his lockjaw.'

'Well, well, look who the cat brought in! Gidday, Ryan,' the second security man called out, coming over. 'Your mum, she okay?'

'Oh, hi, Johnno,' Ryan said slowly and pointed to where Billy lay doubled over on the floor with the other man squatting beside him. 'No, it's me friend, he's broke his wrist and he's real crook.' He turned and looked at the receptionist, 'She give us a hard time just because he's a derro and can't read and write!'

The receptionist brought her hands to her hips, 'I beg your pardon, young man!' she expostulated, 'You said he had lockjaw when I wanted to help him fill out his admission form. You were lying to me!'

'Yeah, well, nobody likes to admit they's ignorant, do they?' Ryan replied.

'It's okay,' Johnno said to the receptionist, placing his hand on Ryan's shoulder. 'Ryan knows Dr Goldstein and is well known here.'

The receptionist clerk drew herself up, her back ramrod straight, breasts sticking out like two traffic cones. She was furious and, refusing to be mollified, proceeded to rearrange the papers in front of her, slapping each piece on top of the other, her lips pulled tight. 'I was just doing my job,' she said primly, 'I don't expect to be insulted by children!' She pointed to the obese woman who was smoking, 'It's bad enough . . . She told me to *ef-off* when I asked her not to smoke.'

Johnno looked sympathetic, 'I know,' he said soothingly, 'You're new here, ain't ya? That's Stella, she's beaten up her husband again, they came in before you came on shift, she's waiting for him to be patched up so she can take him home. It can get pretty grim in here sometimes.' The woman at the desk missed the irony in his voice. Johnno was secretly amused. If she felt insulted by Ryan and Stella, then the future guaranteed a rough passage for the new receptionist, verbal abuse, physical attack, hysteria, histrionics, bad language, threatening behaviour, spitting, vomiting, choking and enough blood in a month to fill a suburban swimming pool. She'd come on duty at seven, the changeover shift known as happy hour, when most of the heroin overdoses and the ecstasy heart attacks, stab wounds, bashings and traffic-accident victims had already been brought in and processed. This was the quiet after the storm, when burns, domestic violence, broken limbs and suspected angina patients politely turned up for treatment and only the occasional geriatric heart attack arrived in an ambulance to disturb the comparative calm of sunrise in an inner-city hospital. 'Christ help her if she ever does a pay-day night every second Thursday,' Johnno thought to himself. He decided he'd open a book on the new receptionist clerk, where he'd offer odds of ten to one in the hospital canteen that she wouldn't last a week. She wasn't the first and she wouldn't be the last.

The remarkable thing about the security men was that they were Bib and Bub, both gay, though one was slightly taller than the other, with gym-muscle physiques, tanned faces and identical peroxided brush-cuts.

'Can you do us a favour, darling?' Johnno now said. 'The triage sister is flat out with the cardiac arrest, will you page Dr Goldstein, please?'

'I've been told I have to process the patient before he sees the doctor,' the receptionist said stubbornly. She paused, 'And for your information, I'm *not* your darling!'

Johnno drew back suddenly, he could usually tell a lesbian. Surely not, he told himself, not with those norks and the blue angora sweater, though the hair was questionable. 'Well, I-am-so-sorry!' he mocked, 'We *are* a bit sensitive then, *aren't* we?'

'I've been a medical receptionist/clerk for twenty years and I'm not accustomed to being treated like this by anyone.' She looked over at Ryan. 'Let alone a precocious little brat like him!'

The second security man had come to stand next to Johnno, 'Private practice, was it, darling? You've obviously never worked in casualty before.'

Johnno turned on him, 'Kevin, you're *not* to call . . . er . . .' he turned and bent forward, squinting slightly as he pretended to read the name tag which lay almost flat on the receptionist's sticking-out left breast, 'Mrs Willoughby "darling",' he scolded. He straightened up and his voice took on a more serious tone. 'There's nothing to process, Mrs Willoughby.' Johnno indicated Billy, who was now seated back on the chair looking very sorry for himself, 'He's an alcoholic, he'll have no medical benefit card, no fixed address, no hospital insurance. He won't give you his social security registration number or even his correct name. You'd have done much better with Ryan here helping you.'

'That's not what I've been instructed to do!' the receptionist repeated again.

'Call Dr Goldstein on his pager, my dear, he'll sort it out,' Johnno urged, this time not without a touch of genuine sympathy. He leaned over the desk and spoke in an undertone, 'He may be a derelict but we manhandled him, there were witnesses. Stella's not backwards in coming forward, and the old bloke would have seen it as well, that could mean trouble, not just for Kevin and me, you'd also be implicated.'

The woman hesitated, then sighed. 'Very well!' she said, trying to maintain her dignity. She dialled the doctor's pager and, when he answered, asked him to come to reception.

'Thanks, Missus,' Ryan said politely. The receptionist glared at him, but remained silent, not sure she wasn't being sent up.

Dr Goldstein appeared a few minutes later. He was a bear of a man, whom even Billy, a rugby union man in his day, recognised as one of rugby league's truly greats. Nathan Goldstein was probably the best-known medical name in Sydney. He'd played in the front row for the Rabbitohs for ten years and had gone on to play for Australia in three test series. He was the son of a Jewish heart surgeon who'd survived the Warsaw Ghetto and the Holocaust and who, after the war, had migrated to Australia, where he'd been required to do the final two years of the medical course at Sydney University. He'd worked with the people in Redfern, helping the local GP, whose qualifications he'd greatly exceeded. When he passed his second medical degree he'd been invited to join the medical faculty, but Moishe Goldstein politely rejected the offer and chose instead to practise in Redfern, not two miles from the university campus and in the heart of Rabbitoh country.

His son, Nathan, had attended Waterloo Public School, where he earned the respect of his peers by belting the crap out of anyone who called him 'Dirty Jew' or 'Reffo!' Later he won admission to Fort Street Boys High, a selective school whose former students included some of Australia's most famous men. There he played rugby union on Wednesdays for the school and for South Sydney Juniors on Saturday. At the tender age of nineteen, much to the chagrin of the university rugby union club, Nathan elected to play first-grade rugby league for South Sydney. He played as a lock, wearing the number six jumper, and despite his dark hair and eyes was predictably known as Goldilocks.

In the seventies and early eighties when South Sydney nearly went broke and, with no money to pay players, almost didn't survive, Goldstein could have played for any club in the competition, earning big bucks, but he stuck with the Rabbitohs. 'In football terms, South Sydney is my mother and father and you don't walk out on your parents when things are getting tough for them, do you?' he'd once told a reporter from the *Herald*.

It was a popular myth among the people of South Sydney that Goldstein had acquired a tattoo showing a rabbit wearing the famous red and myrtle-green football jumper leaping over the crack in his bum with the legend above it inscribed in Latin: '*Nisi cunicularius, pilosus podex es*'. Which roughly translated means 'If you're not a Rabbitoh, a hairy arse you are.' Nathan Goldstein was to become a rugby league legend and be included in the lexicon of South Sydney's greatest players, awarded sixth position behind such immortals as Clive Churchill 'the little master', Harold Horder, Ron Coote, Bob McCarthy, Ian Moir, and then Nathan 'Goldilocks' Goldstein equal sixth with Les 'Chicka' Cowie.

'Gidday, mate,' Dr Goldstein said to Ryan, putting his giant hand on the boy's shoulder, then looked at the receptionist and back at Johnno and Kevin. 'What seems to be the problem?'

Mrs Willoughby was the first to speak, 'This child is a troublemaker, doctor!'

Dr Goldstein looked surprised. 'Ryan?'

'Spot of bother with the paperwork, doctor,' Johnno said.

'Oh? Who's the patient? Not you, Ryan, is it?'

Kevin pointed to Billy, 'Old bloke on the bench. Suspected fractured wrist.'

'The boy lied, said he had lockjaw,' the receptionist interrupted.

Despite himself, Goldstein laughed. 'Lockjaw? What have you been up to, Ryan?'

'Me friend, he fell in the dirt, he needs a needle, tetanus.'

Nathan Goldstein looked over at Billy and immediately understood the situation. 'And his wrist?'

'I think it's broke.'

'I'll take a look.' He turned to the receptionist, 'Don't worry, I'll take care of the paperwork. The triage sister will do his medical details later.' He still had his hand on Ryan's shoulder and turned him to face the receptionist. 'I think you owe . . . I'm sorry, I don't know your name, madam?' he said politely.

'Mrs Willoughby, doctor.'

'You owe Mrs Willoughby an apology, Ryan.'

'Sorry, Mrs Willoughby,' Ryan said in a small voice, bowing the way little kids do at school. It was a send-up and it wasn't missed by the still angry receptionist.

'The boy should learn some manners and could do with a good wash if you ask me,' she sniffed.

Goldstein ignored her remark. 'Righto, come in, let's take a look at your friend, Ryan.'

Ryan walked over and picked up Billy's briefcase. 'Let's go, Billy, see I told yiz, no worries,' he whispered rather too loudly.

They entered casualty, where Goldstein took them through to the treatment room.

'He's real crook, Dr Goldilocks,' Ryan offered.

'Do you know his name?'

''Course, it's Billy.'

'Just Billy?'

'Nah, Billy O'Shannessy without the *u*,' Ryan replied.

Nathan Goldstein walked up to Billy, who rose at his approach. 'What seems to be the matter, Mr O'Shannessy? Ryan here says you've had a fall, hurt your wrist. Have you?'

'I probably just sprained it,' Billy said, looking a bit sheepish, 'We shouldn't have bothered you.'

The doctor looked up in surprise at Billy's accent, it was obvious it was not what he'd expected. 'That's why we're here, sir. Will you hold your wrist out, please?' Goldstein let out a soft whistle. 'Looks ugly, it's badly swollen and you have a large haematoma spreading up the arm.' He touched the wrist lightly with his forefinger. 'How did you get these lacerations?'

'Handcuffs!' Ryan said quickly.

'Pardon?' said Goldstein.

'From the briefcase,' Ryan said and pointed to the set of handcuffs dangling from the handle of the briefcase he held.

Dr Goldstein looked puzzled but recovered quickly, 'Oh, right, that's how you carry it, is it? Good idea around here.'

Nathan Goldstein knew better than to inquire any further, his job at St Vincent's covered the whole spectrum, from heart attacks in the elderly, domestic violence, stabbings, drug overdoses of every description from heroin to the even more dangerous amphetamines. He dealt with just about every other complication known to medical science that could be brought on quickly by human stupidity or sudden frailty. He was famous for a quote he'd once given a reporter: 'If the city of Sydney were to be given an enema, they'd stick the catheter into the front door of St Vincent's Casualty.' Child prostitutes, male and female, who sold their tender young bodies to paedophiles and the other trash preying on children while posing as respectable citizens, knew to come to Dr Goldilocks when they were in trouble.

He'd chosen to practise among what he thought of as the victims of society, the young, the weak, the hopeless, the silly, the unfortunate and the mentally retarded. Nathan Goldstein was a constant thorn in the side of DOCS, and he'd long since given up asking questions or judging his patients. But what he did understand was that these addictions and proclivities usually created a deep sense of vulnerability and a lack of self-esteem that often led to paranoia. Billy's desire to carry his briefcase shackled to his wrist was a mild enough obsession when compared to some he'd come across.

'You'll need an X-ray and then you'll have to wait for an orthopaedic surgeon to examine your wrist. Broken bones are not my area but it looks very much like a Colles' fracture.'

He indicated the lacerations, 'We'll clean up this mess and give you an antibiotic shot and a sling to make you more comfortable, but while you're here I'd like to examine you, is that all right?'

Billy looked alarmed. 'How long will all this take?'

Goldstein didn't try to placate him. 'Most of the morning, I dare say. You look pretty wretched.' Billy's wrist rested in the palm of Goldstein's massive hand and the doctor pinched at the skin on the back of it, pulling it up into a ridge and releasing it. The ridge of skin on Billy's hand remained static for several seconds before slowly resuming its previous position. The doctor also noted the papery dryness of Billy's lips and the blood blister where earlier on he'd forced the pebble into his mouth.

He undid the third and fourth button of Billy's mud-splattered shirt and eased the arm into its interior so that it would act as a temporary sling. 'I just want to check your tongue.' Billy stuck his tongue out. 'Well, you're pretty dehydrated, I'd like to put you on a saline drip, Mr O'Shannessy.'

'I don't think I've got the time for that, doctor. All

morning, did you say? No, I simply can't be here that long. I have business to attend to.'

Goldstein didn't argue with him. 'Sure . . . well then, we'll take it one thing at a time, see how we go, eh?'

'There's nothing wrong with me, just a bit of a strained wrist,' Billy protested. He knew that what he needed more than anything was a drink.

Billy was also worried that he was breaking his routine for the second day running and he was losing his grip, slipping into the twilight zone where so many on skid row passed their lives. It was a part of his paranoia that he believed his sanity could be measured by the precise order in which he did things, and any deviations were a sign of his increasing instability.

'We'll need to take your blood pressure and your temperature.' Nathan Goldstein pointed to Billy's wrist again, 'Clean that up a bit before you go into X-ray, then we can decide.' He turned to Ryan, 'Don't you have school today, young man?'

Ryan looked down at his shoes, then up at Billy. 'I've got to take care of me mate. Can't yiz give me a note?'

Dr Goldstein laughed. 'Ryan, you've got to go to school. You're pretty bright, you know. No point wasting your brains, eh?'

Ryan looked up pleadingly. 'Garn, just this once? I could have lied and told you it was school holidays.'

'And I would have told you that's bullshit, I've got kids of my own, you know. I'll give you a note that allows you to be two hours late, that's the best I can do, mate.'

'School sucks,' Ryan replied, kicking at the toecap of his left shoe.

'So does life without a proper education,' Nathan Goldstein replied.

'The doctor's right, Ryan. I'll be fine and I'm most grateful to you for your help.'

Ryan looked at Billy as if he'd betrayed him. 'I thought we was mates.'

'We are, but the doctor's still right.'

'Fuck, who can you trust around here?' Ryan said, kicking at his toecap again.

Goldstein laughed. 'C'mon, mate, you can sit in on the examination, see we don't harm Mr O'Shannessy. Medical malpractice, you can't be too careful these days.'

Half an hour later, with a note from Nathan Goldstein for his teacher, Ryan said goodbye to Billy as he was going into the X-ray room. 'Termorra, I'll see yiz termorra, Billy.'

A sister arrived shortly after the X-ray had been taken. 'We'll be having to take you through to the triage sister, Mr O'Shannessy. It's a bit backwards, you should have seen her when you came in, but never mind, you're Irish. Let me take your briefcase,' she offered in a broad Irish accent.

'No, no, I'm fine.' He grinned. 'It's a part of me, I'd be lost without it.' He added, 'The only Irish in me goes back to six generations ago.'

The sister grinned. 'You'd not be knowing then, it *can't* be bred out, Irish is forever.'

After he'd been processed backwards by the triage sister,

the same Irish sister came to fetch him and Billy was shown to a bed with a green plastic sheet spread over the hospital linen. 'Just lie on the top please, you'll only be here an hour or two before you see a consultant and then go into surgery,' the Irish sister said.

'Surgery?' Billy looked alarmed. 'Oh, I don't know about that, sister.'

Seeing Billy's alarm, the sister attempted to put him at ease. 'Now we'll not get too fussed, Mr O'Shannessy, nothing's certain yet. Dr Goldstein isn't the one to decide.' She smiled at him. 'Can you get up onto the bed on your own?' Billy nodded. 'You'll oblige me, young man, by first taking off your shoes.' She drew the curtain around his bed. 'Sister will be in soon to put in your drip. Would you like a nice cup of tea and a cheese sandwich?'

'Very kind of you, sister, but no thank you,' Billy said.

The sister picked up the briefcase Billy had placed beside the chair at the side of his bed. 'I'll put this away for you in the cupboard.'

'No, no, please!' Billy said, alarmed. 'Please, sister, I have to have it with me.'

Seeing his agitation, the sister smiled kindly. 'You're quite right, it should be close to you,' she said. 'Do you need help with your shoelaces?'

'No, I'll be fine, sister,' Billy said, somewhat shaken by the prospect of losing his briefcase to some anonymous cupboard.

'Well, then, I'll be off. There's no rest for the wicked.'

Billy sat on the bedside chair and bent down to untie the

laces of his soiled trainers. It proved to be a difficult task as he only had the use of one hand and it was his habit to double-tie his laces. The curtain surrounding the bed stopped short of the floor so that, with his head down near his knees, he could see beneath the bed adjacent to his own. There, under the bed opposite, was a pair of scuffed Cuban riding boots and a battered Akubra he'd have recognised anywhere.

CHAPTER FOUR

Ryan arrived just after sunrise the next morning at the bench outside the library and shook Billy awake. 'Did ya speak to him?' he asked.

'Wha . . . what?' Billy protested, sitting up slowly.

'See, I told you it was broken,' Ryan said triumphantly, 'Yiz got plaster on.'

'Yes, yes, six weeks,' Billy muttered, trying hard to focus. The hospital had given him a pill to take when he went to bed and asked him to try to stay off the grog for one night, a small miracle he'd successfully achieved, so he'd slept well and even survived Arthur and Martha.

'Did ya speak ter him, ter Trim?' Ryan repeated. 'Hey, what happened to your head?'

'Yes, I spoke to him,' Billy moaned, not yet fully awake.

'You've got this big piece of sticking plaster above yer eye.'

'Accident.' There was no getting away from Ryan.

'So?'

'Nothing. It's nothing. I fell at the hospital.'

'But yer wasn't drunk. I know yer wasn't drunk.'

'Just an accident, could have happened to anyone,' Billy lied, not wishing to go into the incident.

Ryan seemed to accept this explanation. 'Have ya talked ter the cat yet? Ter Trim?' he repeated.

'Steady on, lad. Just give me a few moments.'

'Here, I bought yiz some water.' Ryan handed Billy a cardboard cup.

Billy drank most of it. He wasn't feeling too bad, all things considered. He'd have to give Ryan something to go on with. 'Yes, Trim and I had an interesting chat.'

'Yeah? What did he say? Did you ask him my question?'

Billy couldn't quite remember what Ryan's question had been and so he said the first thing that came into his mind. 'He told me about his life on board ship.'

'Cool!' Ryan said excitedly. 'Can you tell us now?'

Billy groaned. 'I just woke up, son,' he protested. 'It's going to take more than a cup of water to get my tongue wagging.'

Ryan drew back, then said accusingly, 'You know I can't go in a pub, kids are not allowed. If I wait outside, you won't never come out 'til yer pissed.'

'No, lad, it's not like that. It's coffee I need. Down at the Quay. I need a coffee fix.'

'I can get yiz a coffee at Martin Place, it's closer.'

Billy looked up and shrugged. 'I'm a creature of habit,

I'm afraid, lad. I've got a Greek mate at the New Hellas Cafe at the Quay who sets aside his first coffee of the day for me. It's . . . well, it's how I start the day,' Billy explained. 'What's the time? When do you have to be at school?'

Ryan glanced down at the oversized rubber-encased watch on his wrist. 'Six o'clock, school starts after nine.' He paused. 'Can you write proper?'

Billy recalled the scene with the receptionist in casualty and realised that the boy knew very little about him. Ryan had assumed that, like some homeless people, he might be illiterate.

'Yes, but I'm not writing a note to your teacher, you've got to go to school.'

'Who says? You can't make me!'

It was a good rebuttal and Billy had to think for a moment. 'Well, no I can't, but I imagine your nana can, she doesn't sound like the sort of person who will let you miss school.'

'Nah, she used to get real cranky, gimme the strap, but now she's too crook to have a go at me.'

'Well, your mother then?'

'Nah, she don't know if I go or not. When they come round last time she told them to fuck off.'

'They?'

'Someone sent by the school, from the department.'

'Was that okay? I mean did you approve?'

'Nah, it was stupid, me mum was drunk. This social worker, she come snoopin' round.'

'What? From the Department of Community Services?'

'Who?'

'From DOCS?'

'Yeah, them.'

'Well, there you are, life gets complicated when you break the rules.'

'It don't for you?'

Billy sighed. 'There aren't too many left for me to break, unless it's jaywalking.' He shrugged and looked down at his knees. 'You wouldn't want to end up like this, would you?'

Ryan was silent for a moment and Billy thought he was being polite but then, true to form, he said, 'Nah, I'm already not that dumb.'

Billy laughed. 'I sincerely hope not, but going to school may help you to avoid just such a calamity.'

'Didn't you go to school, then?'

Billy cleared his throat, it had been a long time since he'd had to accommodate his thinking to a young, questioning intelligence. His new world was brutal and direct, with very little in it coming from a critical or inquiring mind. 'Yes, I did and to university.'

'Well, school didn't help yiz then, did it?'

Billy looked up at Ryan. 'There are more paths to a man's destruction than simply a lack of education, but ignorance certainly qualifies as one of them.'

To his surprise Ryan said quietly, 'Cool. I've still got fifty bucks, we can get the coffee and some breakfast and you can tell me about what the cat told yiz. Okay?'

'Fifty dollars? That's a lot of money to be carrying around.'

'Me mum give it ter me, she don't like ter cook, see, ain't never in the mood.'

Billy nodded, it was not his place to ask questions. He'd kept his mouth shut about the fifty dollars yesterday, but it had worried him and he was grateful for the child's ingenuous explanation. 'And school? Will you go?'

'Yeah, yeah, I promise. What about your ablu . . . ablu . . .' Ryan couldn't quite remember the word.

'Ablutions, it just means having a wash and a crap. I can do it in the toilets at the Quay.'

'Want me to carry yer briefcase? With your crook wrist, the plaster and all that?'

'No thanks, Ryan.'

Ryan pointed to the cast on Billy's wrist. 'Can I write on it? It's lucky if you're the first in.'

'Sure, do you have a pen?'

'Nah, but I'll bring one next time I come, you won't let no one write on it before, will ya?'

Billy knew he had a biro in his briefcase but he didn't want Ryan to look inside. 'Of course, what will you write?'

'You just put your name on it like, all your friends do the same. It's like saying they're sorry you broke your wrist and all that.'

Billy gave a wry grin. 'In that case I think you can safely leave it until tomorrow, lad.' Realising that he was feeling sorry for himself, something he tried never to do, he attempted to cover up. 'Do you know what they said in the hospital?' Not waiting for an answer, Billy continued, 'That my left arm and shoulder was considerably more muscular than my right, which is a bit of a laugh really, and comes from my habit of carrying the briefcase in my left hand. So, I've decided for the next six weeks while I'm in a cast to use my right wrist, even things up a bit, eh?'

Ryan's eyes travelled slowly over Billy's emaciated body. 'Well, ya ain't no superman, is ya? Can ya wipe yer bum now?'

'Don't be impertinent.' Billy laughed. It was the happiest he could remember feeling for a very long time and he told himself to be careful, Ryan was slowly prising open a compartment to which the lid had been firmly screwed down.

They began to walk down Macquarie Street towards Circular Quay. They were several metres from the New Hellas Cafe when Con started yelling at Billy. 'Gidday, myte! Where you been yesterday? Whazamatta? I make a coffee, you don't come? I say the girls, Billy no come, coffee we put, yesterday-bread we put, something maybe is wrong.' He looked at Ryan. 'Who you got? Street kid? Bastards! They steal chewing gums, Chuppa Chup, bloody oaths, fair dinkums, struth!' Con now noticed the plaster on Billy's wrist. 'Bloodyhells! What you do your arms?'

'Morning, Con, this is Ryan Sanfrancesco. I fractured my wrist and he took care of me.' Billy turned to look at Ryan and placed his arm about him. 'Don't reckon I could have done it without him.'

'He's a good kids, huh?' Although Con's expression

clearly indicated that he had grave doubts that such a thing was possible. 'You want two coffee?'

Ryan took out the fifty-dollar note. 'A coffee and a Coke,' he said to Con.

Con looked surprised, then rejected the money with a wave of his hand. 'Keep your bloody money! You want ice in the Coca-Cola?' He took a large Coke container from the dispenser.

'A can! I want a can!' Ryan called out.

Con turned to face Ryan. 'Whazamatta? You don't got no manners! You don't like ice?' He held the Coke container aloft. 'You think I cheats, huh?' He tapped his forefinger on the side of the Coke container. 'I put in here more than they got in the cans!'

'Steady on, Con, it's not like that. The lad simply asked for a can. He prefers to drink from a can.'

'I'll pay,' Ryan said, holding up the fifty-dollar note again.

Billy could see that there was something worrying his friend. 'What's the matter, Con?' he asked.

'Fifty dollar, where that boys get fifty dollar, hey?'

'His mother, she gave it to him to buy food,' Billy replied.

'Food? You think Coca-Cola that foods?'

'It seems she doesn't like to cook, I don't know all the details.'

Ryan held the note out again. 'Yer gunna take the money or what?'

'Jesus Christos! You want to pay? Okay, smarty alecs, you pay!'

'What's got into you, Con?' Billy asked, surprised. Surely Con hadn't changed from his usual friendly self because the boy wanted a can of Coca-Cola and had offered to pay for it?

Con didn't reply. Instead, he leaned over the counter, snatched the note from Ryan and placed it on the ledge above the drawer of the till, removed a can of Coke from the drinks cabinet and plonked it down on the counter next to Billy's already prepared coffee. Then he returned to the till, opened it and was about to give change when he hesitated and gave Billy a strange look, his eyes hard. With a nod towards Ryan he said, 'He your fren, fair dinkums, Billy?'

'Yes, as a matter of fact, he is my friend,' Billy said, still looking puzzled.

Con snatched the note up from the till and waved it at Billy. 'You give that boy fifty dollar?'

'Of course not! It's pension day tomorrow. I'm broke. I told you where he got it.' Billy suddenly knew what Con was thinking and flushed deeply. 'Are you suggesting . . . ? What are you implying, Con?'

'You think me I am stupid? You put your arms round him. Where a boy like this, streets kid, get fifty dollar, eh? You think I don't know? Here, take your bloody money!' He reached for the note and threw it back over the counter at Ryan.

'Con, what's the matter?' Billy cried.

'Billy, you my fren. You help me. I help you. You don't tell me you bloody poofter, Billy!'

'Poofter? Me, a homosexual?' Despite himself, Billy began to laugh. 'Con, I'm an alcoholic, a drunk, I can't get it up. Besides, I'm nothing of the sort.'

But Con was sniffing back his tears and wasn't listening. 'Take coffee, Coke, fuck off!'

'He thinks yiz a rock spider,' Ryan said calmly, using the underworld term for a paedophile. He reached down and picked up the mustard-coloured banknote from where it had landed at his feet.

Billy, trying to recover the situation, turned to Ryan. 'No, lad, Con is concerned about your welfare.'

'I can take care of myself,' Ryan replied. 'But he can stick his Coke up his arse!'

Billy looked up at Con. 'You're quite wrong, Con.' He shook his head slowly. 'Christ, what has the world come to?'

Con was shaking and tears ran down his face. 'You my fren, Billy. You help me!' he lamented again, then he suddenly leaned forward over the counter and through his tears shouted, 'Now, you fucking poofter!' He pointed towards the street, 'Bugger off! You don't comes my cafe!'

'Con?' Billy said, trying to make sense of what had happened. 'You don't understand! It's not . . .'

'Come, Billy, let's go,' Ryan cut in, grabbing Billy by the arm and pulling him away. Then he stopped and turned to look at the Greek cafe proprietor, squinting slightly, his head held to one side. 'Me mum says the Greeks are the worst turd burglars, they do it with girls.'

Billy was shocked, but remained silent until they'd

reached the concourse. 'That was unnecessary, Ryan, it will only make things worse.'

Ryan halted and turned to Billy. 'He called yiz a poofter, didn't he! You ain't never going back, is ya?'

'I don't know,' Billy replied, plainly distressed. 'Con's my friend.'

Ryan was silent for a moment and then asked in a small voice, 'I'm your friend, Billy. You ain't a poofter, is yer?'

The shock showed clearly on Billy's face for the second time. 'No, mate, never was, never could be.' He tried to smile, to reassure the boy, though he now realised that he cared about what the child thought of him.

Ryan smiled. 'Yeah, cool. I didn't reckon yer was.' It was apparent from the tone of his voice that he needed no further reassurance and that the child wasn't in the least put out by Con's outburst.

'Ryan, your mother, she didn't really say that to you, did she?'

'Say what?'

'About Greek men?'

'Yeah, she says stuff when she's pissed, but everyone knows it's true anyway.'

'No, Ryan, it isn't! That's a generalisation!'

'It is so!' Ryan protested. 'Me mum says when men come and ask the girls at the Cross, you know . . . "How much for a short time?", they tells them how much, then they always says, "I don't do no Greek." ' He grinned up at Billy. 'It means they don't do it up the bum, because that's what the Greek blokes want.'

Billy didn't know what to say next. He'd long since become accustomed to the fact that street language was pretty direct, but he'd never been confronted by a young kid, not yet a teenager, who'd lost his innocence to the extent of Ryan's matter-of-fact knowledge and acceptance of how things were in his world.

However, Billy could clearly see that a paradox existed. In fact, Ryan hadn't lost his innocence at all. As evidence of this, there was the boy's willingness, no indeed his persistence and eagerness, to become involved in the adventures of a long-dead cat reincarnated in Billy's dreamtime. This showed both a lively imagination and a childlike belief system still very much intact.

Billy had been robbed on several occasions by street kids, though admittedly they'd been two or three years older than Ryan. Only once had he been hurt, when he'd told a gang of three ferals truthfully that he had no money. It was the day before pension day and he didn't have sufficient money to drink his usual scotch and he'd spent the last of it on a carton of Chateau de Cardboard moselle. They must have been comparatively new to the street not to know that the day before the alcoholics received their disability pension they weren't worth robbing. Anyway, they hadn't believed him and he'd accepted the kicking he'd got as part of his environment, the kids were its natural predators involved in a constant battle for survival.

Ryan, it seemed, had his grandmother to give him love, a sense of belonging and hope in the future, which was what these children lacked. Even though Ryan's mother appeared to have problems managing her life, she gave him money and there was nothing to suggest from what Ryan had told him that she didn't care about him when she was sober.

'What's a generalisation?' Ryan asked.

'Well, in this instance, it's when you say something that includes everyone, when it may only apply to a small number of people.' Ryan looked puzzled and so Billy explained further, 'Well, for instance, some very few men, of *any* nationality, might do what you said the Greek men do, a tiny minority, and so you can't simply include everyone of that nationality in your statement, that's what is meant by a *generalisation*.'

'Like saying all Abos are alkies?'

'Exactly! Well done.'

Ryan ignored the compliment. 'Well, then that's a whole heap of bull, because they are!'

They had reached Billy's usual bench at the water's edge on the eastern side of Circular Quay and directly opposite the Museum of Contemporary Art. Billy sat down. Ryan remained standing, facing him while balanced on his skateboard, knees slightly bent, trundling it a bit to the right and back to the left.

'Ryan, there you go again, it simply isn't true, son!'

'Oh yeah? You ever seen one what wasn't already drunk? And it don't matter what time it is neither.'

Billy had to admit to himself that in the Kings Cross–Darlinghurst area in which Ryan had grown up, the possibility of seeing a sober Aborigine at any time was fairly remote.

'Well, as a matter of fact, I have, only yesterday.'

Ryan glanced down at his watch. 'Hey, you ain't had yer coffee and I'm hungry. I'll go get it.' He stepped down from the skateboard. 'Wanna finger bun?' Billy nodded. He couldn't believe he was actually hungry and didn't have to will himself to eat. His breakfast usually consisted of six teaspoons of sugar in his coffee. Like most alcoholics he craved sugar. 'Pink or white?' Ryan asked and, seeing Billy didn't understand, said, 'The icing! Pink or white?'

'White, but six sugars with my coffee.' Billy dug into his trouser pocket for change. 'Here, allow me.'

'I got plenty.' Ryan grinned, 'That fat Greek bastard I'm not allowed to make no *generalisations* about gimme my fifty dollars back, remember?'

Billy couldn't help himself and burst into laughter. Ryan looked at him, giggling himself. 'I ain't seen you laughing like that before, Billy,' he said, then added, 'Me nana says it's laughter what makes the world go round.' Then, leaving his skateboard in Billy's care, he turned and ran off towards the Circular Quay concourse.

Ryan was still wearing the same dirty clothes he'd been in the first morning they'd met and Billy thought that, like himself, he could probably use a good scrub and a change of clothes. He wondered how he might go about telling Ryan to take a shower but decided he couldn't and shouldn't, it was none of his business anyway. Moments later, he found himself thinking about what it might take to rescue a young mind so clearly intelligent from becoming dulled to mediocrity. With a sudden jolt he brought himself back to reality and remonstrated inwardly, 'Stop it, Billy! Don't get involved, remember Charlie!'

Billy didn't want to admit that the boy had the sharp end of the screwdriver firmly wedged between the lip and the lid of the can of worms that represented his past and that he'd long since sealed, never to be opened again. He forced himself instead to think of Con's reaction to the sight of Ryan in his presence. Billy wondered how he might put things right with the Greek cafe owner.

Though he couldn't condone it, he understood Con's reaction. A derelict and a young boy obviously off the streets, it wasn't a difficult conclusion to come to. Even though the sex drive in an alcoholic is usually severely diminished and very few are sexually active, Billy realised most people would be unaware of this.

Nevertheless, it was a sad world when an old man and a young boy couldn't be seen in each other's presence without people believing something evil was taking place. Since time out of mind it had been incumbent on the old hunter, unable to run fast enough to go out on the hunt, to tutor the young boys in the tribe in the knowledge they would require to survive in the jungle. It was the essential begetting of wisdom and the duty of an elder to pass on the lore of the tribe in order to guarantee its survival.

Nowadays people only saw dirt, the malevolent hand of the paedophile on a young shoulder, rather than the pride of an old man in his grandson or the respect and affinity the older generation has for the young. He must be careful never to touch Ryan, not even in the smallest gesture of affection. Billy now reinforced within his inner self the often declared knowledge that he couldn't love and that he'd consciously cut himself off from all affection.

He mustn't allow a ragamuffin in need of clean clothes and a good bath to creep into his heart where there was no space for him to breathe and grow.

Ryan returned with the paper bag containing the buns gripped in his teeth, a Coke in one hand and the coffee in the other. He handed the coffee to Billy, placed the Coke on his skateboard, took the packet from his mouth and removed the finger bun with the white icing, 'I brought the sugar, how come yesterday you said you didn't take no sugar?'

'Well, it would have been difficult going back. You were very brave going into that coffee shop.'

'Nah, my nana says Cesco's just a bag o' wind, all bluff and no tornado.'

Billy laughed. 'You mean his bark is bigger than his bite?'

'She says me grandpa said when he was in Italy he were just a preliminary boxer, a Joe Palooka. It means he was no good,' Ryan explained.

'Well, I think you were pretty brave going in and getting a coffee for me, lad.'

'No worries,' Ryan replied. He took a bite from his finger bun and as he chewed he examined Billy slowly from head to toe. His mouth still half full, he said, 'You don't eat much, do yiz? Yiz skinny as a pencil, yer could use a bit o' fattenin' up.' Ryan grinned. 'That's what me nana always says about me, "Ryan, yer could use a bit o' fattenin' up, yiz skinny as a pencil."'

Billy washed down a small piece of bun with a sip of coffee. 'Now, about generalised statements and Aborigines always being drunk,' he said, changing the subject.

'How long is this gunna take?' Ryan asked, looking directly at Billy, 'You said you'd tell me about Trim?'

'How much time have we got?'

'You could give me a note,' Ryan said slyly.

'No, Ryan, school's important, I thought we agreed.'

'Yeah, well, okay. But can I choose, then?' He took a bite out of his bun.

'Of course, and I know it's Trim.' Billy smiled. 'You've been very patient, lad.'

Ryan nodded, acknowledging his patience.

'Well, we can't allow the subject of generalised statements and Aboriginal drunks to go away, we'll have to discuss it at another time.'

'Cool. Now can we start?'

'Well, there's something you have to know first.'

'What's that?'

'Trim lived at a different time, almost two hundred years ago, when our language was very different.'

'Different? You mean people talked weird, like thees and thous, what you sometimes hear in them old movies on TV?'

'Yes, but not weird for them, it's just that English is a living language, it changes with each generation. For instance, Matthew Flinders wrote when he was talking about Trim as a kitten: "The signs of superior intelligence which marked his infancy procured for him an education beyond what is usually bestowed upon the individuals of his tribe; and being brought up amongst sailors, his manner acquired a peculiarity of cast which rendered them as different from those of other cats, as the actions of a fearless seaman are from those of a lounging, shame-faced ploughboy".' Billy had learned the passage while a schoolboy playing the role of Matthew Flinders in a play at Sydney Grammar.

'Cool,' Ryan said, 'Trim was different from other cats because he was on a ship.'

Billy looked at Ryan, surprised at his well-summarised translation. 'Well done!'

Ryan shrugged, 'I seen lots of them old movies on TV with me nana.'

'Well, that's just it, Trim didn't speak quite the way we do and there may be one or two things, expressions for instance, I use which are unfamiliar to you. Just ask me if you don't understand a word.' Billy waited, then said, 'That all right with you, Ryan?'

'Sure, cool.'

He wished he could ask Ryan to use some other expression as his constant rejoinder, but he refrained from saying so. In fact, he was quite looking forward to adopting some of the language of Trim's time. Billy was aware that his own syntax and grammar, conditioned as it was by his background and education and honed by his profession, must sometimes seem as contrived to Ryan as the words he'd just quoted by Matthew Flinders. He hoped telling the story with a bit of early nineteenth-century argot might prove a stimulus for them both, it had been some time since he'd been allowed to use his mind.

Ryan seated himself on his skateboard at Billy's feet, his legs crossed. 'Righto,' he said, nodding for Billy to begin, then added, 'Can I ask questions, not just about words and stuff?'

'Of course.'

'During or after?'

'Let's see how we go, eh?'

Billy cleared his throat, then taking a sip of coffee, began to speak. 'It was a time when people and, it must be supposed, their cats spoke in a much more formal manner. Trim was a gentleman and so would have been particular about his language, being polite at all times and when not so, his sharp tongue would be concealed behind carefully chosen words. Although Trim was always referred to as Master Trim by the ship's crew, I shall simply call him Trim.'

'Yeah, that's how they talked,' Ryan confirmed. 'I've seen them old movies, *The Three Musketeers, A Tale of Two Cities*. I liked them two, others also, some were okay.'

'Very well then, shall I continue?'

Ryan nodded.

'Trim was born in 1797 in no place, well not precisely no place, no country, he came into this world meowing and blind in the middle of the ocean on board the *Reliance* while it sailed the Southern Indian Ocean. Captain Matthew Flinders, who most fondly believed he was Trim's owner, which I suppose he was although cats do not see things quite like that, would often remark that being born in that latitude made Trim an Indian, a pukka sahib cat. Though Trim would have made a better African than Indian, he was black as the ace of spades with white tips to each of his paws, a white star blaze on his chest and another smallish snowy dab under his chin.'

Ryan interrupted suddenly. 'What's a pukka sahib and why was he blind?'

'It's an Indian expression for a gentleman and all cats are born blind.'

'How do you know someone's a gentleman?' Ryan asked.

'He has nice manners and is considerate.'

Ryan nodded, 'It's nice how you tell how Trim looked, with them white paws and stuff. You make that bit up?'

Billy pretended to look indignant. 'No, of course not, that's how he is described by Matthew Flinders himself.

'Trim always regarded himself as a sailor, plain and simple, a ship's cat first, then, because he was reared on an English ship, as an Englishman. Of course, at that time there was no such place as Australia.'

'Yes there was!' Ryan interrupted. '1788. Captain Phillip come here in his ship, the *Supply*, we learned it in school. You said Trim was born in 1797.'

'Ah, yes, quite true, but the *Supply* was a convict transport and Captain Arthur Phillip was charged with establishing a convict settlement which was to be named New South Wales.'

'Same thing, they just changed the name,' Ryan persisted.

'Yes, I suppose so, but the convicts didn't see themselves as citizens of a new country, only that they'd been banished from their homeland to the very ends of the earth.'

'Yeah, okay,' Ryan said, accepting the explanation.

Billy could see that the story of Trim wasn't going to be a simple matter of storytelling. Ryan didn't intend to be a passive participant. He was happy with this, we learn better from discussion than simply from listening.

'Perhaps we can keep questions for later, lad, what do you think?' Billy asked.

'Righto,' said Ryan.

'Well, Trim was far from impressed with what he found on these convict shores. The settlement was divided between Sydney Town and Parramatta and a right old mess it all was. There is no record of Trim having visited Parramatta, but Sydney Town was enough to put him in a foul mood, it was quite a dreadful place for both cats and humans. Just 3200 souls shared both settlements and a motley lot they were too. It wasn't as if Trim was a snob, in fact quite the opposite, he was accustomed to strange places and peculiar faces. British sailors at that time were not a handsome breed, most of them being press-ganged into the job.'

'What's press-ganged mean?'

'Well, going to sea wasn't very popular and the navy had a good deal of trouble getting crew to man their ships, so they'd virtually kidnap them. The average jack tar of that time was a pretty miserable sort of person, usually a man living on the streets who was starving and lice-ridden, with his clothes in tatters and probably going about barefoot.

The press gangs would ply such men with grog and get them to sign up before they became unconscious. Then they'd drag them on board a vessel about to leave port and the hapless sailor-to-be would wake up with a fierce hangover to find that they were already out to sea. Conditions on board a man-of-war or even on a merchant ship were terrible and more men died of diseases like typhus and dysentery than were ever killed fighting at sea.'

'And even them sort was better than the convicts?'

'Well, so it seems. Shall I go on?

'The people of the penal colony of New South Wales, with very few exceptions, were drunken riffraff, both convict and trooper with the free citizens hardly much better. The males with hard-favoured faces and the females possessed of a great frumpishness. Misery was their middle name and indolence the central part of their nature. As two-thirds were convicts, one would therefore suppose that they had little reason to work.

'The cats were no better and there was never a more flea-bitten, manged and scrawny example of the feline species. On his frequent journeys of exploration ashore Trim found himself with no reason to spend even an hour in the company of the resident cats. They had no news of the slightest importance, their small-town gossip didn't interest him and, as far as he was concerned, they were, to a cat, country yokels.

'It was not that Trim thought himself superior, a shaggy-tailed upper-class cat, all whiskers and strut, who was critical of the poor examples of the local cat while being himself bone idle. He was a hard-working ship's cat who, among his various employments, was responsible for the demise of the rat population on board. At first he pitied the poor creatures he found on shore. Then he discovered that rats were to be found in abundance in the dockside warehouses of Sydney Town and were there simply for the taking with a minimum of effort. Yet the local cats, like everyone else, seemed too idle to undertake an honest day's labour and thereby procure sufficient sustenance to alter the condition of their miserable lives. It was upon such facts that he based his less than flattering opinion of the local cats.

'Of much more interest to Trim were his explorations, which were many and varied, and there is much to be told about these fascinating excursions into the wilderness. For example, while doing a little exploring of the bush to the east of Rushcutters Bay he'd once chanced upon a group of blackfellows. It was a damnable hot day with the flies a great bother when he came upon a small group, whether family or not he couldn't say. They stood upon a sandy headland leading down to a small harbour beach, three women, two piccaninnies and an adult male. The male carried a long sharpened stick and stood in a most curious manner by placing the sole of one naked foot upon the knee of the other, while resting quite comfortably on the other foot, his balance held secure by means of the stick planted in the sand.'

'I've seen that in a pitcher!' Ryan grinned. 'When we did an excursion to the Museum. Abo standing in the nuddy with his leg up like that, his donger showin' an' all!'

Billy nodded and continued with the story. 'They wore no garments whatsoever and, as a cat, Trim approved greatly of this, the humans he was mostly acquainted with were not fond of bathing and paid scant attention to the laundering of their apparel, adorning themselves in all manner of extremely smelly drapery. Cats are by their very nature fastidious in their attention to their grooming and this lack of personal hygiene was one of the characteristics Trim disliked most in humans, who used their tongues for talking and noisily gobbling down food, but never for grooming.

'By contrast to the convict population, these blackfellows were of a good physical proportion and had about them a most delicious smell. Seeking its source, Trim observed that upon the head of each family member there rested a fish, its entrails cut loose to attract the flies. So dense were the flies that swarmed above their heads and rested upon the fish that it was as if they were a swarm of bees. But here then was the clever idea, not a single fly came to land upon the native fellows themselves, which Trim thought to be a most clever contrivance. What's more, when nightfall came and the flies departed, the family had the means of a hearty meal.'

'Yuk!' Ryan called out.

'Trim took satisfaction in being both explorer and sailor but was ever mindful of his true vocation as a ship's cat. He enjoyed the wilderness and became a great expert on what it contained, the nature of the animals, birds and plants of the land, but he took his official title, Master Trim Flinders, Master Mariner & Ratter, very seriously and worked hard to distinguish himself. He knew himself to be well bred but also well able to rough it with the best. During the course of his life, he faced many vicissitudes and some considerable hardship, which he accepted with equanimity as part of the sailor's lot.

'Trim started his seagoing career as an apprentice sailor and ratter where, I am told, he performed with merit but was often rebuked for asking too many questions. Though this did not stop him, he was a cat with a most curious nature. Trim became a Master Mariner & Ratter and was eventually responsible for inventing several new ways of combating *Rattus oceania*, the notorious ship's rodent known universally to be the most vicious and cunning of its tribe. As Matthew Flinders once observed to him, "To question everything is important, for knowledge is power and ignorance is enslavement. When we accept without questioning, we forfeit the power to control our own lives."

'Trim was very much a cat in control of his own life, but he also carried a second title which he took seriously. The title concerned was Companion to the Ship's Master. Trim always insisted that had it not been in the captain's heart to give him this title he would have remained in obscurity, a good ship's cat and sometime explorer. It was the relationship he shared with Matthew Flinders that brought him to the attention of others and resulted in his gaining a small but secure place in the history of Australia.

'Matthew Flinders was a man bred to loneliness and oft-times needed a friend he could talk to, who, in the best traditions of conversation, took the role of an intelligent listener. There were things he told Trim of a private nature, some of which were not always to his personal credit, such as attitudes and preferences which he would not have admitted even in the letters he constantly wrote to his wife, Ann. One such secret was the disease of love, which he caught on the island of Tahiti while sailing on the *Providence* as a midshipman with Captain Bligh.

'These letters to Ann, which he would often read to Trim, contained a great many ardent declarations of his love and expressed a constant regret that they were so cruelly parted. Trim was inclined to feel that this ardency was intended to be a compensation for their separation, a form of marriage that took place with quill and ink on paper. It was Trim's observation that his master was an awkward man who much preferred his ship and his navigational scribbles to the connubial bliss to be found in an attentive wife ensconced in a rose-covered cottage.

'Trim's opinion of his master must be taken seriously for he knew Matthew Flinders more intimately than probably anyone, sharing his cabin with him while they sailed together for much of the time Matthew Flinders was charting the coastline of New Holland. When he'd completed this extraordinary task, Captain Flinders sought Trim's opinion as to the name he should give to this new territory, pointing out to him that it was known variously as New Holland, Terra Australis and the Great South Land, none of which being satisfactory now that its true dimensions were known. Besides, it had been circumnavigated and charted by an Englishman.

' "What shall we call this territory we have so well surveyed, Trim? What shall we add to this land Australis to make it our very own?" It was late and Trim was half asleep. "Eh?" he said, not fully hearing the question. Whereupon Matthew Flinders clapped his hands together.

' "Capital, my dear! Drop the *s* and add an *a*, what a clever cat you are, we shall call it Australia!" '

'That's dumb!' Ryan protested, enjoying Billy's little joke.

'It was a name that greatly pleased Matthew Flinders' masters in England, who didn't much care for the name New Holland, the name given to the Great South Land by the Dutch explorers. It was a constant reminder to Britain that another country might be entitled to make claims on this vast new territory. The Frenchman La Pérouse had landed in Australia and the French were also making claims to the new land. So Britain proclaimed the land *terra nullius*, called it Australia and demanded that henceforth it be seen as a part of the British Empire.'

'What's terror nullius mean?' Ryan asked.

'Ah, it means "empty land". In Latin, *terra* means land and *nullius* means empty. You see, the British penal colony established on this new land was not strictly legitimate as the Aboriginal people already occupied the land and were, and still are, its true owners. So the British government decided to ignore this small technical hitch and declared that the land was "empty" and that its indigenous people, the Aborigines, were not sufficiently civilised to be included in the human race and henceforth this "empty" land belonged to Britain. Rather a convenient decision, I'm sure you'll agree?'

'I suppose the Abos were all too pissed to care, eh? Them putting a cut-open fish on their head for the flies. Yuk!'

Billy smiled, the boy didn't give up easily. 'No, lad, it was the European invader who introduced alcohol in the form of rum to the natives. Shall we go on, then?

'Now when I say Trim was with Mr Flinders as a constant friend and listener that's not entirely true. You see, the problem was Matthew Flinders was a bit of a dreamer and someone had to run the ship when he was busy looking through his eyeglass and measuring and drawing and scribbling his measurements on a giant piece of vellum with his goose-quill pen, scratching away with degrees of latitude and longitude, rises and falls, depths and shallows, shoals and rocks, coves, cliff-faces and sandy beaches.'

'Vellum?' asked Ryan.

'Vellum is paper made of animal skin, they used it for important charts instead of paper because it lasted longer and was much stronger.

'The point is, the ship could have gone aground or perished on the rocks a dozen times or more had it not been for a certain sharp-eyed cat who constantly watched, steering it out of danger. Mr Flinders always wanted to get closer to the shore so he could draw the dents and measure the bays with his surveyor's instruments. Never looked where he was going, that one. "Closer!" he'd call, not looking up from his eyeglass. "Take me closer, damn you, helmsman!" And Trim would have to yell out to the man at the helm, "Take no notice! Drop anchor now!" As a cat he may have had nine lives but he had no immediate plans to waste them all by means of drowning at sea in one single act of gross negligence. Such a calamitous end could happen simply enough when they had all their wits about them, treacherous shoals and unknown rocks abounded along an uncharted coastline. Trim had no intention of losing the vessel as a result of a bit of navigational scribbling.

'Sometimes they'd drop anchor in some remote bay and go ashore with Mr Brown, the naturalist on board. Mr Brown was very fond of Trim and was always happy for him to go along, knowing Trim was a most sensible cat and not likely to do anything rash. They'd take to the wilderness or the desert to collect plant samples or do a watercolour painting of a specimen and in the process they'd see things you couldn't even imagine. Trees so mighty they would measure four times the height of a ship's mast, some of them possessing a base hollowed out by fire caused by lightning, the cavity remaining sufficiently large to accommodate a cottage.

'Matthew Flinders didn't much like going ashore, all he ever wanted to do was to chart the shoreline and mark the features you could see from the water, though he would venture ashore when some rising ground or hill allowed him to see the topography of the surround, or the flow of a river into the sea might take his curiosity as to depth and width and the strength of the flow. So it was Trim and Mr Brown who were the intrepid explorers. Mr Brown had in his possession a most wondrous and remarkable seeing instrument named a microscope, which wasn't any bigger than Trim's front leg from shoulder to paw. He allowed Trim the very great privilege of frequently taking a peek through this magical tubular device. On the first occasion he did so, he placed at its lower extremity a seed almost too small for the naked eye to see. Whereupon Trim looked through the top of the brass tube to see that it had been transformed into the size of a prize pumpkin. He couldn't believe his own eyes. Cats have excellent eyesight yet the seed was but a tiny dot when he'd seen it shaken on to the glass stand and now it was a sight to behold, all cracks and dents, to be likened to a pumpkin or even a boulder in size and character. "Trim, lad," Mr Brown had said that first time, "together with this little beauty we will unlock the secrets of all the exotic flora of Terra Australis." Then Mr Brown said a remarkable thing. "There is more here to appease the appetite any botanist may have for the exotic discovery than all the plants in Europe should they be put together." Aboard the *Investigator* they had cause to build a greenhouse of quite handsome proportions which was under the care of Peter Good, a man of good character and humour who would allow Trim to make frequent inspections of what he called "Sir Joseph's sprouts", the many botanical wonders of this new land destined as a gift to His Majesty's botanical garden at Kew by Matthew Flinders' benefactor, mentor and friend, Sir Joseph Banks.'

Billy looked down at Ryan. 'We can see many of these plants in the Botanic Gardens if you wish, Ryan?'

Ryan nodded, but didn't appear to be overly eager. 'Sure,' was all he said.

Billy now sensed that all the detail he was putting into the story must sound like a rather tedious history lesson to Ryan. The observations that pleased him might not be so interesting to Ryan. He'd have to watch himself.

'Trim found it most pleasant exploring with Mr Brown. Sometimes they'd see things you wouldn't believe were possible. For example, once they came across these giant rats about half the size of a horse.'

'Ah, bull!' Ryan objected, 'Rats half the size of a horse!'

'Hang on, Ryan,' Billy cautioned, 'wait until you hear the rest of the story.

'As they approached, the rats sat upon their tails and looked at them, calm as you like. "Mighty mother of all seagoing cats!" Trim thought to himself, eyeing the nearest tree for his personal safety, "If the rats are this size, how big then must the cats be?"'

Ryan started to laugh. 'They were kangaroos!'

'Correct,' Billy said, 'Have you ever looked closely at a kangaroo? If you'd never seen one before and you were a cat, then it wouldn't be too difficult to believe they were giant rats.'

'Can we do some of Trim's adventures on the ship, Billy?' Ryan suddenly asked.

Billy had been right. Since Charlie, he'd forgotten how to tell a story to a boy of Ryan's age. 'Sure, life on a ship in those days was pretty tough. You see a ship at that time wasn't a very big place and, as you know, cats are by nature explorers. You may imagine that after a while Trim knew every corner of the ship, foredeck, top deck, main deck and the lower decks, every inch was familiar to him. He didn't even have to look for new places for mice or rats to hide, because they'd all long since been used up.

'There is always good accommodation for rodents available upon berthing at a new port of call. Rats are by nature a cunning and parsimonious lot, they simply cannot resist the prospect of travel and rent-free accommodation, so by the time the ship sailed there'd be a great many freeloaders who had crept aboard under cover of night. So great would this invading population be that it would occasion a major rat-housing shortage below decks.

'Once out to sea again, all Trim was required to do was wait around and the newly resident rats would come scuttling up like a bunch of holiday-makers, falling over each other to sample the delights of life at sea. Trim would see to it that they received a most surprising welcome and, abracadabra, as if by magic, accommodation suitable for a young rat couple at present living with their in-laws and wishing to start a family of their own would become vacant. The newlyweds couldn't pack up fast enough, not thinking to inquire why the previous occupants had thought to leave such a good address, thinking only that they were moving into a nice neighbourhood with pleasant ocean views.

'You may find this strange, but no self-respecting ship's cat wants a rodent-free ship. With the vermin sneaking on board uninvited when the vessel was in port, it would be easy enough for Trim to go on a rat rampage and eliminate them all in the first week at sea. But Trim wasn't that foolish, he'd conserve his rat resources so that they lasted for the entire voyage, the idea being that the ship should be vermin-free just about the time it entered its next port of call. Trim regarded rats, once they realised that the ship under his captaincy was no floating holiday resort, as worthy opponents, naturally cunning and resourceful. His greatest dread was to be left with only a few mice and cockroaches to contend with. Mice, he thought, were rather stupid and too easy to catch. Cockroaches were even more dunderheaded, so there was little fun to be obtained by catching them, except occasionally to amuse the ship's crew when the vessel was becalmed.

'Although, I must say in their defence, cockroaches have survived unchanged for hundreds of millions of years, which makes them one of the ultimate survivors, so they can't be that stupid after all. Trim did not share this opinion and it may well have been that seagoing cockroaches were somewhat inbred for lack of a procreational opportunity among their shore-bound kind, because he considered them positively retarded, proper idiots, not an ounce of commonsense between the lot of them.

'Anyway, as I was saying, Trim always kept a few rats in reserve, not just for sport and recreation during a long voyage, but also for the purpose of human relations. Let me explain, humans can be pretty difficult to manage at times and this was particularly true when tedium set in at sea. Trim would often enough have occasion to remind the crew who was responsible for their general wellbeing and relatively rodent-free environment. In other words, who was the real captain of the ship.

'But being of a feline nature, that is to say, a cat, he couldn't go about the task the way humans do, which is by fighting each other or flogging those who disobey the master's orders. Humans are accustomed to asserting their supremacy with a bout of fisticuffs. "Biff-bang! Thy nose is bloodied and I am master now!" Or "Whack-whack-whack, take a hundred lashes because I'm in charge of this vessel." Trim was much too intelligent for such immature carryings-on and, besides, it was his observation that such tactics only work until the next blighter comes along and knocks the new master over and he's now the one to be obeyed and so on and so forth. Or, in the matter of disciplining the crew by means of the cat-o'-nine-tails, the men eventually grow tired of being flogged and stage a mutiny, as they did with Captain Bligh.

'Ships' cats are a much more sophisticated lot when it comes to the management of humans and one of the methods Trim used was the retention of some well-placed rodents on board. This is how it worked. The ship's galley is where they prepare the food for the crew and, as every sailor knows, ships' cooks are not all that fussed when it comes to cleaning up around food, so there were always plenty of scraps left about, which means a ship's galley is oft-times a land of plenty in the vocabulary of your average rat.

'So, true to one's calling, the ship's cat is duty-bound to disabuse your seagoing rat of this notion to the extent that no rat would venture near it without risking Trim's displeasure. This is a polite way of saying "without the prospect of undergoing a lingering but certain death". "R.I.P." inscribed on a rodent tombstone means Rats in Peace.

'Well, at the beginning of every voyage, when Trim gets his rat mopping-up operation into full swing, the cook can't be nice enough. He saves all the juicy bits of mutton and beef for the grand ratter and Trim lives like a king, his fur sleek and glossy. But, alas, rather typically of humans, when you are no longer useful to them, they are quick to forget their obligations. Once the galley was free of rampaging rodents, the cook's gratitude could no longer be relied upon. No more tidbits, no more bending down to tickle Trim behind the ear, telling him what a handsome fellow he was.

'Cooks are generally cantankerous creatures, as Trim soon discovered after he'd cleaned up the rodents. Feeling peckish, he once decided to stroll into the galley to gently remind the cook how he'd prevented a major rodent infestation and possibly an outbreak of the plague on board ship, but next thing he found himself sailing through the air with a dirty great seaman's boot up his arse!'

Ryan laughed. Kids love an unexpected dirty word from an adult who doesn't usually employ bad language.

Billy smiled, but continued. 'It was on occasions such as this that Operation Spare Rat came into play. It was time to call on the small colony of rats Trim had hidden in the darkest recess at the back of the ship. He would cull them, one at a time, and deposit a fresh carcase every morning at the entrance to the galley to remind the ship's cook to save the mutton scraps for "yours truly". Trim, being of an open nature, always felt a little guilty acting in such a duplicitous manner, but he was essentially a practical seaman and realised that it was sometimes necessary to remind people of their obligations. Good manners and due consideration for others are characteristics too often neglected among humans.

'While Trim loved and honoured his master, he knew him also capable of careless affection. He could become so enamoured of his work or so engrossed in a book that he would quite forget to maintain Trim's rightful position on the ship. So it became Trim's custom to drop a regular rat on the deck beside Matthew Flinders' bunk. This was designed so that when his master awoke from his slumbers and would perchance glance downwards in the process of retrieving his boots, he would see a member of the dreaded genus *Rattus* dead at his feet.

'"Trim, thou art indeed a mighty cat, a feline above all cats that ever was, most affectionate of friends, faithful servant and best of creatures," he would say, giving Trim a bit of a scratch on the stomach while Trim immediately obliged him with a purr, lying on his back with his legs in the air, which wasn't very dignified, but it was Trim's observation that life is full of small compromises and that pleasing a partner in small ways is the prerequisite to a sound and loving relationship.

'The reward for Trim's endeavour would come at dinner in the officers' mess, when he would be seated upon the table to the immediate left of Captain Flinders' chair. There came a moment after the saying of grace when Trim could count on the ship's master telling his assembled officers that he, Master Trim, was the most illustrious of his race and to be much admired as he was, quite possibly, the world's best ratter. Then he would recount the incident of the dead rat on the deck beside his bunk.

'Matthew Flinders was so enamoured of Trim that he failed to observe that his fellow officers around the table were to a man glazed-eyed, having heard the same praise rendered a hundred times before. But they nevertheless clapped politely in the appropriately obsequious manner. "Remarkable, sir!" one would say. "A cat in a hundred," said another. "No, by golly, in a thousand!" responded a third. "Indeed, sir, a reward is called for!" demanded a fourth. "Aye, a reward!" they would chorus.

'"A reward it shall be!" Captain Flinders would say, happy as could be. He'd then turn to Trim, proud as punch. "See how they love you, Master Trim," he'd declare, though Trim had no such illusions and knew that they didn't care a nest of fiddlesticks about him. Life is a practical business and we cannot always seek to win the hearts of everyone before we proceed to make our plans. The dead rat beside the bunk was merely a means of ensuring that Trim didn't have to depend solely on the ship's cook for his meals.

'Trim would rub his head against the gold bands about his master's sleeves, and Matthew Flinders would then cut a tasty morsel of beef from the piece upon his plate and place it on to the end of his fork. With a display of exquisite manners, being careful at all times not to touch the tines with his lips, Trim would remove the beef. "There, I have begun the reward," Flinders would announce. This was intended to encourage the other diners to do the same, which they did with varying degrees of enthusiasm, so that in the process of going to the place of each officer around the table to receive his just reward, Trim managed to obtain a tasty meal.'

'What's obse . . . obseequis . . . ?'

'Obsequious. It means,' Billy couldn't think quite how to put it, 'to suck up,' he said, resorting to a term familiar to Ryan.

'My nana said that was syco . . . sycophantic,' Ryan said accusingly, 'both words can't mean the same, can they?'

Billy was becoming increasingly delighted with Ryan's mind. 'Well, no, not precisely,' Billy paused. 'Let me see, yes, very well, obsequious, *obsequiosus, obsequium*,' he muttered to himself, quoting the Latin roots. 'Ah, compliance! It means to do something in a servile manner, like an over-attentive servant or someone who wants to make an impression on you by obeying your every word. Get the idea?'

'Nope. I think you were right the first time, it means to suck up. I seen girls do that in class to our teacher.'

'Where were we?' Billy asked.

'Trim's just got himself a free feed,' Ryan replied. 'Cats don't have to work that hard for their food these days. I've never even seen a cat catch a rat, or a mouse, or even a cockroach. Once, a moth.'

'Do you have a cat, Ryan?' Billy asked.

'We did, once. It's gorn. We had this cat that my nana used to feed, it was called Nostril. When she got crook she forgot to feed it, and me mum and me also, we didn't. It disappeared and didn't come back. It had half its nose missing from a fight or somethin', maybe a dog bit it.'

'Well, you're probably right about the modern cat,' Billy said. 'They seem to have no sense of responsibility or the need to earn a living, they expect everything to be there for them without having to make any effort on their own. They're out on the tiles all night with their friends, heaven knows where they end up and what they're up to. They come home in the early hours, use the kitty litter and leave it in a mess for you to clean up, then they sleep most of the day and expect to be given everything and to do nothing in return for free board and lodging. Your average dear little pussy wouldn't last two weeks at sea in Trim's world before the rats ganged up on him and shoved him through a porthole one dark night. Even rats have standards to maintain,' Billy said, tongue-in-cheek.

'So we see that Trim understood that life is a difficult process and that it is never a good idea to put all your eggs in one basket. We can never tell how things will turn out and Trim understood that one day you're purring along without a concern in the world and the next the fur is flying everywhere and suddenly you're someone's winter gloves. It's always a good idea to have an alternate plan because if trouble can happen, you can bet your boots it will.'

Reaching out, Billy touched Ryan on the shoulder. 'It's time you left for school, lad.'

'That was real good,' Ryan said, rising from the skateboard, 'Can we do it again?'

'Yes, of course,' Billy said, smiling, just a little pleased with himself. He'd managed to hold Ryan's attention rather longer than he'd thought possible. He wondered if Charlie would have been as attentive. Probably not, he decided. Ryan had none of the advantages Charlie's privileged background had allowed him yet he possessed an exceptional intelligence.

'Will I see you in the mornin'?' Ryan asked, trying not to sound too anxious.

'Not tomorrow, it's pension day. I have to take a shower and change my clothes.' Billy hesitated, 'I don't suppose you'd consider doing the same, you know, bit of a scrub up, fresh gear? Or would that be out of the question?'

Ryan looked down, pursing his lips and examining his clobber critically for several moments. 'Suppose. The washing machine's broke. I'll have to take them to the laundry mat.'

Billy didn't correct him, 'laundry mat' seemed like a nice alternative to that cheerless place where big white boxes growled away and people always looked miserable as their clothes whirled around. 'Cheerio, Ryan, straight to school, that's if you want to be a ship's cat and not a cockroach.'

Ryan gave Billy a cheeky grin. 'You said them cockroaches survived millions of years, nothing wrong with that!' Then, taking his leave in a clatter and rumble of skateboard wheels, he called out, 'See ya, Billy, don't forget I gotta sign yer arm first, it's for my good luck!'

Billy sat in the sun for a while, reviewing Trim's story in his mind, it was still a little formal, he'd used several words that would be well out of Ryan's reach and he told himself he'd have to be careful about that. Then suddenly he remembered how, without thinking, he'd touched Ryan on the shoulder. It was no more than the lightest touch, a sign of his approbation, but anyone looking on might think otherwise.

After a while he rose from the bench and made his way to Lower George Street to purchase a small loaf of bread before returning to the Quay, where he made up the day's ammunition for Operation Mynah Bird and fed the gulls with the remainder of the bread. He was pleased with himself. While out buying the bread, he'd passed two pubs and hadn't gone in. He'd been without a drink for twenty-four hours. While his blood sugar was up due to the heavily sugar-laced coffee, he needed to stimulate it further and stopped to buy himself a Mars bar. The boy and the story of the cat had helped to take his mind from the gut-gnawing craving for alcohol, yet he could sense the tug deep inside him, the need that would grow to be irresistible before the day was out.

Billy thought about the day ahead. He'd go and make his inspection of the Botanic Gardens, then he'd visit Trevor Williams at St Vincent's, which would take up most of the morning, then to the library steps for the mynah birds, so he'd probably be able to hang on without a drink until mid-afternoon. He knew what would happen, first the shakes, a mild trembling and then some sweating, a headache and a sense of anxiety developing, and his heart would begin to race. The craving would only stop when he'd fed his body with the alcoholic infusion it demanded.

Staying off the grog until later in the day would mean forgoing Sam Snatch's free early-morning scotch, but Billy wasn't too sure he'd be all that welcome at the Flag Hotel. It could just be that Snatch would blame him as well as Casper Friendly for letting the blackfella off the hook. Snatch was known to carry a grudge for what he believed was a reasonable period, like a lifetime. Just as well to leave things to cool down for another day or two. Marion would probably defend him if the proprietor of the Flag was still angry, although you never could tell with her, if she'd been in on the deal she might be just as pissed off as Snatch himself.

Yesterday, when he'd seen the Aborigine's hat and boots under the bed next to his own at the hospital, he'd jumped to his feet and pulled apart the curtains around his bed. Then, taking the couple of steps towards where he supposed Williams lay, he opened the curtains. To Billy's dismay, the bed was unoccupied, with the rest of the black man's clobber neatly folded on the chair beside the bed.

Billy was suddenly furious. The anticlimax of finding Trevor Williams and then not finding him was the last straw and now he reached down, picked up the Akubra, jammed it on to his head and started to cry, though his tears were more ones of frustration and self-pity than of vexation. Suddenly he'd had enough, his paranoia took charge and a sense of panic overcame him. He'd found Williams yet he wasn't there, and the stash was still in his briefcase and bloody Sergeant Orr was going to examine it in the morning and he'd be in the clink by tomorrow night. There was only one thing to do, he decided, that was to escape immediately. He'd change into the blackfella's clobber so they couldn't recognise him. Bloody good idea!

But it proved to be a lot easier said than done. The briefcase was attached to his right hand and his left hand was in a sling, while the temporary splint and the bandage that secured it was wound from his wrist down to halfway up his fingers. There had only just been sufficient grip in them to pull the curtains apart and he'd barely had the leverage to pick up the Akubra. Getting to the key around his neck and opening the handcuffs seemed to him much too big a task. Never mind that! He'd attend to that problem later.

Placing the instep of his left shoe on the back of the heel of the right one, he pulled it off, kicking it away, then did the same with his bare foot on the heel of the left runner. He pushed a foot into one of the Cubans, it wriggled around a bit but then gripped. It was a tight fit, plenty of width but the boot was too short and he could feel his toes being jammed at the sharp end while the backs of his heels were slightly elevated. The left boot was a little easier, though still much too tight up front and back.

Putting the briefcase on his lap, so that his hand, chained to the cuff, could reach the buckle, he managed to undo his belt and pull down the zip on his fly. Lifting the case, he stood up, which promptly caused his trousers to fall to his ankles. No problems, he'd have to take the boots off again to get his trousers off, but he'd deal with that later.

Like most derelicts he didn't wear underpants, underpants weren't a part of the clothing-bin contributions that the homeless depended on. People simply don't throw away used underpants, they use them as dusters to polish the dining-room table or clean the car.

Now the big problem, the shirt. Panicked, Billy was having trouble thinking straight. But after a few moments he regained a small portion of his sanity, enough to think. Taking a deep breath, he sat down at the edge of the bed and placed the briefcase on his lap again, then bending forward so that his head was adjacent to the handle, he managed to slip the key over his head. At last something was working for him. But now he realised his fatal mistake, the key was in his right hand and the handcuff was attached to his right wrist, there was no way of opening it.

'Think!' he yelled at the top of his voice. The handcuff attached to the briefcase handle. It had a key slot! Billy's hand trembled as he inserted the key into the second handcuff. But he should have known better, this was the real world where bums and drunks never get an even break. The handcuff hadn't been removed from around the handle of the briefcase for four years and the mechanism was completely rusted up, the lock wouldn't budge a millimetre.

Seated on the edge of Williams' bed, with the Akubra jammed almost down to his eyebrows, the blackfella's Cubans pinching his toes and his own trousers down around his ankles, Billy could take no more. He began to cry again. This was the end of the road, the dark angel of despair had descended upon him and smothered him within her swirling diaphanous black robes. There was nowhere to go. He was trapped, dead meat. The part of his brain that thought and solved problems had turned into a mental stew which boiled and bubbled like a witch's brew inside his head.

'And what in the name of sweet charity have we here?' A voice, as if heard within an echo chamber, reached him. It sounded vaguely Irish, but with the echo effect you couldn't tell for sure. 'And are we not in the wrong bed?' the voice continued.

Billy tried but was unable to stop crying. 'I'm sorry, miss.'

'Nurse, did you not say it was a sprained wrist?' Yes, it was definitely Irish. 'A possible fracture? Did you not say the patient needed an intravenous drip?'

'Yes, nurse, that's what Dr Goldstein said.'

'Well, that's not the only thing we seem to have here if you ask me. Come now, Mr O'Shannessy, we'll be having no more of this nonsense, back we go to our own bed!'

Billy, responding to the undeniable authority in the voice, jumped down from the bed, forgetting that his trousers were still around his ankles and the briefcase around his wrist. He lurched forward and then, as if in slow motion, he was pulled backwards by the weight of the briefcase. Attempting to go forward again, the constraint around his ankles caused his legs to remain nailed to the floor while his torso continued onwards. He crashed forward and his head and shoulders parted the curtains surrounding his own bed. With a resounding clank, his forehead struck against the angular metal frame, bringing him to an abrupt halt. Billy gave a small sigh and sank slowly to the floor, unconscious.

He woke several hours later, he knew this was so because now the ward lights were on. He lay in bed dressed in a pair of hospital pyjamas, his head hurting like hell and his arm in a sling, with his wrist and half his hand up to the middle joints of his fingers encased in plaster almost to the elbow. Billy lay still, trying to focus, to remember what had happened to him. Then he attempted to lift his left arm. It came up easily. He shot bolt upright and saw that a drip had been fixed into his right hand and that the briefcase was missing. His heart started to pound violently and he thought he was going to pass out. Oh, Jesus, the stash! They would have found the stash! He looked around, unable to decide what to do next. Then he saw his briefcase on the chair beside his bed. Holding his hand to his heart, he tried to regain his composure. After a few moments he realised he was by no means home yet, the blackfella's stash may not be inside and now he saw that the wrist handcuff lay open against the side of the case with the key still in the keyhole.

With his hand shaking, he leaned over the side of the bed, clicked open the latch and looked within. All he saw were the notepads and curiously enough the tiger's eye pebble he'd dropped the previous day, the photo album and, protruding slightly behind it, the thick roll of yellow banknotes secured with the elastic band.

Billy fell back into the bed and thought he was going to throw up, it was several minutes before he felt strong enough to lean over to close the briefcase. The shock of finding the handcuff missing from his wrist served to recall his earlier humiliation. He had lost his dignity, the single aspect of his fall from grace that he tried hardest to maintain. Now he was reduced to what he must seem to everyone, just another brain-damaged alcoholic. Billy wondered if indeed his brain *was* going, if he'd finally crossed over the line from the problem drinker he told himself he'd become to a blubbering, mumbling idiot. The idea caused him to break into a sweat and he found he was hyperventilating.

After a few moments he managed to control himself and tried to reach the briefcase but for some reason the drip stand wouldn't move any closer to the bed. He felt his frustration growing. 'Ever since I entered this place I've lost my bloody independence,' he thought. While there wasn't much to be said for being homeless, the one thing going for it was independence. You did what you wished and took the consequences as they came. Now he was trapped in the system. 'That's what I'll do, I'll sign myself out, they can't stop me,' he declared to himself. He'd allowed the hospital administration to control him for long enough.

Suddenly Billy brought his right hand up to his mouth. Gripping between his teeth the edge of the sticking plaster holding the drip needle into the vein, he ripped it off, spitting it out on the bed. Then he did the same to the wing of the butterfly needle and pulled it from the vein, wincing at the sting as the needle withdrew. Somewhat to his surprise, no bleeding followed and all that was left was a small haematoma where the drip had been inserted.

He climbed from the bed and, stooping down, lifted the curtain surrounding his bed so that he could see under the bed opposite. To his joy, the Cuban boots had been placed back under the bed with the battered Akubra on top of them. He heard a cough followed by a groan from the bed above the boots. Wherever he'd been, Williams had returned.

Billy could hardly believe his luck and his hand trembled as he rummaged inside the briefcase to locate the roll of banknotes. He quickly shoved the money into his pyjama jacket and parted the curtains, taking the two steps required to reach the next bed. 'Mr Williams, may I come in?' he asked politely, his voice gravelly as if his throat contained phlegm.

No reply came from the other side of the curtain. Billy cleared his throat, which felt dry and raspy. 'Hmmph! Mr Williams, may I see you, please?' he tried again.

'Who's there?' the voice on the other side of the curtain demanded.

'It's Billy, Billy O'Shannessy.'

'Who? I don't know no Billy!' Williams started to cough but Billy couldn't retreat now, he wasn't going to let the Aborigine escape a third time.

'From the pub, I was with Casper, Casper Friendly, the albino bloke, you may recall.' There was silence from the other side of the curtain and after a few moments Billy said, 'I have good news.'

'Bugger off, yer mongrel, I got nothin' ter say ter your sort!' Williams started to cough again and Billy, taking his courage in his hands, parted the white curtain. Williams was in a paroxysm of coughing, holding his hands to his ribs. His head and one eye were heavily bandaged and so were both hands.

Billy reached for the glass of water at his bedside and held it up to his mouth, allowing the black man to swallow so that eventually his coughing ceased.

Williams lay back on his pillows, panting, though he kept one malevolent eye on Billy. After a while he said, 'I thought I told yer ter bugger off! Don'tcha understan' English?'

'I'm sorry to interrupt you, Mr Williams, but you'll want your money.'

The Aborigine misunderstood what Billy was saying. 'You want me money? You want me fuckin' money! You've took it all, you and yer mongrel mates! Yer beat and kicked the shit outta me and took me stash. Jesus Christ, then yer come here, tell me you want me money!'

Billy took the roll of notes from inside his pyjama jacket and held it out to Williams. 'No, you don't understand me, sir, I'm *returning* your money.'

Williams still appeared unable to comprehend, he looked at the roll of banknotes and back at Billy. After a while he said suspiciously, 'What's happenin' here? What yer doin'? You from the police, crime squad?'

Billy laughed. 'Yes, it's my day off, I thought I'd spend it in the casualty ward.' He opened the drawer of the metal bedside cabinet and put the money into it. 'It's yours, I brought it back, there's nothing missing.'

Williams remained silent for some time, then said, 'What happened, you in a fight?'

'No, drunk, I fell and fractured my wrist, bumped my head.'

'Yeah, okay,' was all Williams said and he fell silent again.

'Mind if I sit?' Billy tapped the bandage on his head, 'I'm feeling a little dizzy.'

'Yeah, righto.' The chair next to his bed held the black man's moleskins and shirt so Billy now sat on the bed. Again there was silence between them. Billy was anxious to explain what had happened but his legal instinct told him to wait a little longer, that Williams was still angry and needed a bit more time to come to grips with the situation, which Billy now saw must seem somewhat bizarre from the black man's point of view.

After a while Williams asked, 'Why you do this, eh? Your mob break all me ribs, one eye's gorn, you jump on me 'ands, break me fingers, me knee's gorn, then yer brings me money back. You gorn crazy or somethin'?'

Billy started to tell Williams the story and when he'd completed it Williams was silent for some time. 'Mr O'Shan . . . ?'

'O'Shannessy, but, please, it's Billy.'

'Billy, yiz a good bloke.' He shook his head slowly. 'Fuckin' oath, who'd a thought somethin' like this could happen, hey? Blackfella, whitefella, blackfella gets drunk, loses his money, whitefella finds it, gives it back ter blackfella, it don't happen like that, mate.'

'Casper Friendly was trying to con you, Trevor, I felt guilty.'

'Yeah, but I thought you was in on it, the two of yiz.'

'I suppose I was in a way,' Billy confessed. 'May I suggest something?'

'Yeah, go right ahead.'

Billy indicated the money in the drawer. 'Don't show it around like that, in a bundle, even an unbroken fifty can get your head kicked in around here.'

'Yeah, mate, I was stupid. Blackfella come into the big city from the bush, needs ter show off, bloody stupid!'

Billy indicated the black man's bandages. 'Have you seen the police?'

Williams laughed and started to cough again, holding his sides and groaning in between bouts of coughing. Billy fed him more of the water. 'Whaffor?' he said gasping, 'Nothin' them bludgers can do.'

Billy smiled. 'Yeah, damned silly question.' He knew what Trevor Williams was really saying was that he was a black man who had been beaten up and supposedly robbed while he was drunk, which in police terms gave him a priority rating of zero.

'Mr O'Shannessy, is that you? And what are we up to now?' The Irish sister stood with her hands on her hips. 'If I may be so bold, what have we done with our drip?'

Billy coughed. 'I'm sorry, but I had some urgent business with Mr Williams, sister.'

'Mr Williams is not to be disturbed, it's pinned to his curtain, clear as daylight for those who care to look.'

'Yes, well, I . . .' Billy couldn't think how to continue. 'I didn't see it, sister,' he said lamely.

'Don't give him a hard time, nurse. He's a good bloke!'

Trevor Williams said, 'Salt o' the earth!'

In his entire life Billy felt he had never received a more sincere compliment.

'Come along now, Mr O'Shannessy, Mr Williams needs to rest. Doctor Goldstein says you're to have a good night's sleep and then you can go in the morning.'

Billy turned to face her. 'No, thank you, sister, but I will be signing myself out.'

'Oh, I don't know about that, Mr O'Shannessy.'

'I am perfectly at liberty to go. With the greatest respect, I do know my legal rights, sister.'

'Oh you do now, do you? Well, we'll have to ask Dr Goldstein about that, won't we? He'll be none too pleased I can tell you that for sure.' The sister turned to a nurse, 'Page Dr Goldstein please, nurse.'

'He's only due in at ten o'clock, sister, he's on the late-night shift in casualty.'

'Then the doctor on duty!' the sister snapped.

'You may do as you wish, but nonetheless I shall be leaving,' Billy said stubbornly. 'There is no point in disturbing the doctor on duty, I won't change my mind.'

The nurse hesitated and the sister held her hand up for her to remain, then she crossed her arms, 'And where will you go then, your report says "no fixed address"?'

'I shall sign myself in at Foster House . . . the Salvation Army,' Billy lied.

The Irish sister now changed tack. Smiling, she appealed to him, 'Mr O'Shannessy, I can see that you're an educated man, can you not understand that we are only thinking of you? That we want to do the best thing for you?' In an attempt to disarm him further, she smiled again. 'I'd be thinking a night's rest will do you the world of good. Fresh as a daisy in the morning, ready to face the world, eh?'

Billy bowed his head slightly, acknowledging her efforts at reconciliation. 'Thank you, madam, I am grateful for what you've done, I'm afraid I have no means of repaying you other than to remove myself as soon as possible.'

The sister's expression changed and her lips drew tight, 'Very well then, you're an Irishman and I'm Irish myself and I know how stubborn you men can be.'

'I'm Australian, madam,' Billy corrected, 'And we are known to be even more recalcitrant.'

The sister turned to the nurse. 'Will you get Mr O'Shannessy's discharge papers please, nurse?'

'Too right, mate!' Williams interjected, 'If I could flamin' walk I'd do the same myself, I got me that clossto . . .'

'Claustrophobia,' Billy said, without thinking.

'Yeah, that!' Williams replied, 'White sheets, white curtains, white walls, white uniforms, white bedpan, white toilet roll, white people!'

The sister ignored the black man's protest. 'Now, come along, Mr O'Shannessy, you'll need to change and I have to take your temperature and blood pressure before you go.' She seemed resigned to Billy's leaving. 'Dr Goldstein says you're to stay away from the grog tonight, you've had medication, antibiotics, it's very important!' The sister guided Billy away from Williams' bed and the curtains closed behind them.

Williams called out suddenly, 'Hey, Billy?'

'What is it, Trevor?' Billy called back, resisting the nursing sister tugging on his pyjama sleeve.

'Can I talk to yiz sometime? It's about me little singing daughter.'

CHAPTER FIVE

It was almost ten-thirty when Billy entered the Flag Hotel the next morning. On pension day, his routine changed, though normally he'd still begin the day by visiting Con, after which he'd set off across mid-town to The Station, a drop-in centre run by the Department of Health.

Even though he told himself it didn't matter about Con, that the very reason he was on the street was to avoid any emotional attachments, it nevertheless pained Billy to think that he'd lost his friend. If Ryan hadn't appeared in his life and Con, for whatever reason, hadn't decided to sever their relationship, Billy told himself, the fight would have been easier to take. After Charlie's death, affection was to be avoided at any cost. The price he'd paid to make this possible was to isolate himself from his family and any other meaningful human contact. Con was an acquaintance, someone he'd helped in a small way and who'd returned the favour, an association conducted at arm's length, no different to helping one of the derros. Now Billy wasn't so sure. The coffee waiting for him of a morning and Con Poleondakis's cheerful ebullience and accident-prone English had become a part of his life. The incident with Ryan and the loss of the cafe owner's friendship now troubled Billy more than he cared to admit.

He left the bench under the ficus tree early so that he wouldn't run into Sergeant Orr, and set out for Martin Place station to buy a cup of coffee. After this he would make his way to the drop-in centre, which opened at seven and where it was his custom twice a week to do his laundry, shave and shower. The centre was known officially as The Station, and it would take him no more than twenty minutes to cross George Street and walk up through Angel Place to where it was situated in Clarence Street.

In the underground at Martin Place he bumped into a derelict he knew slightly who put the hard word on him for a loan. Though Billy couldn't recall his name, he knew him as a metho drinker whom he'd once helped with a family problem. 'Mate, it's pension day, I'm skint,' Billy answered. 'Buy you a cup of coffee if you like?' Billy knew he had sufficient money to buy the alcoholic a bottle of white lightning but his deliberate mention of pension day was a gentle way of reminding him that he should wait until he collected his pension before he got back on the grog.

The alcoholic either wasn't listening or was brain-damaged. 'Nah, yiz a bloody drongo! Won't buy a mate a drink, yiz can get fucked!'

Billy started to walk away, then, remembering the man's name, thought he might as well make sure he realised it was pension day. 'Hey, George,' he called out, 'better stay off the sauce until the banks open.' He smiled, 'Mate, they won't give you your cash if you're blotto.'

'Garn, bugger orf,' the drunk shouted angrily, causing several early commuters to turn around.

Moving over to where he could get a takeaway coffee, Billy smiled ruefully. 'Welcome to a beautiful new day, Billy O'Shannessy.'

The Station was a two-storey sandstone terrace house with a small verandah and a green wrought-iron fence. A homey little place on the corner of Clarence and Erskine Streets, it was perched on the corner like an oversight and surrounded by city skyscrapers. No doubt a hugely valuable piece of real estate, it seemed incongruous to Billy that the terrace house was given over to the day care of the city's homeless.

Billy thought The Station one of the few social-welfare institutions that worked well, in fact he regarded it as an altogether admirable organisation. Though he was asked to sign himself in when he entered, he was not required to give his own name and the book was full of invented names. Smith, Jones and Brown were always prominent, with Ginger Meggs and Fatty Finn both popular choices, as well as an occasional Clark Gable or some other movie star. Once he'd seen Darth Vader, Donald Duck and Mickey Mouse. Paradoxically, the only legitimate names in it were those of people who were illiterate. People who couldn't read and write had nevertheless learned to write their signatures and they could be observed painstakingly labouring over the book, which appeared simply to be a head count of the drop-outs who dropped in so that the Salvos could receive their government subsidy.

The Station was especially popular among those alcoholics who stayed at the 'Starlight Hotel'. In other words, those who, like Billy, slept rough. For a single payment of five dollars, a steel locker could be hired with a stout padlock to store possessions for as long as its recipient wished. Two free phone calls were permitted per day and the place could be used as a permanent address for the homeless. The staff were generally helpful and would happily take messages. Showers and laundry facilities were available and equipped the same as any family bathroom or laundry. There was a recreational room furnished with brown tables and vinyl-covered chairs with the usual TV channels as well as Foxtel.

There were few rules to observe, though the ones that existed were strictly kept, no fighting, no drinking, no violence, and there were designated smoking areas. Billy found the latter rather amusing as The Station's clients were mostly alcoholics and he was a very rare example of a derro who didn't smoke. None of them was likely to make old bones so that death by passive smoke inhalation was hardly an issue.

The centre also required that the torso be covered by some sort of shirt. Curiously enough, this had nothing to do with decorum but had been brought about because of the television. Intimidation was strictly forbidden and anyone who threw his weight around was banned from the centre, so some of the derelicts wishing to change a channel habitually removed their shirts and paraded around the room, flexing their muscles and showing their mostly prison-acquired tattoos while loudly proclaiming the channel number they preferred to watch. This was meant to frighten the more timid guests, usually among the mentally retarded, who preferred cartoons and were apt to spend endless hours staring at the television set though not necessarily watching it. Billy had long since observed that it was one of life's truisms that no matter how desperate the situation a collective mob finds itself in, a pecking order of some sort always exists.

Billy signed in and went over to the receptionist, a young lady in her early twenties named Sally Blue. He greeted her politely, asked for a towel and extended his left arm so that she could drape it over his plaster cast. 'Oh, you poor old thing, Billy,' she cried, observing his arm. 'Had an accident, have you?'

'Entirely my own fault, my dear,' Billy grinned, 'but thank you for asking.' He always thought her name particularly pretty, speculating that her parents couldn't possibly have known she'd keep her violet-coloured eyes when they'd named her. The name suited her well, Sally Blue was blonde, attractive and very popular among the homeless.

'The usual?' Sally asked. Billy nodded and, as well as the towel, she draped an old dressing-gown over his arm. The dressing-gown wasn't standard issue and Sally had brought it from home, claiming her father had received a new one for Christmas. Billy carried no spare clothes other than the plastic raincoat he kept in his briefcase, so he needed this dressing-gown in order to launder the clothes he was wearing. She automatically reached for a sachet of instant coffee and a small packet of biscuits, then laughed. 'Don't suppose you can carry these?'

'Thank you, I'll get them later,' Billy replied and turned towards the shower block.

'Wait on!' Sally suddenly cried, 'You'll get your plaster wet.' She rose and walked down a small hallway, up a set of stairs to the kitchen and came back with a roll of gladwrap. Removing the towel and gown, she made Billy hold out his arm while she waterproofed his plaster cast, sealing each end with a rubber band. 'There's a go,' she said.

Billy washed his clothes and waited in his dressing-gown while they dried. The gown was old and somewhat threadbare, but he thought of it as a small luxury, something he'd enjoyed in his past that he didn't need to forget. Cosy in the dressing-gown and enjoying the fuggy solitude of the laundry, he decided to wash his runners as well. He put an extra portion of soap powder into the washing machine to compensate for the fact that they were in a mess but hadn't thought about how much louder they'd sound in the big drier. Now he watched embarrassed as they bumped and thumped, making a fearful racket for the better part of an hour.

With his shoes clean but still somewhat damp, he went upstairs to breakfast, where he had a mug of tea and asked the kitchen attendant if she'd wrap the four slices of bread which served as the regular breakfast. It wasn't an unusual request and she added two more slices. 'Butter, jam, peanut butter?' she asked pleasantly.

Billy shook his head, 'No, just the bread, thank you, Monica.' Billy's legal training made him good with names and he constantly surprised staff with his memory. Billy knew he was popular at The Station, the reason being the simple courtesies he affected without thinking. Most alcoholics have poor memories and are, for the most part, untrained in the social niceties. Besides, they usually feel they have very little to be thankful for, particularly in the morning when they invariably suffer from a hangover. His mannerisms would have gone largely unnoticed in polite society but here they were remarked upon and, because of them, he was afforded a number of small privileges, the dressing-gown being one such, the extra slices of bread another. Billy wondered what the kitchen attendant would think if he explained the true purpose of the bread.

Leaving the dining room, Billy went through to the recreational room to watch the nine o'clock news and, shortly after this, took his leave. He stopped to say goodbye to Sally, who had her head down writing. She looked up and smiled, her smile was likely to be the nicest thing to happen to him for the remainder of the day.

'I hope you have a very pleasant day, Sally Blue,' Billy said. He always called her by both names just to hear the sound of it. It was like some tiny flower you might find tucked into a crack on a lichen-covered boulder. Sally Blue flashed him another brilliant smile and Billy turned towards the door. Despite the inconvenience of the damp runners, he was shaved, showered and happy that this part of the day had turned out well.

Sally jumped up from behind the desk, 'Oh, Billy, I nearly forgot, you must let me sign your arm,' she called, 'It's good luck to be first.'

It should have been easy, a simple explanation that he'd promised the first signature to someone else. But now she was advancing on him, her pen held at the ready, her face showing her delight. Billy tried to say something but found he was struck dumb, saw his left arm going up and Sally Blue accepting it, stooping over it, her blonde hair falling over one eye and touching his elbow, holding the cast steady in her left hand while she wrote her name across the plaster. 'Oh, this is so nice. You see, I need all the luck I can get, there's a job in a computer company I've applied for and they said they'd received fifty-two applications.' She looked up at him with her lovely, smiling blue eyes and said, 'God bless you, Billy, I know you'll bring me luck.' Her expression grew serious for a moment, 'You will tell me if you'd like to see someone, won't you?' She was referring to a drug and alcohol counsellor and the detox and rehabilitation programs available. It was not the first time she had asked but it was always said with such ingenuousness that he found it impossible to take offence.

Billy found his voice at last, 'Yes, thank you, Sally, I will,' he said, barely above a whisper.

Outside on the pavement Billy couldn't believe what

he'd done. He'd broken his promise to Ryan and betrayed the boy's faith in him. He felt simply dreadful, 'How could I ever have done such a thing?' he asked aloud, shaking his head in dismay. It was Charlie all over again. He looked down at the plaster cast. Sally Blue had scrawled her name in a large bold signature down the centre. The Pentel pen she'd used appeared to have soaked into the slightly porous plaster to become indelible. There was simply no chance of his erasing it without Ryan noticing it immediately. Billy tried to tell himself it was a tiny thing, he'd explain it to Ryan, who would understand, but he knew it wasn't so, that the past was coming back to haunt him and he could find no reason why the boy should trust him ever again.

Billy was close to first in line when the bank opened and it immediately upset him to see that the teller had changed. The young bloke behind the counter, who looked hardly old enough to have broken out of his teens, glanced at him for scarcely a moment and then looked away again.

'Good morning,' Billy said, 'Miss Partridge not in today?'

The young man grunted. 'Gone upstairs.'

'A promotion, is it? Please give her my regards.'

'Yeah,' he muttered, still not looking up.

Why was it, Billy wondered, that young men so often lacked the fundamental courtesies that seemed to come naturally to young women of the same age? It was something he'd heard called 'attitude'. There was probably a new equal-opportunity law which allowed pipsqueaks like this to be rude with impunity. He wanted to shout at the little bastard, get rid of his self-loathing by transferring his anger to someone else. The young bloke counting out the banknotes pushed them across the counter to Billy without a word.

'I asked you to give Ms Partridge my regards!' Billy repeated, 'My name is O'Shannessy.'

'Yeah, righto,' the teller said, looking over Billy's shoulder to the next customer in line, 'I heard you the first time.'

Billy shook his head, his chest felt constricted and his stomach churned. 'What is it with you?' he shouted angrily. 'Who the hell do you think you are? I'm cleanly dressed, am I not! And freshly shaved. My hair is combed. I have shoes on my feet. I asked you politely to pass on a message. For God's sake, I'm a customer!' Billy turned around, pointing to the people standing in line behind him. 'I have two ears, a mouth, two eyes and a nose just like them. Quite remarkable, isn't it? Because I'm on a disability pension you think you can treat me like a piece of dirt. Well, you can't. I demand to see the manager! How dare you treat me like this.'

The young bank teller looked up at Billy in astonishment, his mouth half-open. 'Excuse me, sir, what did I say?' he asked, genuinely bewildered.

'You were rude. Bloody rude!' But the fight had gone out of Billy as suddenly as it had come. He was a piece of dirt and he'd overreacted. The teller's manner, brusque and unpleasant as it had been, hadn't merited the outburst. He was ashamed, aware that he'd been railing against himself and that the young teller had got in the way. Billy swallowed hard, then, attempting to save face, he said somewhat breathlessly, 'I want an apology.' Speaking very deliberately, he said, 'I want you to say in as pleasant a manner as you are capable of, that you'll tell Ms Partridge that I congratulate her on her promotion. Can-you-possibly-do-that?' Billy peered at the name tag on his coat, 'Mr Titsok?'

'Yes, sir.'

'Yes, sir, what?' Billy repeated.

'Yes, sir, sorry . . . I'll tell Suzanna Partridge what you said.'

'And my name?'

The teller had already logged off on the transaction and it was at once obvious that he'd forgotten Billy's name. Using the protruding fingers of his left hand, Billy reached for the banknotes still on the counter. The teller must have caught sight of the name scrawled on the plaster and, taking a gamble, said, 'I'll tell her, Mr Blue.'

'It's O'Shannessy, Billy O'Shannessy.' Billy had salvaged a small victory from the fiasco and now felt able to leave with a modicum of hastily gathered dignity.

He had only taken a few steps towards the door when the teller called out to him, 'Do you still want me to call the manager, sir?'

Billy couldn't tell if the young bloke was being facetious or was simply stupid. 'No, lad, if he was responsible for hiring you, he's obviously incompetent and unlikely to be much help,' he called back.

To Billy's surprise the people in the queue started to clap

and a young bloke in jeans, a white T-shirt and a scuffed leather bomber jacket standing directly opposite Billy grinned. 'That was awesome, really cool, man!'

Billy walked out into the sunlight, wondering how it was possible for his tongue to turn into a great fleshy appendage, choking his ability to speak when he'd been confronted by Sally Blue but could now, under greater pressure, effortlessly fashion a reply the young teller would probably recall with an inward wince for several days.

Billy needed a drink. His complimentary scotch would be waiting for him at the Flag Hotel, though it occurred to him that he still had the problem of the Trevor Williams walkout and that Sam Snatch might not welcome him with his customary exuberance. On the other hand, it was pension day and the proprietor of the Flag was always happy when the derros dutifully lined up in the bottle shop and all the way out to the pavement.

Billy took his usual route through the Botanic Gardens. It was a glorious sunny day and he was sweating lightly when he entered the cool darkness of the Flag Hotel. The interior of the hotel still had its morning-after-the-night-before smell, the slightly sour odour of hops mixed with stale cigarette smoke, both somewhat masked by the heavy application of the late-night cleaner's room deodorant.

Marion was alone at her bar when Billy walked up. 'Missed you yesterday, Billy,' she said, reaching for a glass. Then she saw the plaster and the dressing above his eye. 'What happened? Had a fall?' And more directly, 'Somebody do that to you?'

'No, my dear, all my own work, I'm afraid.'

Marion knew better than to question him. There were three common reasons for broken bones among derelicts: they became the victim of a mugging, they fell when intoxicated, or were hit by a car while attempting to cross the road.

'The blackfella got away, then?' Marion said casually, placing Billy's scotch on the bar in front of him.

Billy's heart leapt, the incident hadn't, as he'd hoped, been forgotten. 'Where's Sam?' he asked.

'Licensing Board.'

'Nothing serious, I hope.'

'Nah, he wants to extend out the back, put in a bigger kitchen.' Marion's eyes lifted briefly towards the ceiling, 'Having a bistro is all the go in pubs nowadays. Sam thinks with the development of the Finger Wharf into apartments, he'll be onto a winner.'

'He's not angry about the Aboriginal bloke, is he?'

Marion smiled. 'Ropeable would be a better choice of word, he wasn't real pleased.'

Billy shrugged, trying to make light of the incident. 'Casper had something going, his own agenda. The blackfella got suspicious.' Billy shrugged. 'Nothing much I could do, it never got as far as getting involved.'

'Yeah, we thought as much, Sam isn't blaming you. Casper got what he wanted anyway.'

'What was that?'

'The blackfella's money.' Marion gave a disparaging little laugh. 'Which doesn't make Sam any happier, he was that angry with Casper he threw him out, scotch bottle an' all. Casper kept yellin' out that he'd get the black bastard and it seems he did.'

'How do you know that?'

'Ambulance bloke comin' off shift, always comes in around lunchtime, said they'd picked up an Abo who'd fallen down the McElhone Stairs. Reckoned he was a right flamin' mess.'

Even though Billy knew what had happened to Williams, his training as a lawyer wouldn't let it go. 'What makes you think it was Williams? There are lots of his kind around the Cross.'

'Ambulance bloke said he was a bushie, moleskins, riding boots . . . his hat.'

'But he also said he'd fallen . . . down the steps?'

Marion sighed. 'He was speaking euphemistically.' There it was again, Marion's command of language. 'He's an Aborigine, ambulance blokes know the police are gunna do nothing. Lots of unnecessary paperwork and a waste of taxpayers' money.' Marion sighed. 'You know the drill well enough, Billy.'

'And you think it was definitely Casper Friendly?'

Marion laughed. 'Not on his own, the deadbeats that hang around with him.'

'Poor chap, seemed like a decent sort of bloke,' Billy said, acting concerned.

Marion reached for a cigarette. 'I guess that's life in the big city.'

Billy smiled, 'Sam will be sorry he threw Casper out.'

Marion inhaled and blew the smoke through her nostrils. 'Don't tell me, mate.'

Billy grinned, not displeased with the thought of Sam Snatch missing out. 'With all that suddenly acquired wealth, chances are that Casper would have spent a fair bit of it here.'

Marion laughed. 'Yeah, that thought hadn't escaped Sam. He says if you see Casper to tell him he's sorry, that he was a bit hasty, sudden rush of blood, tell him he's always welcome in the beer garden, no hard feelings, eh.'

Billy looked up surprised. 'Me? Tell him? Why would I do that? We're not exactly bosom pals.'

Marion lifted the bottle of Johnnie Walker on the bar. 'You'd be doing Sam a big favour.'

Billy grinned, he'd almost finished his drink and now tapped the rim of the glass. 'Would an immediate token of Sam's appreciation be out of the question, my dear?'

Marion laughed. 'You've got all the instincts of a con man, Billy, but of course you are a lawyer.' Reaching for a fresh glass, she poured Billy a second scotch.

Billy thanked her and took a small sip of the fresh scotch and thought of Trevor Williams in hospital, swathed in bandages, a small black man in agony in his white-on-white world.

Knowing that Casper didn't have the stash was a comfort, a small victory over the collective greed.

Marion was silent for a while, then she took a drag and carefully placed her cigarette down on an ashtray. 'Billy, there's something.'

Billy looked up. 'What is it?'

'Well, I don't suppose it's any of my business, but you know how it is, there's more big mouths around here than you'd find at a lipstick convention.'

Billy looked at her anxiously, Marion's tone suggested trouble. 'Tell me, Marion, what is it?'

'You know how derros are, how they see everything?'

'I ought to, I am one, what are you trying to say?'

'It seems you've been seen walking around with a young boy.'

'So, what's that got to do with the price of fish?' Billy's heart skipped a beat, surely he wasn't hearing this correctly?

Marion pulled back, surprised. 'It's true, then?'

'What's true? That I've been seen with a young boy? Yes, that's true.' Billy was suddenly angry. 'But if you're thinking something else, then don't!'

Marion reached out and picked up her cigarette. 'Hey, take it easy, Billy, I'm your friend, remember?'

Billy regained his composure. 'Marion,' he sighed, 'this is ridiculous. I have never had a prurient thought about the boy. Who told you?'

'The boys were all talking about it in the beer garden this morning.'

'I thought you weren't supposed to work out there?' Billy said, trying to gain a few moments to think.

'I don't. Sam Snatch and I had a bit of a contretemps. I told him putting a bistro in when there'll be five restaurants in the Finger Wharf development is plain bloody stupid. He shouted at me and, well, I shouted back and it was all getting a bit toey, so I went out back to cool down.'

Billy had always suspected that there was more to the ownership of the pub than Sam Snatch's lottery windfall and superannuation money. Marion arguing with him about a bistro suggested a different relationship to that of owner and employee. 'That'd be right,' Billy sympathised, 'That's Sam, not exactly a candidate for Mensa.'

But Marion wasn't to be sidetracked. 'Billy, you can't ignore it. This is a union pub. The derros have the story, soon enough it will be known to the wharfies, they're working-class blokes and that means trouble.'

'Marion, he's a young lad!' Billy protested, 'Not quite a street kid, but with a lot of the same instincts. He gets out on his skateboard early, they all go down to Chifley Square for a workout. He stops by and we talk about cats.'

'Cats?'

'Well, a particular cat, actually. Trim, Matthew Flinders' cat.'

'Come again?' Marion exclaimed, then added, 'Matthew Flinders has been dead nearly two hundred years, so, I imagine, has his cat.'

Billy accepted that Marion was probably the only bartender in Sydney who knew that the story of Matthew Flinders came equipped with its own famous cat.

Billy tried to explain the relationship between himself and Ryan but soon accepted that the story told to a third person didn't make a lot of sense. 'His grandmother is dying and, well, his mother seems to have problems of her own. As far as I can make out, the boy has to pretty well look after both of them,' he concluded.

'What's his name?' Marion asked, suddenly curious, 'His surname?'

'Sanfrancesco. Why do you ask?'

'Jesus, Billy!' Marion said, alarmed. She stubbed her cigarette down hard into the ashtray, grinding the spent butt. 'Do you have any idea what you're getting yourself into?'

'Into? I'm not sure I know what you're implying, my dear.'

Marion reached for another cigarette and remained silent until she'd lit it and taken a puff. 'Billy, the boy's mother is dog turd!'

Billy blinked, not sure he'd heard correctly. 'I beg your pardon?'

'She's a whore and a heroin addict as well as an alcoholic, the whole bag of shit, you name it!'

Billy had half expected something like this, he'd hoped that the remarks Ryan had inadvertently made weren't true, his comment about the circus-tent erection and blokes coming home, the references to her similarities to Billy's own condition when he'd brought him water the first time. The two security men at St Vincent's inquiring if his mother was all right. He'd said she was asthmatic but he'd never indicated that she was a drug addict as well.

'How sad,' Billy said, 'How very sad for a small boy.'

'Billy, ferchrissake stop! Listen to me, she's an exotic dancer and still a very good looker, though Christ knows how she manages it. She knows everyone, all the heavies, the baddest blokes in town, if she thinks you're interfering with her little boy, you're dead meat!'

Marion made a point of talking tough, it was part of the persona she worked on, male talk from a female's mouth, but Billy could see she was deadly serious. 'Poor little bugger,' was all he could think to say. After a while he looked at Marion and said, 'You know her then?'

Marion spoke through clenched teeth, 'Yes, I know her.' She tapped the ash off the end of her cigarette. 'Take my advice, Billy, stay away from the boy. She's a nasty piece of work. Smiles like an angel but has a heart dark as hell's gate.'

At that moment a large, well-groomed man in a conservative grey, three-piece, pin-striped suit, a blue-striped shirt, and a tie in excruciatingly bad taste, and in complete contrast to his sartorial correctness, came up to the bar. Billy could see him in the mirror behind the bar and stared in some amazement at his choice of neckwear. The man was dressed like a senior counsel in all respects other than for his taste in ties. The pink silk tie was emblazoned with bright-purple rats.

Marion took a hasty puff of her half-smoked cigarette and stubbed it in the ashtray. 'Excuse me, Billy, I have to go,' she said. She glanced at the newcomer and quickly back at Billy. 'See you tomorrow,' she said in a half-whisper.

'I'll be on my way, then,' Billy said, speaking to Marion's back. 'Thanks, Marion.' Though he wasn't sure if he was thanking her for her advice or simply as a normal courtesy. He swallowed the rest of the scotch and got down from his bar stool. He'd been so taken with the stranger's neckwear that he'd hardly looked at his face but thought he'd seen him somewhere, a politician, someone like that, someone in the public eye anyway. Then he remembered some idle talk that Marion had a boyfriend who was some sort of politician. If this bloke was her boyfriend then he certainly made her nervous.

Billy made his way round to the bottle shop but when almost there he turned back and hurriedly left the pub. He'd promised to visit Trevor Williams to talk about his daughter. If he was drunk, they wouldn't let him into the ward. Billy needed to think and a bottle wasn't going to help him sort out the mess he was in. He crossed the road and made his way up the Domain steps and back to the Botanic Gardens. His emotions threatened to overwhelm him. He had a growing sense of panic. The urge to retrace his steps to the bottle shop was tremendous. He found he was biting his lower lip. The two drinks at Marion's Bar had barely been enough to steady his nerves after the incident with Sally Blue and the quarrel at the bank. Marion's warning not to go near Ryan was a much larger concern. He couldn't imagine how he'd managed to get himself into such a mess and he was afraid. He needed to stop, to think, to sit among the flowers and hear the sound of water over stone until the information whirling around in his head stopped long enough for him to make some sort of sense out of it.

Instead of making his customary inspection, Billy made straight for his bench beside the pool, where he could sit in the shade cast by the Moreton Bay. He'd heard that if you went to a certain office in the Town Hall, they'd give you a bus ticket anywhere you wanted to go as long as it was a long way from Sydney. It was something to do with the Olympics coming in 2000, and the city fathers were testing the idea of getting all the derelicts away from the city during the Games. He could go to Surfers Paradise, stay there until the boy had forgotten about him.

Billy went over the whole litany again, his abdication of all responsibility so that he owed nothing to anyone. He was a drunk, plain and simple, and was permitted to enjoy the rights of a drunk, which were to be completely unreliable and irresponsible. What did it matter to him whether the black man found his daughter or, more importantly, the boy was saved from a perilous future? Billy even reprimanded himself for thinking that he could make a difference or change the seemingly inevitable course of the child's life.

'For Christ's sake, who do you think you are?' he chided himself. If there was illness and addiction in Ryan's family which seemed likely to lead to problems in the future, that was the concern of the Department of Community Services. This last argument, Billy knew, wouldn't stand too much cross-examination. DOCS was known to be hopelessly inadequate and he'd recently read somewhere that it was in such a bureaucratic muddle it currently had some seven thousand reports of child neglect on its books that were uninvestigated. Almost every month in Australia a child was murdered through neglect or by a parent or a de facto while intoxicated or under the influence of drugs and usually long after the department had been made aware of the danger the child faced from repeated mistreatment or neglect. Ryan, with a mother and grandmother still alive, living under an apparently safe roof, with only a record of minor truancy and without reports of physical abuse, had no chance of even getting onto DOCS' books.

Billy tried to persuade himself that while Ryan's grandmother seemed very ill, perhaps in the terminal stages of cancer, his mother obviously still cared about him and gave him money for food. While it was not perhaps the ideal situation, the boy seemed to be coping and it was well known that some heroin addicts managed their addiction for years. He'd only known the lad for a few days, far too little time to forge a strong, caring and mutual relationship, so why should he take any unnecessary risks?

Billy had almost convinced himself that there was nothing to be concerned about except for the danger that threatened him. Derros were generally uninterested in the moral standards of society, being as they were on its fringes, but the one thing they would react to is paedophilia. They would hunt down someone in their ranks who was thought to be corrupting an innocent young boy and more than likely they would kill him. This was Billy's first great danger. The second was, of course, the wharfies at the Flag, where he could very easily find himself wrapped in a length of anchor chain and dropped to the bottom of the harbour.

And there was Marion's warning to beware of Ryan's mother and her associates, perhaps the greatest one to worry about.

Billy knew that the murder of a homeless person and, in particular, an alcoholic, was of no concern to anyone. In his case it might receive a few lines tucked away in the back of the *Sydney Morning Herald* and the *Telegraph*, '*Once-prominent barrister found dead, believed to have been murdered, the police are making inquiries, etc, etc, ho-bloody-hum.*'

The uncaring nature of society in general was often talked about among the homeless and by derelicts in particular. They loved to tell the story of the time during World War II when the Japanese midget submarines came into Sydney Harbour and two of them were captured. It seems the navy was concerned that they might be booby-trapped and so a bomb-explosion expert was called in to examine the wiring. However, the navy weren't prepared to take the risk of sacrificing a valuable expert, so they sent two navy policemen up into the Domain to find a couple of derros, whom they threatened with a fate worse than death and frog-marched down to the docks, where they were made to enter the submarines with instructions to tug on wires and generally crawl about. The reward, if they made it back, was a bottle of scotch each, a commodity in very short supply during the war.

The story had long since entered the folklore of the homeless and was often enough told for laughs among the derros. It would usually end with the statement that the navy never did come good with the scotch and, instead, substituted a kick in the arse and two bottles of cheap overproof rum. Billy had always believed that behind the laughter lay the recognition that society thought the two men weren't worth a pinch of shit. He doubted that things had changed very much since that time. Killing him or, as in the case of Ryan's mother, having him killed wasn't a very big deal.

Billy could think of no other way out of his predicament than to take the bus out of town and decided to make inquiries at the Town Hall first thing in the morning. He'd get blotto tonight and then book himself into Foster House and the drunk tank so that he'd be safe. He told himself that the primary reason for doing this was so that Ryan wouldn't find him in the morning. He even managed to persuade himself that, because of the complications involved, the sooner the boy was rid of him the better. If he was murdered and the story got out, as inevitably it would, it might have a far-reaching impact on the boy's life.

Feeling he'd at least made a decision, even though a tiny voice deep within him protested that as usual he was copping out, Billy now busied himself making poison pellets with the six slices of bread he'd garnered from the drop-in centre and shortly thereafter set out for the library steps to do his worst.

After this, Billy crossed the Domain and made his way up Bourke Street to William and up the hill, where he turned right into Victoria Street and headed towards St Vincent's. Passing Cesco's, he noted that the bicycle wankers were long gone and now an altogether more ordinary-looking citizenry occupied the pavement tables and the interior. Billy purchased four Florentines, remembering how surprised he'd been to see that just about the only part of Williams that seemed not to have been injured by Casper's mob was his mouth.

Trevor Williams seemed both surprised and pleased to see him. 'Gidday, Billy, how yer bin?'

'Never been better,' Billy lied, reminding himself that he was a whole heap better off than the Aborigine. He grinned down at Williams, 'How's the white-on-white world treating you, old son?'

'Could be worse, mate.'

'Brought you a special treat,' Billy said, resting his briefcase on the bed and reaching in for the biscuits he'd bought. 'Florentines, fruit and nuts, a bit chewy, how's your teeth?'

'What's left o' them's real good,' Williams grinned. 'When them mongrels had a go at me, all I could think was ter protect me 'ead and mouth. If I can think and sing, it don't matter if they've broke me ribs and kicked me in the balls so there's no more little Williamses gunna be runnin' about the bush.'

Billy placed the bag of biscuits on the locker beside the bed and noticed that a harmonica lay on it. 'Harmonica, eh? You play the harmonica?'

'Yeah, well we're a musical family, like. Me missus was Irish and she had this real good voice, contralto, and me little daughter's even better. I sing a bit, you know, go along,

harmonisin' and that and . . .' he nodded his head towards
the harmonica, 'use that for the accompanying.' Williams
smiled shyly. 'I done them a little concert in here last night.'

'Concert?'

'Yeah, some o' the old bush ballads and a bit o' country,
sister says they're all askin' that I do it again ternight.'

'Mate, that's great, you must be feeling a bit better?'

'Ribs hurt a fair bit when I'm blowin', but it ain't too
bad.'

'You say your daughter sings?'

Williams' eyes lit up. 'She's the one's got the talent, jazz,
the blues. A man don't want ter brag, but she's got a voice
get yiz crying every time.'

'Jazz, eh? I used to sing a bit myself, university revues and
later at amateur concerts.' Billy laughed. 'More bravado
than basso profundo, I'm afraid.'

'Yeah? You sing, eh, Billy?' Williams was plainly delighted.

'No, not any more. Now, tell me about your daughter.'

'You ever heard of Billie Holiday?' Trevor asked.

'Of course, the blues, there's never been anyone better,
not even Ella, tragic life though.'

'Well, that's me daughter, the new Billie Holiday,'
Williams said proudly, then thinking Billy might feel the
comparison inappropriate, hastily added, 'Well, that's
what this Yank at the conservatorium said.'

'Conservatorium? Your daughter has a trained voice?'
Realising this might sound patronising, Billy quickly
added, 'That's unusual in a jazz singer.'

'Grazier's wife, Mrs Johnson out Wilcannia way, she heard

Caroline singing when she were twelve years old and put her in for the country eisteddfod. At sixteen she gets this scholarship. Yer know, ter go ter the Adelaide Conservatorium of Music.' Williams paused. 'Her mum were that proud, pleased as punch, me also, mate, our own little daughter.'

'Don't blame you,' Billy said. 'It's lovely when the kids turn out well.' He'd no sooner spoken when he realised he'd made a mistake. Williams, he now remembered, had come down to Sydney to try to find his daughter, who Billy guessed was in some sort of trouble.

The black man was silent and Billy was about to stammer an apology when Williams turned and picked up the harmonica and started to play. From the opening refrain it was immediately obvious that it was a blues number, a haunting melody that Billy thought he recognised, though he couldn't quite place it. Trevor Williams withdrew the harmonica and started to sing in a strong and well-modulated voice.

Southern trees bear a strange fruit,
Blood on the leaves and blood at the root.
Black body swinging in the Southern breeze,
Strange fruit hanging from the poplar trees.

Williams picked up the harmonica and played the refrain, then continued singing. As his voice rose above the white curtains screening his bed, the ward grew silent. It was as if everyone held their breath so that they might hear his clean, strong voice.

Pastoral scene of the gallant South,
The bulging eyes and the twisted mouth,
Scent of magnolia sweet and fresh,
And the sudden smell of burning flesh!

The refrain followed and then Trevor Williams continued.

Here is a fruit for the crows to pluck,
For the rain to gather, for the wind to suck,
For the sun to rot, for a tree to drop,
Here is a strange and bitter crop.

A few moments of complete silence followed and someone started to clap and then more clapping followed and someone whistled, thinking the concert had started early. Billy saw that Williams was crying, silent tears running down his pocked and wind-roughened cheeks. 'It's her song,' he said after a few moments. 'Billie Holiday sung it first and then she took it up, she done it as her theme song. It's what started all the trouble for Caroline.' Williams grew silent, his dark blackfella eyes bloodshot and, although no sound followed, the tears continued to slip down his cheek and onto the white sheet. 'She's lost,' he whispered. 'She don't sing no more, she's gorn, been took away from us by the strange and bitter crop, our little daughter.'

The tragic song written by a New York Jewish schoolteacher, Abel Meeropol, as a protest against the lynching of Negroes by white Southerners in the thirties had been turned into a different lament, a black man in search of a child who had tasted the strange fruit and had been possessed by it. Billy reached out with his left arm, his Sally Blue plaster-cast arm, his blonde-and-blue-eyed smiling arm, and placed his hand on the back of the black man's. 'You poor bastard,' he said quietly.

CHAPTER SIX

Billy sat at the back of the bus going to Queensland. He'd arrived at Sydney Town Hall at ten that morning from Foster House after spending the night in the drunk tank, a windowless dormitory with twenty-six men in white beds a metre apart puking, hawking and crying out in their sleep. Although he had money in his pocket and could have afforded scotch the previous night, he'd chosen a cheap 'n' nasty cask of moselle designed to put him off the air as quickly as possible. He'd taken the cask to where he knew the Mission Beat van would call and by midnight they'd dropped him, legless and forlorn, at Foster House. It was the only way he could face the prospect of spending the night in the safety and horror of a roomful of his own kind.

Cliff Thomas, the Salvation Army major in charge of Foster House, had given Billy the number of the office at the Town Hall to apply for a travel voucher. The office was the last in a row down a long, brown, polished corridor with the word 'Travel' hastily scribbled on a temporary sign outside it. Billy stopped to unlock the handcuff around his wrist before knocking. 'Come!' a voice called out. He entered to see a large, red-faced man seated behind a desk.

Billy stopped, unsure whether to approach. 'Good morning,' he said.

The official didn't return his greeting but looked him over carefully before indicating the vacant chair opposite him. Without further preliminaries he asked, 'Where to? Perth? Alice Springs? Not Tasmania, there's no bus to Tasmania.'

'Surfers Paradise,' Billy replied.

The official shook his head and, as if talking to himself, said, 'The derros and the Jews.'

Billy hesitated, he had a hangover and was not prepared for a confrontation. He'd taught himself over the years on the street to be obsequious. There seemed little point in reacting to rudeness or insults as he knew some officials gave vent to their frustration by abusing a derelict. Billy half understood this, the public could be difficult to handle and the appearance of a derelict often allowed a clerk to let off steam. Had Billy not been carrying the self-anger he'd felt when he'd let Sally Blue sign his plaster cast, he would've let the young bank clerk get away with his offhand manner. Billy had come to accept rudeness as part of being a nobody, but he hated racism. He accepted that while most people are covertly racist to some degree, the overt kind not only showed ignorance but also a prideful and belligerent attitude challenging people to contradict the perpetrator. He couldn't let the man's anti-Semitic retort go unanswered.

'Are you also encouraging Jews to leave town?' he asked.

'Joke, mate, joke. Surfers Paradise, Jew-heaven,' he said, not looking up, his pen poised. 'Name?'

'Joe Homeless,' Billy replied.

The official shook his head and clucked his tongue, then looked up and asked, 'Some personal identification, please.' He held out his hand, an uninterested look on his face.

'I have none,' Billy said. He lifted his plaster arm and indicated the patch above his eye, 'Mugged, they took my wallet.'

The official scribbled something on the travel voucher. 'Your name's Brown, Joe Brown.'

'Thank you, that will do nicely,' Billy said, satisfied that he'd gained a small advantage.

'Don't thank me, Mr Brown, just don't come back.' The official pointed to the wall on his left, 'Now, will you stand in front of that little window, feet on the yellow line.'

'Why?' Billy asked, immediately looking anxious.

'It's for your travel voucher, your picture, so you don't sell the voucher to another Mr Brown.' The clerk shrugged, knowing he'd regained the upper hand. 'No photo, no voucher,' he smiled, 'them's the rules.'

'Yes, of course, the rules, must have the rules.' The system had got him after all. Billy's paranoia told him that the picture would have more than this singular purpose. He rose, far from happy, and walked over to the yellow line, which was a strip of plastic taped to the floor. He wasn't the first by any means, the tape looked scruffy and worn at the edges. 'What about make-up?' Billy asked facetiously.

The official didn't respond. 'Look straight at the camera, Mr Brown.' Billy looked through the little window to see a camera lens pointed directly at him. A moment later a flash went off. The clerk must have activated the camera somehow, because Billy couldn't see an operator behind the window. 'If you'll come back here, there's one more thing,' the official called out.

Billy returned to sit at the desk, where the travel clerk pushed a clipboard across to him and slapped a biro down beside it. 'Write your name and the reason why you chose the destination, then sign it,' he instructed.

Like all street people, Billy disliked giving his personal details to anyone, even if they were bogus. It was a question of principle, a freedom only the homeless enjoy. 'Does it matter to anyone where I go and why?' he queried.

The official sighed. 'Are you being difficult, Mr Brown? Just sign the friggin' thing, will you, use your new name.'

'I'd rather not,' Billy said.

'Look, I don't care where you go, providing it's out of the metropolitan area and you stay away as long as possible, for instance, the rest of your life.' He pointed at the clipboard. 'The mayor wants to know your choice of preferred destination and it's not my business to know why. If you fill it in and sign it, you'll get ten dollars travel allowance.'

'This about the Olympics?' Billy asked.

'Who told you that?' the official asked, immediately suspicious.

'I can't recall, I heard it somewhere,' Billy answered.

'Yeah, that'd be right, little birdie told you.'

'Is this a practice run?' Billy persisted.

'Practice for what?'

'The Olympics.'

'Yeah, it's a new event, first time ever in the Olympics, a race to see who can get out of town the fastest, derros, alkies, druggies, psychos, schizophrenics, intellectually handicapped, the no-hopers and the useless, the whole shambolic. Finish line is, you guessed it, Surfers Paradise!'

Billy had to hand it to him, the man had a certain bizarre wit. His eyes met those of the official and held, 'What about the Jews? They not included in the race out of town?'

The official looked surprised. 'You trying to be funny?'

Billy placed the biro down on the clipboard and pushed it across the desk. 'No, sir, there's nothing funny to say about a racist.'

At that moment the door opened and a young woman walked in and handed the official an envelope. He extended his hand and took it from her without saying thank you or even glancing up. She left, an obvious look of distaste on her face. Billy noted that he wasn't the only person to find the man odious.

The official held up the envelope. 'I'll ignore that last remark, Mr Brown,' he said as he pulled open the flap. The light played through the back of the envelope and Billy could see three postage-stamp-sized squares showing through. The official dipped his fat fingers into the envelope and withdrew a single passport-sized photograph. He opened a drawer and produced a glue stick, applied it to the back of the photograph and stuck it to the travel voucher. Reaching for a rubber stamp, he pushed it into an ink pad and stamped the corner of the photograph, careful not to obscure Billy's face. Later Billy would see that it contained the month and the words 'Exit Sydney'.

The man pushed the travel voucher over to Billy.

'What about the other photographs in the envelope?' Billy asked.

The official didn't deny their existence. 'Keepsakes,' he said, smiling blandly, 'to remind me of you.' Then to Billy's surprise he stood up. He was even bigger than Billy had supposed, the buttons on his white shirt straining fit to bust, the material between each button scalloped to reveal a thick matting of dark hair. He pointed to the door, 'Garn, bugger off!' he growled.

Billy shook his head slowly. Taking the voucher, he folded it carefully and placed it in the breast pocket of his shirt. Bending down, he clipped the handcuff back about his wrist, picked up his briefcase, rose from the chair and walked unhurriedly towards the door. As he opened the door he turned to face the official, who was now in the process of sitting down. Billy clicked his trainers together, shot his left arm towards the ceiling and shouted, 'Heil Hitler!'

He went directly to the interstate bus depot at Central Station to discover that the bus for Queensland and Surfers Paradise was leaving in three-quarters of an hour and he'd arrive there in the early hours of the following morning. He had time to kill so found a railway cafe, ordered a takeaway coffee and bought six Mars bars to keep up his sugar level on the journey. Paying for them and the coffee, he asked the bloke behind the counter for a large plastic milk container. Billy knew these were readily available, all cafes used them. Con always had them on hand. But the proprietor was mean-spirited, or perhaps just weary of the many derelicts who made their home in Central and begged him for money or goods. 'No got! You go now!' he said to Billy.

Billy was quarrelled out, so he crossed the road to Our Lady of Snows, the government-funded restaurant that dispensed food to the homeless. The lady there, grey-haired with a pleasant face, produced a plastic bottle and Billy explained that it would need to be a two-litre milk container so he could grip the handle with the fingers protruding from the plaster cast. She found one in the fridge and transferred the milk from it into the bottle she'd originally offered him, washed out the container and filled it with water. Billy thanked her. 'You're welcome,' she said, then, noticing his takeaway coffee, added, 'You could have had a coffee here, it's free.'

Billy grinned. 'Thank you, I don't wish to seem ungrateful, madam, but even free it's not a viable proposition.'

The woman laughed. 'You've been here before then, it isn't very good, is it? I think it must be the urn, they boil it. Taking the bus out, are you, love?' Billy nodded. 'Cold weather comin', you'll be better off up north,' she said, then added, 'You'll need some sandwiches to take with you.' She produced a used plastic bag and dumped into it five thick-wedged white-bread sandwiches, each pre-wrapped in gladwrap. 'There you go, peanut butter, two jam and a cheese, that should see you through. Wouldn't mind going with you, my rheumatiz plays up something terrible in the cold weather.'

Billy laughed, affected by the woman's chatterbox cheerfulness. 'You're a fine-looking woman, madam, I take that as a compliment.' He put the sandwiches into his briefcase.

She left him to take care of a couple of street people who'd come in for an early lunch so Billy sat quietly and finished his coffee. He rose and called over, 'Thank you, madam,' lifting the water with his left arm in recognition of her generosity.

'Cheerio, then,' she called over. 'You know where to find me when you come back, name's Gracie Adams,' she laughed, 'unmarried and ready to be kick-started!'

Now as he sat in the bus, Billy thought about the man at the Town Hall. With his background in criminal law Billy had spent most of his adult life thinking about why people behaved in certain ways. Over the years he'd observed how attitudes were built out of an accumulation of small incidents and influences. If a series of negative influences resulted in making a criminal, would the same idea work within a society?

The official at the Town Hall wasn't really a Nazi, but given the benefit of the doubt, he was probably an unthinking racist, a Jew-hater, possibly without ever having experienced any harm to himself from someone who was Jewish. Ryan's attitude towards Aborigines and his bias against the imagined sexual preferences of Greek men was a first planting of the seeds of racism, the tiny beginnings of the merry-go-round of hate.

Billy now turned his attention to the coming Olympic Games, whose largesse he was currently enjoying in an air-conditioned coach flying along the Pacific Highway. When it was announced that 'Sid-en-nee' had won the bid for the Games the nation had gone wild with joy, which was shortly followed by a great deal of officialdom waxing lyrically and much pontificating.

It seemed to Billy that the Sydney Olympics weren't just the usual bread and circuses designed for the pacification of five billion people locked into their lounge rooms for two weeks, but was instead the opportunity to show the world what Australia had to offer. Its major purpose was to attract new overseas investment and increased tourism. If the original purpose of the Olympics had been to create a celebration of youth, this didn't seem to merit too much current mention in the newspapers. The main objective seemed to be to add infrastructure and hence increase potential wealth for the city.

The city of burnished light was already encouraging its

citizens to practise wearing their 'nice' faces, to become perambulating smiley badges. Sydney wanted the world to see it as the cleanest, neatest, sunniest and most welcoming destination in the world. Not for what it mostly was – a deeply divided and superficial city concerned at the top stratum with individual greed and the carrying-ons of a social pecking order dictated by personal wealth and largely consisting of cultural airheads, while at the middle and bottom strata there was a growing sense of anger and despair.

With his bum ensconced on a plush coach seat heading for Queensland, he was now playing a part in the clean-up, with the evacuation of the hopeless and the senseless from the streets of the city. Billy hadn't the slightest doubt that, as the Olympics drew closer, what he was doing willingly would eventually become a 'highly persuasive' exercise.

While Billy was enjoying this bottom-feeder's view of society and, he admitted, conducting a highly generalised discourse with himself, he was secretly aware that what he was really trying to do was to avoid the issue of his own cowardice. On the journey to the north, he was attempting to keep his mind sufficiently busy to delay the moment when he was forced to confront himself.

On leaving the hospital the previous day, Billy had returned to the library steps to do his daily worst. Though he recited his poem at the usual aftermath, he'd done so with less conviction than normal, knowing that the flying shit factories would have time in his absence to repopulate.

After that he'd crossed the road to the Gardens and made his way to his bench, where he composed a letter to Ryan.

My dearest Ryan,

By the time you get this letter I shall be well on my way to Queensland, where I plan to stay for a little while, perhaps for the duration of the winter. I am getting old and cranky and my bones hurt in the morning. The thought of spending the coming cold weather cooped up in a small, airless room in a hostel for derelicts is much less attractive to me than following the sun to the north.

I truly regret that there was no chance to say goodbye, but an opportunity arose for me to travel to my destination immediately and I felt compelled to take it.

We have known each other for a very short time, less than a week, but I count this time as very enjoyable and most helpful. You were generous and kind to me and I will always remember that.

You are a young man of exceptional intelligence and I urge you to continue with your schooling. I truly believe you are capable of achieving anything to which you set your mind.

As for me? You must try to see us as ships passing in the night, an old man with a drinking problem and a young man who showed him great kindness. You made a big impression on me and I shall find it difficult to forget you. I shall particularly miss telling you further stories of Trim.

Now I urge you to think of me as a very small incident

*in your life, which I hope will lead on to great happiness
and achievement.*

*If you go to the Mitchell Library and stand in the
centre of the top step and look directly across to the
Botanic Gardens, you will see a mighty Moreton Bay fig
tree. I have cut a small notch in one of its buttress roots.
Concealed under fallen leaves, directly below the notch,
you will find a book that tells you the story of Matthew
Flinders and his circumnavigation of Australia and many
more of his grand adventures. I hope you enjoy it.*

*I leave you with the hope that you will grow up to
be a splendid human being. To have known you, if only for
a short time, was a far better thing than never to have met.*

*I am attaching a small poem which was taught to me
by my first teacher and while, alas, I have not lived up to
it myself, it is a way of behaving in life to which we
should all aspire.*

I remain in your debt.

Yours,
Billy O'Shannessy (without the 'u')

On a separate page Billy wrote:

I shall pass through this world but once,
any good thing I may do,
or kindness show, to any human being,
let me do it now,
for I shall not pass this way again.

After completing the letter and its attachment, Billy visited a large bookshop in George Street and purchased the book for Ryan. He stopped off at the bank in Martin Place and waited patiently until the teller was alone. The badge on her blouse said her name was Fiona Mills.

'Good afternoon, Ms Mills. I wonder if you could do me a favour?'

Fiona Mills smiled, 'If it's bank business, certainly.'

'Well, it's just that I've been coming here for some time and the teller who usually looks after me is Suzanna Partridge and, well, I have some particular business to conduct and I wondered if you would be kind enough to see if she's in?'

'Oh, but Suzanna's been moved upstairs,' she smiled. 'It's a big promotion.'

'Yes, I know, but I would particularly like to see her.'

The teller looked uncertain. 'I'll see if she's in. Would you excuse me for a moment, please?' She walked to the rear, entered a small cubicle and picked up the phone. Billy watched as she nodded her head and smiled. She then returned and said, 'Suzanna will be right down, sir.'

'Thank you, Ms Mills,' Billy said, relieved, remembering his previous experience with the testosterone-loaded young male teller.

Suzanna Partridge appeared shortly and greeted Billy with her usual enthusiasm. 'Congratulations on your promotion, my dear,' Billy said.

'Oh, thank you, Mr O'Shannessy, but I must say I quite miss the contact with people like you. Come through and we'll sit in the customer interviews office.' She laughed, 'Only it's called something else now, Client Interface Facility.'

Billy explained to her that he was contemplating spending the winter months in the sun and wanted his account transferred to their branch in Southport where his future pensions would be sent. He also told her he wanted to withdraw all the money, with the exception of a hundred dollars, from his current account.

After visiting the bank, he returned to the Botanic Gardens where he buried the book for Ryan. What remained of the day he spent visiting all his favourite walks and places within the precincts of the Gardens.

In the fading afternoon, to the sound of magpies carolling in the trees, Billy made his way down the Domain steps to the Flag Hotel. Marion, he knew, knocked off promptly at five o'clock and Billy needed to see her before she departed. As Sam Snatch wouldn't permit any of the derelicts to approach Marion's Bar, except for Billy's usual morning visit, Billy would have to take the chance that he'd be able to talk with her. Otherwise he'd have to wait outside the pub and catch her as she left. His need to see Marion had been one of his more compelling reasons not to allow the sadness within him make him reach for an early bottle.

'Hi, Billy, what brings you here?' Marion called as he approached. There were several people seated at the bar and Billy, anxious not to attract attention, flinched at the sound of her voice.

He moved quickly to the bar, 'I apologise, Marion,' he said in an undertone, 'but it's important that I see you.'

Marion smiled. 'It's okay, Sam's not here, what is it, Billy?'

'It will take a few minutes.'

Marion glanced at the men seated at the bar. 'They're regulars, they won't mind you being here. Scotch?'

'No, thank you,' Billy replied.

Marion raised one eyebrow. 'It *must* be important,' she said.

'Marion, I'm leaving,' Billy said.

'Leaving?'

'Town.'

Marion looked surprised. 'There's no need to do that, Billy.'

'Yes, yes . . . I've made up my mind.'

Marion sighed. 'Billy, I only told you for your own good, mate. All you have to do is stop seeing the boy.'

Billy thought for a moment, 'It's not that simple, my dear.'

Marion's lips drew tight. 'Why not? You and him, you told me you're not . . . ?'

'For God's sake, no!' In a calmer voice, Billy added, 'No, Marion, there's nothing like that.'

Marion relaxed. 'I believe you, Billy. But why can't you simply reject him? He's a tough little kid, they all are around here. He'll soon forget you and get on with his life.'

'No, I couldn't do that!' Billy exclaimed, then lowered his eyes and said softly, 'I did that once before with another child. I . . . I couldn't do that again . . . ever.'

Marion nodded sympathetically. 'We'll miss you, Billy.'

Billy looked up, surprised at the tone of her voice. 'No, I promise you, we really *will* miss you,' she repeated.

'Thank you,' Billy replied. 'Marion, will you do something for me?'

'Of course, if I can.'

Billy produced the letter to Ryan. 'Can you somehow get this to Ryan Sanfrancesco? I'd deliver it myself, but I have no idea where he lives. You said you knew his mother, I was hoping . . .' His voice trailed off.

Marion's face grew stern. 'Billy, are you sure this is a good idea?'

'No, that's the point, I'm not,' Billy said quietly. 'I've left the envelope unsealed so that you may read it.'

Marion looked doubtful. 'Billy, it's not that. It's, well, it's just that the boy's mother is a truly nasty piece of work. It wouldn't matter how innocuous the letter seemed, if she got hold of it she could quite easily get the wrong impression.' She looked steadily at him. 'Let me put it as frankly as possible, I don't want the bitch coming after me.'

'But, Marion, I'm only asking you to get the letter into the boy's hands, to deliver it. Surely his mother will never know it was you who gave it to him?'

Marion turned her head to one side, her arms crossed, her lips drawn tight. 'Billy, I'm sorry. I'd like to help you, but I can't.'

'I see,' Billy said, suddenly lost for words. It had never occurred to him that Marion would refuse, or that she could possibly be placed in danger by simply arranging to deliver the note to Ryan. He picked the envelope up from

234

the bar and dropped it back into his briefcase. 'I quite understand, Marion,' he said, turning to go. 'It was inconsiderate of me to ask.'

Marion didn't reply. 'Look after yourself, Billy. We'll miss you,' she called after he'd retreated halfway to the door.

'Yes, thank you, Marion,' Billy said, trying to conceal his frustration. There had always been something about Marion that worried him. It couldn't be the business upstairs. Selling knickers to cross-dressers and transvestites might be slightly on the nose but it was hardly a criminal offence and certainly nothing to hide.

He stood outside the Flag Hotel, wondering what to do next. Two children, both girls, chatting and laughing, totally absorbed in themselves, were approaching. They seemed to be about Ryan's age. He cleared his throat, 'Excuse me, girls,' he said, stepping directly into their path. Both stopped and looked up in fright, then without a word to each other they started to run, jumping to either side of him before setting off. 'Do you know Ryan Sanfrancesco?' Billy shouted after them.

They stopped about six metres away from him, a safe distance should they have occasion to make a second run for it. They looked at Billy. 'What's it to you? Bugger off, you stupid old bastard!' one of them called. Then, hugging each other and giggling hysterically, they ran off in a clatter of school shoes, disappearing around the corner of the pub.

Billy grinned, children who lived in Woolloomooloo grew up fast. At least they knew not to talk to strangers. Though, of course, Ryan hadn't observed this rule when they'd first met. Billy had seen all he needed to know, both girls had been wearing the light-blue cotton tops with the school badge embroidered on them to show a sailing ship set in an oval frame with the words 'Pring Street Public School' and the motto 'Togetherness' stitched around its circumference. From the way the girl had responded to his question, Billy was fairly certain they knew Ryan. The years in the criminal courts had taught him to translate innuendo into accurate meaning.

Pring Street Public School turned out to be adjacent to Forbes Street, a street historically notorious for its brothels, which after legalisation had mostly moved to more salubrious accommodation. To Billy's surprise, because he'd expected the usual dreary brown-brick establishment set within a macadamised wasteland, the school appeared to be a modern building, painted yellow with doors and window frames in lime green, and within pleasant grounds. It possessed a garden, which was contained within a dark-green fence with casuarina and sheoaks, while the playground area, painted red and yellow, had a covering of woodchips.

It was just after five o'clock and the schoolyard was empty but Billy could hear the sound of a piano coming from somewhere within the building. The pianist was playing a Chopin étude, though if a child was playing, it was a very accomplished one. The piano was a further surprise, he'd expected Ryan's school, judging by his attempts to play truant, to be pretty average, not the sort of place where children learned music.

He entered the gate, conscious that he might be seen as an intruder. He would often forget that he no longer resembled the dapper little lawyer he'd once been. He entered the building, hoping to see a cleaner or caretaker, but except for the piano sounds the building appeared to be empty. He passed several classrooms, each leading into another and noted that they contained no blackboard or even traditional school desks scarred with generations of patiently carved initials. Instead, each pupil appeared to have a small cream table and red chair and these were placed, seemingly at random, around the room. The walls were brightly coloured and a line of eight computers sat on a long table which ran along the far wall. It was a far cry from anything he'd experienced in his day at primary school. After searching the ground floor for someone to whom he could introduce himself and ask directions, he retraced his steps to the stairs and made his way, a little fearfully, to the second level, where he saw that a covered walkway led to a second building from which, he now realised, the music came.

Billy finally reached the music room. His heart was beating a little faster, he was too far into the building to beat a hasty retreat and should someone come upon him and ask him to explain his presence he knew his explanation would be difficult to believe. The door was slightly ajar though he couldn't see the piano or its player. He knocked tentatively but nothing happened, so he tried a second time, this time a little more loudly. The music stopped, 'Who is it?' a woman's voice asked.

'May I come in?' Billy asked.

The sound of a cultured voice must have put the woman somewhat at ease, because she said, 'Yes.'

Billy opened the door wider and saw the shock on the

young woman's face. She stood up, backing away from the piano chair. He was surprised to see that the instrument she'd been playing was a baby grand. 'It's quite all right, my dear, the plaster and the patch, a small accident. You were playing Chopin, an étude I used to play as a child, though never of course with your proficiency.'

The woman seemed to relax a little. 'Who are you?' she asked warily.

'My name is William O'Shannessy and I confess to being a derelict, though a perfectly harmless one.'

The young woman's eyes went to the handcuff around Billy's wrist and she backed further away. 'Mr O'Shannessy, I don't think you should be here.' She looked around, suddenly conscious that she was alone.

'Billy, please call me Billy. William is an entirely inappropriate name in my present calling.' He lifted the briefcase showing her the second handcuff attached to the handle. 'In my vocation it is as well to be security conscious.' He grinned, then, trying to put her at ease, Billy said, 'I shan't keep you long, madam, I am simply inquiring if you have a Ryan Sanfrancesco in your school. I am leaving town and I wish to leave him a letter.'

'A letter? Are you a relation?'

'No, madam, we are old friends. Ryan is a quite remarkable child.'

'Could be if he tried harder,' the young woman replied.

'Ah! Then you know him,' Billy cried. 'That's splendid.'

'Yes, he attends music lessons,' she paused. 'When he can be bothered.'

'He plays music? I didn't know that.'

'Ryan has a glorious voice, a boy soprano of exceptional range and clarity.'

'Well, I never,' Billy said, pleased.

'It's very frustrating. We want him to sing in the St Mary's Cathedral choir. The choirmaster, Monsignor Fiorelli, is very keen to have him, but he won't have a bar of it. The principal went to see his mother accompanied by the monsignor, but she sent them away with a flea in their ear.'

Billy sighed, 'Yes, I know, it is for that reason I'd like you to give the letter directly to Ryan. Do you think you could do that, Ms . . . ?'

'Sypkins, Sylvia Sypkins.'

'Nice to meet you, Ms Sypkins.'

'I will have to show the letter to the principal, Mr O'Shannessy.'

'Yes, of course, it's unsealed and she *must* read it and so may you. I appreciate your taking such care over the matter.' Billy opened the briefcase and withdrew the letter, handing it to Ryan's music teacher.

'Thank you, Mr O'Shannessy,' Ms Sypkins said. 'It's been, er . . . interesting meeting you.'

Billy, amused, thought how young and pretty she was. He remembered his own music teacher, Miss Roseblatte, a terrible old dragon who rapped him frequently on the knuckles with a twelve-inch ruler from which the steel edge had been removed.

'I crave your indulgence, Ms Sypkins. There is just one more thing.'

The music teacher glanced at her watch. 'I really must be going,' she said, a little nervously.

'It won't take a minute.' Billy produced a second envelope, this one thicker than the last. 'Ryan's grandmother is dying of cancer, though how soon that might be I can't say. His mother . . .' Billy paused, 'Well, she has problems of her own and I don't believe she can cope. Ryan, it appears, is often responsible for taking care of them both, which may explain somewhat his attitude to school.'

'Oh? I was not aware of that.' Ms Sypkins showed concern. 'Only that his mother was difficult.'

'There is a little money in here. Fifteen hundred dollars precisely. Would you please give it to the principal and ask her to use it to help Ryan, should this become necessary in the next few months?'

Ms Sypkins threw up her hands. 'Oh, I don't think I can take that responsibility. Ms Flanagan has already left for the afternoon.'

Billy smiled. 'The money hasn't been stolen, there's a withdrawal slip signed by the teller, whose name is Partridge, Suzanna Partridge, I've written her telephone extension number on the slip.'

Ms Sypkins still seemed reluctant. 'Really, Mr O'Shannessy, I couldn't. I wouldn't sleep a wink all night knowing it was in my flat. Could you not return in the morning to see the principal?'

Billy shook his head. 'That would be quite impossible, my dear, I leave first thing.' Realising her anxiety over safekeeping the money, he tried to keep things light. 'The usual recommendation is to put it under your pillow, but I suggest the mattress, that's always a safe place, my grandmother used to say. A thief may manage to place his hand under a pillow while you slumber but it's a lot more difficult to dislodge a mattress with you asleep on top of it.' Billy pushed the envelope towards her.

Ms Sypkins accepted it reluctantly, and walked over to the piano, reached for her handbag and placed the envelope inside. 'I'll do my best,' she said, 'but I'm terribly nervous.'

Billy laughed, 'I should be the one who's nervous, I may never see you again and I've just given you fifteen hundred dollars.'

'A receipt! Of course, you must have a receipt!' Ms Sypkins cried.

'No, that won't be necessary, the Chopin étude you were playing and your concern for Ryan is receipt enough.' Billy paused and appeared to be listening. 'Ah, the currawongs are calling, it's getting late, I must be off, my dear, though there is one more small thing.'

Ms Sypkins looked apprehensive. 'Yes?' she said tentatively.

'It's Ryan's eyes, the boy is short-sighted. He's a skateboarder who, I imagine, can't see much more than five or six metres ahead of him, sooner or later he's going to have a bad accident. Do you think the school could arrange to have his eyes tested?'

Ms Sypkins looked relieved. 'Yes, we know about Ryan's eyes, the community nurse has picked it up on two occasions and we've sent a form home with Ryan twice and then posted one. You see, we need permission from a parent to take him to the eye hospital,' she explained.

Billy sighed, shaking his head, 'Same old problem, eh? Ms Sanfrancesco does seem to be a very difficult woman.'

'Don't worry, we'll keep trying,' the music teacher assured him.

'Thank you,' Billy said quietly. 'Well then, I'll take my leave.' Billy bowed slightly, 'You have been the soul of kindness, Ms Sypkins.'

Ms Sypkins smiled at Billy's old-fashioned manners. 'Nice to have met you, Mr O'Shannessy.'

Billy walked towards the classroom door and, as he reached it, Ms Sypkins called out, 'Your money will be safe. I'll put it under the mattress!'

Billy had given Ryan the money he had intended for his own funeral. Over the period he'd been among the homeless, Billy had carefully put aside a small part of his disability pension to pay for his gravesite. Suzanna Partridge, at the bank in Martin Place, had helped him, and had also placed in safekeeping a letter with his burial instructions.

Billy was most anxious to avoid a destitute's funeral conducted by the state, where he'd have to share the gravesite with four others, each coffin placed next to each other. The Salvation Army would bury him decently, and alone, at a cost of fifteen hundred dollars, or for that matter, at their own expense.

He didn't want the final act in his life to be a handout so he'd paid an initial deposit of two hundred and fifty dollars to the Salvos after making the trip out to Rookwood Cemetery, where he'd asked to see the plots they'd been allocated. These were positioned on the eastern extremity of the cemetery with plenty of morning sun and seemed ideal for Billy's purpose. The position was important because for another fifty dollars, which he'd already paid to a nursery, he'd arranged for a sapling to be planted over his grave in place of a headstone.

Billy wanted the remains of his earthly body to act as nourishment for the sapling's roots. *'These are my roots of heaven,'* he'd written in his will, *'the beloved spotted gum will rise up a hundred feet into the air and release oxygen to make the clouds and the rain and I shall be a part of the forest and the deserts, pure and clean, with all the human malice washed from my bloodied soul at last.'* It was, he admitted, a somewhat melodramatic notion, written in an over-flowery manner, but he allowed the indulgence, telling himself a man's last gesture should be one of putting back, a thing of the heart and not of the head, a sentimental thing and an apology to nature for the shabby way we have treated it.

The particular sapling he'd requested was important to him. The spotted gum, *Eucalyptus maculata*, was the eucalypt varietal that had been used to build the first locally constructed sailing ships as well as in the construction of Sydney's streets. Cut into blocks, it had been the foundation paving for all the city's major thoroughfares and most of its inner-suburban streets.

He was vaguely conscious that what he was doing

for Ryan was really for Charlie and that the envelope contained conscience money, though he quickly buried this notion into his subconscious, unwilling to face the fact that he was running from his responsibilities once again. He could clearly see the looming tragedy about to envelop the child, but tried to convince himself that, given his present position in life, he would be of no use to Ryan by being present when it occurred. It was better for the boy to forget him now than have to depend on him later. The money would be more useful anyway. Billy wasn't at all sure he could handle any sort of dependence on him by another human being. He had trouble enough looking after himself. If he was killed because people thought he was a paedophile, it might damage Ryan's perceptions of life permanently. This was his greatest excuse.

On his way to St Vincent's he stopped off and bought a packet of roll-your-own tobacco and cigarette papers of the brand he'd seen Williams smoking in the pub, three small chocolate caramel bars and a large block of Cadbury milk chocolate. It wasn't very imaginative, but his sugar craving was always best served by these two particular confections and both were easy to suck or chew. He hoped Trevor Williams would feel the same way.

In the reception area of St Vincent's Casualty he bumped into Dr Goldstein. Somewhat to Billy's astonishment, the doctor greeted him by name.

'Mr O'Shannessy, how's the wrist coming along?' Goldstein immediately asked and without waiting for a reply said, 'Here, let me see.'

Billy held out his arm and, observing Sally Blue's signature on the plaster, Nathan Goldstein grinned, 'Girlfriend?'

'I should be so fortunate,' Billy smiled. 'Good evening, Doctor Goldstein.' He was strangely pleased that the doctor had remembered him by name. 'Please call me Billy, doctor.'

'Move your fingers for me, will you, Billy.'

Billy did as Goldstein instructed. 'That's good, plenty of movement. As long as it doesn't give you pain, you must try to exercise the hand as much as you can. What brings you here, anything I can do?'

'Thank you, doctor, I'm here to visit a friend, Trevor Williams.'

Goldstein laughed. 'We'll be sorry to see him go, his concerts the last couple of nights have been such a buzz for the ward that we're thinking of putting him on broadcast throughout the hospital. We had an old bloke in last night, heart attack, fortunately we brought him round successfully, although he was pretty groggy when we wheeled him out of the theatre on his way to the intensive-care ward. As we passed the public ward, Trevor Williams was giving a recital, at that very moment singing "Summertime". The old bloke suddenly sat upright, nearly bringing on another heart attack. "Is this heaven?" he asked.' Goldstein smiled. 'He's got a pleasant voice, though, hasn't he?'

Trevor Williams was delighted to see Billy. 'Gidday, mate, how's yer bin, orright?'

Billy realised that he was going to miss Williams, the

little blackfella had a nice way about him, a gentleness which Billy had almost forgotten could exist in a man. Billy placed the bag containing the chocolate and tobacco on the locker beside the bed, then reached for the key around his neck and unlocked his handcuff, putting the briefcase on the floor. 'How are you feeling, Trevor? The doctor tells me you're the current singing sensation, that broadcast rights and a contract are being negotiated as we speak.'

'Ah, it's nothin', a bit o' amusement for the folks, that's all,' Williams said in a self-deprecating way. 'Wish me little daughter were here, then you'd hear summin' else, mate. Yiz'll see for yerself when we finds her,' he added modestly. 'But they like me here, dunno why, bit of a singsong ter keep them happy when they's feelin' crook, I suppose.'

'The doctor says it's by popular demand, ward's never run better. You're giving them another concert tonight he tells me.' Billy said, 'Well done, Trevor.'

'Yeah, some the older folks back yonder,' he indicated the end of the ward with a thrust of his chin, 'say they can't hear me too good. So, there's these two real nice poofter security men, good blokes, muscle men, built like a brick shithouse, they look identical, same haircut, same colour, they's bringing in the microphone from reception.' Williams laughed. 'They both crazy about country music, so ternight I'm gunna mix a bit more country into me repertoire. Bin thinking all day, tryin' ter remember some o' them lyrics Slim Dusty sings. Them old ones, y'know, "A Pub with No Beer" or "When the Rain Tumbles Down in July". Bin a while since I sang any of them numbers.'

Billy's admiration for Williams had been growing steadily since they'd first met in the Flag. Now his heart skipped a beat at Williams mentioning his daughter, indicating that, when they found her, he would see her talent for himself. He realised, going right back to the abortive meeting with Casper Friendly, in the black man's mind there had always been a tacit understanding that he'd help in some way. Billy was silent, trying to think of how he might break the news of his departure to Trevor Williams.

'What've you brought me?' Trevor asked, reaching for the bag. He opened it. 'That's real nice of yiz, Billy, fair dinkum. Them biscuits yiz left last time, real good, mate.'

'Florentines, traditional Italian delicacy,' Billy replied, realising he'd told Williams this, that he was simply stalling for time.

'Italian, eh? Italian is good tucker.'

'Trevor, I've come to say something. It's . . . well, it's not necessarily good news.'

Trevor Williams looked up at Billy. 'What's the problem, mate?'

'I've decided to leave Sydney, go up north, to Queensland.'

'Whaffor? This your home, Billy!'

'It's a long story, some complications have arisen.'

'The police? You got trouble?'

'No, nothing like that. It's just that I have to get away for a while.'

Trevor Williams was silent, looking down at the white sheet covering his lap, then he slowly attempted a smile.

BRYCE COURTENAY

'I thought it was only blackfellas needed to go walkabout, eh?'

Billy tried to smile but was becoming increasingly upset. He could feel the disappointment in Williams, though the black man was trying hard not to show it. 'Trevor, I know you feel I might be able to help with your daughter, but I can't. What legal knowledge I once had . . .' Billy searched for the right words, then finally gave up. 'Well, anyway, I'd hate to be represented by someone like me in a court of law.'

'Yeah, you said that before, when we was with that mongrel albino. It was bullshit that time, I reckon it's still the same.'

'No, I'm afraid it's true.' Billy sighed. 'It's been seven years since I defended anyone in court and I lost my last three cases. I should have been disbarred for incompetence.'

'Yeah, you said that also,' Williams replied.

Billy could think of nothing more to say, short of telling Williams the true reason for his departure. 'I'm sorry, mate,' he said lamely.

'There's no need, Billy. Yiz the best whitefella I ever met. Yer had me stash ter yerself and yiz returned it ter me. Yer come ter see me in the hospital. Yer listened to me story of why I come here. White bloke like that don't need t'explain hisself.' Williams smiled. 'When I'm an old bloke, no teeth, I'll be sitting around the fire with my people. "There's this whitefella," I'm gunna say, "done something you wouldn't believe a white bloke would do for a blackfella in all your born days." Then I'm gunna tell them the story of Billy O'Shannessy. Maybe make a song, hey? "The Ballad of

Billy O'Shannessy", do it country, sing it round the fire, I can play the guitar a little bit.'

Billy, despite himself, began to cry. 'Trevor, that's the second time you've made me bawl,' he said.

'She's right, mate, no worries, man can have a blub, don't do no harm to no one else. Me mum, she'd say, crying's been given us for washing out the sorrows.'

Slowly Billy found himself telling Trevor Williams the story of Ryan and Trim the cat, and the friendship that had quickly developed between himself and the boy, then of the accusation that had followed. When he reached the point where Marion had refused to help deliver his letter to Ryan, Williams interjected for the first time.

'That one, she's got a great arse, but butter wouldn't melt . . . Don't never trust her, Billy,' he warned.

'Ryan's just a scrap of a boy, a nice little kid, bright as a button, just the thought of harming him in such a vile way is utterly repugnant.'

Williams was silent for a while. 'It's a shit of a world, mate. Youngster like that needs a daddy who can tell him things. What's gorn wrong when a man can't do that? Can't help a little bloke avoid finding trouble.'

Billy reached down and dried his eyes on the edge of the sheet. 'I'm truly sorry, Trevor. I've no right burdening you with all this, you have your own problems, and they're a lot more serious than mine.'

Trevor Williams didn't reply at first, his eyes downcast, then he raised them to look directly at Billy, 'Yeah, that's true, we all got troubles of our own, mate. But we saw our little daughter grow up decent. Her mum don't touch the grog and me, only sometimes, not at home, sometimes when I'm away. Only once me little girlie seen me drunk, she was eight years old and she cried for three days. I told meself that ain't never gunna happen again. She had a good home and she done good winning that scholarship to the conservatorium in Adelaide. Never gave her mum and me no trouble, always singin' round the place like a canary bird. I know if I can find her, the love we's always had will come through. Heroin, that's bitter fruit, man. A bloke's just gotta hope that what she knows in her heart, that's gunna come through for her.'

'What will you do, Trevor?' Billy asked. 'I mean, when you get out of here?'

'I'm goin' back home to Wilcannia, get meself well again, then I'm comin' back. I ain't givin' up on her, she's somewhere and I'll find her, I give me word to her mum.'

They were silent for a while. 'Trevor, I really should be going, mate.'

'Yeah, me too, I got to give these folks a concert.' Williams held out both arms, one still heavily bandaged. 'Take me hands, Billy, both o' them.' Billy gripped the little Aborigine's arms. 'You're my brother, I won't forget you, mate.' Billy saw that Williams' eyes were bright with tears.

'You've made me cry twice,' Billy sniffed. 'Fair go, mate, not again. Is there anything further I can do for you?'

'Yeah.' Still holding Billy's hands, Williams indicated his hands with his chin. 'They's crook, can you write to me missus, tell her the old bloke is okay, that I'm comin' home real soon?'

'Of course!' Billy cried, happy that he could do something for his friend. He released Williams' arms and reached into his briefcase for a pad and biro and wrote down the address Williams gave him. 'I'll do it tomorrow, post it from Queensland.'

Trevor Williams pulled open the drawer to his locker, took out his stash and peeled four fifty-dollar notes from it, 'For the journey, mate, take care.'

'No, I couldn't,' Billy protested, throwing up his hands. 'No, really it's lovely of . . .'

Williams' expression grew suddenly stern. 'You don't take money from a blackfella, that it, eh?'

Billy accepted the money. 'Thank you, Trevor.' It was all he could think to say.

'Ha, gotcha!' Williams barked, wiping his eyes on his bandaged arm and attempting a grin. 'That's called reverse psychology!'

BOOK
TWO

CHAPTER SEVEN

With each perfect day rolling in with the surf, Billy became increasingly depressed in Paradise.

He had spent almost five months in Surfers, where the sky was more or less perpetually blue and the generous daily quota of sunshine persisted in ratifying the local slogan that each day was better than the one that had preceded it.

Billy had confronted his demons a hundred times and each time declared himself guilty of being weak and, worse than this, of avoiding any sort of responsibility. But he'd always concluded that he'd paid the price for the right to abdicate from a conscience-driven life.

What he was having difficulty facing was that this time his running away wasn't simply an abdication of responsibility, it was cowardice. There was no other way of looking at it. He'd run before he'd been threatened. He'd fled like a timid creature at the sound of a breaking twig. He'd made no attempt to mount a defence against his accusers nor demanded they show him proof of his guilt. He'd made no denial or even lodged a protest. Instead, he'd run from the enemy at the first wisp of smoke on the horizon.

Billy didn't wish to see himself as a coward. He didn't want to accept and live with a coward whimpering pathetically within him, his alter ego beaten and quivering.

He'd told himself again and again that he'd done the honourable thing and in the process of his life he'd always settled things properly. The proof was there for anyone to see. As a result of his departure, his wife had lost forty-five kilos and discovered that behind the layers of lard lurked a very handsome woman. She'd cut and styled her hair, grown and painted her nails, gone to the gym to tighten the loose parts, adopted the very best of haute couture for the forty-plus woman, wore achingly high heels and jammed her toes into shoes that cost five hundred dollars a pop.

As a good Catholic girl, she'd denied Billy a divorce but demanded and got a hugely generous settlement, which included the heritage-listed family mansion on three-quarters of an acre in Bellevue Hill. With her life beginning again at forty-nine, she'd found a man five years younger than herself and, so she couldn't be seen by the bishop to be openly living in sin, she'd installed him in the renovated servant's cottage at the bottom of the garden.

What was left of his worldly goods, still a considerable amount in shares and property, Billy had given to his lawyer daughter. She had accepted his remaining assets without feeling the slightest obligation to keep in touch or the need to introduce him to his two grandchildren. As far as she was concerned, it was payment in return for the embarrassment his drinking had so often caused her as a junior in his own chambers.

Then, as his final act of contrition, Billy had accepted all the blame for Charlie and politely removed himself from the scene so that he would no longer be an encumbrance.

So, what more could he possibly do? Nothing, came the reply. Whereupon he'd begin convincing himself all over again ad nauseam – he'd swapped a warm bed for a park bench, status for nonentity, money for poverty, old friends for vicious strangers, a family for a life alone and a life of ease for one of extreme discomfort. Billy argued that what he'd done wasn't cowardice, but true remorse. Only a real penitent would deliberately fashion for himself a hairshirt of such unlikely and difficult contrasts.

But every way he argued or whichever angle he looked at it, the guilt persisted. He'd forsaken a ten-year-old child who was trying to come to terms with a dying grandmother and a heroin-addicted mother. Billy was finally forced to admit that he'd done what he'd always done, paid the money to salve his conscience and made a run for it. He *was* a coward, the argument was over.

However, an admission of guilt is not necessarily acceptance. Guilt is not always assuaged by confession, the road to self-acceptance is rocky, rutted and long, and its end is as often self-loathing as it is self-forgiveness. Not every road to Damascus ends in an epiphany. And so, as alcoholics so often do, rather than tackle his cowardice head-on, Billy turned to Mr Johnnie Walker. The wee Scotsman with the big stride, in his polished leather boots, smart cutaway coat, top hat and silver-tipped cane, was always there for him. They had walked side by side through triumph and disaster, in good times and bad, Johnnie was no Johnnie-come-lately.

Billy started to hit the bottle hard. He could no longer pretend he was a problem drinker skirting the peripheries of alcoholism. He was drowning in self-pity for the new guilt he had taken on board. Billy soon lost his habit of doing his ablutions daily and now bathed and shaved every fortnight on pension day. He grew dirty and unkempt and what remained of his hair reached down to his shoulders and became infested.

In his fourth month in Paradise he was arrested for exposing himself in public. He'd been discovered wandering through a beachside shopping mall with a bottle in his hand, his fly unzipped and his willie peeping out at passing patrons. Fortunately for the late-night shoppers, his appendage was of such small dimensions that it lay buried in the shadows and general camouflage of his dirty apparel. That is, until a small boy of fly-zipper height pointed it out to his mother. In his state of advanced inebriation, Billy had taken a leak and neglected to make himself decent before leaving the toilet block. He'd weaved and stumbled a fair distance along the mall before he was finally apprehended by a very large Maori on the security staff. When Billy had attempted to resist him, the Maori had picked him up, tucked him under his arm and hailed a passing police van.

Billy spent the night in the watch-house in Southport where he was charged with wilful exposure. He was put into the drunk cell, which contained a cement bench and several cubic feet of stale air. Later the next morning he was arraigned in front of the magistrate, where his obvious remorse and pleas for forgiveness seemed to make less of an impression than his good manners and cultured accent, and he was let off on a good-behaviour bond.

While the dangling of his willie in public left Billy devastated, it also served to send him back to the bottle in an attempt to obliterate the terrible shame he felt. Drunks often repeat their actions by attempting to forget them.

In Billy's sober moments, which were growing increasingly further apart, he was dimly aware that he was slipping inexorably towards the point in his life when he'd wake up one morning clutching an empty bottle of sting (metho) and mumbling gibberish. He slept where the bottle took him, usually in the doorways of shops or sitting with his knees up around his chin on the floor of a phone box. Or, if he was still capable of hearing the sound of the surf, he'd attempt to stagger onto the beach. Through all of this Billy hung onto his briefcase, now handcuffed back where it belonged, to his left wrist.

The Salvation Army drug and alcohol rehabilitation counsellors in the William Booth Institutes will tell you that an alcoholic will only agree to a detox and rehabilitation program after they've hit the wall. That is, after they admit they can't give up the grog by themselves and need outside help. But they always say that an alcoholic rarely seeks rehabilitation to save himself. It is invariably an external event that triggers his resolve and it is *always* a thing of the heart.

At the William Booth Institutes they have a saying, *'Treat the person and you may win, treat the addiction and you'll always lose.'*

Billy's emotional jolt came in the form of a letter from Ms Flanagan, the principal of Pring Street Public School. It had been forwarded to the Surfers Paradise branch of his bank by Suzanna Partridge, his favourite bank person in Martin Place, and was handed to him when he went in to get his pension money.

The back of the envelope had been stamped 'Pring Street Public School' and at first Billy was afraid to open it. He left the bank and walked over to a small park close by, where he found a bench beside a stone picnic table. Placing the letter on the table, he walked around looking at it for several minutes. With a pocketful of pension money, he was tempted to buy a bottle in case the news was bad. Billy's mind was overcome with anxiety, the worst of his roiling imaginings being that something terrible had happened to the boy; the best, that the letter on the table in front of him was simply an acknowledging and accounting for the money he'd left in the school's care. His stomach churned and his throat constricted, he could feel his panic growing to the point where he thought he was going to throw up.

Finally Billy sat on the bench, moving the letter so that it was placed on the table directly in front of him. He reached for the key about his neck, only to discover that his hands were trembling so badly that it took him nearly two minutes to remove it and unshackle his wrist. A further minute followed as he furiously scratched around in his briefcase to locate his glasses. At one stage he shouted out, 'See, I can't find them, it's not my fault I can't read the letter!' He was consumed with the need to flee, leaving the unopened letter on the table.

When he finally found his glasses, the process of opening the envelope proved so fraught that it fell from his grasp on two occasions. Billy was whimpering when he eventually succeeded in withdrawing the three sheets of paper. With the pages now in his hands, they began to tremble to such an extent that he was forced to lay them on the surface of the table and hold them flat by placing his palms firmly on either side of them.

11 June 1996

Dear Mr O'Shannessy,

I respect your need for privacy and I wouldn't be writing this letter if I didn't think it important. Of course, I accept that you may choose to ignore it.

Ryan Sanfrancesco has become an increasing concern to myself and my staff and has, on two recent occasions, been returned to the school by a police officer when he was discovered in the Botanic Gardens during school hours. These are only two occasions in what has become constant truancy. Now he comes to school only on music days.

Naturally we have informed the Department of Community Services of our concerns. They point out that a file can only be opened if Ryan has been placed in physical or moral danger, or is subject to continued neglect. As we have no proof of this, other than his truancy, there is very little that can be done. Our private inquiries reveal that Ryan's grandmother is in the final stages of cancer and was moved to St Vincent's Hospice yesterday, so we may be able to persuade DOCS to do a risk assessment.

However, since Ryan received your letter, which, at your suggestion, I duly read, he has changed markedly. His first reaction was extreme disappointment and silent tears. But he is a brave little soul and seemed, at first, to recover from the disappointment of your departure quite well.

Then approx. two weeks later he appeared at my office and asked me if I'd received a letter for him. He seemed convinced that you would write to him and was unable to accept that you have gone from his life forever.

For the following two months he made regular appearances at my office asking if I had received any mail for him. Abruptly he stopped coming and, shortly after this, his teacher reported that he had grown morose and increasingly troublesome in class. Then his present truancy began.

I'm not sure why I am writing this letter to you, but Ryan Sanfrancesco is an exceptional and talented child and, heaven knows, there are few enough of them. He is burdened, like so many of our children at Pring Street Public, by family influences which are, to say the least, in many cases unfortunate. We would hate to lose him and my fear is that we are close to doing so.

Yesterday Ryan was apprehended by the police again, this time for stealing a set of skateboard wheels from a shop in Oxford Street. I have used a small part of the money you left in my care to pay the proprietor and he has agreed to drop the charges.

It is now obvious to us that you have had a profound and disproportionate effect on Ryan's life. Yesterday, in his school locker, we discovered the remains of a book, the pages ripped from its covers and then further torn into tiny pieces. With it, intact, was a drawing, which I enclose. It seems to clearly indicate his present distressed state of mind.

I don't quite know how to put this, but do you think you could write to him? I am aware that you haven't known each other for very long and that you make an odd couple, but children can sometimes be instinctive about these things. I confess that it would have been a neglect of my duty if I hadn't first checked on your background, to ensure that there was nothing of a prurient nature to be concerned about.

Mr O'Shannessy, if you can find it in your heart to write to this small boy, you could well be making the single difference between saving him or losing him. My experience as a teacher has taught me that sometimes the most fragile threads bind the tightest.

I remain,
Yours sincerely,
Dorothy Flanagan
Principal, Pring Street Public School

Billy, his spectacles misted with tears, came at last to the third page, stopping to clean his glasses and to wipe his eyes on the sleeve of his shirt. Replacing his spectacles, he saw that the third page, a piece of yellow A4 lined notepaper, contained a drawing using grease crayons of the kind younger children are given in kindergarten to scribble on sheets of butcher's paper. Considering the crudeness of the medium, the sketch was carefully done and it showed a briefcase half submerged in waves with a set of handcuffs dangling from it, one of the cuffs below the scalloped wave lines and the other attached to its handle. The briefcase was open and sitting in it was a black cat with only its head and shoulders showing. A speech balloon came from its mouth and floated above the cat's head. Inside the balloon were two words:

BILLYS GONE.

Billy remained on the bench for nearly four hours, intermittently chastising himself and weeping. It was late afternoon when he arrived at Resthaven, the Salvation Army Bridge Program premises in Southport, and asked if he might see a counsellor.

Within a few hours Billy O'Shannessy's real nightmare would begin. He was cordially welcomed and taken to a small office where he was introduced to Major Turlington, himself a reformed alcoholic. The Salvo major offered Billy the seat in front of his desk and Billy sat down, placing the briefcase onto his lap. 'How long since you've eaten, Mr O'Shannessy?'

Billy tried to think, he couldn't remember. 'Yesterday, no maybe the day before, I can't think, major.'

'Much easier if you use my Christian name, it's John.' Major Turlington hesitated a moment, 'And yours is?'

'Billy. I don't think I could eat anything quite yet, major . . . er, John.'

'That's all right, cuppa tea then? We'll throw in a sandwich, see how you go, eh?' The office door was open and he called out, 'Penny, can we have a cup of tea and a sandwich, please?' He turned to Billy, 'How many sugars, Billy?'

'Six,' Billy replied.

'Six sugars, thanks, Penny, I'll have a cuppa as well.' He turned back to Billy. 'While we wait for Penny to bring the tea, why don't I take down a few particulars, nothing too personal.' The major grinned, 'Though I guess we have to know who you are, surname, marital status, religion, next of kin, I'll need your social security registration number, that sort of thing. Got any problems with that, Billy?' Billy told him he had no objections and the Salvo major withdrew a form from the drawer of the desk and commenced asking questions. At one point Turlington asked, 'Are there any legal complications, you know, past criminal convictions?'

Billy hesitated, then, somewhat shamefaced, he confessed to the recent charge of indecent exposure while under the influence. 'I'm most terribly ashamed, I'm afraid I was very drunk, major.' Billy was having some trouble calling the tall Salvo by his Christian name.

Turlington laughed, 'Billy, if you saw some of the

reports we compile here, that is the very lightest of raps on the knuckle, you got a "good behaviour" and that's all that matters.'

At that moment Penny entered with a tray and placed two cups of tea in front of Major Turlington and Billy. 'If you don't mind I've added the sugar and stirred it, sir,' she said, smiling down at Billy. This was standard procedure, alcoholics often have the shakes and it saved them embarrassment.

'Thank you, that's fine,' Billy replied. Penny left, closing the door behind her.

'Now one of my last questions, are you on any current medication?'

'Nothing that doesn't come out of a whisky bottle,' Billy said, then immediately relented, 'I'm sorry, that wasn't very clever.'

Turlington laughed. 'But honest. Which is a damned good beginning and I guess that's why you're here. Which brings me to the next question. Was there a particular incident that brought you to this point? Brings you here today?'

Billy was silent for some time. 'Ah, I . . .' but he could go no further. He made several more attempts to say something but his throat constricted on each occasion and finally he gave up and looked down into his lap. He thought he'd exhausted his self-recrimination but now the tears rolled silently down his cheeks.

'You haven't touched your tea, Billy, try the sandwich, do you good,' Turlington suggested quietly.

Billy picked up the cup in front of him, but his hand

shook so violently that half its contents immediately soaked the sandwich and spilled onto the desk. 'I . . . I'm so sorry,' Billy said, distressed. The cup rattled against the saucer as he attempted to place it back. Ashamed, he tried to wipe the desk clean with the sleeve of his shirt.

'No, please,' Turlington said calmly, 'No harm done, mate. This place is heartbreak hotel, you've got a fair distance to go before we get concerned.'

'I'd like to try and detox, major,' Billy blurted out.

'That's the spirit, Billy, and we're going to be on your side all the way. We'll get back to why you're here later, but I need to explain to you what's involved. You'll be kept here for seven days, although, depending on your condition, this could be up to three weeks. We need to monitor your overall health and get you over alcohol withdrawal.'

'I'm not sure I could spend that much time in a dormitory with people like me,' Billy said nervously, 'I have great difficulty with the drunk tank.'

Major Turlington tried to reassure him. 'It's not quite the same thing here, Billy. We don't have a drunk tank, only a clinic and a recovery ward, just like a hospital. You'll be required to stay in bed for the first two or three days at least. Although, for the first forty-eight hours, you'll be in our detox clinic where you'll be under constant twenty-four-hour supervision by nursing staff and, of course, a doctor. Now I have to ask you, have you ever attempted detox before?'

'No, this is the first time,' Billy admitted.

'Well then, you'll need to know what to expect. But I

have to ask you to sign an admission contract before we can go any further.'

'I beg your pardon, major, a contract, I don't understand?'

Turlington smiled. 'That's what we call it. As you can imagine, we get all types coming into Resthaven and there has to be a clear understanding of the conditions under which we operate.'

'Oh, the rules,' Billy said.

'Well yes, but most people coming in wanting our services don't much like the word, so we call it a contract instead. You sign it, we sign it and then we can proceed. Pretty simple really.'

By submitting himself voluntarily to an institution for detoxification, Billy hadn't expected to be in a position to haggle over his rights, but he was still a lawyer by nature and signing a contract of any sort without reading it was anathema to him. 'May I see it, please, major?'

'Of course.' The Salvation Army officer handed Billy a single sheet of paper and Billy scratched around in his briefcase until he found his glasses.

The contract contained eleven clauses, all of which were designed to protect the institution as he had expected. He was not allowed to bring any drugs or alcohol onto the premises, gamble or have sexual liaisons with any other patients, destroy property or behave violently or steal. He was required to submit to a random search at any time and an inspection of his personal property. Finally he was required to give the medical staff a sample of his urine for analysis. It was all pretty basic and Billy signed the contract and handed it back. Several other sheets of do's and don'ts, rights and wrongs, instructions and procedures, freedoms and limitations were handed to him and Billy read them, signed them and handed them back. There was no hidden agenda.

Turlington smiled, 'Congratulations. That's the first time I've ever seen anyone read through every document in the ten years I have been here.'

'In another life I was a lawyer, old habits die hard,' Billy replied. 'I apologise if I took too long.'

'No, no, not at all, it's surprising what people will sign without first finding out what they're getting themselves into,' the major said. He appeared to hesitate a moment before continuing. 'Billy, this isn't going to be easy and you're going to feel pretty rotten for the first little while. I'm afraid there's no simple way to detox.'

Billy had often enough heard detox stories from drunks who had attempted it and he knew it would be difficult. 'Don't expect it will be easy, major,' he now said, having given up trying to call the Salvation Army officer by his first name.

'Perhaps now you can tell me the reason you are here, Billy?'

Billy began to tell the major the story of Ryan and why he had run away from New South Wales, finally handing him the letter to read. He managed to stay dry-eyed through the process and at the end of it felt a little stronger. 'I'm not sure I have the strength to take on any responsibility at the moment, major.'

The Salvo grinned and tried to turn Billy's anxiety into an abstract. 'Now why doesn't that surprise me? Very few people do. I guess it's hard enough just taking care of ourselves. In the meantime, try not to think about what you're going to do about Ryan. Your coming here is the first step, the only one we need to concern ourselves with for the moment. For the next few days, try only to concentrate on getting well again.'

Billy knew that he was being expertly handled, in different circumstances he might have said 'manipulated'. But he sensed that he'd reached the stage where his famous intellect wasn't going to help him. Whatever he thought wasn't going to make a difference. He was emotionally exhausted, the justifications and the arguments were over, he knew if he ran away from this battle, there would be no others to come. Charlie was Ryan and Ryan was Charlie, there could be no more self-pity, no more excuses, no more taking the blame for everything with the secret nobility that this implied. This time he had to choose sides, there was no middle ground, no no-man's-land in which to play dead until the battle was over and he could crawl to a dishonourable safety from where he'd cower in an emotional shell hole while the fighting went on.

'I see,' Billy said quietly. 'What happens next?'

'Does that mean you wish to continue with us?' Turlington asked, 'Go on the program?'

'Well, the detox, yes,' Billy answered.

'That's good,' the Salvo said, not making a fuss. 'You'll need to take a shower and we'll give you a pair of pyjamas. Then you'll see the doctor for a medical examination.'

Turlington rose from the desk and opened the door. 'Penny, will you take Billy through to the shower block, please.' He handed her the interview form. 'On your way back, give this to Major Tompkins.'

Billy rose and moved towards the door. 'Thank you, major,' he said.

'Oh, Billy, your letter, you'll want that,' Turlington said, taking the four steps back to his desk. 'I must say, Ryan's principal sounds like a very nice person.' He folded the letter carefully, placed it back into its envelope and handed it to Billy, who rested his briefcase on his knee, clicked it open and dropped the letter inside. 'We'll see a bit of each other over the next few days, Billy. Remember, we're on God's side and that's a winning team.'

Penny, Billy never did get her other name, was waiting for him at the door and took him through to the shower block where she introduced him to an attendant named Nick. Nick wore a set of very faded and worn racing silks and jodhpurs with a pair of heavy workman's steel-capped boots. 'Nick will take care of you, Mr O'Shannessy, and when you've had your shower he'll take you through to the clinic,' Penny said kindly, then bade them both goodbye.

Nick was a tiny, battle-scarred man of an indeterminate age, certainly over forty, but too physically weather-beaten for Billy to venture a more accurate guess. It would later turn out that he'd been a jockey, though never in the big time, scraping a living out of country racetracks and spending too many long, lonely nights propped up at the bar of small-town pubs. He was severely bow-legged, so much so that it cost him a good two centimetres in height. It transpired that his pins had acquired their shape less from sitting in the saddle than from falling out of it. Billy was to learn that Nick's entire body was a reassembly, a poorly patched-up job of multiple mended fractures and badly knitted bones. He seemed unable to keep still, shifting from one leg to the other, as if neither leg could tolerate his weight for more than a few moments. The heavy steel-studded boots would crash down onto the cement floor every few moments to announce his whereabouts. He also had a shiny purple dent in the right side of his temple so that the eye below it sagged noticeably and appeared permanently inflamed. Nick had accepted the Lord Jesus Christ in the process of an alcohol rehabilitation program and had subsequently joined the Salvation Army as a witness to his redemption.

'What she say the name was, mate?' he asked, when Penny had left. 'Sheilas does that to me, I get that nervous I don't listen to nothin' they says.'

'It's Billy.'

'Yeah?' Nick seemed amazed, 'That's gunna be real easy, praise the Lord. I used to 'ave a parrot called Billy. Billy Parrot we named him, he were bald, see.' He extended a hand on which several fingers pointed in slightly different directions. 'Gidday, mate, pleasetermeetcha, here to take a nice shower, is ya?'

Billy nodded, too emotionally worn out to do much more. Nick seemed harmless enough, though he may have taken one knock too many on the head.

Nick hopped from one foot to the other examining Billy.

'There's bad news and there's bad news, which you want first?' he asked, chuckling at his own joke.

'Seeing I have a choice, the bad news,' Billy replied, forcing himself to play the game.

'Righto then, London to a brick yer got nits. Know what the real name is?'

'No, I don't think I do, Nick.'

'*Pediculus humanus!*' Nick said gleefully. 'Nasty them little buggers, bitin' and itchin'. Now, I can shave yer head off *or* we can rub it with Banlice mousse, supposed to work pretty good, but that's kids, blokes like us, that's different I reckon, but yer need a haircut anyway. That's both the bad newses,' he concluded happily.

'As I'm already bald I don't suppose it matters too much if you remove the rest of my hair, but I'm rather anxious to retain my head,' Billy said. He was beginning to feel that he was losing control of his life while, at the same time, he kept reminding himself that, for the present anyway, this was probably the best thing that could happen to him.

'Praise the Lord!' Nick said, delighted, this time not simply evoking the Almighty's name as a figure of speech. 'I'll get me trusty clippers.'

Nick disappeared into a small room to the side of the shower block and moments later returned carrying a pair of barber's clippers and dragging a steel chair behind him. He indicated that Billy should sit down. To Billy's surprise, Nick was wearing a short white barber's jacket. 'Afternoon, sir, nice to see you back. The usual?' he said in a formal, well-spoken voice.

Billy glanced anxiously at Nick, not sure what was happening. 'You will be careful, won't you?' he asked a little tremulously, having noted the condition of Nick's fingers.

'Of course, sir, here at the Ritz we take great pride in our hair.'

Billy couldn't believe his ears. 'Shouldn't I have a towel? I mean, something around my neck?' he asked.

'Nah, no worries, gunna burn yer clobber. Body lice!' Nick exclaimed, instantly forgetting his barber's act and resuming his own vernacular. 'They's different, see, can't see them much, little buggers live in the seams of your clobber, come out, have a nip and nip back in.' Without asking permission, he pulled the sleeve of Billy's shirt up to his elbow to reveal his inner arm. 'See them red marks, that's 'em. They likes the soft parts. There's also crabs, *Pediculosis pubis*.' Nick paused and came to stand directly in front of Billy, clipper in hand, hopping from one foot to the other. 'Mate, I'm your expert. You been a naughty boy lately, Billy?'

Billy smiled. 'It's been so long I can't remember.'

'Me too, mate, shit me britches just thinkin' about it.' Billy wondered briefly what might have brought Nick to the stage of being terrified by the opposite sex. 'So, there yer go then, yer home and hosed. Don't want to be shaving down where the goolies hang, does we?' Nick said. 'Take me word, burnin' yer gear, quickest way ter catch them little buggers kippin' in yer seams. We'll keep yer shoes, if they's still good enough we fumigate them.'

Billy was so tired he was having trouble following

Nick's rapid patter, but the little ex-jockey who'd turned to Christ was as good as his word and, without a nick or even a nasty pull, removed the hair that grew from the base of Billy's bald pate down to his shoulders. 'There yer go!' Nick said enthusiastically. 'Good as new, praise the Lord.' He stood back, admiring his handiwork. 'Fair dinkum, yer looks just like Billy Parrot.' He made no attempt to explain his suddenly assumed and abandoned bit part as a barber at the Ritz Hotel.

Billy was given a towel, a pair of pyjamas and a small square packet that looked like clear plastic. 'Soap's in the shower,' Nick said, 'Rub yer scalp good with the antiseptic shampoo. Gives a call when yer finish, don't forget to wear yer slippers.'

'Slippers?'

'Yeah, them plastic ones, in the little packet.'

Billy emerged from the shower in his pyjamas, wearing his disposable plastic slippers which looked remarkably like shower caps. He carried his briefcase, having shackled it back to his wrist. Nick now seemed to see it for the first time. Pointing to the briefcase he said, 'Dunno about that, mate. Them yer things in there?'

'Yes,' Billy replied, immediately defensive. 'I couldn't be parted from it.'

'Handcuffs, eh? Bloody good idea!'

Billy looked down at his briefcase, then up at Nick, concerned. 'They'll not burn it, will they?'

'Nah, have to inspect what's innit, that's all, praise the Lord.'

'Oh? But there's nothing . . .'

'Substances, mate! Harmful substances,' Nick said interrupting. 'Major Tompkins's pretty strict on harmful substances. C'mon, I'll take you through, but I can't go in with yiz, it's me woman thing.'

'Major Tompkins is a woman?'

'Yeah, mate, you wouldn't want ter cross her, bad news,' Nick warned. 'Real tough cookie.'

A tough cookie seemed about the last term one might think of to describe Major Tompkins. She may well have been durable but she was a large woman of an institutional kind now obsolete, yet once found in every hospital wearing a white uniform, starched veil and sensible shoes with a watch pinned to her rigidly starched breast. Although Major Tompkins wore a pale-blue shirt, navy skirt and the same sensible shoes, and her steel-grey hair was cut short in a no-nonsense style that showed a lot of scissor work and very little skill, her old-fashioned medical pedigree was unmistakable. She'd made the transition from hospital matron to the title of Team Leader of the Southport Salvation Army's Resthaven detox ward without having to draw breath.

She motioned Billy to a chair in front of her desk and glanced at the form Penny had given her. 'Mr O'Shannessy, welcome, my name is Major Marjorie Tompkins.'

Billy sat down and, as usual, placed his briefcase on his lap. 'Thank you, major.' There was no suggestion he call her Marjorie and Billy couldn't imagine anyone, not even Major Turlington, doing so.

'Goodness gracious, is that a handcuff about your wrist?' she asked, surprised. 'Whatever is it doing there?'

'Oh, it's to secure my briefcase,' Billy said softly. 'My things, keep them safe,' he added, a little lamely.

'Well, never in my born days!' she exclaimed. 'Your things will be quite safe here, Mr O'Shannessy. We can't have you walking around handcuffed to your belongings! Will you please remove it from your wrist so that we can inspect the contents?'

'There are no harmful substances in it, major,' Billy protested. 'Only my personal things.'

'I'm quite sure you're right, but I'll need to see for myself.' Then, tight-lipped, she said, 'Those are our rules, Mr O'Shannessy! Without rules, Heaven only knows where we would be.' She pointed to the handcuff, 'Do you have a key for that contraption?'

Billy removed the key from around his neck and opened the handcuff. 'Splendid,' Major Tompkins replied, 'I'm very glad to see that you've agreed to have a haircut, saves a lot of bother all round.'

Billy started to put the key back around his neck. 'No, no, I'll take that,' she said, holding out her hand. 'Can't have you swallowing it now, can we?' Billy didn't feel sufficiently strong to resist, and handed her the precious key. With the evening approaching, his body was now screaming for alcohol and the first of his withdrawal symptoms was cramping at his gut, his tongue sticking to the roof of his mouth. 'Will you place your briefcase on the desk now, please, Mr O'Shannessy.' Again Billy did as he was told. 'Open it, please,' Major Tompkins instructed. In the meantime, she'd slipped on a pair of surgical gloves.

Billy opened the briefcase and she commenced to examine it, hauling each item out and checking it separately, putting Billy's knife, fork and spoon to one side along with the bottle-opener, corkscrew and the various bits of wire and different-sized corks. The remainder of the contents she placed on the desk to her right. 'Goodness!' she said in surprise as she withdrew the packet of surgical gloves, 'Whatever are these for?'

Billy was glad that he'd long since thrown away what remained of the rat poison. 'They're for scrounging in garbage bins,' he said, thinking quickly.

Major Tompkins looked up in surprise. 'Well, I never!' she said. She examined his notepads and his newspaper clippings, though in a cursory manner. Not wishing him to think she was being overly curious, she did not open the photograph album. 'Perhaps, when you're feeling a little better, you'd like to write again,' she said, not unkindly. Then, turning to the pile on her left, she said, 'We'll have to keep these for you and after we've fumigated it, we'll return your briefcase and these things here,' she pointed to the pile on her right. 'The dangerous objects you may get when you leave.'

'And my key?' Billy asked.

'No, no, I'll keep that until you leave, you have a locker beside your bed for your things.' Anticipating his next question, she added, 'It has a combination lock.'

Billy knew that Major Tompkins was a relic from a

different time and if he'd cared to assert his rights, the over-officious woman would have been forced to back down, but he was too crushed by the events of the afternoon to protest. By abandoning his briefcase, he was making as much of a commitment to his rehabilitation as the admission to Major Turlington that he was not capable of giving up alcohol on his own and needed help. Without his briefcase, he was finally stripped naked.

Billy pointed to the envelope containing Dorothy Flanagan's letter. 'I'd like to take that letter with me now, please.'

Major Tompkins seemed to hesitate for a moment before she handed him the letter. 'If you have any money on you, you may leave it with us for safekeeping or keep it in your locker.' She smiled at Billy, 'It says on your report you haven't eaten for two days, we'll give you something to eat and then you'll see the doctor.'

Billy's resolve was weakening by the minute, he would have liked to ask for his clothes to be returned, run away and fled to the nearest pub. But he was in the hands of experts, his clothes were probably being incinerated by Nick, who'd be praising the Lord and burning the bug eggs in the seams. Any attempt to escape in his pyjamas, wearing his plastic slippers and with his head plucked like Billy Parrot, he didn't think would get him too far. The Salvos had him by the short and curlies.

Billy was given a bowl of thick beef broth and two slices of white bread before being taken through to the detox clinic by a male nurse for his medical examination. He was to discover that most of the nurses were male. Most derelicts felt very uncomfortable around women. Life on the street for an alcoholic was almost exclusively a male experience and contact with females was rare except for an occasional short and often wordless sexual encounter with a prostitute in an alley or an equally brief and only slightly more personal contact with a barmaid in a pub. Females in the bureaucracy such as social workers or the people at Centrelink, where they applied for a pension and other concessions, were not regarded as having a gender. They were simply neuters who asked questions and, in turn, received answers in monosyllables, their eyes averted.

The doctor seemed pleasant enough, he was young and possessed an easy manner. He introduced himself as Mike Todd, a simple name to remember, but Billy, despite the soup and bread in his belly, was now beginning to feel decidedly the worse for wear and somewhat agitated, so immediately forgot it. This was unusual, for Billy took great pride in remembering people's names. It was not only his massive hangover and the start of his withdrawal symptoms but he was also emotionally drained. Dorothy Flanagan's letter had simply blown him out of the water.

By the time the doctor had completed examining him, giving him a medical that included a blood test, his malnutrition status, respiratory problems, dental problems, an assessment of his alcohol and nutritional intake, and examination for bronchitis, diabetes (very common in alcoholics) and pancreatic inflammation, it was almost eight o'clock. Billy had broken into a fairly heavy sweat on his face and chest and was experiencing small and constant tremors of his upper extremities.

'Mr O'Shannessy,' the doctor said after completing his examination, 'you are a highly intelligent man, but you are also a very sick one and we're going to try to make you better. It won't be easy and you're in for a rough ride, which we'll try very hard to make as easy as possible. I'm going to prescribe 20 mg of Valium every two hours until you're fully sedated. You'll start to feel sleepy and hopefully relaxed. A senior nurse will also give you a vitamin B injection each day for the first three days and we'll be watching you carefully, checking your progress constantly.'

'Checking me for what?' Billy asked. 'Withdrawal symptoms?'

'Exactly.'

'I'd like to know what to expect, doctor.' Billy shivered, his mouth so dry he was having trouble articulating.

'Could be almost anything,' the doctor replied. 'Exaggerated shaking. I see that you're perspiring now. That, for instance, could get a lot worse, so could the tremors. Nausea may be present, we'll treat that. High blood pressure, heart palpitations, some diarrhoea, dehydration, insomnia.' The doctor spread his hands. 'Mr O'Shannessy, you're in good hands, we'll be checking you constantly for the next three days.'

'Is that all, doctor?' Billy asked, his expression doubtful.

Mike Todd smiled. 'Oh, I see, you're thinking of delirium tremens? The Valium will usually take care of most of that but, yes, some hallucinations can and do occur, though not as often as before. You're almost certain to feel some degree of anxiety and agitation and, perhaps, disorientation.' He shrugged, 'You're an alcoholic, Mr O'Shannessy, and we can't predict what will happen. But be assured, there will be someone near, or at your side, all the time.'

Billy was escorted to the detox ward, which was freshly painted and very clean, each bed covered by a dark-blue doona and fitted with fresh bed linen. A tall wooden locker stood beside his bed with a combination lock fitted to it. His bed contained a typical hospital tray of the kind that could be wheeled away when it wasn't needed. The most remarkable thing about the ward was the huge painted sign in fire-engine red against the white end wall facing the door as you entered. It read:

THERE IS HOPE.

Billy was given a shot of vitamin B and of Valium and put to bed. He needed sleep but he was still conscious of sweating and waited for the Valium to take effect. He had gone longer than this before without alcohol, he could do it again. But when he tried to think when that might have been, he couldn't. The thought of never again walking with wee Johnnie Walker crept into his mind and soon became unimaginable.

He'd been drinking more than was reasonable since university when he'd entered law school at the age of seventeen. He was fifty-six years old, he'd been drunk at his graduation, drunk at his wedding, drunk at Charlie's funeral, drunk at his daughter's graduation, he'd been drunk when he signed the deeds to the family home and the settlement he'd made with his wife, drunk when he'd made the financial arrangements for his daughter, drunk when he'd bade them all adieu and walked away from everything. But he hadn't been drunk when he'd made the decision to walk away from Ryan. That was the only mistake he'd made, running away while sober. Now they were taking away his support, his emotional crutches, before he could walk. He'd been using them for thirty-five years, matching strides with Johnnie Walker, and now they were expecting him to walk alone without a friend in the world. It wasn't fair!

Two hours later, when he received a second shot of Valium, he was still awake, the night nurse asking him if he was all right. Billy nodded. He didn't know if he could speak, but he didn't wish to do so, speaking was out of the question, his mind was turned inward and all he could think was that the lights in the ward didn't go out. The bloody lights never went out. The fucking lights never went out! A great spotlight was beamed on him and its heat was making him sweat but instead of feeling hot he was freezing. That was it, ten thousand candlepower burning, focused on him, like a magnifying glass concentrating the sun's rays, white light burning into the ice of his soul, demanding he do something he couldn't do.

By morning he'd had 80 mg of Valium and had barely slept at all, the constant coming and going of nurses sounded to him like a troop of horses stampeding down a tarred road. The medication they gave him became lost in the confusion of whirling lights, mixed with faces, groans and sighs and occasional screams from other patients. The accumulated terror, his, theirs, the terror of every drunk he had ever known, now aggregated, then clumped together tighter and tighter until it seemed to become a ball of light roughly the size of a tennis ball that proceeded to bounce against the white walls of the ward, each bounce harder, faster, louder, more furious, until he became exhausted attempting to follow its frenetic cat's cradle progress.

Suddenly, without making a conscious decision, he'd shoot upright in bed and catch sight of the sign on the back wall, but instead of giving him courage, he grew furious and cried out, 'Scrub it! Scrub it off!' Then he had a cunning thought, he'd get the yellow ball to wipe out the sign, direct it, make each furious impact eliminate a tiny portion of the sign, until he'd blasted and bounced the scary message off the wall.

Billy worked on this new plan, concentrating, directing the ball onto the bright-red paint. *Whack! Whack! Whack!* It seemed to go on for hours and when the day-shift nursing staff came on duty only the three letters OPE remained. He kept whacking them with the ball but they remained stubbornly on the wall. He tried removing them by creating different words, COPE (He couldn't!) DOPE (That's what he was! Stupid!) SLOPE (He was tumbling, falling head over heels down, down, down!) ROPE (He was hanging from a tree. *The bulging eyes and the twisted mouth!*) Then it turned back into HOPE and he started to scream.

Twelve hours after he'd taken the first 20 mg of Valium, Billy's alcohol-withdrawal symptoms rating scale, based on a maximum score of four points in each of six categories, reached eight points and the alarm bells went off and the doctor was called in. The rough ride they'd promised him was beginning.

Mike Todd sat with Billy, asking him questions. 'Do you know where you are, Billy?'

'Yes, the drunk tank. Scrub it off, scrub it off!' Billy begged. The ball was still bouncing, though now it had gone haywire, nowhere near the sign on the wall. He could no longer direct its erratic behaviour.

'And where is the drunk tank?' Mike Todd asked.

'Foster House, scrub it off! Please scrub it off!' Billy pleaded. He was waking up in the drunk tank in Sydney, but this time his hangover was a hundred times worse than anything he'd ever experienced before. *Whack! Whack! Whack!* The ball was coming at him, it was going to turn on him, he knew it for certain, it was going to kill him!

Mike Todd injected Valium directly into Billy's muscle. 'He's not too bad, but I'd like him monitored every twenty minutes, nurse. Has he complained of nausea yet?' he asked.

'No, doctor.'

'He probably will at some stage, or he'll start to vomit, you know the drill. I'll call in around five tonight.' Mike Todd turned to Billy and touched him on the shoulder. 'Hang in, mate, you're not doing too badly.'

'Scrub it off! Please scrub it off!' Billy cried.

'Tactile hallucination,' Mike Todd said quietly to the nurse as they left the bed. He had mistaken Billy's pleas to scrub the sign from the wall for the most common hallucination in alcoholic withdrawal, described in medical terms as *'a sense of false movement or sensation on the surface of the skin'*. In other words, a sense of something crawling all over your skin. This is a part of the total sensory overload that withdrawal from alcohol brings about.

The usual effect of alcohol is to dull the senses and in an alcoholic this eventually numbs them to the point where they can withstand quite severe shock or trauma. Badly festering ulcers remain untreated, the pain of a bad sprain or even minor fractures are left unattended, or they will tolerate problems, such as bronchial infections, which would send most people to hospital. They may often be medically in an extremely poor, sometimes life-threatening, condition without seeking help. Alcoholics seldom die from alcohol poisoning or liver and kidney malfunction, it is usually from something they've neglected to attend to.

However, when alcohol is withdrawn from the system, the system begins to experience sensory overload. Every condition is massively exaggerated, sensory perceptions increase, sometimes a hundredfold, dull lights appear as blazing floodlights. Footsteps sound like a herd of buffalo passing, the mild sting of an injection needle feels as though a sharp, probing dagger has entered the skin, smells hitherto unnoticed become suffocating, what on the outside appears to be a slight trembling has the effect of feeling as if a goods train has rumbled over muscle and sinew and crushed the internal organs, so that, almost inevitably, the mind is affected and hallucinations begin to follow.

Shortly after the doctor's departure, Billy's headache,

already severe, started to increase in intensity until the throbbing sounded like artillery fire and the pain was as if he was being beaten over the head every few seconds by someone using a pick handle.

This was followed by a massive, all-consuming feeling of nausea, though he was too far out of it to tell the staff monitoring him, so they were unable to give him medication to calm his stomach. The first sign of the nausea was a sudden convulsing, pushing the contents of his stomach up like an erupting volcano. Billy had only the remains of the soup and bread in his gut, and after this came up as a gruel, there was nothing left to follow, although the muscles continued to convulse, bringing up a burning bile that seared his throat. He became dehydrated and the nursing staff hurriedly set up a saline drip.

Then, despite the Valium, Billy's legs started to cramp and jerk wildly, the muscles cramping and releasing, the pain so unbearable that he cried out constantly.

And always the light, Billy was drowning in the light.

The hours went by and he kept getting injections of Valium, but the sensory overload continued. Five o'clock arrived but the doctor had been delayed and Billy, already confused and disorientated, knew he was dying. He tried desperately to concentrate through the intense pain, beating his arms against his chest and stomach to rid himself of the lice he imagined covered him in a moving, itching, thick grey blanket. But the harder he tried, the more confused he became. In the early evening, though of course Billy had no sense of the time, he became totally consumed with fear and shortly afterwards went into a full-blown panic attack, gasping for air, his eyes bulging, his body completely soaked with perspiration.

By the time Mike Todd arrived it was eight o'clock, Billy's heart rate had soared, pumping so hard that it filled his chest and throat and threatened to bring on a heart attack.

'Can you hear me, Billy? It's Mike Todd. Hold on, mate, it's going to be all right.'

The ball was back, flying through the air, this time a small meteorite, blind with malice. It smacked into the wall time and time again, each time tantalisingly close to the word HOPE, though never again touching it. 'Scrub it off!' Billy sobbed.

Doctor Todd immediately administered the Valium through Billy's rectum to get it into his bloodstream more effectively. He'd absorbed a massive amount into his system without it seeming to slow him down.

Mike Todd stayed at Billy's bedside for the next two hours, waiting to administer the next dose of Valium. An hour after midnight, twenty-nine hours after he'd been given the first injection, the sedative finally overcame him and Billy watched the ball bounce into the wall before it fell to the floor and rolled away under one of the beds. He fell into a deeply sedated sleep.

Finally Billy had come out of the delirium tremens. It had been fifty hours since his last drink. He'd taken the first small step towards rehabilitation. In his tiny office near the detox ward, Dr Mike Todd fell asleep writing up the patient's notes. He'd written: *The patient has responded well to treat . . .*

CHAPTER EIGHT

Billy, still in his pyjamas and shower-cap slippers, sat in a small enclosed courtyard behind the detox ward in Resthaven munching a bar of chocolate with a Coke at his side. The sun was high enough to enter a corner of the courtyard and this was where Billy was ensconced, writing with the sun at his back under another relentlessly blue sky.

It was six days since Billy had arrived and he'd been allowed out of bed for the past four. Over the four days following the delirium tremens, the dosage of sedative had been gradually decreased until this morning, when he'd finally been weaned off Valium. With drugs no longer present to mask his condition he was feeling battered and intensely weary but he was nevertheless anxious to be up and about, as he was to be discharged the following morning.

The chocolate bar and Coke business was run by Nick,

the shower attendant, who was aware of the craving for sugar patients experienced coming off detox. He kept a supply of both in his little room off the shower block. The Coke rested in a yellow plastic bin containing ice which Nick hauled twice-daily from the party ice dispenser at a nearby service station. On a hot day, which was almost every day, he'd unwrap the chocolate bars and plunge them in the ice bin and sell the combination as Sip 'n' dunk. He made no profit, selling his wares at the price he paid for them as his witness to the Lord, or as he put it, 'It's me Christian duty, mate, them fellas is cravin' somethin' sweet and with Gawd's help I can give it to them.'

Billy, still fearful, was writing to Ryan. Detox had been a horrendous experience and perhaps its only advantage was that he had been left too ill and too sedated to think about anything very much. Even now he didn't feel strong enough to talk directly to the boy about the passage of time he'd been away, nor was he sure what his immediate future might bring or whether he would ever post the letter.

Billy had been brought to the point where he'd been reduced to nothing. He could no longer harbour any illusions about himself, there were no more comfortable boltholes in his past behaviour where the always honourable gentleman could crawl when things got tough. Quite simply, he was an alcoholic, a nobody on the way out, he'd reached the point where the excuses and self-justifications were all used up and he was going to have to start at the beginning again or slide into oblivion. The letter to Ryan would assume that he had something to say that was valuable and important to the child and Billy wasn't at all sure that he had the right to make such an assumption. The values that Ryan needed were not ones that Billy believed he truly possessed and in writing to Ryan, his fear was that it would seem as if the devil had taken up preaching the gospel.

This time he couldn't hide behind the fact that he'd once been a famous barrister with seven generations of First Fleet pedigree behind him and a considered opinion on just about everything.

The starting point for Billy now was the same as it was for every other derelict on skid row. He had to learn to crawl, then walk, and then come against a hard-faced world that didn't care if he lived or died, and he had to do this without the help of Doctor Bottle.

As a drunk and a derelict Billy had fashioned a world to live in and while it was grim, unpredictable, dangerous and difficult, it nevertheless had quite specific parameters. Sober, he faced a life that had no defined boundaries and in which he would be shown no mercy. Whatever the weakness that had caused him to become a drunk, it was nothing to the strength of character he would now require just to stay sober. The detox clinic may have been the big dipper, but the bumpy ride was by no means over.

Billy took three days to write the letter to Ryan, not knowing if he would ever have the courage to post it.

My dear Ryan,

Since last we talked, much has happened to Trim and not all of it good. With a master like Captain Matthew Flinders, who seems prepared to face any hardship to achieve his objective, this has meant facing danger and living under extremely difficult circumstances.

Trim was a ship's cat born and bred, he accepted that some days were fair sailing with a fine breeze, the cirrus clouds on the horizon the only smoky smudge in the blue of an everlasting sky. Then there would be days when the weather turned foul and the wind howled in the topsails with the decks awash with foam, the sputum of an angry and malevolent ocean.

There were times too when they faced hunger and, unless a dolphin or a large ray might be hooked or netted, they would go without, as smaller fish were not always plentiful and the seine, a fishing net cast out in shallow water and used to encircle fish, didn't always supply food for the eighty-eight men on board.

On one expedition, Trim's fine glossy black coat turned to grey and his ribs stood out for all to see. It was greatly feared that Master Trim would not recover from such onerous times but, as it transpired, when conditions were plentiful again, the darkness of his fine pelt returned to its full burnish. Trim did not see his needs as superior to those of the ship's crew and he suffered, with never a meow of complaint when times were bad, which was more than may be said of some of the crew when their stomachs cramped for need of sustenance.

It was generally supposed that the natives, for they were not called Aborigines but were referred to as natives or often as Indians, were of a cowardly demeanour, by nature timid and fearful. But this was not the case. Although they soon developed a hearty respect for the musket ball, they were prepared to defend their territory from intruders with their spears of strong, resilient sapling, the tips hardened by means of fire. Though primitive to our eyes, these 'sticks' were not to be disparaged as weapons and were as capable as well-forged metal for the purpose of penetration into the chest or stomach of a victim or to bring down a kangaroo or giant lizard.

Trim could recall one occasion when the Indians were not pleased to see them. They had been preparing to do a survey of Cape Barrow and had moored the ship on the leeward side of Woodah Island where the botanical gentlemen and Captain Flinders had gone ashore, the former to examine plants and Mr Flinders, as always, to survey the surrounding land and to observe the shoreline of the bay that formed the mainland. Trim had not accompanied Mr Brown and Mr Good, the two botanicals, nor followed his master, deciding to take a bit of a kip on board, his stomach still a little upset by a rough passage the previous night.

However, the next morning a wood-collecting and fishing party were sent out and the botanicals as well. Once ashore, Mr Brown called out, 'Trim, wilt thou be part of our expedition today?' Trim shook his head and expressed in meowing terms that he was afraid that they must do without his feline company on this bright and cloudless day, that, alas, he felt it his duty to accompany the working party.

This was not an altogether honest response, Trim had been fantasising about a tasty morsel of fresh-caught fish and the prospect was more than he could resist. Feeling just a little shamefaced, he branched off with the wood and the fish, leaving the floras to fend for themselves. He was soon running ahead, enjoying the light clean air, stalking a bird or small lizard, chasing a clicking locust and, generally, having a fine old time. Although soon the sun grew exceedingly hot and he found himself seeking the shade of the bushes. On one such occasion he came across a small patch of washed sand and upon it, clear as daylight, were to be seen the footprints of Indians, broad and barefooted and not to be mistaken for anything else. Trim sat firm and commenced meowing mightily to attract the attention of the working party.

'What is it, Trim?' Mr Whitewood, the master's mate, called, then came over to inspect the reason for Trim's caterwauling. 'Aye, thou art surely the finest of thy breed, Master Trim, we shall keep a careful lookout for these Indians and our weapons shall be at the ready, though we are cautioned by Captain Flinders to treat the natives with friendliness, it is as well to keep our muskets primed.'

Soon after they passed through a small wood not suitable for gathering timber and commenced to a second further up a ridge where the trees seemed of a more mature appearance. There, not more than half a mile away upon the ridge, stood five Indians, all in the peculiar stance Trim had first observed in Rushcutters Bay, the instep of one foot resting on the knee of the other, their spears pinned to the ground and held vertical to maintain their balance.

'Ahoy, Master Trim, we have found your Indians, a small party not of a sufficient size to cause alarm, we shall approach them in a friendly manner for this is their territory and it is we who trespass,' Mr Whitewood explained.

Trim was the friendliest of all creatures and feared nothing and no man at sea, but on land he was prone to sensible caution. Once, when somewhat younger and while in Sydney Town, he had observed a chain gang proceeding along the Quay, a string of such utter human misery where the clink of shackle and chain and the groaning of the men near broke his feline heart.

Trim knew that nothing touched the human soul more deeply than the stroking of his fur against a leg accompanied with a purring resonance to indicate an affection and a bond between fellow creatures. On board ship there were sailors who would be brought near to tears if rewarded in such a manner for a clean-scrubbed deck or well-tucked sail.

With this small and harmless charity in mind, Trim picked out a particular fellow who seemed even more woebegone than the rest of the wretched line and commenced to rub his glossy coat against the man's naked ankles. In a trice, a hand shot down and grabbed him, lifting him off the surface of the road and holding him aloft and directly to the front of the man's foul-smelling breath. With both hands about Trim's throat, the convict set about choking him, this to the greatest possible mirth of his fellows in bondage.

But Trim was not so easily dispossessed of his life and he lashed out with his claws to the demonic, bloodshot eyes of the miserable villain and rendered him sightless, no doubt condemned to wander blindly for several days. With a scream of anguish, the convict allowed Trim to fall to the ground and escape, though Trim did so by walking away with dignity, tail flicking in anger at such a gross attempt to humiliate him. He could hear the jeers and laughter of the men now turned upon the evil perpetrator, this time they seemed even more pleased at the merry japes they'd witnessed and the swift comeuppance of their murderous colleague.

And so it was with a modicum of caution that Trim followed the wooders as they went to meet the Indians on the crest of the hill. There was, he observed, little attempt to prepare the muskets as it seemed Mr Whitewood had not informed the men to do so and had simply spoken of taking the precaution to humour Trim. Somewhat to the surprise of the party, the natives stood their ground.

As they drew closer they could see a smile on the face of the leading Indian. 'They seem friendly enough,' Mr Whitewood remarked. 'It is the captain's wish that when the natives appear docile we must return their goodwill and encourage them to visit the ship to receive trinkets.'

The foremost Indian held his wooden spear in such a manner as to suggest that it might be a gift for Mr Whitewood, though Trim did not care for the look in his eye and took a cautionary step to conceal himself behind a clump of spinifex. As the master's mate stretched out his hand to receive the spear, the 'friendly' Indian ran the spear into his breast. Mr Whitewood, with the spear embedded in his chest, raised his firelock and aimed it at his assailant. Though the weapon fired and the range was point-blank, such was the shock of the spear in his chest that the officer missed. Pulling the spear from his chest he retreated, only to receive three more spears to his back and thigh. The men, hastily retreating, and Mr Whitewood, still able to run, attempted to fire upon the natives, but the marines, charged with the protection of the party, had paid scant attention to the preparation of their weapons. It was only after some little while that two were made to fire and the natives fled, taking with them a cabbage-tree hat dropped in haste by one of the crew.

Still, some among them were able to witness how Trim, seeing the spear pierce the chest of Mr Whitewood, flew from where he was hidden and leapt to the shoulders of his assailant, his claws striking lightning blows to the Indian's eyes from behind. The native gave a howl of pain and fell to his backside, clutching at his eyes as Trim made good his getaway. This astonishing act of bravery was to be seen the next day, in circumstances I will shortly tell you about.

Mr Whitewood was carried aboard and the prompt attention of the ship's surgeon saved his life. It was most fortunate that the Indians, unlike those of South America, applied no poison to the tips of their spears and thus his life was saved. But not so lucky was a marine by the name of Thomas Morgan, who had foolishly left the ship without his hat and suffered what at that time was known as *coup-de-soleil*, but which we call sunstroke, and he died in a frenzy that same night.

It was not in the nature of the British navy to tolerate such a mischievous and unprovoked attack, so a party was sent out to hunt for the Indians who had wounded Mr Whitewood. Trim was most severely told to remain on board, Matthew Flinders having heard somewhat of his derring-do, though privately putting this down to the exaggeration normal to members of the crew when talking about Master Trim.

At sunset they came upon three Indians who immediately took to a canoe at the water's edge. Wasting no time to inquire whether they belonged to the same group as those involved in the attack earlier in the day, they fired on the natives who were paddling furiously for the mainland. One of the Indians was seen to drop while the other two dived from the canoe and swam strongly for the distant shore.

'Hooray!' shouted a seaman, 'It is my shot that got the bugger!' Whereupon he immediately plunged into the water and swam for the canoe. Reaching it, he boarded to find a dead Indian and also the cabbage-tree hat that had been lost earlier. By some strange circumstance it proved to be the seaman's own. He placed it on his head and standing up in the canoe hailed the shore, 'A dead Indian and my hat returned to me!' he yelled with such enthusiasm that he capsized the canoe, tipping the dead native into the water as well as himself.

The canoe was later rescued, but they had to wait until morning when the tide washed the body of the dead Indian to shore. It was then that they all witnessed proof of Trim's courage on the previous day. The seaman's musket ball had passed through the native's heart, a neat hole that left him otherwise undamaged. The man lay with one arm across his face and when this was lifted there was a gasp from the men, the dead man's eyes were greatly damaged, the lids scratched and torn as were the eyes themselves. This was the testimony of Trim's bravery for all on board to witness and it became part of a legend, a tale seamen still tell whenever the merit of a ship's cat is raised.

The body was taken to the boat for scientific purposes, the ship's surgeon wishing to dissect the corpse for anatomical reasons. The shipboard artist, Mr Westall, wished also to record the body and features for comparison with the natives found in other parts of this vast and primitive land. In his sketch he was most careful not to show the wounds to the chest and neck or the scratching to the eyes, although he showed the eyes closed whereas in death they should have been wide staring open.

Of immediate interest to Captain Flinders himself was that the body had been circumcised and had lost the upper front tooth on the left side whereas with the natives of Port Jackson it was the upper tooth on the right that was knocked out at puberty.

My dear Ryan, you are probably finding much of this tedious, it happened such a long time ago and the dangers present today are so very different to those faced by Matthew Flinders and the inestimable Trim. But as you grow older you will see that danger is an element in our present lives that has very little to do with an outcome decided by musket ball or spear. The danger we face today is that we lack the confidence or even the permission to act bravely by listening to our consciences. The real bravery in today's world is doing for each other what is right and proper. In the end, this courage is far more powerful than the spear or the musket, the stealth bomber or the nuclear weapon.

Billy was conscious that in writing to Ryan about bravery he was the perfect example of the cowardice he was showing. He didn't quite know how to tell the young lad that he was aware of his gutless behaviour and that Ryan should see him for the unreliable and cowardly creature that he was. More and more, he was recognising his own shortcomings and his own lack of the virtues he was writing about. He wondered if he should quit writing for he was increasingly feeling the hypocrisy behind his moralising. The letter had taken a turn he'd never intended and it was as if it was being dictated by some inner self with whom he needed to make contact. After some thought he decided to continue, though not without real misgivings.

At your age, the lack of loyalty and bravery of conscience may be as difficult to understand as it was for Trim when he was shipwrecked. Trim was a seagoing cat and his first loyalty was always to his crew and then to all the sailors afloat. They were a fraternity of brothers, men who faced the same hardships, cast asunder from the land, they placed their trust in each other when in distress. This is the law of the sea and it has ever been so.

But now of the shipwreck. The *Investigator*, worn out and no longer reliable for the purposes of circumnavigation, had returned to Port Jackson for lighter work. As there was no suitable vessel to replace her it was decided that Matthew Flinders would leave for England to obtain another ship to complete his work of charting Terra Australis. He was to sail under the command of one of his own officers, Lieutenant Fowler, and with many of his former crew, to England where he would report to the Admiralty. The vessel chosen for Lieutenant Fowler was the *Porpoise*, a ship well overdue for a refit. It had been brought from Van Diemen's Land where it had been employed in coastal work. The sailor in Trim wasn't at all happy with this arrangement and thought the *Porpoise* ill-suited for the voyage to England, having seen out the best of her days at sea. He made his opinion known to Captain Flinders by rushing ahead of him while the inspection of repairs took place and pointing out with much meowing those parts of the old tub which were not to his liking.

Matthew Flinders shared Trim's anxiety and on one occasion had thrown up his arms, 'Trim, thou art correct in thy survey, but we have no choice, England prepares for war against France and all His

Majesty's seaworthy warships are gathered in England, this old gunpowder trap is all they have available for us to use to sail back home. Alas, if the war were to take place in these antipodean lands, then the use of my charts would allow us to command the latest man o' war, but the coast of Europe is well charted and we must be happy with this mended old bucket well past her fighting days.' He had stroked Trim to reassure him, 'There are much worse sailing the seven seas, my friend. The *Porpoise*, at the least, is not leaky nor crank and, given fair weather, will do us well, what say you, eh?'

Trim, with a cat's instinct for survival, wasn't too keen to put another of his nine lives to the test but he had no choice, he was obliged to go wherever his master went. But he was not a happy pussycat. He had climbed the *Porpoise*'s mast to find it was too short and thought her beam too narrow and she creaked to his ears like the bones of an old lady.

On the 10th of August 1803, the *Porpoise* sailed down the harbour and through the heads accompanied by two merchant vessels, both bound for Batavia as their first port of call. They had asked permission to sail with the *Porpoise* as they were anxious to test the Torres Strait, a shorter passage first charted in the *Investigator*. Flinders was only too pleased to have them along, as it would give him the opportunity to prove the advantages of this new route and so bring it into general use. Captain Palmer was master of the *Bridgewater*, a ship of 750 tons, and Mr John Park commanded the *Cato*, a smaller ship of 450 tons.

Billy was becoming increasingly aware that if Ryan had been present and seated on his skateboard while he told the story, he would have omitted some of the detail which might prove tedious to the youngster. Billy, a keen sailor in his better days, had sailed in the Sydney to Hobart yacht race on six occasions and, like all serious yachtsmen, found it almost impossible to leave out what others might think of as superfluous detail. It was, he knew, self-indulgence and he told himself he intended to make a clean copy and would leave out the nautical bits 'n' pieces.

All went to plan for the first two days and on the morning of the third day they sighted a sandbank but continued on all day and by nightfall were thirty-five miles (50 km) from it with a good depth of water under them. Lieutenant Fowler decided they were well clear and, rather than lose sailing time, they would run through the night under easy working sail. With the topsails double-reefed and a fresh breeze blowing, all seemed well enough. The night was cloudy and visibility slightly down, though not too badly so there was no cause for concern. The *Porpoise*, with the two merchant ships on either side a good distance away but with their lights clearly showing, was making steady progress when suddenly the master of the watch shouted from the quarterdeck, 'Breakers ahead! White water!'

Trim rushed to the quarterdeck rail to confirm the sighting. There it was, a surf crashing in the half-light against an invisible shore. The helm was immediately put down, the intention to tack away from the crashing waves, but with the topsails double-reefed they lacked the canvas to pull the vessel around. 'Oh my God!' thought Trim, 'there goes another one of my poor lives!' For he was too good a sailor not to know what would happen next.

And happen it did, the sails were shaking in the wind with the ship being pulled towards the huge breakers fifty metres away and in less than a minute the *Porpoise* was among them. Then came a mighty thump as the ship hit the coral reef and immediately heeled on her larboard beam ends. Men clung on desperately and there was a great deal of yelling out. 'Fire a gun! Fire a gun to warn the other ships,' Matthew Flinders shouted. But the surf roared over them and threw men every which way so that the firing of the small cannon was impossible. Then the foremast crashed down and was carried away, another bump followed and the bottom stove in and the *Porpoise* started taking in water.

'Bring up the lights!' shouted Lieutenant Fowler, 'We must warn the other vessels with our lights!' But before the lights could be brought up, Trim saw that the two merchant ships, the *Bridgewater* and the *Cato*, had both realised the danger to themselves and moved each on the opposite tack, 'Holy puss 'n' boots!' Trim meowed, 'They're going to collide!'

The men on the *Porpoise*, drenched from the spume and spray as the breakers broke over the ship's beam, watched as the two merchant vessels drew closer to each other. If they collided, as it now seemed they must, there could be no rescue for the men on the *Porpoise*. Even Trim held his breath and closed his eyes as the two ships were about to ram. By some miracle of the deep they passed each other, their hulls lightly touching but moving each away from the other. 'Hooray, we are saved!' someone shouted, but moments later they saw the *Cato*, the lighter of the two merchant vessels, caught in the breakers two hundred and fifty metres away. She fell onto her broadside and her masts immediately disappeared in the white water. With her profile no longer set against the sky, she was now too far away to be seen in the darkness.

Trim was drenched but unafraid, he could swim if he must and beyond the breakers there would be a shoreline. The *Bridgewater* is still safe, she will rescue us, he thought, she's big enough to take us all if we should survive. Just then the *Bridgewater*'s lights came on at her masthead, this to show she had cleared the reef. 'Hallelujah, we are saved!' the bosun, a religious man, shouted 'Praise be to the Mighty Redeemer, we have been snatched from the darkness of the sea!' It was thought by all that it was only a question of time before the *Bridgewater* would tack and send boats to their rescue.

In the meantime Matthew Flinders was in a fine pickle, he had missed Trim and thought he might have been washed overboard. 'Trim! Trim! Where art thou?' he shouted, looking wildly about and making inquiry of all. Whereupon Trim hurled himself from the quarterdeck, a wet and soggy pussycat, landing with a lightness of tread precisely on his master's right shoulder. 'The *Bridgewater* is not coming to our assistance!' he meowed into his master's ear.

'Steady on, Master Trim, it is night and too dangerous, she will come at first light, any good ship's master would not risk his ship in the darkness.'

Trim knew that Matthew Flinders would not have waited for the dawn but would have set about the rescue while taking all necessary caution. He had once caught sight of Captain E. H. Palmer Esq. on the Quay at Port Jackson and had noted the shiftiness of his expression, his eyes were dull as soaked raisins and he was observed treating two of his seamen aboard the *Bridgewater* in a decidedly churlish manner.

Well, what a night for one and all it turned out to be! Though some good fortune favoured them, the *Porpoise* had not foundered in a storm and, furthermore, had heeled towards the reef so that the incoming surf now crashed against her turned-up side and flew high over her decks and hadn't the strength to wash anything very much off them into the sea. The boats were intact and the smooth water under the leeward side looked promising enough to attempt to launch them.

Beyond the breakers there seemed to be clear water, for they had struck a reef and not the shore. In terms of good seamanship and given good light, all the *Bridgewater* needed to do was to sail until she found a break in the reef to move through. If no suitable passage could be found, then she could sail to the end of the reef, anchor and send her longboats into the tranquil water on the far side of the breakers. After which, it would be a simple task to row to the rescue of the *Porpoise* and the *Cato*.

Matthew Flinders volunteered to take a gig, a light boat for rowing, with the intention of marking a possible course and then communicating it to the *Bridgewater*. It was Trim's expectation that he would go along, but his master, ever fearful of his safety, denied him this passage. 'Master Trim, I must needs swim and it is not safe, lad.'

Trim was not amused, Matthew Flinders was aware that he could swim, for often, when a kitten, he had become so taken with playing and jumping that he'd been thrown overboard by his own enthusiasm and while the crew set about his rescue he had discovered he could swim. Once or twice as an adult cat the hawser line had jerked suddenly while Trim was in the process of going ashore and he'd plummeted into the sea, only to swim to the Quay with calm dexterity.

Sensing Trim's disappointment, his master said, 'These surfs pounding upon the reef are cruel and I vouch too strong for such as me,

I cannot take the chance, for your life is most precious to me, Master Trim.' He could see Trim remained unconvinced and so he added, 'There is responsibility sufficient to attempt this rescue, with thy safety added to my concerns the burden would be too great for me to bear.'

Trim was not a cat who sulked and so he hid his disappointment, for he would rather have been consigned to Davy Jones's locker in the arms of his master than live to a ripeness of age without him. He would have gladly sacrificed what remained of his nine lives, but must needs follow his master's orders for Trim was a master mariner cat and lived by his captain's commands.

At first a six-oared cutter was lowered but she was immediately caught up in the roaring surf and thrown against the sheet anchor and damaged, filling with water. Flinders then proposed a four-oared gig and this was duly cast, though well clear of the ship so that the incoming waves would not also damage it.

Captain Flinders, with four oarsmen selected by Lieutenant Fowler as able to swim, dived into the sea and swam towards the gig. Once seated in the boat, Matthew Flinders discovered that only three men had boarded. The fourth, thinking it too risky, had remained on board the ship. Furthermore, two of the four oars in the smaller boat were of the wrong selection. Then, to add to his frustration, Matthew Flinders discovered three stowaways crouched under the thwarts, the armourer, the cook and a marine.

'Damn thy eyes! What are you doing here?' Matthew Flinders cried out.

It was the armourer who spoke first, 'We are done for, sir! That is, if we remain on the *Porpoise*. She will break up soon and we cannot swim, the three of us. It is far better a chance we take to find the shore with thee than to wait for our certain destruction.'

'Fools! Bumpkins! I go to find a passage past the surfs to rescue us all! There is no shore but a coral reef, we row towards the *Bridgewater* as it is not my purpose to save my own skin, nor yours, while others are in danger!' Matthew Flinders was very angry, but there was no time to deal with the men at that moment and, besides, he was not master of the *Porpoise*. 'Can you row?' Flinders sighed, thinking them at least in this respect useful.

'No, sir, as you are well acquainted, we are not seamen, but armourer and marine and myself a cook,' one of them replied.

'I have a good mind to tip thee overboard and let thee drown,' Matthew Flinders said, greatly annoyed at this new inconvenience. The delay in getting them back on board the *Porpoise* would be too great and so he was obliged to take this useless human cargo along with him.

With Matthew Flinders himself manning one of the inadequate oars, they made for the surf, and were fortunate to catch an incoming wave which swept them on to the clear water. The only problem being that, in the process, they had taken enough water aboard to nearly sink the gig.

'You must bale or we are sunk,' Matthew Flinders told the three stowaways.

'There is no baling bucket, sir!' said the useless marine.

'For God's sake, man! Use thy hat and shoes, but get to it lively if you wish to save your miserable hides!'

Baling furiously with hat and boot and keeping sight of the *Bridgewater*'s lights, they rowed towards the rescue ship. The ship was standing to the leeward and Flinders soon saw that any attempt to get near her before she tacked would be fruitless, with two oars not working as well as they might, and in the now overloaded boat, even when the *Bridgewater* tacked, the seas would be too strong to reach her on the windward tide.

Matthew Flinders turned furiously to the three stowaways, his frustration plain. 'Your presence has denied what chance we had to make this rescue, you are scoundrels and have much to answer for!' Although, when daylight came he realised that the attempt to reach the *Bridgewater* had been prompted more by the desperation of their circumstances than by the practical application of seamanship.

Matthew Flinders decided they would see out the night between the *Porpoise* and the *Bridgewater*. This he decided for two reasons, in morning's light he would be in a position to guide the boats from the merchant ship towards the stricken vessel or, if the *Porpoise* should break up, he was ready to take what crew he could to the distant shore beyond the reef. He observed how Lieutenant Fowler burned blue lights every half hour from the *Porpoise* so that the *Bridgewater* would not lose sight of their presence, but at around two o'clock in the morning the lights of the *Bridgewater* were lost to them. The young lieutenant put this down to a slight shifting of the other vessel's position and thought no further of it. The *Porpoise* was in calm conditions and there now seemed little chance that she would break up before daylight came.

In the time available until dawn and in case a further flooding was to come, Fowler had worked his crew hard to fashion a large raft from the spare topmasts and yards and any timber he could employ for this purpose. To it, he attached short lengths of rope so when the raft was launched it would carry a full load while dragging members of the crew along by means of holding fast to the ropes. On the raft was lashed a barrel of water and provisions enough to see them through until the *Bridgewater* effected their rescue and then he added a sextant and the *Investigator*'s precious logbooks.

Matthew Flinders had also seen the lights of the *Bridgewater* fade from sight, but his mind was not as easily put at rest as had been the case with Lieutenant Fowler. He started to plan a rescue that did not take the *Bridgewater* into consideration.

The men in the small gig were drenched and miserable, a fresh wind blew from the south-east and they became very cold. Matthew Flinders, despite his growing doubts but observing their consternation, assured them of their rescue by the *Bridgewater* in the morning. He pointed out that from the decks of the *Porpoise* he had seen several breaks in the reef where the water seemed deep enough to allow the rescue vessel to run to the leeward, and there anchor or lie. After this it would be a simple matter to send her boats to their rescue. The three oarsmen were considerably cheered by this prospect and while the stowaways were not consulted, they too sat with backs straightened and baled with renewed energy whenever a wave splashed across the sides of the gig.

The story of the unfortunate *Cato* that had so narrowly escaped collision when approaching the *Bridgewater* on opposite tacks was to come out later. As it happened, it was Captain Park of the *Cato* who, by means of astute seamanship, had avoided the prospect of the two ships colliding and being carried together onto the reef. By not continuing to set his mainsail, he bore away to the leeward, allowing the *Bridgewater* to tack and avoid the impending breakers. But the *Cato* herself was then placed in mortal danger. Unable to tack herself, she struck the reef upon the point of a great rock that drove in under the larboard chess tree.

The unfortunate vessel, unlike the *Porpoise*, fell over to windward where her decks were exposed to the thundering waves driving hard and fierce onto the reef. In a short time her decks were ripped and thrown about and her hold torn open so that everything was washed away. The only place left for the crew was the larboard fore-channel where they crowded together to survive against the furious sea.

Of the two wrecked ships the *Cato* was in the greater predicament, for every time the sea struck her she was twisted about on the unpitying rock with such violence that all who clung to her expected the stern, already below the waterline, to part and they would be thrown into the waves. Furiously they clung to whatever remained of the vessel, some lashing themselves to the timber heads so if the next wave should carry them away, the roaring surfs would drive them to some distant shore. Others clung to the chain plates and the dead eyes, and even some, the one to the other, so that as shipmates they might drown together. And always the thin thread of their hope remained attached to the chance of rescue by the *Bridgewater*, which they had so gallantly saved at their own expense.

And so Captain Park, a religious man, prayed vehemently that the Almighty, who controlled both the firmament and all the creatures below it, would show them mercy.

At dawn's light Matthew Flinders faced the spume-flecked waves again and, with a frantic baling from his three stowaways, crossed the roaring surf to reach the *Porpoise*. Here, he and his crew clambered across the fallen masts to find themselves once more on board. Despite the despair at being wrecked, there was a great deal of rejoicing, for all had thought the gig lost.

'See there, sir!' shouted one of the oarsmen, a man named John Robertson, who, having climbed from the gig and mounted a fallen mast, pointed to where an albatross, its great wings lazy in the pewter-coloured morning sky, circled the stricken ship, 'We have the wings of good fortune above us!'

Trim was among the first to welcome his master's return by leaping into his arms. His normally glossy fur was wet and much bedraggled, but he made up for this with the loudness of his purring, which warmed the cockles of his master's heart.

Daylight revealed that the *Bridgewater*, though now under sail, still stood towards the reef. It also showed a sandbank beyond the reef no more than a half-mile distant that was large enough to receive them all while they waited for rescue. With the water and provisions saved, it was thought no great task to achieve the safety of its beach.

Matthew Flinders found himself well pleased that he had agreed to the suggestion that the two merchant vessels accompany the *Porpoise*. While the *Cato*, like the *Porpoise*, was lost, they would nevertheless be saved by the presence of the *Bridgewater*. He silently castigated himself for his unseemly thoughts regarding the intentions of Captain Palmer.

And then, unaccountably, the *Bridgewater* disappeared across the horizon. Waiting only for daylight, she had sailed away, leaving them to their fate.

The crew watched as the *Bridgewater* dipped below the horizon and they could scarcely credit their eyes. Surely she would tack and then return? The wreck of the *Porpoise* as well as that of the *Cato* was not the work of a fierce storm where all was clearly lost in the fury of an angry and destructive sea. They had foundered on a coral reef, which would always suppose that some might survive such an encounter. Any master in charge of a vessel at sea would find himself beholden to make an attempt at rescue if such should save but one life.

Daylight showed quite clearly that Captain Palmer would not place his ship at risk by crossing or circumnavigating the reef. Once crossed, the water beyond was calm and deep. Such an action did not call for extraordinary valour nor even seamanship of a high quality. The weather was benign and the *Bridgewater* was sturdy, well canvassed and so easy to sail, not so large that she would risk striking the sides of several available channels that breached the reef. After which, rescue would have been a matter of routine.

However, there was no time for consternation, at that time of the year the weather could turn quickly and the sooner they reached land the better. Unless Palmer had returned to Port Jackson to report their mishap, they were in a great deal of trouble. Though, after only a moment's reflection, it became obvious that he would not do so. The first question the governor would ask was the most obvious, 'Why, sir, did you not effect the rescue yourself?' Furthermore, the Torres Strait was a seagoing passage only just charted and not yet used by other vessels, so there was no likelihood that they would be discovered by a passing ship. Palmer had knowingly left them to die.

Preparation was now made to launch the raft and the boats to get to the safety of the sandbank as soon as possible. Matthew Flinders had earlier gone out in the gig once again and returned to say that the bank, though free of any vegetation, had the eggs of sea birds scattered upon it with some close to the waterline, so that it must be safe and its major parts above the high-water mark.

The two cutters and the gig were then sent to check what had happened to the *Cato*. They were seen by the crew of the second wreck while some distance off and greeted with loud cheers. The men still clung to the masthead and other convenient appendages but now they launched themselves willy-nilly into the sea. Swimming or clinging to any piece of plank or spar they could find, they made their way to the rescue boats. Captain Park was the last to climb aboard, having ascertained that all his men, but for three young lads who were drowned in the attempt, had been safely rescued.

Captain Park later spoke of one of these unfortunate lads, a boy named Tom Turtlewood. The *Cato* had been the fourth voyage he had made to sea and he had been shipwrecked on each occasion. Throughout the night he had declared his presence that of a Jonah. He was, he lamented, the reason for their misfortune.

The master of the *Cato* had tried to comfort the poor lad, who was beside himself with grief. 'Steady, lad, thou art no more Jonah than I. You must ask yourself, "Is there another Tom Turtlewood aboard the *Porpoise*?" For she too is wrecked. Many a calm voyage you shall have before you hang your hat beside some quiet hearth. Dame Fortune, like all her female kind, both smiles and frowns, each is a part of every sailor's life. Cheer up, boy, you have had an over-share of the bad, henceforth thou can expect more than a fair measure of the good.' And then, to cheer the lad, he sang to him a ditty much loved by the costermongers of London which he had learned from a servant girl when himself a child.

Duck-legged Dick had a donkey
And his lush loved much for to swill.
One day he got rather lumpy,
And got sent seven days to the mill.
His donkey was taken to the green-yard
A fate which he never deserved.
Oh! It was such a regular mean yard
That alas! The poor moke got starved.
Oh! Bad luck it can't be prevented,

Fortune she smiles or she frowns,
He's best off that's contented,
To mix, sirs, the ups and the downs.

Soon the entire crew had learned the words and throughout the night someone would begin the chorus and others would join in, the men singing as they clung for their lives. So when the cutter from the *Porpoise* was seen approaching, Captain Park turned to Tom Turtlewood, 'Lad, you shall come with me, we will share the same broken spar and whatever fortune holds, it will be the same for each.'

They had jumped into the sea together and were immediately overcome by a wave that broke over them, the spar swirling about and dipping briefly beneath the thunderous sea and then shortly resurfacing, but minus Tom Turtlewood, who had lost his grip and was never seen again. Of the two other young lads, the sad story of their final moments was never witnessed.

At low water, about two o'clock in the afternoon, the reef was dry and the able-bodied men from both crews worked feverishly to get all the provisions and water they might onto the reef and then to the distant sandbank. By five o'clock in the afternoon, with the men weary beyond all possible belief, they had transported five half-hogsheads of water, some flour, salted meat, rice and a half-hogshead of spirits to the safety of the sandbank.

With no ship to command, the seniority fell to Matthew Flinders who took control, though with the willing consent of Captain Park and Lieutenant Fowler. A most tricky question had arisen. While the men from the *Porpoise* belonged to the British navy and so remained under the command of the senior officer present, this did not pertain to the crew of the *Cato*. When a merchant ship is lost, the seamen not only cease to be paid but they also lose all wages due to them after leaving their last port of call. Matthew Flinders was now faced with men over whom he had no legal command and who could do as they wished without fear of prosecution or punishment.

However, it was a problem to be embraced in the morning, for the ninety-four men saved, many of them bruised and cut by the coral, were too tired to stand much less think of a reason to revolt, and they fell asleep on the beach, even though some had not eaten for a night and a day.

Trim was glad to rub himself dry in the warm sand and set off immediately to explore. It didn't take him long to realise that he had landed in the middle, so to speak, of the proverbial jam pot. Birds' nests abounded and in many of them fledglings chirped and quarrelled, each of which would serve him as a complete dinner. There might also be an occasional fish to vary his diet so he knew he wouldn't starve. He returned to the encampment about nine o'clock to find his master already asleep and, curling up into his arms, he too fell to slumbering under a fresh-risen moon.

After breakfast Matthew Flinders stood the men to, though six of the *Cato*'s crew, sore and battered, their limbs stiffened from the night's sleep, seemed reluctant to take a part in the muster and sat to one side with their backs to the rest of the men. Flinders had feared as much, he knew that the only authority he had at his command was his strength of character. To argue at this point would not serve him well and so he held back, knowing that tension was as much on his side as it was against the recalcitrant crewmen.

The master of the *Investigator* knew that if they were to be saved a collective discipline was necessary and it was his duty to impose it on both crews. This was a contest of wills he dare not lose and he was aware that in such cases it is often a single moment that may count for victory or defeat.

It was at such a moment that Trim took charge. Dried and fluffed, his obsidian coat gleaming in the morning sun, his four white paws as neat as a guardsman's gloves, the star upon his chest equal in brilliance to a burst of shining light, he leapt within the small half-circle of resistance. With his tail held high at the vertical, his legs stiff, his chest thrust out, he paraded before the six men, inspecting each as if he were judging their merits in preparation for some reward. Then he proceeded to jump over each, twisting in the air. In passing, he flicked off the second man's cabbage-tree hat and finally landed with all four paws perfectly balanced atop the head of the last. The men burst into laughter and, with their former resistance now trapped into laughter by this very clever cat, they joined the rest of their comrades, shaking their heads in wonder that they had been so simply charmed. Trim, congratulating them for their repentance, stroked against their legs and purred.

'Aye, welcome, gentlemen,' said Captain Flinders, then after a pause, he added, 'We have a simple enough rule here on Wreck Reef, those from the *Cato* who would share His Majesty's provisions should be willing to work with us to make our predicament as bearable as is possible under the circumstances.'

Thus, by giving his authority to Trim's clowning, Flinders had established his leadership and added earnestness to his intention to keep them alive and ultimately effect their rescue. Yet he had not threatened them, allowing their stomachs to do the talking for him, starvation being a harder taskmaster than any authority Matthew Flinders might invoke in the name of the King. Though Matthew Flinders preferred to deal with his men by appealing to their intelligence, he was not afraid to exert discipline if he thought it necessary. On one occasion, shortly after they had landed on the sandbank, one of the men from the *Porpoise*, an ex-convict whose freedom Flinders had personally requested from Governor King, was guilty of misconduct and so he was tied to the flagstaff and the articles of war read before he was severely flogged. It became immediately clear to all that Captain Flinders, who ruled with a light hand, could also bring it down most heavily when required.

There was little to recommend the sandbank other than that it had provided them with safety from the sea. No plant or tree or blade of grass destroyed the baldness of the sea-washed sand and only a few clumps of saltbush could be observed. There was no natural shade and the sun beat down on the white sand to blind the eyes. Those who had lost their hats made new ones from scraps of canvas and all were made busy constructing tents. A spar was used as a flagpole and the blue ensign was hoisted to its top and turned with the jack upside down to indicate their parlous state.

All this, of course, took several days, but as the weather remained mostly benign with some evening rainfall to replenish their water supply and the seine cast out to bring in a good feed of fish, mostly bream, the men felt not entirely forsaken. Matthew Flinders knew that the greatest problem they would face would be as the days wore on. With little to do, they would become despondent and thereafter quarrelsome. And so he made clear his plans to them all.

'There is no chance of rescue from outside and so I propose that we rescue ourselves by firstly sending one of the cutters to Sandy Cape, sixty-three leagues distant, and from there along the coast to Port Jackson,' he declared.

There followed a look of disbelief in the eyes of some of the men, while others looked to the ground and shook their heads. There were experienced seamen among them who knew that at this time of the year strong winds prevailed from the south that would carry the cutter away from the shore, and the likelihood of a favourable outcome was small.

'Cap'n Flinders, some of us know you learned your skill of navigation from Cap'n Bligh hisself and we do not doubt that you are his equal, but you cannot fight the wind from the south with so slight a boat and the small amount of canvas she can be made to carry,' said Thomas Kirstin, a master mariner who had sailed with both Bligh and then with Flinders on the *Investigator*. He was holding his hat in both hands and cupped to his knees while he said this.

'Aye, Thomas, thou art correct in this, it will be difficult, that much I'll grant you, but not impossible. If you volunteer to accompany me I shall show you how it might be done.'

'Yes, sir, cap'n, but if we are perchance lost?'

'Ah, the Doubting Thomas is always with us!' Flinders quipped, then grew serious. 'And this is how it should be, one plan is not sufficient, we must have more than one cat in the bag.' Trim thought this an unnecessarily familiar remark but chose, under the circumstances, to forgive his master. 'There are sufficient carpenters and skilled men to build two boats from what we may salvage from both wrecks, two small decked boats with sail sufficient to navigate under difficult weather conditions. These we will commence immediately and will require all hands to the labour. We will build them large enough to take you all, with only one boat's crew (four men) and an officer left behind to be later rescued.'

'Why would we not take all, sir?' came a voice from the back.

Matthew Flinders smiled, 'I have every hope of getting to Port Jackson in the cutter, but if after two months no rescue ship has arrived for thee, you will know we were lost, so you will proceed in the two boats to Port Jackson with a good chance of success. But nothing is certain and in three months the prevailing winds will change and take the remaining cutter and the crew we leave behind to Port Jackson with almost certain success.'

Matthew Flinders could see that they could not follow his logic, why not have everyone on the two boats?

'You force my hand, gentlemen, I confess there is part logic and part lively emotion in my reasoning.' He paused, looking, it seemed, into the eyes of every man assembled. 'Of the logic, it is my contention that of three attempts to rescue ourselves, one must succeed. Putting logic aside for a moment so that I may express my innermost feelings, you would not be in this predicament were it not for the perfidy of one man who, without conscience, left you all to die on this reef. What happened to us must be spoken of. I am determined that there are some who will remain to bear witness to this man's crime against his fellows. I swear to you all that, while breath remains in my body, the name Captain E. H. Palmer must forever remain a blasphemy on my lips and I charge you to do the same. Should only one of us remain to tell the tale, let him bear witness, so that as long as men go down in ships to the sea they will damn this coward and condemn him to the everlasting fires of hell!'

Trim thought this a capital speech, one of his master's better efforts, he wished only that he could meet the miscreant Palmer and give him the white-claw treatment by thoroughly boxing his eyes.

There was a roar of approval from the men and then three cheers for Captain Flinders was called out. 'Don't thee worry, sir. We will build two stout ships to take us back where all can tell the tale!' the ship's chief carpenter announced. And so the men were put to work, cheerful that by means of their own hands, they would rescue themselves and that each of them now carried in his heart this story of infamy that would last forever in the minds of men. It gave them great comfort to think that whatsoever should happen, the despicable coward Palmer would never again raise his head high among men who sail the seven seas.

I am sure, Ryan, you would like to know what happened to the coward, Captain Palmer? So I will digress for a few minutes to tell you that part of the story. It is always the case with the moral coward that he attempts to justify his actions. In plain language, he makes excuses for his behaviour. The curious thing about excuses of this sort is that not even the gullible believe them. In their hearts even the most contemptuous villains know right from wrong when they have committed a cowardly act or when they hear of one.

So, naturally, Captain Palmer, having sailed to Batavia and then on to Bombay, had plenty of time to construct a story that suited his version of the events. Now, think about this, in Bombay there would be no possible knowledge of the wreck taking place. Only Palmer and his crew knew of the circumstances and so he had no need to tell anyone until months later when he reported to his owners in England. But he couldn't get the story out fast enough. Not the real story, of course, but his much thought-out and reworked version. He had changed this fact a little and that one a little more, bending and twisting the story to suit his purpose, so that by gradual degrees he strayed from the truth while sounding plausible and fair-minded. He ended it by saying how he had suffered and in his own words said he was filled with the '*most painful reflections on the suffering of the shipwrecked [about whom] . . . it was too late, had it been in our power to give any assistance*'. He had written the events of the night and the morning following with an eye to his own vindication and when he berthed in Bombay on the 3rd of

February 1804, five and a half months after deserting the *Cato* and the *Porpoise*, the first thing he did was to send his written version of the events directly to the newspapers.

But as so often happens when cowards try to justify their actions there are honest witnesses who are willing to reveal the truth. The third mate of the *Bridgewater* wrote in his journal of the events at Wreck Reef. Let us hear now how it seemed to those on the deck of the *Bridgewater* from Mr Williams' journal. He is speaking of the morning after the night when the two shipwrecked vessels had observed the *Bridgewater* under sail and this is what he wrote:

> *At half-past seven a.m. (Aug. 18) saw the reef on our weather bow, and from the masthead we saw the two ships, and to the leeward of them a sandbank. The weather abated much, we set all our sails and every man rejoiced that they should have it in their power to assist their unfortunate companions . . . The ships were very distinctly to be seen from aloft, and also from the deck; but instead of rendering them any succour, the captain ordered the ship to be put on the other tack, and said it was impossible to render them any relief.*
>
> *What must be the sensations of each man at that instant? Instead of proceeding to the support of our unfortunate companions, to leave them to the mercy of the waves, without knowing whether they were in existence or had perished! From the appearance of the wrecks there was every probability of their existing; and if any survived at the time we were within sight, what must have been their sensations on seeing all their anxious expectations of relief blasted?*

Well, my dear Ryan, truth seems always to find a way of wriggling through even the most closely knit fabric of a lie. Of all the people Captain Palmer should choose to deliver his carefully written lies to the newspaper, he chose Mr Williams.

Now here is an interesting point for you to consider. Does Mr Williams stay loyal to his captain? Or does he show true bravery of conscience, the kind of bravery I talked about earlier? You see, all our actions, good or bad, have a consequence and often the consequence of telling the truth is seemingly not the best outcome for the person with the courage. For instance, if the third mate, Mr Williams, told the truth he would lose his job and the pay due to him and find himself in a strange country with little prospect of finding a ship back to England. If he kept his mouth shut, he would be safe and even if it did come out later that Captain Palmer had behaved in a treacherous way his crew could not be blamed for following his orders. And so you see, telling the truth can be very difficult and it sometimes takes a very brave man to expose a cowardly or criminal one.

But Mr Williams proved to be a truly brave and honourable man and he told the truth of what happened on Wreck Reef and, of course, he lost his job and his wages and even his spare clothes and, if he had a family, he risked being parted from them perhaps for years until he found his way back to England. But there are some men who preserve the higher truths in all of us and prove that while man can be a vile creature, he can also be a noble one.

Now, here is the end of that story. Mr Williams was left on shore with nothing to his name and Captain Palmer sailed away from Bombay bound for Europe with the *Bridgewater*'s holds full of valuable cargo for his masters in the East India Company. But the ship never arrived back in her home port and was never seen again.

Somewhere in the vast ocean the ship went down with all her crew. Captain Palmer died knowing that his name would always be associated with infamy. It must have been a terrible moment when he had to face his conscience, knowing that sailors forever would celebrate his timely death.

Of Matthew Flinders and the crews of the *Porpoise* and the *Cato*, I will tell you more at a later time if you wish. But here are some details in the meantime. The carpenters worked on the larger of the two cutters and fitted her with masts and sail while maintaining her rowlocks and oars so that she could be rowed if needs be. Now a seagoing vessel needed a name and Matthew Flinders christened her *Hope*. In all, fourteen men were to sail with her, two crews of six for rowing, Mr Park the captain of the doomed *Cato* and Trim's master himself. Thomas Kirstin, the master mariner who had earlier doubted the wisdom of the voyage, did not accompany them, his skills too important in the navigation of one of the two ships yet to come.

On the morning of sailing, Trim had gone out early and partaken of a good breakfast of plump fledgling knowing that anything could happen at sea and that a full stomach upon departure was the only certainty. He cleaned his fur, paying particular attention to his snowy paws, and presented himself, ready for departure, at the good ship *Hope*.

It was August the 26th and a glorious day, with the sky cloudless and a light wind blowing from the south. Trim thought that the flimsy vessel, *Hope*, was loaded too deeply but he understood why his master would want to take two crews. If the southerly blew strongly from the shore, it would need two crews taking turns at the oars to keep the little vessel on her course.

The moment came to launch their perilous expedition and all the men were gathered to witness the departure of the *Hope*. 'I leave you only sufficiently long to bring about our rescue, my good companions,' Flinders said. 'I shall be among you again in a short passage of time. While I am gone, I charge you to complete the task of building two stout vessels and if I do not return in the time I have stipulated you will effect your own rescue. May God be with us all.'

Just then a seaman quit the crowd and ran to the flagpole where the ensign was flown with the union jack upside down, a signal, first to the long-departed *Bridgewater* of their predicament, and now simply as a sign of their distress and need of rescue. The seaman lowered the flag and righted it with the union in the customary top left-hand corner. It was a signal to all that they had taken charge of their own destiny and, with God's guidance, would, by their own skill and perseverance, bring themselves back into the fraternity of other men. They would, by their own hand, see their dear ones, their wives and children once again. It was a small gesture of defiance and a grand moment when men condemned to die on a barren sandbank now did spit in the face of the cowards, the Captain Palmers of this world.

'We shall survive!' shouted Matthew Flinders.

'Aye!' shouted the men and then repeated, 'We shall survive!'

Trim jumped into the bow of the cutter as some of the men on shore began to push her from the shallows into deeper water.

'Wait!' Captain Flinders shouted out. The men pushing the boat paused in their endeavours as he picked Trim up and held him to his chest, rubbing his chin into the cat's glossy fur. 'Alas, Master Trim, you cannot accompany me, for we embark on a most hazardous journey.' He stroked poor Trim and sighed, 'I promise I shall, with God's help, return for thee, but now you must be that part of me that remains on Wreck Reef as a symbol that I am gone only a short time.'

In all his life Trim had not experienced so great a disappointment. And now he meowed pitifully, convinced in his heart he would not see his beloved master again. 'Take me with thee, I beg,' he meowed, 'I would willingly sacrifice what remain of my nine lives, some six, I think, and these pledge to thee. Please, master, I beg thee, let me be a comfort and a support on your voyage so that together we face our single destiny?'

But Matthew Flinders shook his head sorrowfully. 'Thou must stay, dear Trim. It is thy duty to keep the men in good cheer and, as my surrogate, to supervise the building of two ships and then, if I should not return, to lend thy expertise in seamanship for their own expedition to safety. Is thy name not Master Mariner Trim Flinders? How would they accomplish their journey to Port Jackson without the navigation skills I have taught thee?'

Trim tried very hard to restrain himself and the closest observation of his face showed no emotion, but as for his tail, he could not bring this part of his anatomy to equal good account. It flicked and twitched, held at the vertical, for that is how a cat shows extreme emotion.

Trim leapt from Matthew Flinders' arms and, making small puffs of sand rise as he ran, fled to the furthermost corner of the sandbank where he might be alone to grieve.

The letter to Ryan was never posted. Instead, Billy took it to Nick and watched as the shower attendant fed it into the incinerator. He now realised that the letter had not been intended for Ryan, but was written to himself. The story of Wreck Reef was simply a ploy to get to the central issue, his own weakness, cowardice, disloyalty and irresponsibility, the four things that had destroyed his life. In writing it, Billy O'Shannessy had taken another step in the long process of his own rehabilitation.

CHAPTER NINE

Although Billy had destroyed his letter to Ryan, it had served a purpose beyond simply forcing him to face up to his many shortcomings. It had also given him a tangible reason to stay on the wagon. He told himself repeatedly that if he went back to drinking, it was the equivalent of the *Bridgewater* sailing away into oblivion. While Ryan might live on, as did the ninety-three men on Wreck Reef, his promising young life could well be compromised forever. He'd patently deserted the child, and although there was nobody to report his cowardice, except possibly for Trevor Williams, he knew that unless he attempted to make amends, he could well become the Captain Palmer in Ryan's life.

Billy was aware that, ghastly as the detox had been, the hard part lay ahead. To this point he had simply put himself into the hands of others and his own willpower had not been involved. He'd submitted to and been committed for treatment and the clinic had done the rest. Now he must fight his addiction on a daily basis and this time he must conquer his demons alone. While the detox had allowed him to climb onto the wagon, it was now his responsibility to hang on for dear life on what would prove to be a very bumpy ride.

They had counselled him at Resthaven, suggesting that he undergo a program of rehabilitation. They'd congratulated him and told him that the detox was a noble battle but warned that the war with himself had yet to be won. Again they asked what his motive had been to agree to detoxification and this time he was able to articulate it.

'There is a young lad who is going to need my help.' Billy didn't explain that the young lad wasn't only Ryan, but also Charlie and his own life, past and present. He had been granted a second chance, or perhaps he could even one day be able to claim that he was giving himself one.

Even though Billy's body had been cleansed of alcohol, the psychological pressure to drink was enormous, hardly a minute passed when he didn't think of grog. What his mind simply refused to embrace was the prospect of a life where alcohol didn't play the major part. Billy couldn't imagine not removing the top from a scotch bottle in anticipation of the rush he would get the moment after the golden liquid touched his lips. Our lives are very largely controlled by ritual, they are the habits we form to suit our emotional needs or even to survive the painful process of life, and when they are removed what often follows is psychological trauma resulting in a deep sense of loss.

Billy couldn't stay in the clinic beyond seven days so he

transferred to Stillwaters, a Salvation Army hostel about five kilometres away, where he was able to get a room. This was done very much against the advice of the clinic, who urged him to go on to a rehabilitation program immediately.

Major Turlington had also asked him, almost pleaded, 'Billy, we've cleaned out your system, the alcohol is out of your body, but it's still in your mind, the next few days are critical, you *must* have support.' Several counsellors had joined in, telling him that it was not a matter of willpower, that the psychological craving would override his will.

But Billy remained stubborn. 'I have some thinking to do, I must have a little time to myself,' he insisted.

Quite apart from the horror of the first forty-eight hours, it had been a strange few days in the clinic. He'd found himself overwhelmed. With his body still heavily sedated, he hadn't been able to think beyond the instruction and the talks he was forced to attend, and now he needed time alone to think about his priorities.

On the third day, the day after he'd finally surfaced from the delirium tremens, he'd been placed in a group to learn the rules of the unit. No drinking, no leaving the premises, blah, blah, blah. The only thing Billy had noticed about the group was that, apart from a quick look at his companions, he, like everyone else, sat hunched over, elbows on knees and eyes to the floor. They all had one thing in common, their eyes were turned inwards as they dealt with their own personal demons. He knew he wasn't ready to face the world outside and imagined the others felt much the same. He had never before realised what a shield alcohol provided and he now found himself vulnerable, naked, inadequate and quite incapable of coping with even the simplest details of ordinary life. Had he been made to leave the clinic at that moment he would have headed straight for the pub.

The second day of therapy had consisted of Bible readings, which Billy put down as the price he was required to pay for the tender loving care he'd received. Apart from their obvious sincerity and deep commitment which showed in their daily witnessing for Christ, the Salvos seldom rammed their faith down your throat. Besides, he was still on 60 mg a day of Valium and the Godspeak had seemed rather comforting. It was nice to know that someone up there was going to stretch out His hand and guide him through his darkest hours. Billy had once seen the forefinger of God stretched out to start all of creation in Michelangelo's painting on the ceiling of the Sistine Chapel. Billy could only hope that when the Almighty reached out and took his hand, he wasn't blown away by the first touch of that all-powerful forefinger.

The next day brought collective counselling and held warnings of what lay ahead. Billy soon lost the sound of the instructor's voice and began to think of what it would be like never to taste a drop again. Despite the effect of the Valium, he felt really depressed.

Day four had been more of the same, though this time he had learned about the nature of his addiction. By then the heads had started to rise, the 'calm juice', as Valium was called, was almost out of their systems and they were all, more or less, coming back to real life. The first tentative questions were attempted and soon the evening became a lively discussion that continued until the week ended and Billy was discharged.

During that week at Stillwaters, Billy sent a letter to Trevor Williams.

Dear Trevor,

I trust you are well on the mend by now and are back home with your dear wife. Surfers Paradise was not the best decision I've made, or to put it differently, running away from Sydney was quite wrong and, to say the least, cowardly. I suspect you knew this all along, but were too wise and well-mannered to say so.

However, in one respect it has been good. After making a thorough mess of things and sinking well below my already low expectations of myself, I submitted myself to a detox clinic.

This was not an experience I hope to repeat and I find myself on the wagon for the first time in some thirty-five years. That is, if you don't count the time as a teenager when I stole a regular nip of scotch from my father's liquor cabinet.

I well recall the incident the ever-diminishing level in the bottle provoked. I am ashamed to admit one of our maids, who was Polish, was blamed. My mother believed that, as a foreigner, she was obviously not to be trusted. The poor girl was Jewish and a victim of the Holocaust, which my mother simply didn't believe. She reasoned at the time that the child could only have been eight when

*the war ended and was simply telling a sob story to gain
her sympathy. We now know the story was completely
plausible and that many children did survive the
concentration camps. Anyway, she was promptly
dismissed, even though she had probably never tasted
a drop of scotch in her life. I regret I didn't own up and
the poor girl, her name was Rebecca, who had suffered
so terribly, was once more a victim of racism. This was
probably the first sign of things to come and a tangible
example of my moral turpitude and innate cowardice.*

*I am returning to Sydney as soon as possible where I
hope to undergo further treatment and attempt to make
amends for my recent behaviour. I am submitting myself
for rehabilitation and I don't know how long this process
will take, but once I am out I would like to help you find
your daughter. I am not at all sure that I will be of any use
in the search, but if you are returning to Sydney, as you
suggested you might be, and wish to contact me, you
may do so at the following address:*

The Station
Cnr Erskine and Clarence Streets
Sydney NSW 2000

*In case you have forgotten my surname, it is
O'Shannessy. We were only, I recall, formally introduced
on one occasion with Casper Friendly at the pub. If you
can't make it to Sydney in the next little while, perhaps
you could tell me a little more about your daughter? Her*

*first name as well as any professional name she may have
assumed? Is her surname still Williams? Does she have a
police record? Hospital record? Last address? Childhood
friends? Boyfriend? Known associates? Previous
theatrical booking agent? Can you describe her?
Birthmarks? Scars? Distinguishing features? Nickname?
Any sentimental jewellery she would never part with,
a locket or chain, ring or bracelet? A sample of her
handwriting? Does she have a tattoo? Expressions she
likes to use? Manner of speech, fast, slow, considered,
excited? Is she an introvert, extrovert? In fact, anything
else you think might be useful for me to know.
I greatly look forward to hearing from you.*

Yours sincerely,
Billy

He had also written to Ryan, addressing the letter to the
Pring Street school.

My dear Ryan,

*I am sorry I haven't written to you and I have no real
excuse. Perhaps you will find it in your heart to forgive
me and we can resume our friendship? I would very much
like this to happen. I have given up the grog and will be
returning to Sydney in a week or so. I will leave a message
for you at your school. It may be some time before we can
meet as I am going into the William Booth Institute for*

rehabilitation. Just let me know if you'd like to see me again, I will take it from there.

By the way, I have a new Trim story. It is about a shipwreck where Trim and his crew are left to die on a desert island by a wicked Captain of a ship who could have rescued them. It is a grand story of courage and betrayal and, of course, it is absolutely true.

I hope that you will forgive me for running away and that we can be friends once again. If you would like to write to me, my address is:

The Salvation Army
Foster House
5–21 Mary Street
Strawberry Hills NSW 2010

In the meantime, look after yourself.

Your friend in Trim (the Master Mariner cat and famous explorer),
Billy O'Shannessy (without the 'u')

Billy purchased an overnight bus ticket to Sydney. Arriving at Central Railway Station the following morning, he walked from the terminal to Foster House. He'd only just entered the foyer when he saw Major Cliff Thomas coming towards him.

'Hello, Billy, you must have come in early, we were going to send someone to meet you.'

Billy looked surprised. 'You knew I was coming?'

'Well, hoped, there's many a slip between the bus and the lip,' Thomas quipped. A Welshman, he was ex-British Army and very popular with the men who used Foster House. 'Yes, we knew. Major Turlington gave me a call, said to look out for you, said you'd toughed it out on your own at the hostel after you left the clinic. That can't have been easy.' The Salvo stuck out his hand, 'Well done, congratulations, you've made a great start. Come into my office, let's have a chat.'

The week in the hostel after leaving Resthaven had been hell and the only way Billy had been able to stay out of the pub was to have them lock him in his room and only let him out for meals and to go to the bathroom. The fact that he'd made the bus ride without a bottle was another miracle and Turlington had phoned to say Billy should be met as he didn't know how much longer he would be able to hold out on his own.

In Cliff Thomas's office Billy handed him an envelope which contained his clinical notes from Resthaven and details of his stay. The Salvo major took it, putting it to one side. 'Have you had any breakfast?' he asked.

'Yes, thank you, the bus stopped at McDonald's in Newcastle, I had a cup of coffee and something I think was called McMuffin.'

Thomas laughed. 'Well, I have to say you look more as if you've been hit by a Mack truck than a McMuffin.' He leaned forward and appeared to be looking closely at Billy's face. 'Although that could be a smidgin of white in the corner of each eye. Detox takes a lot out of one. How are you feeling?'

'Not too bad,' Billy replied, although he had hardly

slept on the journey down and had a fierce headache and a stomach pain that had been with him for the past three days. 'Bit of diarrhoea, headache,' Billy grinned. 'I've had hangovers a great deal worse.'

'Ha! Chocolate! I'll bet you've been eating a fair bit?'

Billy smiled. 'It's the craving for something sweet after the detox.'

Thomas laughed. He was around the same age as Billy and it was comfortable talking to him. 'I know what you mean. When I came out of detox, a week later they needed to choco-tox me. How about a cup of tea? Sugar? We'll throw in a couple of Panadol, that'll help, I'll see if we've got something for the squits.'

Billy looked up, surprised, he hadn't realised that Cliff Thomas was a recovered alcoholic. 'Thank you, major, you've given me renewed hope.'

Thomas grinned. 'We all need a bit of that, although you've managed a week on your own, that's remarkable in itself.' He picked up the telephone and asked someone named Kylie to bring in a cup of tea with six sugars and a couple of Panadol and to ask the nurse for something for diarrhoea. Then putting down the receiver, he said, 'Now, how can we help you, Billy?'

At first Billy didn't answer. He'd done a week cold turkey without anyone to help him, but it had nevertheless taken its toll. His nerves were shattered and he didn't know how much more of the same he could take. Now that he had reached the point of changing his life by agreeing to undergo the full journey to rehabilitation, the enormity of what he was attempting struck him. He could feel the panic growing in his stomach. What he was attempting to do, he now saw clearly, was impossible. He felt a sudden and tremendous urge to rise from his seat and leave, run away.

In the past week he had audited his life dozens of times and always with the same bottom line. He was weak, he'd covered it up all his life by being a nice bloke, but underneath he knew he was gutless. How could he possibly think he, of all people, could survive the process of rehabilitation? In the end he would let everyone down. Might as well do that now. *On your bike, Billy, much easier on everyone.* He started to rise . . . *You're sailing away on the* Bridgewater, *Billy,* a second voice cried from deep inside him. He looked at the Salvo major then averted his eyes again. 'I . . . I think I'd like to . . .' but he could go no further.

Cliff Thomas, a big teddy bear of a man, reached over and took Billy's hand. 'Mate, we're all like that, wondering how we can possibly rehabilitate ourselves. Billy, look at me please. Look at me.' Billy, fighting back his tears, reluctantly met the other man's eyes. 'The answer is we can't, but with God's help and one day at a time, we shall,' Thomas said gently.

'I'm a coward. I'm a weak bastard, I don't know if . . .'

'Shush! Don't talk dirty, boyo! We're all weak, but that's not the problem this time. The problem is that you have an illness, a disease, that's what we have to treat. If you had cancer, I mean, think of it like this, imagine I'm your doctor, okay?' Thomas's voice dropped half an octave. *'Mr O'Shannessy, I'm afraid the news isn't that good, you've been diagnosed with cancer.'* Thomas's affected voice continued, *'But if you are willing to undergo the right treatment we can almost guarantee we can get you into remission in eight months.'* Thomas looked at Billy and, in his normal voice, said, 'What would you say, Billy?'

Billy didn't reply and simply shook his head, understanding what it was the Salvo was telling him.

'No, Billy, I want a reply!' Thomas insisted, waiting for Billy's first affirmation. 'What would you say?'

Billy sniffed. 'Well, I'd have to say yes.'

'Of course, be crazy if you didn't. Thankfully you *haven't* got cancer, you've got another progressive illness, but one that usually takes about the same time to fix. Fix is quite the wrong word, of course. Like cancer, you'll be in remission, but *unlike* cancer, *you* decide how long your health will last. You, not the disease, will decide whether you want to go back to being very sick or want to stay healthy, hopefully for the rest of your life.'

'Thank you, major, I hear what you're saying. It's just that . . .'

'One day at a time,' Cliff Thomas interrupted, 'that's all you have to pledge and you don't have to do it all on your own. In fact, you can't. We now know that the problem with this particular chronic disease is that it's progressive and irreversible, it is not a question of willpower or weakness. A psychological definition of alcoholism is that it causes you to drink *against* your will. Total abstinence will halt it in its tracks but won't cure it. It takes only one drink to activate the illness again and send you off on a binge.'

'Thank you. Yes, I'd like to go on the program, major.'

Just then Kylie, a young woman who looked no older than eighteen, knocked and entered, carrying a small tray. She placed a cup of tea and two Panadol and a small brown pill in front of Billy and then a glass of water. 'Six sugars! I bet your dentist likes you,' she said, grinning. She pointed to the tiny pill. 'Nurse says this little one is to prevent a messy nappy,' she giggled.

'Thank you, Kylie, that will be enough from you!' Thomas said, laughing. 'Don't put any calls through until I let you know and close the door behind you, please.' Thomas waited until she'd left before saying to Billy, 'She's a bit forward, but I'd rather have 'em full of beans like that than down in the mouth. Kylie's a great little example, she's been off heroin now for eighteen months and she's kicked methadone as well.' Cliff Thomas pointed to the closed door, 'It's kids like that who make me want to cry out with joy.'

Billy nodded, thinking of Trevor Williams' daughter. 'Well, she's perfectly right, of course, a trip to the dentist is long overdue.'

'Billy, you do know that we don't do the rehab here, don't you?' Thomas asked. Billy nodded. 'It's done at William Booth which is down the road a bit. Major Harris is in charge there, a good Christian and a nice chap all round, but you'll mostly work with Vince Payne, the pocket dynamo, he's not a Salvo, but is the program director. You'll be in safe hands. Do you know anything about AA?'

'Alcoholics Anonymous?'

'Yeah.'

'Just the usual, the meetings they hold for reformed alcoholics.'

'Right, well, perhaps reformed isn't quite correct, you see you will always be an alcoholic but one who doesn't drink. There's a bit more to it than attending a few meetings, AA is your support group, your strong right arm.' Cliff Thomas looked at Billy. 'When you sign on, well, it's not just for the next eight months, it's for the rest of your life.'

Billy hesitated. 'I understand there's rather a lot of appealing to God. I'm afraid I'm not very good at that, haven't attended church since I was married.'

The Salvo major laughed. 'I know what you mean. Although my early life was Methodist, my drinking life was atheist. Now, of course, I'm a born-again Christian, the Big Bloke and me are on very personal terms. Perhaps I can put it to you a little differently. AA has a central premise that seems to work, one they've tested tens of thousands of times. I'll put it to you as bluntly as I can. Chaps like us, alcoholics, don't successfully rehabilitate without the help of someone or something, a Higher Power, we can believe in. For me, it's God, but in the AA group I attended there was a greenie who had as her Higher Power a tree she once saw in Tasmania, a giant red gum. Another chap, a cow cocky from the country, used a blue heeler he once had. He'd say, if you'll excuse the French, "That bloody mutt was possessed of an intelligence and a spirit bigger than any bloody human!" So you see, for me it's the Lord Jesus and for someone else it's a tree or a superior cattle dog.' He grinned. 'Whatever you choose as your Higher Power, you're going to need one to come out of the other end sober.'

The idea of a tree as his Higher Power appealed to Billy and he wondered if he should use *Eucalyptus maculata*, the spotted gum he'd intended for his grave. After some thought, though, he chose Trim. After all, it was Trim who had brought Ryan into his life and, like the blue heeler used by the bloke from the bush, there was no doubting that Master Mariner Trim Flinders had been a superior being in his time. His spirit most certainly lived on. Any cat who had survived two hundred years of history was worthy of being regarded as a Higher Power. After all, the ancient Egyptians had regarded cats as gods, so why shouldn't Billy choose the first cat to circumnavigate Australia?

Billy wasn't being blasphemous, he had never doubted the faith of others, in fact, quite the opposite. He had admired his wife's complete dedication to her Catholic faith and her absolute belief in the sanctity of the Pope as God's disciple on earth. He greatly admired the Salvos and their faith in a loving and compassionate Jesus Christ. It was just that he hadn't paid his dues and now that he was in need of help he didn't feel he had earned the right to be a supplicant.

Of course, those with complete faith would constantly point out to him, often pedantically, that this was the whole purpose of a loving God, who didn't count fealty and compliance as the requisite for redemption. His love was all-embracing, all-forgiving, '*Come to me all you who are weary and burdened and I will give you rest.*' It was a simple matter of total faith, total acceptance, total surrender to a Higher Power.

But Billy, much as he would have loved to hand his life over to this highest of all the Higher Powers, knew that he lacked the faith required to commit his everlasting soul to God's mercy and love. In his own eyes he had been a phony all his life, this time he would need to be honest and trust in himself. *To thine own self be true*, it was a mantra he kept repeating.

'You'll be staying at William Booth for the next three weeks,' Cliff Thomas said.

Billy had been told at Resthaven that this would be the case and so he nodded. He'd greatly miss waking up at dawn to Arthur and Martha and the singing in of the light by his glorious avian choir. It was something he had hungered for while he'd been away. He comforted himself with the thought that after the first three weeks he could still work around the AA program and resume some of his routines, his morning inspection of the Botanic Gardens, Operation Mynah Bird at the luncheon break, and his writing seated on the bench beside the pond and opposite the mighty Moreton Bay.

Billy felt a sudden stab of pain when he thought of Con at the New Hellas Cafe. Such a good bloke really, he'd have to attempt to patch things up, though he couldn't think quite how this might be done. He suddenly realised that for the first time since he'd run away he had a tiny sense of hope, a sliver of light. Now all he had to do was hang on for dear life and crawl towards it.

But Billy's hopes were about to be severely dashed. Cliff

Thomas dialled the William Booth Institute and asked for Vince Payne. When Vince came to the phone, Cliff went through the usual courtesies, then said, 'Billy O'Shannessy is with me, he arrived on this morning's bus from Surfers Paradise, is it convenient to bring him over now?' Vince must have said they'd send someone, because Thomas said, 'No, no, I'll bring him myself, I could use the exercise.'

On the way to Albion Street, Cliff Thomas told Billy his own story. He was one of fourteen children. His father had died three months before his youngest brother was born and his mother had to raise the eight of them who were still too young to work. She was strict and pious, a God-fearing woman who insisted they all attend Sunday School. Cliff Thomas smiled. 'If you used a coarse word you got it over the head with the broomstick.' It was a pretty tough life and at the age of fourteen, Cliff, big enough to pass for an eighteen-year-old, found himself increasingly in the pub with his older brothers.

'By the time I was eighteen and decided to join the army, I had acquired a taste for drink. No, worse than that, I *needed* to drink. With an army salary three times as much as I'd previously earned I could drink three times as much. I now realise that three years into military service I had become an alcoholic, though, of course, army discipline and hours hid this from my superiors, perhaps even from myself. I was one of the lads, a good man to be with when you needed a busy elbow at your side. I told myself I had a bit of a problem, but nothing I couldn't manage, young blokes always think they're invincible.'

'Ah, don't I know! A problem drinker, definitely not an alcoholic, give it up any time I like,' Billy interrupted.

The Salvo smiled. 'I guess denial is something we learn very early in the game. But I was about to be flushed out into the open. My battalion was sent overseas, to Cyprus, where we'd go on extended, what were called dry exercises, no alcohol allowed.' Thomas shrugged and turned to Billy. 'In a big family you learn to take care of yourself, I was ever the resourceful one and started to make my own booze.'

'What, beer? Home brew?' Billy asked.

Cliff Thomas laughed. 'No such luck. Metho, brasso and melted-down boot polish, it had a kick like a mule and the ingredients were always available. It soon became my preferred drink. By the time I was in my mid-twenties the battalion M.O., not knowing of course that I was drinking metho, told me that my health was breaking down, and if I didn't give up going to the canteen I wouldn't see the ripe old age of thirty.' Thomas then asked Billy, 'You a Catholic, Billy? What I mean by that, did you have early religious instruction?'

'No, Protestant, my wife is Catholic, O'Shannessy spelled my way comes from the north of Ireland. Church in my family was for formal occasions, births, deaths and marriages, my father called himself an agnostic.' Billy laughed. 'Which was rather amusing, he was a Supreme Court judge and was forced to swear allegiance to God every day of his life.'

'Well, it was different for me. For us, early Methodist training leaves you feeling guilty all your life. I knew I was sinning, going against God's will by being a heavy drinker, so I solved that problem quite easily.'

'You did?' Billy's headache was lifting slightly and the walk, in the mid-winter sunshine, was pleasant.

'Certainly, I went to my company commander and had the word "Methodist" removed from my army records and the word "Atheist" replace it. I was free to drink without feeling guilty.' Cliff Thomas shook his head. 'The mind plays funny games, boyo. I never get over the ability we all have to justify our actions no matter how bizarre. It seems most of mankind is in some kind of denial.'

'How did you get to Australia?' Billy asked quickly, hoping to avoid the subject of denial.

'Well, I could see the writing on the wall, so I purchased my discharge from the army before they kicked me out. There was nothing for me back home, my friends had all married, my brothers and sisters had scattered around the world and my mother had gone to Methodist heaven.' Thomas stopped and gave a cheeky grin, 'Australia seemed a highly suitable destination for a drunk.'

Billy laughed. 'History proves you right. Most of our male citizens spent the first hundred years pissed, and the second hundred hasn't been enough of a contrast for any of us to notice a significant difference.'

'You're right, it was like a homecoming.' Thomas then went on to tell Billy the usual story of a drunk's progression down the slippery dip of life until he finally landed in the gutter where a Salvation Army officer stretched out a hand and offered to pray with him. 'It was the first time in my life somebody had offered to pray with me and for me. We knelt down together right there on the grass in Hyde Park and prayed that I would be healed.'

Billy braced himself for the sermon that was to follow, though much to his relief Thomas now said, 'I won't bore you with the details, salvation is a deeply personal experience but, to cut what's been a long story shorter, that was thirty years ago and with the help of the Lord Jesus Christ in my life, I haven't touched a drop of alcohol since the day I got grass stains on my knees from praying alongside the Salvo.'

They had arrived at the Albion Street address and Cliff Thomas put his hand on Billy's shoulder, 'Good luck and God bless, Billy.' He returned the Resthaven envelope he'd been given earlier but hadn't opened. 'You'll need to give this to Vince Payne, they'll probably ask for it at reception.' He extended his hand. 'Remember, we're on your side, no matter what happens.'

The two men shook hands and the Salvo major walked away, but then stopped. 'Oh, Billy, you can call me at any time,' he paused fractionally, 'for the remainder of your life.'

Billy walked up to a window beside the front door and pushed a button set into the wall. Moments later, a pleasant-looking woman in her forties came to the window, which was covered with clear perspex with a slot for sliding stuff in or out and several small holes at mouth level for talking through. Billy would later learn that it was bulletproof. 'What can I do for you, sir?' she said in a friendly manner.

'I've been sent from Foster House, madam. My name is O'Shannessy, William D'Arcy, I'm here . . .' Billy hesitated for a few moments, he'd never had to spell it out to a stranger before, '. . . for the alcohol rehabilitation program.'

'Just a moment, please,' the woman replied and turned away, to return a few moments later. 'That's right, you're on the list, come in.' Billy heard a buzz and a click as the door opened. He was suddenly possessed of an enormous urge to run, but the lady seemed to understand. 'Welcome, we've been expecting you,' she said.

Billy entered and the door closed behind him. He stood for a moment, his eyes adjusting to the light. He admitted to himself that he was frightened, it felt like the first few minutes at boarding school after his parents had dropped him off. Although the reception office was to his immediate right, the first thing his eyes focused on was a small blackboard positioned against the wall to his left, on which was written the lunch menu in pink and white chalk. Someone had taken the trouble to do it in a cursive script so that it looked quite decorative, almost like the daily specials in a restaurant.

Lunch

Lamb chops – gravy
Mashed potato
Mixed veg
Banana custard

Billy was strangely comforted by the menu, banana custard had been a favourite of his when he'd been a child. He turned towards reception, which consisted of wood panelling up to the counter level and then the same perspex that covered the outside window. Once again, there was only a small opening through which to push things and the cluster of speech holes.

The woman at the window now stood waiting for him on the other side of the opening. Billy approached and she pushed out what looked like a large ledger, with a biro attached to it by means of a piece of string. 'Please sign your proper name, date of birth and the name and address of your next of kin,' she instructed.

'Is the last bit, I mean the next of kin, really necessary, madam?' Billy asked.

The receptionist seemed to expect the question and she said sympathetically, 'There's usually someone our clients want us to contact if it becomes necessary, sir.'

Billy filled in the details and under next of kin he thought for a moment before he wrote: *N/A*. He had committed himself to a new start and if something should happen to him he didn't want to be remembered for his past. He didn't believe that his wife or his daughter should be burdened with any more memories of him or the responsibility of seeing him decently buried. He closed the book and pushed it back through the slot. 'Do you have any papers, Mr O'Shannessy?' she asked, taking the book.

'Oh, yes, of course,' Billy said, handing her the envelope Major Thomas had returned to him.

'Thank you. Take a seat in reception, please,' the receptionist said, pointing further down the small corridor.

Billy walked through to the reception area over a carpet patterned with small two-toned grey triangles that were intersected every once in a while by one of a brighter colour. Woven into the centre of the carpet was the Salvation Army red shield. There appeared to be offices on one side of the area and on the other the dining room with the banana-custard menu outside the door. The area contained a dozen old-fashioned red-vinyl lounge chairs, most of them occupied by silent men.

Billy chose a chair that concealed from him a large terracotta pot which contained an arrangement of pink and green artificial lilies made of silk with stamens of a sharp orange. Artificial flowers, though not quite in the mynah-bird category, were among his pet hates. Man's attempts to emulate the perfection of a single blossom, even non-indigenous flora, was an exercise in the debasement of nature. As he eased himself into the chair there was a sudden escape of air from the vinyl-cushioned seat and he was tilted backwards, so that his eye line was drawn upwards. On the wall directly above the dining-room door was a large sign painted in Salvation Army red.

Jesus said – You must be Born Anew – John 3:7

While Billy knew it was a call to repentance, nevertheless it didn't seem to him somehow appropriate. This, after all, was to be a new start for him, his own personal born anew.

Although, looking around, he could have hoped for a more pleasant environment in which to be reborn. The William Booth Institute had a forbidding nineteenth-century atmosphere that wouldn't have been out of place in a Charles Dickens novel. He imagined the silk flowers were intended to soften the effect, give it a contemporary feel. Then he noticed a more concerted attempt to modernise the surroundings. Positioned between two office doors sat a very large fish tank containing half a dozen extremely well-fed goldfish. Above the tank was a notice, which, with exclamation marks added, read more like an admonishment, 'Don't feed the fish!!'

Billy looked around for something to read but apart from a few dog-eared brochures exalting the work of the Salvation Army, there was nothing else. With nothing to occupy him, he quietly observed the men seated around him, each of them with a small nondescript sports bag or backpack containing his belongings beside him. While the area was fairly large, the red chairs and the silent men seated in them made it appear as if they were all lost in a vast grey ocean, every man on his own small island.

The sense of being utterly alone caused Billy to feel an almost physical sense of isolation. It was as if the air surrounding his immediate presence had congealed and sealed him into his own space, excluding him from reaching beyond his vinyl-covered prison.

Most of the men were gazing blankly at the fish tank. Although people moved past, going into offices or down a corridor to the side, they seemed to pass without any sense of movement. Only the fish moved in a hypnotic somnolence, mindlessly floating forward, never increasing momentum, turning, gliding at the glass, backwards or sideways, responding to some eternal rhythm that seemed as if it were rolling in from eternity itself.

A door opened to the office directly in front of him and a small man wearing glasses with lenses rather thicker than normal appeared. Perhaps it was because of the sense of everything being slowed down that he seemed to be spring-loaded, the energy radiating from him piercing the air surrounding Billy.

Vince Payne stood framed in the doorway of his office, scanning them all, and then fixed his bifocals on Billy. Having found his quarry he started forward, 'propelled' was a better word. With his arms slightly bent at the elbows and held away from his body, his fingers extended, he paddled through the air on either side of him, his body swivelling left and then right. It was as if he too sensed the containing air and was making a concerted effort to break through it to reach Billy.

'You must be the lawyer?' he said, smiling. He came to a stop in front of Billy, his hands still paddling slowly, treading the air.

'Was once, but how did you know that?' Billy replied, not sure whether he was required to stand, half rising.

Vince signalled for him to remain seated. 'We've had blokes in here who've talked about you, can't be too many Billy O'Shannessies who help the brotherhood get around the bureaucratic minefields.'

'Oh, I see. I'm not sure I've ever helped all that much.'

'Vince Payne, I'm your program director.' The pocket dynamo stuck out his hand, 'Welcome to the house of pain.'

Billy grinned. 'Thank you. Yes, I have to agree, it does look a bit Dickensian.'

Vince grinned back. 'Nothing that a couple of million dollars wouldn't fix, or maybe tear the whole place down, eh? Start all over again. Probably be cheaper in the long run.' He had an easy manner and Billy found himself liking him immediately. 'Come to my office,' Payne said and then caught sight of the handcuffs about Billy's wrist and the briefcase. 'Crikey! What have you got in here,' he exclaimed, pointing to the briefcase, 'the flamin' crown jewels?'

Billy shrugged. 'It's an extension of my arm, my way of not losing it.'

'Damn good idea, but I'm afraid we're going to have to take it off you while you're here.' Vince Payne understood immediately that Billy, like so many homeless, had no concept of storage. The idea of deserting their possessions, meagre as they might be, was beyond their comprehension. Drawers, lockers and cupboards served no practical function in their lives. You were what you carried and an attachment to a bag or a backpack was often the only certainty you knew. Getting Billy to part with his briefcase was going to involve intervention therapy, the first bridge they would need to cross together. He waited for him to reply.

Billy had already been through the process at Resthaven and it had troubled him greatly to know his precious briefcase was in the care of someone else. When it had been restored to him it had been as if an old and trusted friend had come back into his life, his eyes stung with tears as he grabbed it, hugging it to his chest. Now he was threatened with losing it a second time.

'It really isn't any trouble, sir. You may search it for contraband,' Billy said, hoping his voice didn't betray his concern.

'Okay, come into my office,' Payne said, appearing to relent. 'I need to clear up a few details and brief you on your program.'

Billy rose and followed Vince Payne into an office that wasn't much bigger than a cubicle and contained a desk on which sat a computer, while the remainder of its surface was covered in paper and files. Two dark-green filing cabinets, an office chair and a straight-backed kitchen chair completed the furnishings. On the wall was a cheaply framed photograph of a man with an old-fashioned haircut under which appeared the words:

Bill W.
Alcoholic
Founder: Alcoholics Anonymous, 1935

Vince Payne motioned for Billy to take the chair before he seated himself on the old and slightly lopsided typist's chair behind the desk. The office looked worn-out and lent its owner no authority, although it was already abundantly clear to Billy that the program director didn't need any of

353

the usual trappings to assert himself, he was one of those people who simply assumed control and got on with it.

'Cup of coffee?' Payne asked.

'No thank you, I've just had a cup of tea at Foster House.'

'You sure?' Vince asked again.

'Yes, quite sure.'

'Just as well, the coffee here is atrocious, the staff drink it, but I reckon you have to draw the line somewhere. There's a little place across the road, Rocco's, good bloke, makes great coffee. If you're ever desperate for a caffeine fix, don't take the chance of being poisoned, ask someone to get one for you.'

'Thank you, I will,' Billy said, enjoying the honesty.

'My credentials first,' Vince Payne now said. 'Apart from running the counselling in this joint, I took seven years to fail two years of law.' He grinned. 'Good thing too, I reckon I'd have made a lousy lawyer.'

'You'd have been in good company, there are plenty of us around. I'm not sure I was any great shakes myself.'

'That's not how I've heard it told,' Payne said, then abruptly altering his tone, he said, 'Okay, let's get on with it.' He looked down and picked up the notes from Resthaven that Billy had given the receptionist. 'How the hell did you manage to stay in the hostel for a week on your own after you'd detoxed?'

Billy attempted to explain. 'I can't say it was easy. Mostly I asked the manager to lock me in my room. I discovered that being conscious of not drinking and still desperately wanting a drink is just about as distracting a state of mind as being, well, you know, blotto.'

'Well, all I can say is that you've made a damn good start, mate. Congratulations, so far you're ahead in the all-important mind games.'

'Thank you,' Billy said. 'But I think it was probably foolish.'

'Damn right it was foolish! But there you go, you're here and you made it in under your own steam, miracles will never cease.' Billy liked the no-nonsense manner Payne affected. 'Now the good news is that you won't be on your own here. In fact, I'll be perfectly frank with you, there are going to be times over the next three weeks when you'll wish you could be, but there's no privacy.' He paused. 'Introspection is a luxury we can't afford while we deal with several more important things out in the open in a group atmosphere.'

'I'm not sure how I'll cope, Mr Payne, I've kept my own company for a good while now.'

'Yes, of course, there's two kinds of alcoholic, the social ones who enjoy company and the loners. Your kind are in the minority. It's much easier for the gregarious ones, in a sense they've come from a group environment and understand the *gestalt*.' Billy thought immediately of Casper Friendly's mob. 'The loners find it difficult at first,' Vince Payne continued. 'It will take a bit of getting used to but I hope you'll try. Group discussion is the basis of most of our therapy. Are you acquainted with the Twelve Steps of Alcoholics Anonymous?'

'You hear a fair bit around the traps and Major Thomas explained some of it to me this morning, but not really.' Billy thought for a moment. 'I guess it's something I've always thought of as being for someone else.'

'Ah, I see, *they* are alcoholics and *you* are a problem drinker?'

Billy grinned, surprised. Vince Payne certainly couldn't be accused of patronising him. 'Yeah, something like that.'

'Okay, the anonymous part of AA is taken very seriously. From the moment you leave this office you will simply be known as Billy, or William if you prefer.'

'No, no, Billy is fine.'

'You'll hear a lot more about AA over the next three weeks as we try to practise what we preach. Briefly, there are twelve steps to sobriety, they embrace the following principles, or concepts. An admission of powerlessness is the starting point, after that the program asks you to take a damn good look at yourself. It's called "taking a moral inventory", very American, I'm afraid.'

'I think I've done a fair bit of that already,' Billy said.

Vince Payne scratched the tip of his nose. 'I think you'll find there's more to come, mate. Looking inwards isn't that much fun and it usually takes a bit of pulling out. I guess we've all done things in the past we're not that proud of, so another area is called "restitution for harm done", by that we mean simply saying sorry to the people you've hurt on the way to being what you've become. Then we believe that we need to help each other, our experience is that alcoholics work best with alcoholics. Straight people, even psychiatrists, don't really know what goes into being an alcoholic, but another alcoholic does. He, or she, has been through the same hell, they know what's going on in the other person's head.' Vince Payne absently picked up a biro and tapped it against the computer screen. 'So we become a service industry to each other.' He looked directly at Billy. 'Now for the hard part. The concept most of our more intelligent clients have some difficulty getting their minds around is the idea that we must surrender to some personal God, some Higher Power.'

'Yes, Major Thomas touched on that this morning.' Billy was beginning to realise that the God business couldn't be taken lightly, it seemed to be the central pillar on which the entire program was built. He wondered if Vince Payne would let him get away with Trim as his Higher Power the way Cliff Thomas had explained to him.

'Righto, Cliff Thomas probably told you, who or what you choose as your Higher Power is up to you. But make no mistake, whoever or whatever your choice, it has to be serious. You must surrender completely, *you* can't influence your Higher Power, but it must be able to influence you, guide you, even talk to you. Do you understand, Billy?'

'I think so,' Billy replied. 'It's not an easy idea to grasp.'

'I know it sounds a bit dodgy at first, but you'll soon grow accustomed to it all. Try to think of it as less a religious precept than basic psychology. We've learned that you need certain things to hold on to if you are to get through to the other side. When all is said and done, you have to replace your need for alcohol with something else.

Some say alcohol is a negative power and can only be overcome by a positive power. The positive power, in this instance, is something greater than the addiction, *and* greater than the sum of the parts of you trying on your own to give up alcohol.'

Despite what Vince Payne had said, Billy couldn't help feeling that it still sounded like old-time religion, Billy Graham in full swing – *Confess your sins, be saved, washed in the blood of the lamb, free, free, free at last!* But it was obvious to him that Payne knew what he was doing and that he wasn't a religious nut. While he spoke with conviction and force, and was a very skilled proselytiser, he didn't appear to be a religious bigot. It wasn't Jesus *über alles*.

The program director asked Billy to read and sign the admission sheet, commit to the non-returnable hundred-dollar admission fee, and read the rules, which were not all that different from those of Resthaven. Having done all this, Payne began to outline the entire rehabilitation program.

Billy would never know whether this procedure of leaving the explanation of the course to last was standard. As Vince Payne told him what was to come, Billy's heart sank. Although he now saw that there had been several indications that the process would be protracted, he hadn't realised just how much his freedom would be curtailed. He'd reconciled himself to the three weeks of incarceration at the institute, but thereafter he'd imagined he would be free to conduct his own life while attending regular AA meetings, perhaps even remaining at the institute or at

Foster House, but nevertheless in control of his own affairs. Now it was obvious that this was not the case.

'When you've completed your three weeks here you may need to be transferred to Newcastle, depending on vacancies down here,' Payne continued.

'Newcastle! Transferred?' Billy couldn't believe his own ears.

The program director paused. 'But surely, Billy, you were aware that therapy takes ten months?'

'Yes, but not that I'd be sent away, have no personal freedom, not be able to come and go as I wish?'

'But don't you understand, *that* is the rehabilitation? You have to learn how to crawl, then walk, then live your life free of alcohol, learn the business of coping with an outside world that doesn't care if you go to hell in a handcart!'

'Don't patronise me!' Billy shouted, losing his temper. 'By being sent to some sort of reform school, I'm going to learn to cope? Do me a favour!' Billy was aware that he was being unnecessarily aggressive but he couldn't restrain his anger. The tentative plans he'd made to resume his relationship with Ryan, who, he was certain, was running out of time, and the need to help Trevor Williams find his daughter, were being swept away. This pompous little man sitting in front of him, with the annoying habit of hitting the screen of his computer with a biro, was telling him how he had arranged his life for him. It was simply more than Billy could take.

Billy had seen Ryan and Trevor Williams' daughter as

the way he would eventually redeem himself, *they* would be his rehabilitation. 'Bullshit! I'm leaving!' he cried, rising from his chair.

Vince Payne's expression didn't change as he said softly, 'Before you run away, may I . . .'

Billy was too angry to allow him to continue. 'Damn you, I'm not bloody running away! I have things I must do. Commitments! People who need my help!'

'Ah!' Vince Payne said, placing the biro down. 'Let me ask you something. These commitments, were they not the reason why you submitted yourself for detox?'

'Yes! Bloody stupid of me in retrospect,' Billy replied, still furious.

'And now you'll be able to achieve those commitments when you resume your old life?' Payne asked.

'I can manage my own life, thank you,' Billy said, realising that he was sounding truculent and childish.

'That why you ran away to Surfers Paradise?' Payne saw the look on Billy's face, 'It's in your notes.' He tapped the Resthaven report on the desk in front of him with his forefinger.

Billy had now risen. While he wasn't a big man, he seemed to loom over the diminutive program director seated in the rickety office chair. He was about to say, 'Why don't you mind your own bloody business!' when he became conscious of a third voice. *'You're sailing away in the* Bridgewater, *Billy.'* The difference this time was that it wasn't his own inner voice that suggested this to him, it was quite distinctly a cat's voice. He was perfectly aware that cats don't speak, but he also knew, with absolute conviction, that he'd heard Trim, loud and clear. His Higher Power had kicked in.

Billy sat down again and began to weep. 'I don't know what to do, I don't know what to do, I'm such a weak bastard,' he sobbed. 'Nothing's changed, I'm still going to let everyone down!'

Vince Payne waited until Billy was back in control. 'Billy, I've got a problem.' He waited for Billy to respond and when Billy didn't, he added, 'I need your help.'

Despite himself, Billy was forced to ask, 'What is it?'

'The program, it's pretty full on and I'm afraid you won't be able to manage it with one hand tied behind your back.'

'What do you mean by that exactly?' Billy asked.

'The briefcase, it renders your left hand more or less ineffective.'

Billy was silent, the logic was irrefutable. 'Will it be locked away so nobody can get to it?'

'Tell you what I'll do,' Payne said. 'We lock all personal belongings in a filing cabinet in the office, each drawer has its own big brass lock, then the admin office is deadlocked when the staff go home, so your stuff will be safe.' Billy started to object, but Payne held up his hand, restraining him. 'Not only safe, but we will also give you the key to the drawer, to the padlock. How about that?'

'Ha! There are two keys to the padlock!' Billy cried.

Vince Payne laughed. 'Good one! Righto, we'll give you both.' He spread his hands, 'Have we got a deal?'

Billy knew he'd been beaten and he nodded his head. 'Okay.'

Payne smiled mischievously. 'But now *I* have a problem.' Billy waited, not asking what it might be. 'What happens if you lose the keys?'

It wasn't an unreasonable question, although Billy knew that such an idea was impossible, the keys were his briefcase incarnate. He also sensed the program director was sending him up, albeit gently. 'Tell you what I'll do,' he said, imitating Payne, 'I'll get my ears pierced and wear a key dangling from each earlobe, then we'll both know where they are at all times.' Billy's ability at repartee was returning, it had been some time since he'd felt entitled to give as much as he got.

Vince Payne gave a little nod, acknowledging Billy's return serve. 'Excellent suggestion, we'll attend to it right away.'

He escorted him up two flights of stairs and they turned into a short corridor, which passed a small lounge on which several men were seated, some reading, others chatting quietly. 'Gidday,' Vince said as he passed, though he didn't wait for them to return his greeting. They continued down the corridor, which turned left into a large room with a counter immediately beyond a small entrance foyer. Beyond the counter sat several people working at computers along the rear wall. As it turned out, they were the group counsellors whom Billy would progressively meet during his stay.

In the centre were three desks, also manned, though by office staff. Against the right-hand wall were three creamy-coloured filing cabinets fitted with a stout-looking brass lock on each drawer. The filing cabinets were the first thing Billy saw, mentally checking the strength of the brass locks.

Vince Payne introduced him to Don, a clerk, whom he instructed to give Billy both padlock keys after he locked his briefcase away.

The clerk looked reluctant. 'It's against the rules, Vince,' Don said, somewhat embarrassed to be talking in front of Billy.

'It's okay, write down that it's on my instructions.'

The clerk shrugged. 'Whatever you say.'

Vince Payne turned to Billy. 'You'll see plenty of me, Billy. I'll leave you in Don's hands for the time being.' He shook Billy's hand before departing. 'I'm glad you decided to stay.'

'I'm sorry I made a fuss,' Billy apologised.

'You're an amateur, mate. That was barely a conniption.' It was a strangely old-fashioned word to use.

Billy, pre-warned that they would take his precious briefcase, had unlocked the handcuff and waited while Don examined the contents. The man went about his job in a serious and deliberate manner, not even remarking on the box of surgical gloves. He carefully noted each item on a form, leaving it on the counter to check against the list later. He then asked Billy to read the list and sign it. When Billy came to the little leather bag containing his three hangover stones, he couldn't bear the thought of never using them again. He pointed to the tiny drawstring bag on the counter. 'The little leather bag, it contains three polished pebbles, may I take them with me?'

The clerk hesitated, reached for the bag and, opening the drawstring, upended it to let the three pebbles spill onto the counter. He picked each up and tapped it against the wooden surface, making sure it was what it appeared to be. 'Not supposed to,' he mumbled, returning the pebbles to the bag and handing it to Billy.

'Thank you, Don,' Billy said politely.

The clerk then placed the briefcase in the drawer of a filing cabinet and locked it. Returning, he wrote Billy's name on an envelope and placed the key to the handcuffs into the envelope together with the contents list and put it into a small safe. 'Please remember to reclaim your personal belongings when you leave,' he instructed. He opened a drawer and took out a small square plastic-covered badge with 'Billy' written on it. 'This is your name badge, you are to wear it at all times. Please put it on now.'

'The keys, please?' Billy said, holding out his hand. The clerk hesitated and shaking his head, handed the two padlock keys to him.

Billy was given a towel and toilet kit and signed for them. 'Wait here,' the clerk instructed, pointing to a chair adjacent to the door. Billy sat with the towel and toilet kit on his lap, not quite knowing what to expect. After about five minutes, a man came through the door and turned to him, 'Hi, I'm Hamish, I'm a nurse, you must be Billy?'

Billy, holding onto the towel and the kit, stood up. 'Yes.'

'Come with me, Billy,' Hamish instructed. Billy noticed that he held a specimen jar of the type they use in hospitals and a folded, green-plastic garbage bag.

He followed Hamish back down the corridor and turned left into a wider corridor at the end of which was a bathroom.

Billy had seen a few institutional bathrooms in his time and this one competed impressively with them all for the title of 'most depressing'. It looked and smelled wet, a peculiar and permanent damp and a coldness that pervaded everything. If a room could be said to have bones, then the damp was in its bones. Billy gave an involuntary shudder.

While Billy had grown accustomed to the harshest living conditions, old, tired bathrooms filled him with a peculiar kind of despair. Even new, this type of institutional bathroom was always intended to be a miserable place, although such places came into their own as they aged. Stained and cracked yellowing tiles, leaking shower heads, mouldy, grey slate urinals that smelled of camphor balls and piss. The only thing that seemed to be missing was the proverbial hissing toilet. This being the Salvation Army, things like that got fixed, water after all costs money. But toilet blocks like this one, with its dark, damp corners, were a convincing testimony to humankind's failure on the planet earth. Why was it, Billy reflected, that in such places the light took on a gloom so deep that electric light bulbs, cowering under old-fashioned green-enamel coolie hats, gave off an incandescence redolent of misery and despair?

'This part isn't going to be very nice,' Hamish said, not unkindly. He pointed to a small room beside the shower recesses. 'You'll need to strip.' Billy looked to where he was pointing. The cubicle was without a door and, in the gloom, he could only just make out a wooden bench along the far wall and a floor that consisted of narrow wooden slats of the kind customarily found in school gyms and the like. Tinea traps, he remembered they were called, they never quite dried out and had a sense of always being dirty. 'Please remove whatever you want to keep from your pockets and leave your clothes behind when you come back out,' Hamish instructed.

'Why is that?' Billy asked, it didn't seem to make sense to him.

'I have to burn your clothes,' the nurse replied.

'Burn them? But they're practically new.'

'It's the rules, we can't make exceptions.' Hamish ran his eyes over Billy. 'Look, I admit you look pretty clean, but we can't make exceptions, you'll get new gear from the Salvation Army shop.'

'But these came from the Salvation Army shop in Queensland,' Billy protested.

'Sorry, mate, I'm just doing my job,' the nurse said. 'Now, if you'll please strip.'

'You mean, strip *everything*?'

'Yes, I'm afraid so, I have to give you a complete body inspection.'

Billy rubbed the stubble on his head. 'I've already been deloused and checked for scabies at Resthaven,' Billy protested again.

'Sorry, mate, gotta be done,' the nurse said, shaking his head sympathetically.

Billy, shivering in the damp atmosphere as he stood in front of the nurse, was examined front and back. He hadn't noticed that Hamish was wearing a surgical glove on his right hand. It wasn't hard to understand that anyone examining him would regard him as, he couldn't think of the right word and finally settled for contaminated.

'Bend over,' the nurse asked, standing behind him.

Billy hesitated. 'What for?'

Hamish sighed. 'I've got to check your rectum for drugs.'

'No!'

The nurse looked relieved. 'Thanks, it's not compulsory.'

Billy had expected an argument. 'Why didn't you tell me I had a choice?'

'Yeah, I'm sorry. We have to try. The young blokes don't mind, most of them have been in prison so they know the drill. Not nice though, is it?' Hamish smiled. 'I'm pleased to report that bodywise there are no creepy-crawlies.'

Billy, who was still annoyed at the nurse's rectal presumption, said, 'I already told you that, son.'

Hamish didn't protest. 'Nearly through, Billy. I have to take a urine sample and it's over.' He picked up the specimen jar from the floor. 'I have to watch while you piss into this.' He sighed, anticipating an objection. 'Sorry, them's the rules.'

Billy wondered fleetingly whether this was why Vince Payne had urged him to have a cup of coffee. 'Is this optional?'

'Afraid not, thank you for co-operating, Billy.' He handed Billy the jar and then stepped in front of him. 'Do your best.'

'What's this for?' Billy asked.

'Same as the shunt in the rear. Drugs. We need to know a bit more about your immediate past.'

Billy turned on him, his expression ingenuous. 'Might as well admit it now, I'm taking *Theobromaecacao*!'

'What's that?' the nurse asked. 'Never heard of it. New drug, is it?'

'No, very old. Chocolate. It's the Latin name for chocolate.' Billy knew it was a cheap shot, but as he attempted to empty his bladder into the specimen jar, it served to regain a small portion of dignity.

Taking the bottle, the nurse said, 'Latin, eh? We don't hear of lot of that spoken here.'

The kid was sharper than he'd supposed. He realised he was getting old, he'd always rather patronisingly thought of nurses as general factotums, glorified housemaids. Now, he realised, they needed a university degree to work. Hamish was sending him up, though somewhat gently. 'I'm sorry, son, it was a cheap shot,' Billy apologised.

'That's okay, Billy, I'm the one should be apologising. All this isn't very nice for an educated bloke. I'm damn sure I wouldn't like it done to me.'

Hamish then explained that he'd need to take a shower and get into pyjamas ready for his medical. 'You only need one shower and I won't have to scrub you.'

Billy didn't need to have this explained to him. He'd been around derros long enough to know that cleanliness wasn't prized among the fellowship. Casper Friendly and his mob probably took an average of one shower annually between them. After a while some drunks actually took pride in their unkempt condition, it became an affirmation that they were outcasts, different. Dirt became a badge of defiance.

'I've already had a medical at Resthaven, the results are in the papers I brought in,' Billy said.

'I'm sorry, Billy, it has to be done. House rules, you spend the first day here being showered, deloused, medicated, examined, analysed and observed and then you'll spend the rest of the day in bed in the clinic.'

Billy didn't suppose he minded all that much. The trip down south had been exhausting and while his diarrhoea and headache seemed to have ceased, he felt weak.

Dressed in his pyjamas, he was taken through to the clinic where a second nurse, who introduced herself as Christine, weighed him and measured his height. Like most alcoholics he was considerably underweight. 'Billy, we're going to have to put some flesh on those bones! While you're here, you have to try to eat more.'

'May I start by having banana custard for lunch?'

The nurse laughed. 'Of course! But try to combine it with a couple of chops and a helping of mash, will ya?'

With the nurse still in attendance, a young doctor examined him, checking his heart and lungs and taking a blood test. 'You're a bit dehydrated, Billy. I'm going to put you on a saline drip. It's into bed for you, young man, you'll stay in the clinic until tomorrow and then you'll go to your dormitory.'

'Dormitory?' Billy asked fearfully, thinking of the drunk tank in Foster House.

Christine laughed. 'It isn't too bad, four to a room, and you'll probably be the only one who snores.'

Billy wasn't sure he understood. The drunk tank, apart from all its other gastrointestinal disturbances, was a cacophony of snoring that would have put a rainy-season frog chorus to shame. He was to learn, as an alcoholic only, that he was more the exception than the rule. The days of the gregarious and harmless drunk manipulating the system and attempting to rehabilitate were largely over. Most of the clients at the William Booth Institute were a new kind of addict, they were young, aged from eighteen to their mid-thirties, often married with kids and addicted to both the bitch and the witch.

In the language of the street, the bitch was grog and the witch heroin or amphetamines. Taken together, they made for a very difficult and dangerous mind-altering combination. Nerves were shot, tempers were often on a hair trigger. These were desperate young men, many of them in and out of prison all their adult lives. As a general rule, most of them had led reckless and difficult lives. They suffered from low self-esteem, were alienated, confused, angry and, when under the influence, very dangerous. AA had spawned a new organisation, NA, which stood for Narcotics Anonymous, a whole new ball game.

'Tell you what, Billy,' Christine said. 'Tomorrow, when you come out of the clinic, we'll give you bed seventeen in room five, it's tucked around a bit of a pillar, it'll give you just a tiny bit of privacy. I'm afraid the intake is just about all young blokes, there's not going to be a lot of private space to go around, they're a pretty noisy mob. If it gets too bad you can come into the clinic during your free time, have a bit of a lie down, be by yourself behind a curtain.'

Billy, despite being exhausted, lay awake all afternoon. He was worried about Ryan and the letter he'd sent to Trevor Williams. He'd have to think the whole thing out again. It would be ten months before he would be free to be useful to either of them. For God's sake! They might send him to Newcastle! Send him away again. He felt panic growing in the pit of his stomach. He began talking to himself, 'Christ Almighty, Billy! Anything could happen to the boy in ten months. His grandmother is probably dead and his mother . . . ?' He wouldn't allow himself to think what might occur if Ryan was alone in the house with his heroin-addicted mother. He would, he decided, need to write urgently to the principal of Pring Street Public School. She was a decent and concerned woman, she would agree to be a link between himself and Ryan and help to hold the line until he got out. No, she wouldn't. Yes, she would. She had too much on her plate to care about one child. Yes, she would, she was that sort. What sort was that? His mind spun with contradictions, each thought cancelling the previous one.

Towards evening, Billy fell into a fitful sleep, waking often with the singular thought that he should leave William Booth in the morning. His mind raced from one thing to another. Surely that would be the decent thing to do? Somehow he'd stay off the grog so that he could help the boy. By staying in rehab, wasn't he simply doing what he'd always done? Wasn't this just another case of copping out, retiring from the scene for ten months? 'Nice one, Billy!' he remonstrated with himself again. 'If something happens to Ryan you can say it wasn't your fault, *your* conscience is clear, you're doing the best you can, all you were trying to do was to rehabilitate yourself so you could help the boy. What rotten luck it turned out the way it did!'

Billy was stretched to breaking point. His mind was filled with confusion and self-loathing, the coward was back. So much for his Higher Power. It was Charlie all over again. *Run rabbit, run rabbit, run, run, run!* At last Billy's mind reached overload, he could cope no longer and he fell into a deep, exhausted sleep.

Christine arrived some time later with a bowl of banana custard left over from lunch. 'Poor old bugger,' she said, smiling down at Billy. 'Never mind, mate, tomorrow's another banana-custard day.' She looked at Billy. 'But I can't say I like your chances, mate.'

CHAPTER TEN

The careless shouts of the two garbos working a truck on the street below woke Billy. It seemed to him that garbagemen, as a breed, were born with a compulsion to deny the rest of humanity any attempt to sleep beyond six a.m. The constant stopping and starting of the truck, the grind and whine of its bin-lifting mechanism, the crash of the impactor, the clink of bottles and the hollow clunk of plastic bins hitting the ground invaded the early morning air. Billy, as he always did, lay still, trying to listen for a snippet of birdsong through the racket, the call of a currawong or the carolling of a magpie. But then he realised that he was in the heart of the concrete jungle, the grey, sleazy end of Darlinghurst, where only the flying rats and the airborne shit factories, the pigeons and the mynah birds, were to be found.

With no Arthur and Martha to wake him, Billy had no

idea of the time, though it was only just coming up light and he judged it to be about six-thirty. He could vaguely remember someone making him sit up while they removed his drip during the night. Billy rose, parting the curtains around his bed, and stumbled towards a window. The winter's morning seemed to be struggling to wrestle free from the night, the light in the street grey and uncertain, and the road wet from earlier drizzle. The garbage truck had moved on. The street, now thoroughly awake, was reduced needlessly back to silence. This was to be another of the rest of the days of his life, his sixteenth day without a drink, and while he felt physically a little better and his body stronger, his mind was still completely preoccupied with his addiction. His hope for a scrap of birdsong was so strong that he could block out his waking thought, the urgent desire to find something, anything, alcoholic to drink. He could understand Cliff Thomas's need to concoct a mixture of metho, boot polish and brasso when on a dry exercise in the army. Billy would have gladly accepted this offering had it been available to him at that very moment.

Not quite knowing what to do and with no street clothes to wear, Billy returned to his bed. He would need to write to Ryan at some time during the day and inform him that it would be six weeks before he would be allowed to visit Billy in the institution. The letter would be awkward to write as he was still uncertain whether the boy would accept him back into his life. To a young boy six weeks is a lifetime and it would be four weeks before Ryan could ring him or Billy could attempt to call the school to inquire about him.

After the week spent at Resthaven, Billy had some idea of what was waiting for him and Vince Payne had told him he was required to do it again, as the procedure was somewhat different at William Booth. This didn't trouble him too much. At Resthaven he'd been so zonked on Valium and preoccupied with the letter he was writing to Ryan that he'd hardly concentrated on the lectures and made almost no contribution to the group discussions.

At seven o'clock, and still in his pyjamas, Billy was permitted to go downstairs to breakfast, which was a plate of oatmeal porridge with sugar and milk and a cup of sweet tea. Directly afterwards, he was taken to the Salvation Army shop to choose two sets of clothes and a pair of shoes. Though second-hand and no doubt from the charity bin, the clothes were in excellent condition and Billy chose a pair of blue jeans, a pair of khaki cotton pants, two well-washed, soft-blue cotton shirts, two long-sleeved jumpers and a couple of T-shirts. Socks and underpants were optional and supplied new by the Salvos, but Billy hesitated. It had been more than four years since he'd used either, but he decided to give them a go. It would be part of his rehabilitation, his return to normalcy. Finally he chose a pair of almost new, rather over-the-top red-and-white basketball boots, which he thought rather snazzy and which Ryan might think were cool.

Billy was then taken to his dormitory, although it was referred to as a room and accommodated four men. He was given bed seventeen, the nurse's promised intervention for a bed that had a little privacy. It was tucked away behind a pillar and allowed his head and shoulders to be concealed from the other occupants. Billy was to find that sixty centimetres of private space would prove to be one of the most important aspects of his recovery program. It allowed him to hide his emotions from the others, read and write without interruption, even to have a quiet weep when things got too much for him. He was yet to meet his room-mates as they were out on their first exercise program, so he waited in a small area on the first floor that was used by the men between activities.

At eight-twenty he was ushered by a counsellor into the lecture room where there were about thirty men all wearing name tags. Billy recognised the look in some of their eyes, they were still on 20 mg of Valium and just out of detox and their minds were turned inwards. Most mumbled a half-articulated greeting and, at the suggestion of the counsellor, they all sat down.

'Righto, everyone, my name is Jimmy,' the counsellor announced. 'Just so you know, I came into William Booth two years ago for the second time, having messed it up the first time. Like all of you, I am an alcoholic and addict. At the time I was on heroin.' He looked around, his eyes taking in each of them. 'I only say this so you'll know I know what you're going through. Also, I'm not Salvation Army, I'm a trained psychologist and I'm paid to do this job. Having said that, I like what I do and I'm on your side.'

Billy's ability to read between the lines heard the translation as 'Don't try and pull a swift one on me, I know the score'. It was a good start, most drunks and many addicts become expert at conning and manipulation, and practise it almost without thinking, always probing for an advantage. Jimmy, who appeared to be in his mid-thirties, was making it clear that there was no point trying it on.

The counsellor smiled. 'This joint is run by the Salvation Army, the salvation part is up to you guys, but the army ain't. They've got rules, strict rules, and if you're gunna stay here, you're gunna have to do it their way. Okay, guys?'

What followed was a chorus of 'yeah', 'no worries', 'sure', 'cool', which surprised Billy as most of the men had looked a bit totalled coming in and he'd expected a muted and morose response. He was considerably older than the rest of the group, the youngest of whom appeared to be no more than a grown boy and the eldest perhaps in his late thirties or early forties. Perhaps the younger men had more physical reserves and this accounted for their reaction.

'For a start,' Jimmy continued, 'don't throw anything out of the windows. It's been happening and if you're caught doing it you'll be discharged. The eight a.m. morning walk is compulsory. If you're feeling crook you'll need permission from the nurse and, I warn you, that ain't easy.' He grinned. 'Hamish is easier than Christine.' This caused a laugh and Jimmy let it subside before continuing. 'You've all been given a set of rules, please read them. Like I said, they're strict and ignoring them is going to get you into trouble, it's just the same as if you were in the army. Okay, sometimes there's blokes come in who can't read, no worries, catch me sometime and I'll go through the rules with you. You've also been told this before, but I better warn you again, no bad language, no *effing*, *b's*, *c's* or *s's*. The Salvos won't tolerate it, so keep your language clean at all times. Oh, one last thing, you've also been told this before but sometimes blokes forget, the Salvos take seventy per cent of your dole or pension while you're here. That just about leaves you enough for smokes and the odd Coke, so do yourself a favour, don't try to borrow money from anyone, it always leads to trouble. Got me?'

This last warning was received with less alacrity. Cadging, borrowing and bludging were accepted behaviour among derelicts and, in particular, heroin addicts, who were masters at it. Billy wondered to himself how successful this warning would prove.

'Okay, guys, now I'll give you a bit of a talk where I'll keep stopping to ask questions and after tea you'll go into groups of ten and discuss what's been said in more depth. I'm afraid you have to sit through this first part, but I appreciate some of you are just out of detox and may be feeling pretty crook. If you can't hack the group discussion, you can leave and go back to your room.'

Jimmy moved over to a small table, on which rested an overhead projector. The word 'Denial' flashed onto the screen. 'Here's a word you're going to hear a lot. *Denial*! What's it mean? Anyone here tell me what it means?'

The group remained silent.

'Come on, somebody, please.' There was still no response so Jimmy said, 'Come on, guys, this isn't a flamin' examination, you're not back at school.'

'It means making excuses for yerself,' someone said tentatively.

'Yeah, not bad. What kind of excuses?'

More silence followed. As the oldest man in the room, Billy didn't want to assert himself, and there was the question of his accent, but finally he said, 'We deny to ourselves that we are unable to cope with our addiction.'

'Spot on!' Jimmy called. 'Good answers, both of you.'

He showed the next transparency: 'Denial ain't a river in Egypt.' Billy and one or two of the others laughed, but for most of them it took Jimmy to say the words out loud before they got the pun. 'Denial is the number-one symptom of all addictions, it isn't even something we think about a lot, it's the unconscious component of addiction of any kind.' Jimmy stopped, 'So what am I saying? I'm saying that we've been denying stuff since we were knee-high to a grasshopper, so denial is an automatic and unthinking response. It's who we are and we can't ever remember being any different. Now, if this is true, what's the most natural thing for us to do?'

'To deny what we are?' the bloke next to Billy volunteered.

'Seems pretty simple, doesn't it? To deny that we are addicts. You, me, every bloke in this room is an addict and the funny part is that we addicts are usually the last to accept this fact. We continue with our addiction, often until we're insane or dead, and we blame anyone or anything except the disease for what we've become. Anyone disagree with that?'

'Yeah, mate, me old man were an alcoholic and that's why I'm one also. It's like me born personality, I don't have no choice.' It was the young bloke who looked no more than eighteen, though already he had two teeth missing, one on either side of his mouth. His blonded hair was worn spiked and set with gel. He also wore an earring and Billy would later see that he had four letters, *F.U.C.K.*, crudely tattooed on his right hand, one on each knuckle. Although fairly light-skinned, he clearly had Aboriginal blood.

'What are you saying? That the addiction is passed on from father to son?'

'Yeah, mate.'

'Let me ask you something, Davo. Why are you here?'

'Judge sent me, mate. Bastard wouldn't gimme bail but said if I done this I could stay outta the clink 'til me case comes up.'

Billy admired the young bloke's honesty, it couldn't have been easy to say what he'd just said, but he could also see where Jimmy was taking him.

'So, given the choice . . . Oh, and by the way, cut the bad language, you've just used one of the *b's* . . . You wouldn't be here if you had a choice?'

'Too right, mate.'

Jimmy turned to the group. 'Anyone recognise what's going on?'

'Denial,' several of the men called out.

'What's that supposed to mean?' Davo said, looking around.

'Well, there's no scientific evidence to suggest that alcoholism is inherited, but you could be right in another way, Davo. You see, we learn our behaviour patterns from our parents at a very early age, and very often the way they behaved towards us is how we grow up to behave ourselves. You didn't inherit your addiction but you acquired the pattern from one, or both, of your parents. Perhaps you can think about that while you're here.' He looked back at the group. 'What Davo's just said is rationalisation, just another aspect of denial which we'll get to soon.'

Jimmy turned back to the young lad. 'Thanks, Davo, that was useful stuff.'

It was clever footwork and Billy admired Jimmy for not putting the kid in his place, it had taken real skill to answer without making the boy seem young and foolish.

'Denial is one of the major reasons why recovery from a chemically-dependent addiction is seldom effective if the person doesn't come voluntarily into treatment.' Jimmy spread his hands. 'It's pretty simple really, you can't work on a problem unless you accept that it exists, can you?'

Billy felt sad for the young bloke. What Jimmy was saying was that it was highly unlikely that Davo would benefit from the magistrate-enforced rehabilitation program. The lad was likely to regard his stay at William Booth as preferable to going to gaol. You couldn't blame him for that, he'd made the right choice.

'Okay, everyone, it will come as no surprise to you that step one is working through your denial. This means allowing yourself the idea that you are powerless over your addiction. The next step is to recognise that it is the addiction that is bringing the chaos into your life. Anyone got anything to say about this?'

'You mean, if we give up the grog or whatever, everything will be sweet?' said someone whose name Billy couldn't read.

Jimmy laughed. 'This isn't Puff the Magic Dragon and the world is suddenly beautiful, mate. Most of us have spent most of our adult lives destroying relationships and messing things up for ourselves, our partners and our families, and blaming it on anything or anyone but our addiction. Your admission that you're an addict and can't give up your dependency on your own means you can start repairing the damage.' He turned to the group. 'That's the truly amazing thing, when we acknowledge our powerlessness over our addiction, we are suddenly empowered to take the first steps to an addiction-free life.'

'Like now we've got the strength to face up to things?' someone asked.

'Exactly, by admitting we're powerless and can't manage, we give ourselves the strength to look for help in facing up to ourselves and begin to rehabilitate.'

Jimmy moved on to the next transparency, which read:

- PROJECTION
- RATIONALISATION
- INTELLECTUALISM
- MINIMISING
- SUPPRESSION
- WITHDRAWING
- GEOGRAPHIC ESCAPES

'So, here are some common types of denial. You may recognise one or two in yourself. Okay, let's look at *Projection*. This one goes like this: "I don't have a problem, it's you that's got the problem. It's a free world, I can do as I damn well please. If you think I have a problem with grog that's your problem, not mine." That familiar to anyone?'

There followed a grunt or two and several of the men nodded before Jimmy moved on. '*Rationalisation*, we're all good at this one. "I drink because of my crummy job, my wife, growing up, my parents and so on." The reasons are endless and we learn to defend them to the death. Hands up anyone here who's blamed someone or something for his addiction?'

Hands shot up everywhere. Billy seemed to be the only one who didn't put up his hand. While he was now willing to admit that he was powerless against his addiction, he couldn't remember ever blaming anyone for what he'd become. How could he? He'd had a privileged background and had lacked for nothing in his childhood.

'Okay, we have lots for rationalisation, that's a good start.' Jimmy turned to the screen. 'How about the next denial? *Intellectualism*. This simply means that you tell yourself that all your problems are in your head. For instance, "I'm not an alcoholic, I'm a problem drinker. All I have to do is make up my mind not to drink and it's all over, no worries, it's all about my willpower." The problem here is that we never quite get around to making up our minds to give up and if we try we always seem to fail.' Jimmy paused. 'The point is that intelligence has nothing to do with addiction. Clever people, judges and lawyers, doctors and professors, may have no more willpower than anyone else, because addiction isn't about willpower or intelligence, the big nobs in society are just as vulnerable as the rest of us if the circumstances are right.'

Although Billy had responded to one of Jimmy's questions earlier, as the oldest person in the group he could sense that some of the younger blokes were waiting for him to take the lead. 'I can vouch for that,' he said quietly, then realising that they might get the wrong idea and think he was saying he was smarter than them, he added quickly, 'Not about being more intelligent, but the bit about judges and lawyers being just as vulnerable.' Billy found himself blushing.

Jimmy was quick to respond, covering up for him. 'Yeah, funny that. Most of us lack self-esteem and sometimes it comes from our backgrounds. You know, a poor education, getting into trouble with the police, bad things happening to us at home when we were young, so we come to accept that maybe we're not as clever or as good as other people. Billy's just told us that's crap. The people *we* think are always in control, given the right circumstances, are just as susceptible to becoming addicted.

'Here's an example I read about recently from America. This family seemed to have everything, wealth, leisure, education. The father was a world triathlon champion and a Harvard Law School graduate. This guy was a world-beater, everything he touched he conquered, except for his two boys. He was so busy being a champion of everything, he didn't notice that his sons, realising they were expected to live up to his standards and couldn't, were pulling in the opposite direction as fast as they could, deeply resenting his success. At fourteen and sixteen, both boys were addicts, both on heroin, both using the drug to substitute for what they thought was their inadequacy. It isn't always the kid with the drunken father and broken home that ends up addicted.'

Billy now realised that he'd been sitting back, taking it all in, judging both the lecturer and the responses from the group without recognising that he was himself involved. This was, in itself, a kind of intellectual superiority. He was no better than any of the men seated around him and it was time he got involved. He was guilty of making assumptions, for all he knew he might be sitting with a roomful of computer gurus, young doctors, lawyers, teachers, stockbrokers and accountants. The derelict and addictive world wasn't simply made up of Casper Friendly and his mates. He silently chastised himself, 'You of all people, Billy O'Shannessy, what right have *you* got to make judgements?'

'So let's get on to the next form of denial. *Minimising*.' Jimmy grinned. 'Well, you wouldn't be here if you were still doing this one, but it's also something most of us go through at some time or another, with grog in particular, which appears to have a slow addiction time, but also with other drugs. It goes like this, "Sure, I drink a few beers each day but it's not a problem I can't manage." For the guys on heroin or the various pills, their argument is, "I mostly only shoot up for parties, it makes me feel great. Yeah, sure, sometimes I just do it because I'm feeling crappy, so where's the problem?"'

There were grins all around the room and Billy could remember saying precisely this about scotch when he'd still been a law student.

'*Suppression!* This one's a real doozy, I don't know about you guys but this was me all the way. This is where you abuse family, friends, steal the housekeeping money, snatch handbags, roll drunks and act badly without any sense of responsibility and force yourself *not* to think about what you've done. You make the memory go away, often by getting pissed or taking a pill or a needle all over again. Anyone here share this little denial technique with me?'

Several hands went up. 'Yeah, the tricks our minds get up to,' said Jimmy.

Billy liked the way the counsellor included himself with the rest of the mob, admitting to his own failings so that they'd feel a little easier talking about their own.

Jimmy turned back to the screen. '*Withdrawing.* This is when it all gets too much and rather than face your problems you leave a relationship or a job.'

Billy put up his hand. 'It's called running away and I'm currently the world record-holder in this denial subdivision,' he said.

This brought a big laugh from the group. Jimmy waited until the laughter had died down. 'Thanks, Billy, that leads on to another denial sub-type known as *Geographic*

Escapes. "My life is unmanageable, but if I move to some other place where I'm unknown it will get better."'

'Guilty again!' Billy said, raising his hand. 'Surfers Paradise, here I come!'

They all turned, laughing and grinning. The old bloke was joining in and to Billy's surprise they seemed happy about this.

'Well, that's about it for today's lecture. Are there any questions? Anything you didn't understand?'

'How come you know so much about me?' said a bloke with a name tag that read 'Morgan'.

Another laugh all round. 'No, Morgan, it's all of us, everyone ever born. The foundation of the addictive personality is found in all humans. It's part of a normal desire to live life with the least amount of pain and the greatest amount of pleasure. It's part of our defence mechanism, our distrust of others, it's also natural to be somewhat pessimistic about life. But when negativism and pessimism, and a lack of self-esteem, take control that's when we try to fix the whole calamity called "life" with a substance.' Jimmy put up his hand. 'And that's the whole sad point, the substance works! It makes us feel better, it allows us to cope, it diminishes our fears, and while we have it under control, it even improves our relationships. But here's the problem, first we use it, then we abuse it, and then it uses us and we become addicts.'

They were free to go, though most stayed to listen. 'I'm not sure I understand,' Billy said. 'Are you saying that we don't know when enough is enough? When we use whatever, alcohol or drugs, to hide some emotional injury, we don't see the lights go red and so we don't slam on the brakes?'

Jimmy thought for a moment. 'That's not a bad explanation. Let me put it another way. The fundamental belief that drives any addiction is centred on what we secretly believe about ourselves, the things we'd never tell anyone else about ourselves, because if they knew what we were *really* like deep down they wouldn't like us.'

'Don't we all secretly think that?' Billy asked.

'Of course, but with the addict there's no up side, no normal life going on. In the addict these beliefs are always negative, we believe we are intrinsically flawed, bad, unworthy, defective, and don't have the right to be loved and so, obviously, we can't establish any meaningful relationships with other people. When we are unable to endure a relationship or even undertake one, this confirms, reinforces our convictions, what we think about ourselves. We settle for a love affair with alcohol or drugs, and our mindset becomes physically altered so we no longer feel loneliness or despair, or think we must be stupid or inadequate, or feel inferior or hurt. Like I said before, at first it works. The substances we take sometimes make us feel powerful, superior and angry, comforted that it's not our fault but the fault of others.'

'But that's not how I feel when I'm drunk, I don't feel powerful or superior, or even angry,' Billy protested.

'That's because addicts soon enter into another aspect of substance addiction known as "toxic shame".'

'I beg your pardon? Toxic shame? Sounds American.'

Jimmy looked at the others, realising that he was a little

ahead of himself and that Billy was leading him into areas that some of the others might take some time and more explanation to grasp. 'You're right, it comes from the American AA. You see, rooted in the addict's core belief that he is fundamentally flawed is the tragic emotion of shame. This we now call "toxic shame", the increasingly dependent we become on alcohol or other drugs the more we internalise the shame we feel for simply being alive. Any emotion – anger, grief, despair – can be internalised but when we no longer *feel* anger or despair, we've *become* completely angry or completely despairing. Now, shame is the same, we no longer feel it as a transient emotion like everyone else does, we have become wholly shameful. Once this happens, we simply live our lives as shame-based identities. We accept our shame without questioning it, feeling it. It's like never taking a wash, after a while dirty is the normal way to feel and the idea of washing, of being clean, is completely foreign to us.' Jimmy paused. 'And that, Billy, is why you don't feel powerful or superior or even angry when you're drunk.'

Billy was beginning to realise that he had a long way to go before he was a healthy little Vegemite again. Jimmy turned off the overhead projector. 'Sorry about that, we've been going for an hour and an extra bit, thanks for hanging in. Better hurry or morning tea will be over. Hey, don't forget, unless you're feeling pretty awful, be back here . . .' he looked at his watch, 'in twenty minutes. Go to your groups where you'll discuss the things we've talked about this morning in some depth.'

Billy soon slipped into the routine at William Booth. After all, he had always been someone who liked a regular daily pattern and, although this one was forced upon him, he preferred, unlike most of the other men, the predictability of the day's outcome. Breakfast, lecture, morning tea, group discussion, a small break for a smoke or a chance to go back to your room or have a chat. Lunch at a quarter to twelve was followed by an afternoon group, then an hour and a half of free time for ping-pong, pool, cards, chess or backgammon, with another group session and thereafter a break for a smoke or a visit to the clinic for medication. Dinner was served at a quarter to five, after which they could watch television before another meeting. The only variation of this routine was on Wednesday, when chapel replaced the evening group discussion. Chapel was also held at nine-thirty on Sunday mornings. It was lights out at ten-thirty and wake up at six.

Billy was to discover that talk was the essence of everything. As the men began to feel better, the group discussions started to open up and blokes who hadn't talked about their problems to anyone for years, some of them never, found themselves bonding with others who had shared similar lives. Secrets that lay buried deep within their hearts now came out and the support, the one for the other, was touching and often heart-warming. They soon learned not to be ashamed or afraid to cry, that childhood sexual abuse was shared by a number of them and a drunken father who'd beaten and humiliated them was almost commonplace. Some spoke of mothers who'd had de facto relationships, with every new 'bastard' treating them worse than the 'uncle' before, although the men, the fathers and surrogate uncles, in their lives seemed to play little or no part in the general discussion other than to be dismissed as villains. Those moments in childhood when they had felt safe and loved were invariably associated with a female, usually their mother, who was the only control most of them had known that hadn't been harsh and punitive.

Billy spent his first evening in his room writing to Ryan. During the course of the day he'd received tremendously heartening news that, while he was not allowed to have visitors for six weeks, he could invite someone to chapel of a Wednesday and Sunday, and after chapel the men could mingle in the foyer with their families or friends for ten or fifteen minutes.

Billy was tremendously excited by the prospect of seeing Ryan again and he couldn't wait to send off a letter care of the school inviting him to visit. He visited the shop downstairs to purchase writing materials and stamps and his hands shook as he took them back to his room and placed them in his bedside locker. But, when the time came to write a note to Ryan, he was suddenly filled with trepidation. He'd had no word from Ryan, who hadn't replied to the letter he'd sent from Queensland. Billy told himself that Ryan, or even the principal at Pring Street Public School, would have only just received the letter and wouldn't have had time to reply. Ought he not wait? Ryan might not wish to see him. His advances might not be welcome any more. In his present state Billy couldn't bear the idea of being rejected, yet that's exactly what he'd done to the boy. Ryan had every right to kick him out of his life.

Billy was beginning to realise that he'd fondly supposed he was helping the boy in all of this, that his rehabilitation was because Ryan needed him, but now he saw that it was he who needed Ryan. The boy was as much a part of saving him as he was of saving Ryan.

William Booth Institute
Albion Street
Strawberry Hills

My dear Ryan,

This has been my first day here and I must say it has been a busy one. It's a bit like being back at school and I am finding it all rather strange, but the good thing is that I am feeling a lot better and have been off the grog for sixteen days, my all-time record since the age of fourteen.

In my last letter I told you that I wouldn't be allowed to see you for six weeks as the rules here are very strict. But, hooray, there's a loophole in the law! We are allowed to have guests come to chapel at seven o'clock on a Wednesday evening and half-past nine on a Sunday morning.

I don't suppose you're much of a churchgoing person but this is just singing and stuff and then afterwards we can talk for about fifteen minutes. What do you think?

If you are busy or have something better to do, I understand. But I would very much like to see you if you have the time. I look forward to hearing all your news.

All the best to you,
Billy O'Shannessy (without the 'u')

P.S. We may even be able to begin the new Trim story
I told you about in my last letter.

His room-mates turned out to be Davo, the kid the magistrate had sent for rehabilitation, Morgan, the bloke who'd made the crack about Jimmy knowing him so well, and a young male prostitute named Freddo, not, he explained, because he was christened Fred. 'Lookit me, will ya? Me mouth's spread across me face and I've got these lubra lips, I were born to give good head.'

'Not here, you weren't,' Morgan said, hastily backing away, then he added, laughing, 'You ain't pretty enough . . . On the other hand, after a while in this dump, you could get prettier,' he joked.

'I ain't gay, mate!' Freddo protested. 'It's better than stealing or mugging old ladies, it's how I paid for me addiction! I got one strict rule, nobody gets it for free, I got "Entry $100" tattooed on me arse. Wanna see?'

'What happens if the cost of living goes up?' Morgan cracked.

It was true about Freddo, his face was decidedly peculiar-looking, his mouth stretched almost to the outside edges of each cheek and both his lips protruded. The surface of his face was almost entirely flat with only a vague outline indicating a bridge to his nose, though his nostrils were wide and distended. His eyes seemed too large for the size of his head and they bulged noticeably. His head was shaved, so he had a distinctly amphibian appearance.

Later he would explain to Billy how, as a three-year-old, his 'uncle' had, in a drunken fit, smashed his fist into Freddo's face to stop him crying, crushing and flattening the still-soft bones of his cheeks and tiny nose, and spreading his mouth across his face. The Freddo-Frog look (his description) he wore for the remainder of his life was the result of inept plastic surgery.

Davo, the reluctant guest, remained silent and truculent for the first week and made no attempt to co-operate. He didn't think he belonged and it was obvious he was taking very little from the lectures and not contributing to the group discussions. He seemed to have the single response, 'It sucks', to anything he was asked to comment on.

Billy had frequently tried to be friendly but Davo had rebuffed him on each occasion. On the last attempt he'd called Billy a 'fuckin' old poofter', though out of earshot of anyone in authority. Billy, who was having enough trouble sorting himself out, finally gave up.

Two days later Billy was seated on his bed trying to work out how to sew a missing button on his shirt and constantly pricking his finger and making a real hash of the task. 'Gis that!' Davo called impatiently, his hand extended to take the shirt.

Billy looked up, surprised. 'It's a button,' he said and shrugged.

'I know it's a fuckin' button, mate!'

'It's a tricky business, I had no idea,' Billy said, ashamed of his ineptitude.

Davo accepted the shirt, rethreaded the needle, knotted it at the end, and expertly sewed on the button, biting the cotton off at completion. 'There yer go, mate.'

'How excellent!' Billy said. 'Thank you, Davo.'

'No worries, mate,' Davo replied, his voice flat, although Billy could sense he was pleased at the compliment but didn't wish to show it.

'Your mum teach you?'

Davo's head jerked back, surprised, and he gave a bitter little laugh. 'Osmond Hall, mate.'

The name rang a bell somewhere in Billy's mind, though he couldn't remember quite why. 'Osmond Hall?'

'Juvenile Detention Centre.'

'And they taught you to sew?'

'Occupational therapy, yer got the shit beat outta ya if yer didn't. Laundry duty, sewing on buttons, patching, hemming, darning socks and then darning the fuckin' darn.'

'Mailbags? Did yer do mailbags?' Morgan called from his bed. It was meant as a joke but Davo missed it.

'Nah, just mendin' and stuff like that. The screws would bring their gear from home and yid get into the shit if it weren't done perfect.'

Billy looked down at the button on his shirt. 'Yes, I can see you're an expert.'

'Nah, it's only a button. We had this matron, real bitch

395

with a moustache, we hated her, she were there the first time I done Osmond. She'd make yiz sew on a button, you were eleven years old, see, and you'd sew it and she'd take the needle . . .' Davo hesitated, 'Like you know there's four holes in a shirt button so you makes an X with the stitches, sewing like from one hole to the diagonal opposite, like you seen I just done. She'd take the needle and, with its point, separate the stitches, countin' them. If they weren't the same number o' stitches on both the crossovers, yer didn't get no dinner.' Davo laughed. 'Count 'em, mate, betcha there's the same number on both arms o' the X.'

'I'll take your word for it, Davo. I'm afraid my eyes aren't up to it.'

'Give it here,' Freddo called. 'Okay, who wants to make a bet? What odds you offerin', Davo?'

Davo looked momentarily confused. 'Er . . . two to one.'

'Righto, gennelmen, Morgan?'

'Ten bucks says they ain't,' Morgan cried.

'Ten to win twenty, how about you, Billy?'

'I'm on the kid's side,' Billy said. 'Ten dollars says he's right, both sides are even.'

'Hey, wait on! I ain't got no money,' Davo cried.

'Don't matter,' Freddo said. 'I've got a bet each way. The book, that's me, takes ten per cent.' He turned to Billy, 'Here, 'and me the flamin' needle, mate.'

'Hey, just a moment!' Morgan said. 'If *you* count, you can make it come out any way you like!'

'That's denial, you don't trust anyone,' Billy laughed.

'Too right! Who says Frog Face here can be trusted?'

'Well, as a matter of fact, I do,' Billy said.

'Oh? On what authority? You don't know him from a bar of soap.'

'His terms are not negotiable, he isn't an opportunist and can be trusted.'

'Eh? And how would you know that?'

'Quite simple. The er . . . tattoo on his rear, it's a firm price, he doesn't take advantage of his customers, it's one price for everyone, that means he can be trusted.'

'You mean the same for all *comers*!' Morgan said, unable to resist the pun.

Davo was laughing and Freddo laughed as well. 'Good one, mate! If I go back on the game I'll have that tattooed as well – "One price for all *comers*!"'

Using the point of the needle to separate them, Freddo now set about separating each strand of cotton on first one diagonal of the newly sewn button and then on the other. 'Billy wins! They're exactly the same,' he announced.

'Told yiz, didn't I!' Davo cried, pleased with himself.

Morgan paid up reluctantly and Freddo deducted twenty cents and gave the remainder to Billy.

'Thanks,' Billy said. 'That was lucky, a dollar eighty, that's what you said it cost to sew on a button, didn't you, Davo?' he said, handing the money over to the young bloke.

The ice had been broken and a much easier relationship developed between the four men, though each had times when they slipped off to the clinic to hide behind a curtained-off bed and fight their demons. They would return red-eyed and often still trembling but the others would pretend not to notice. The nights too were noisy affairs with one or the other shouting and calling out in his sleep or weeping quietly in the privacy of the dark. The drug of their particular addiction was out of their systems but it remained firmly in possession of their minds.

Davo and Billy became friends and one afternoon Davo explained how he'd turned eighteen and was now eligible for a prison sentence and how frightened this made him. 'Osmond Hall, I shit it in, didn't care nothin' about that, mate. I been going there since I were eleven, there's nothin' them bastards can do to hurt me no more. But this time they gunna throw me in with the big boys and I'm shittin' me daks.'

'What have you been charged with?' Billy asked.

'Motors. Stealin' motors.'

'You mean cars?'

'Yeah, motors.'

'What do you do when you steal them? Sell them?'

'Nah, drive them, go for a burl, then crash 'em, drive 'em off a cliff or somethin'.'

'Crash them! Whatever for?'

'I hate them fuckers, them BMs!' Davo said with vehemence.

'BMs?'

'Yeah, BMWs.'

'What, that particular make or just expensive cars?'

'Nah, not the motors, I love 'em, they's things of beauty. The wankers that drive BMs.'

'What? You love the cars but you hate the owners?' Billy shook his head. 'All the owners?'

Davo nodded. 'They're wankers. They makes me mad, that's all. I want to hurt them, see how they feel when it's done to them.'

'Done to them? What is done to them?'

Slowly the story of Davo's one-man war against BMW owners emerged. At the age of eleven his alcoholic father had deserted the family for the umpteenth time and at the same time his mother had lost her job as a cleaner at Central Station when she'd found a wallet that had been planted by the cleaning contractors in a railway carriage with forty dollars in it and because she'd kept it they'd dismissed her. 'We was living in these two rooms and a sort o' kitchen in South Dowling Street and when the landlord comes around for the rent she don't have it and he's already given her a week to find it and when he comes back she still hasn't found the money, so he tells us to leave.' Davo went on to tell how his mother had pleaded with the landlord and when he wouldn't listen she had attacked him.

'He was an old bloke, about your age,' Davo said. 'Fat, and he wore this black overcoat and hat like you see in them old movies and he don't speak like us, he's foreign, like he's a Lebbo or something. Me mum don't hurt him but she's half-pissed and pretty aggro and he's frightened and he's backing out onto the street and she's following him, abusing him, calling him names, she wants to kill the bastard. He jumps in his BM and me mum's bangin' on the roof and kickin' at the door and I'm trying to pull her away. Next day these three big Maoris arrive and they take all our stuff and throw it on the pavement, mattresses, chairs, blankets, everything. We've got this old TV and they put it with the rest of our gear, bringing it out last and putting it down. Then one of the Maoris says, "This is from Mr Malouf, you black bitch!" and he kicks in the screen o' the TV and they gets in this old Holden station wagon and drive off.'

'And the landlord drove a BMW?'

'Nah, that's not what done it. Me and me mum are sitting on the pavement with all our gear and there's people lookin' out their windas and standing in the doorways watchin' but nobody's doing nothing to help, because we're Abos and me mum's crying. It's getting real cold so I'm sitting next to her wrapped in this doona. I'm eleven and I don't know what to do. Me mum says looks like we're gunna have to sleep on the pavement and she needs fags, to go get her a packet o' B & H at the shop. The shop's like two blocks away and as I get near I see the landlord and the three Maoris standing on the pavement outside and he's paying them. His BM is between him and me, there's workers digging up the pavement using them jackhammers so I find this big piece o' cement that I have ter lift with both me 'ands and I smash the windscreen, then I smash the cement lump hard as I can into the bonnet and the doors and the roof and the boot and I do all the windas. The jackhammers are going, hammerin' away, digging up the pavement, so the Maoris and the Lebbo don't hear me doing the deed. When I'm almost finished wreckin' the BM, they catch sight o' me and they come running and I run for me life. They don't catch me, but I got to go back to me mum, don't I? But she ain't there and so I can't leave because then she won't know where I am. The Lebbo musta called the cops, because they come in the wagon and I'm took away.' Davo paused. He'd told the story almost without drawing breath. 'That's the first time they put me in Osmond Hall.'

'And your mother?'

Davo shrugged. 'I ain't never seen her since.'

Billy didn't know whether he should believe Davo or not, but told himself it didn't matter, that he wasn't there to be his judge, but that Davo was pretty damaged and needed help, although Billy had no idea how he might get it from the justice system. His only hope seemed to be if he could kick drugs and alcohol, but even then what was waiting for an Aboriginal kid like him in the so-called straight world?

Billy could see Ryan on the same path, his life already had all the ingredients required, a mother who was a heroin addict, his grandmother, the one steady influence in his life, probably dead, nobody to watch over him. Billy was suddenly filled with a terrible fear and sense of helplessness. Davo had shown him almost precisely what would happen to Ryan. He was beginning to see clearly that time was running out, that ten months in rehabilitation was too long. He'd have to do something soon. But how could he? He wouldn't last five minutes out there on his own. If he tried to rescue Ryan, he'd only destroy himself and do nothing for the kid. Billy spent that night in the clinic behind the bed curtains knowing that whatever he did, he was going to fail Ryan.

The following evening the men were watching the rugby league game of the week when the camera turned onto the crowd and showed a close-up of Jeff Fenech, the ex-featherweight champion of the world, who was sitting in the Channel 9 commentary box. 'He's the best there ever was, mate!' Davo said to Billy. 'Pound for pound!'

Billy hadn't been concentrating and only caught a glimpse of the boxer before the camera turned away. 'Who?'

'Jeff Fenech, mate! He's me idol.'

It was the first time Davo had ever mentioned anyone in a positive vein. 'Why don't you write to him?' Billy suggested.

'Nah.'

'Why not, have you seen him fight?'

'Every one of them from 1988 when I were only ten years old, mate. On TV that is. I seen all his title fights since then, Victor Callejas, Tyrone Downes, George Navarro, Marcos Villasana. Azumah Nelson in Las Vegas, that were for his fourth world title. It were a draw but he was gypped, he won it easy, everyone said so. It were a Don King decision, the big boys had their money on Azumah.'

'Oh, yeah, what about when he fought the return in Melbourne? The black bloke KO'd him in eight,' said Morgan, who was sitting close by.

'Jeff was crook, mate, he shouldn't never have fought that day, he had asthma real bad.'

'Fight's a fight, mate. He took it, he lost it, it's down in the books,' Morgan replied in a dispassionate voice.

'Yeah, but his hands, they was RS as well.' Davo was clearly upset.

'Should've given it away then,' Morgan countered. 'Didn't he lose to the next bloke as well?'

'Yeah, Calvin Grove. Like I said, his hands were ratshit, he retired straight after,' said Davo, defending his idol. 'Can't take his record away from him, mate. No Australian boxer ever done better, never will neither. Twenty-nine fights, twenty-six wins, one draw, two losses when his hands were gone.'

Morgan turned away to watch something on TV and Billy said again, 'Well, write to him, Davo. Look, I've got a pad and pen and stamps, it shouldn't be too hard to find his address.'

'Nah, that sucks. No way, mate.'

Billy had left it at that. They'd all learned that Davo couldn't be coerced. But a couple of days later he sat beside Billy at breakfast. 'Porridge sucks, I hate it.'

'Have some toast,' Billy suggested.

'Yeah, suppose,' Davo said, continuing to spoon the oatmeal into his mouth. 'About Jeff Fenech, you fair dinkum?'

'What do you mean?'

'About writin', mate? Yer know, sendin' him a letter like?'

Billy put his spoon down. 'I said, *you* ought to write to him.'

'Nah, can't.'

'Can't what? What can't you do?'

Davo was silent, tapping the back of his spoon against

the plate of oatmeal in front of him. In a small voice he said, 'See, I ain't no good at writin', mate.'

'That's okay, tell me what you want to say and I'll write it for you,' Billy said, trying to sound casual while realising at once that Davo was confessing he was illiterate.

'Yeah?'

'No problems,' Billy said.

'What'll I say?'

Billy pretended to be thinking. 'Lots of things. How you admire him. How you've never missed any of his fights on television, that sort of thing. You could tell him something about yourself.' Billy made a logical guess. 'Maybe how you want to be a boxer?'

'Shit no! He don't want to hear that.'

'Do you want to become a boxer?'

'Yeah, I can fight, man. I ain't scared.'

Billy knew not to push him. 'Think about it for a couple of days, let me know when you're ready.'

'Thanks, mate. Thanks a lot!' Davo said, reaching out and lightly touching Billy's shoulder, then drawing back, suddenly aware that he'd touched another human being affectionately.

It was during a lecture in the second week that Billy began to see a pattern emerging that began to explain his own life. The subject being discussed was codependency and his own past began to open up for him. He had always thought of codependency as something to do with substances. For instance, the cook and housemaid when he was younger didn't need to take a Bex powder with their morning tea but they were codependent on Bex and simply had to have one. They believed that without the powder they would not be able to cope with the day ahead. But now he learned that the meaning of codependence was much more, it was a vicious and insidious psychological disease. He'd been somewhat doubtful when he'd first been told this, these days there seemed to be an explanation for everything and nothing was anyone's fault any more.

But he began to sit up and take notice when the lecturer said, 'Remember when you were a little kid, all the messages you got were that there was something wrong with you, you were bad? You didn't know why you were bad, you just were. If your parents fought, it was because you hadn't been good, it was your fault. You were told you had to be a good boy, perfect, you shouldn't cry, only sissies cried if they skinned their knee or bumped their head. If you made mistakes you got yelled at and this told you that you were unlovable and flawed and not the little boy your parents wanted. Sometimes your mother comforted you and sometimes she turned on you, aiming her rage and anger at you, blaming you for her misfortunes in life. "I wish I'd never had you!" "You're a little shit!" "You're just like your father, no bloody good! You'll grow up to be a bastard, just like him!" Your father had very little to do with you, he'd shout at you to be a man, that you were a sissy and a coward. If you didn't excel at sport you were a failure, no good to anyone and, even if he didn't say so openly, you could sense his deep disappointment in you.'

Billy had interrupted at this stage. 'But isn't that all part of the business of growing up? You know, the rough and tumble?'

'Yes, of course, that's because your own parents were subjected to the same thing when they were kids. They're only following a pattern, but that isn't to say it isn't a flawed design. That it isn't wrong to act in this way.'

'Sure, but it's a real world out there. Isn't what happens, like I said, the toughening-up process to prepare us for what's to come?'

'Right again, Billy!' Though they'd had several counsellors for their lectures, it was Jimmy's turn again. 'That's how we justify it, but the result isn't always a stronger person, it's often a person who has learned to live in a codependent society.'

'Codependent society? What's that mean?'

'Okay, instead of believing in yourself, in your own intrinsic value as a human being, you devalue yourself. You learn pretty quickly that value is assigned by society as a list of comparisons, such as richer than, prettier than, sexier than, cleverer than, more spiritual than, healthier than, and so on. You relinquish your right to be yourself and you allow others to judge you. These comparisons inevitably lead to a feeling of separation, which can lead in its extreme form to resentment, violence, hopelessness, despair, to being an outcast. Codependence is vicious because it causes us to hate and abuse ourselves.'

'Hang on, don't we have choices? Are you saying that the process of childhood as it is conducted in our society corrupts the inner child and robs him of his intrinsic power?'

Jimmy brought his hands together and applauded. 'I wish I'd said that, Billy.'

'To be truthful, it sounds like a bit of a cop-out to me,' Billy countered.

Jimmy frowned. 'How old are you, Billy?'

'Fifty-six, though sometimes I feel a hundred.' The men around him nodded.

'Okay, so your father was born, let me take a guess, around 1917?'

'1915,' Billy replied. 'He was a last pleasant act before his father went to Gallipoli.'

'Well, your father's generation did it tough, many of them lost their fathers, and those who didn't grew up with silent, uncommunicative men. Today we'd call it post-traumatic stress disorder, but at that time it would simply have been known as your grandfather's 'moods'. His silences and irritability would have been almost constant and the only way he could've shown his frustration was by losing his temper. Your father's dad was a war hero, he had to be perfect, except for his anger, which his wife and his son grew to fear greatly and would go to great lengths to avoid. Am I making any sense?'

'I can't say, I didn't know my grandfather, but you're doing a pretty good job of describing my father.'

'Aha! Let's skip a generation then and go on to your father. Did your father go to war?'

Billy thought of his father, whom he'd always seen as the

stern-faced judge he'd greatly feared and who had often spent the whole night drinking alone in his study. 'Yes, he was captured in Singapore and was sent to Changi.'

'Righto, with the usual superficial differences found in the next generation, he was probably a lot like his own father, what we used to call the strong, silent type who only expressed himself fully when he was angry. He probably didn't communicate very well with you but had unreasonable expectations of his only son, and when you didn't achieve these he'd disparage and humiliate you.'

Billy had picked up a number of expressions in the group discussions. 'Right on!' he said.

'So your mother tried to compensate,' Jimmy continued. 'She told you how she loved you, how you were all she had. You watched how she too was humiliated by your father and would do anything to appease him. She loved you but he came first. Everything was for your father. But nothing helped your father's rage or indifference or drunkenness or cruelty. You felt responsible for your mother's wellbeing and ashamed that you couldn't protect her from his raging or the pain she suffered in her life.'

Jimmy shrugged. 'So there was the evidence you needed. Here was someone who loved you and who thought you were worthy of being loved, but you couldn't protect her from her husband, your father, from being humiliated or hurt or having an awful life. As a small child this was all the proof you needed that you were flawed and unworthy. You knew that she was going to find out that you were no good, and too weak and unworthy to help her. When she became exasperated and desperate and deeply depressed and screamed at you or blamed you for her plight, this was the moment of truth when she found out your unworthiness, when she told you what you knew all along, that you were useless.'

Jimmy spread his arms. 'I'm hypothesising, of course. But if these were your circumstances, Billy, then you may have unknowingly begun the continual cycle of shame, blame and self-abuse that would manifest itself in one of many ways in the adult you. The pain of being unworthy and shameful is so great that we eventually learn to avoid it, disconnect from our feelings. We look for a way to protect ourselves from hurt with drugs and alcohol, food, cigarettes, work, relationships and obsessions such as perceived body image. We become codependent and, in the end, it destroys us.'

'Isn't that universal, I mean the Christian church teaches that we are guilty of original sin?'

'No! We are made to *believe* we are guilty. Yes, you're right, the Church has been doing this all along, we are told we are born sinful and unworthy. The family environment encourages this idea and adds to it in the way I've just described and so guilt and shame are passed on from one generation to the next.'

Jimmy stopped suddenly. 'Look, I'm making it sound too complicated. Let's take a simple example, eating too much. Right, I'm a bit overweight; so others start pointing this out, at school, my father. I feel ashamed but I keep eating, I don't know why. Now I judge myself, call myself a fat slob; I mentally beat myself up for being fat; then I feel the terrible hurt that comes with being a fat slob and decide

I must do something to stop the pain. But willpower doesn't work, I'm too weak I tell myself, too useless, so to nurture myself I buy three hamburgers with cheese and bacon and a double portion of chips; I judge myself again for being weak, unworthy and a useless fat slob, and the cycle begins all over again.' Jimmy looked around. 'But the reason I became fat wasn't because I was intrinsically an unworthy human being but because I was made to *believe* that I was.'

This was something the men could understand and they clapped and whistled. They'd all been there a thousand times before with their codependent drug of choice.

Then Morgan said, 'Yeah, Jimmy, you know how you, like, made the case for Billy, his old man givin' him a bad time and his mum lovin' him but also abusing him when she got cranky?'

'Yeah, what's the question?' Jimmy asked.

'Well, I don't know about the others here, but I reckon I'd have thought I was on easy street if that happened to me. Me old man was always drunk, he'd come home and beat the shit out of me mum, then he'd rape me and beat me up. My mum said we had to forgive him because it was his nerves from the war. But when I was about seven she also became a drunk.' Morgan started to weep and Billy, seated beside him, put his arms around him.

That evening while they were waiting to go into chapel, Davo came over to Billy and sat beside him. 'Mind if I sit with yiz ternight, mate?' he asked.

'No, of course not,' Billy replied.

Davo was silent for a while then he said, 'You know how Morgan said about his dad, you know, what he did to him and then his mum?' Billy nodded, not speaking. 'You know I told yiz I'd never seen me mum again after I run away from smashin' the BM?' Billy nodded again. 'Well, it weren't true. Last year I'm in this pub when this Abo woman comes up to me, she's drunk and she says ter me, "Gimme ten bucks you can fuck me."' The tears started to run silently down Davo's cheeks. 'It's me mum. She don't recognise me, her own son.'

Billy put his arm around him, 'You ready to write that letter to Jeff Fenech tonight, Davo?' The kid sniffed, knuckling back his tears, and nodded.

That evening Billy sat with Davo while the young bloke dictated the letter to Jeff Fenech. Billy tried to put it down as it was spoken, thinking that if he corrected Davo's grammar he would lose some of the feeling that came through in the spoken word. There were frequent stops and starts as Davo tried to work out what he wanted to say, often turning to Billy to ask his opinion. 'Just be honest, Davo, tell him what's on your mind.'

William Booth Institute
Albion Street
Strawberry Hills

Dear Mr Fenech,

I'd like to call you Jeff but I got too much respect.
My name is Davo Davies and I'm doing rehab here.
The judge sent me to detox, like instead of going in

remand 'til my case is heard. I hope yer 'aven't got a
BMW cos that's why I'm in the shit, stealin' and wreckin'
them. It's cos somethin' happened way back and I can't
help meself. But now I'm clean, man, and even if I get
time I'm gunna try to stay clean this time.

The reason I'm writing to you is that yiz always
been me idol.

Even though yer no longer boxing, yiz still in the
game, coaching blokes. Yer putting something back in
the game. That's real good. I seen every one of your title
fights since I was ten years old and there's never gunna
be anyone better than you, mate. I'm sorry about your
broken hand, yer would've beaten Azumah Nelson the
second time like yiz did the first time and got gypped,
if yer wasn't that crook yiz could hardly lift a finger.

I think I'm going inside. I done this BM 740 and
I reckon I'm gone, cos I'm eighteen and no longer a
juvenile offender. I done a bit of fighting in juvenile
remand but then I got hooked (grog and amphetamines)
but when I'm clean I hope to go back and have a go.
Maybe they'll let me box inside?

I'm sorry to go on like this, but I just wanted yiz
to know you're the best, mate. They don't make two
Jeff Fenechs in a hundred years.
Your number one fan,
Davo Davies

Billy hadn't heard from Ryan and he was now almost three
weeks into the first stage of rehabilitation. Ryan's failure to

answer his letters was a constant preoccupation of Billy's. Whenever chapel occurred and the wives or girlfriends of some of the men would turn up and mingle afterwards in the foyer for a few minutes, Billy would be especially disconsolate and confused as to what to do next.

Chapel was the best thing that happened to the men all week, although it was intended as a religious gathering where they might come to terms with their saviour Jesus Christ. While every gathering included a short sermon aimed at repentance and a reading given by one of the men from the blue *Selective Readings* book, it was the singing they most looked forward to. The very act of singing is a strong bond between people, and the chapel was an opportunity to let her rip, to get their emotions out into the open. The singing, while not always tuneful, was lusty and surprisingly uninhibited given the lyrics. Although there were many favourites among them, such as 'One Day at a Time', 'To God be the Glory', 'Just a Closer Walk with Thee', 'Put Your Hand in the Hand', 'Count Your Blessings' and 'Amazing Grace', by far the most popular of the 133 songs in the book among the men was 'Power in the Blood'.

Would you be free from your burden of sin?
There's power in the Blood, power in the Blood;
Would you o'er evil a victory win?
There's wonderful power in the Blood.

Chorus

There is power, power
Wonder-working power
In the Blood of the Lamb
There is power, power
Wonder-working power
In the precious Blood of the Lamb.

Would you be free from your passion and pride?
There's power in the Blood, power in the Blood;
Come then for cleansing to Calvary's tide;
There's wonderful power in the Blood.

Chorus

Would you be whiter, much whiter than snow?
There's power in the Blood, power in the Blood.
Sin stains are lost in its life-giving flow,
There's wonderful power in the Blood.

Chorus

Would you do service for Jesus your King?
There's power in the Blood, power in the Blood;
Would you live daily His praises to sing?
There's wonderful power in the Blood.

Chorus

Nothing quite matched the gusto of this hymn with its easy tune and strident chorus and, while there may not have been a single born-again Christian as the Salvos would define one, the men's eyes shone with conviction after completing it.

On his final Sunday at William Booth, and two days before Billy completed the first stage of rehabilitation, the chapel was packed. They were about to be transferred to the St Peters rehabilitation centre for the lengthy second stage. Billy was relieved that he didn't have to go to Newcastle after all. This would be the last time for two months that families and partners would see each other and there was a great deal of tension and apprehension in the air.

This second stage was a truly frightening prospect, seven months of complete introspection one-on-one with a counsellor. They would be required to write every day, addressing their fears, flaws, assets, resentments, past sexual conduct and the harm they had done to others, specifically answering hundreds of related questions in minute detail. They would have to work through each of these, dredging up the past since childhood, facing every nightmare they'd ever experienced. They would even at one stage have to seek out and face up to all the people in their lives whom they had harmed and ask for their forgiveness, perhaps the most harrowing experience of them all.

The second stage was where most men baulked and left the program, heading for the nearest pub or fix, telling themselves that the pain of dredging up long-buried and deeply hurtful memories was too much to ask them to endure. In fact, experience showed that while certainly harrowing, the pain didn't come from working through the past, it came from resisting doing so. Alcoholics and other addicts would often rather go back to their addiction than openly face some of the inner truths in the process of rehabilitation. It was Jimmy's initial point all over again, when on the very first day he'd said that freedom from the addictive self is impossible if we hold on to the fears and secrets we've been harbouring all our lives. The way of gaining strength and hope is, paradoxically, to make ourselves vulnerable.

The chapel was packed to the rafters on this final Sunday. Billy had checked the strangers coming in and watched the look of joy on the faces of the men who had someone they could call their own. Ryan hadn't come again and it was with a heavy heart that Billy took a seat in the front of the chapel so that he didn't have to look at any of the visitors. He was deeply confused. If he agreed to go to St Peters in two days he would be even further removed from contact with the boy, who now appeared not to want him in his life anyway.

A short message was given by the Salvation Army chaplain, who congratulated the men who had completed the three weeks of the first stage in their rehabilitation. Each was asked to come up to receive a Bible, the traditional parting gift from the Salvos before they were transferred to one of the other venues chosen for the next stage in their rehabilitation – St Peters or Miracle Haven, a working farm outside Morisset. This was followed by a reading from Morgan, who spoke in a surprisingly well-modulated voice, somewhat different from his usual manner. Morgan hadn't talked much about himself. Despite his wisecracks and his flip manner, he was the least forthcoming of Billy's room-mates.

After the reading, there was a call from several of the men for 'Power!' as 'Power in the Blood' was called. A lusty and wholehearted rendition followed and then others nominated various hymns. Almost to his own surprise, Billy found himself calling out 'Amazing Grace' for the final hymn.

The pianist started the refrain and the congregation began to sing the beautiful hymn when suddenly Billy became aware of a voice that rose above them all, a voice so pure and perfect that it didn't seem possible. The rest of the congregation stopped and the single voice, a boy soprano, rose to fill the hushed chapel, the words perfectly, gloriously enunciated.

Billy turned to see Ryan standing at the doorway, singing alone, clutching his skateboard under his arm, his dirty little face raised to the ceiling. His voice rose higher and higher, then dropped, until the congregation felt sure it must falter. Billy found himself weeping uncontrollably. Ryan had come at last. The lad had forgiven him.

At a signal from the chaplain, the congregation resumed their seats and Billy was forced to turn his back on Ryan. A final short prayer followed, which seemed endless to Billy, who could hear his heart thumping in his chest. Sunday chapel was finally over. Billy rose, barely able to contain himself, but Ryan was no longer standing at the door.

Billy pushed people out of his way as he ran from the

chapel and down the stairs to the foyer below and towards the door. 'Ryan! Ryan!' he shouted. Vaguely he heard the buzzer as the receptionist locked the electronically controlled door and Billy slammed into it, breaking his nose and falling to the floor. 'The boy! Did you see a boy?' he shouted, oblivious to the blood pumping from his nose.

'You can't leave, Billy,' the receptionist said calmly. 'You are not allowed to go after him.'

Billy looked down to see his nice soft-blue cotton shirt stained with blood.

CHAPTER ELEVEN

Billy was taken to the clinic and from there to St Vincent's where they reset his nose. He asked to see Dr Goldstein but he was off duty. The reception clerk was also different and he learned that Mrs Willoughby, Ryan's opponent, hadn't lasted the distance and had long since departed. He had hoped to hear something of the boy, thinking that perhaps his mother had been a patient in Billy's absence, but even the two gay security men were off duty and there was nobody who could help him.

When Billy returned to William Booth, his mind was made up, he would leave the rehabilitation program and find Ryan. The boy's appearance, and then abrupt disappearance, could only mean one thing, he was extremely confused. Billy told himself that an eleven-year-old child wouldn't come all the way to see him and then run off. There had to be something very wrong.

Back at William Booth, Billy was told that Major Cliff Thomas from Foster House had called to deliver three letters for him. Not finding him present, he had left a note.

Dear Billy,

How can I apologise to you? These three letters have been waiting for you at Foster House, the first for two weeks, the second for over a week and the third one arrived yesterday. I just happened to notice the one yesterday and then looked to see if there were any others. I am not normally responsible for the mail, and the person who is, not knowing your present whereabouts, simply assumed you'd call around in due course to collect it. I can only pray they are not important. I hope your nose is all right and that you're feeling better.

Yours in the blessed name of Jesus,
Cliff Thomas

When writing to the principal of Pring Street Public School and to Ryan, Billy had used the Foster House address in Mary Street, Strawberry Hills, not at the time knowing the correct one for William Booth. He'd neglected to make arrangements with Cliff Thomas to forward his mail. Such a small mistake might have had disastrous consequences and Billy's hands shook as he tore open the first letter, which was written in an educated hand on light-blue paper using a fountain pen.

Pring Street Public School
22 July 1996

Dear Mr O'Shannessy,

Thank you for your letter in which you showed concern
for the welfare of Ryan Sanfrancesco. I only wish that the
news I could give you was positive. Ryan's grandmother
passed away and since then his attendance at school has
been irregular. We have tried to talk to him about it, but
he refuses to speak to us other than to say 'It's cool, she
told me she was gunna die'.

We are aware that he needs counselling, but the
school's facilities are very limited and we have informed
the Department of Community Services of the situation
with his mother. As there have been no formal complaints
of abuse, they have noted Ryan's case as Priority One.
Do not think that this means they consider his welfare
a priority, this category simply means they will open a file
and if there are no further reports in twenty-six days,
his case will be closed.

Your letter to Ryan has been duly received and, as part
of my responsibility as his principal, I have been obliged
to read it. I have passed it on to the Department of
Community Services, who have issued instructions that
Ryan may not receive your letters until you have
identified yourself personally to the appropriate
Community Services District Officer.

I know that in my previous letter I encouraged

you to write to Ryan, as I was convinced your friendship was both important and honourable and I remain of that opinion. I am personally sorry that this is the outcome as I feel sure that your association with Ryan is very important to the boy. I hope you understand my hands are tied in this matter and I am in no position to disobey the department's instructions.

In the meantime we all worry about Ryan, who is such a bright and talented boy, and it would be a terrible shame to lose him. It is such a pity that your present circumstances make it impossible to see him, although of course I fully understand your situation. If it doesn't seem presumptuous, may I wish you every success in what you are personally attempting to do with your life.

Yours sincerely,
Dorothy Flanagan
Principal

Billy's first reaction was one of utter dismay. Ryan hadn't received his letters and, worse still, the Department of Community Services had forbidden them. In his present emotional state, Billy felt betrayed. He hadn't met Ryan's principal and now he felt she'd simply, as Morgan would have put it, 'covered her arse'. It wasn't until much later that he realised that, under the circumstances, it had been a responsible attitude for her to adopt.

Billy sat for a while thinking, not opening the second letter. How the hell had Ryan tracked him down if he hadn't received either of his letters? Why had he appeared suddenly in the chapel and then run away? Billy opened the second letter, and glancing quickly at the bottom of the page he saw that it too was from Dorothy Flanagan but this time it was typed on the school's letterhead.

Dear Mr O'Shannessy,

I have received your second letter to Ryan and as you must have received my last letter I cannot understand why you would write a second one. You must understand that my position in this matter is quite clear, I cannot disobey my instructions from the Department of Community Services. Your letter to Ryan would have been studied by a qualified child psychiatrist and I am not at liberty to go against their decision. I am very sorry but I must ask you not to write to Ryan again care of this address.

Yours sincerely,

Ms D. Flanagan - Principal

cc. Mary Kennedy, School Counsellor - DOCS

A second page was attached and on it appeared a single typewritten line in a different typeface.

I have told R. of your whereabouts.

Ryan's principal, God bless her, was covering her tracks. Billy's heart soared, Dorothy Flanagan had seen Ryan and spoken to him.

Billy now opened the third letter, this one again handwritten.

Dear Mr O'Shannessy,

Today has not been one of the better days in my teaching career and I have no idea why I am writing to you other than that you have shown that you care about Ryan Sanfrancesco and God knows very few people seem to. Please forgive me if I appear over-emotional. I have been teaching for thirty-two years and I keep telling myself that I am beyond being surprised. Pring Street is not an easy school to administer, but having been offered several so-called better choices, I chose this school to see out my career, my motive being that I thought I might be able to bring my experience to bear and in the process help maintain some sort of balance in the often topsy-turvy lives of so many of our children.

Occasionally we are rewarded with a gifted child such as Ryan, so it is especially distressing when we lose the battle to save him because of circumstances beyond our control.

This afternoon I had a visit from the police looking for Ryan and, while I don't know the full story yet, they explained that Ryan had called the ambulance service, saying that his mother was having an asthma attack and needed to go to St Vincent's. The operator told the police that the child sounded very distressed, convinced his mother was dying. One of the paramedics who had picked her up on a previous occasion remembered that she was a heroin addict and that there might be complications, so they responded immediately with a full resuscitation unit.

When they arrived, the front door was ajar and they found Ryan's mother dead. There was no sign of Ryan. The police have been looking for him for several days as the post-mortem on his mother showed that she was ill from Hepatitis C. According to the police, she had not been to work for ten days (I am told she was an exotic dancer) and the cause of death was not an asthma attack but a heroin overdose. Apparently the heroin she had injected in her weakened condition was too pure and she died of a massive heart attack.

I am not at all sure that there is anything you can do. We have asked all the children here at Pring Street to report to me if they see Ryan and to assure him that if he comes to me I will make sure that he is safe and cared for. If he should in some way try to contact you, please let me know as we both have his welfare at heart.

Yours sincerely,
Dorothy Flanagan

Billy had gone to his bed to read the letters and now, with his torso concealed behind the pillar, he couldn't stop trembling. Ryan was a brave and capable child, he'd taken his mother to St Vincent's on numerous occasions so why had he fled the house at such a critical moment? Was it the shock of seeing his mother die? Did a child know when someone was dead? The way Dorothy Flanagan had described it, Ryan's mother must have died while the ambulance was on its way. Or was it just the child's way of alerting the authorities to his mother's death? It didn't sound like the Ryan he knew, that child didn't run away. He recalled how he'd first met Ryan, who'd been standing squinting at the statue of Trim on the window ledge of the Mitchell Library. He hadn't even flinched when Billy had shouted, threatening him. Then there had been the incident with the receptionist at St Vincent's when Billy had broken his wrist, and, before that, the brazen boldness he'd shown in going into the Cesco Bar to buy him a cup of coffee. Billy also recalled how he'd stood up to Con at the New Hellas Cafe. Ryan simply wasn't the sort to run away from anything. It just didn't make sense. Despite everything, he'd loved his mother and he even seemed to take responsibility for her. It was almost as if she was the child and he the adult. Why? Why? Why? None of it made any sense to Billy.

Billy spent a sleepless night driving himself to distraction and in the morning he was already waiting outside the office of Vince Payne, the program director, when he arrived at work at eight o'clock.

'Morning, Billy, here to see me?' Payne asked.

'Yes, if I may, please.'

'How's your nose? You've got two bonzer black eyes, mate.'

'Fine, thanks.' Billy had been so distressed that he hadn't shaved or even glanced in the mirror when he'd attempted to wash his face.

'Come in, come in,' Payne urged, unlocking his office. 'Sit!' He indicated the straight-backed kitchen chair. 'Make yourself comfortable.'

Vince switched on his computer as a matter of habit. He'd brought in a styrofoam mug of coffee from Rocco's, which he balanced precariously on a bundle of papers among the many that covered his desk. 'Would you like a decent cup of coffee, mate? You look like you could use one. I'll send someone?'

'No, thank you, Vince, I've already had breakfast.' Although he'd been to breakfast, Billy had been unable to eat or drink anything.

Vince leaned back in his rickety office chair. 'So, what's on your mind, Billy?'

Billy cleared his throat, his nose throbbed and one eye felt as if it was only half open. 'I'm afraid I have to leave the program, Vince, I won't be going on to St Peters.'

Vince Payne looked shocked. 'Why, Billy?'

'It's private, there's something I have to do.'

The program director looked serious. 'But there's something you have to do at St Peters, Billy. Something very important!'

'I'm sorry, but I can't explain. I just have to leave.'

Vince Payne had heard it all before, the life and death assignation, wife dying, kids ill, they were the most common lies, but there were many more. Many of the alcoholics were schizophrenics and had used alcohol to stop the voices in their heads. When they detoxed, the voices returned and their reasons for leaving the program could be anything from a call from Spiderman to help save the world from certain disaster to a message they'd received saying that the William Booth Institute was a hotbed of communist activity and was about to be blown up by the CIA.

In Billy he thought he recognised the usual underlying reason, simply a desire to get away because he was unable to face the idea of a further seven months spent in an institution. The street drunks who lived in the so-called Starlight Hotel, the open air, were particularly vulnerable. After three weeks incarcerated at William Booth, they had a desperate need to break out. As program director there wasn't a lot he could do under the circumstances, it was unlawful to hold a client against his will. He'd have to try a delaying tactic, anything to give Billy time to reconsider, or it sometimes helped to read the riot act and make a firm appeal to commonsense, which in Billy's case seemed the more productive course of action.

'Now listen here, Billy, you're not being fair to us or to yourself,' Vince said, his voice firm.

'Oh?'

'Billy, I'll be perfectly frank with you. When you came in I told myself you'd be lucky to last a week. Old blokes, confirmed alcoholics, don't usually rehabilitate. Well, one in a hundred, anyway.' Vince had located Billy's file among the clutter on his desk and was flicking through it. 'Your counsellors' reports are outstanding, only yesterday at the end of the course meeting Jimmy said, and I quote: "Billy has made an outstanding contribution to the group and his attitude suggests that he will do well at St Peters."' Vince stopped and turned the page. 'Ah, here it is.' He turned back to Billy. 'We give every client a prospective rating, a recovery potential, your rating is a full twenty points above the norm. For an old bloke that's outstanding.'

'Thank you,' Billy said quietly, 'but I have no choice, I must leave.'

Vince Payne picked up the biro and started the annoying business of tapping on the frame of his computer. 'Is it over the incident in chapel yesterday?'

'Yes,' Billy admitted.

'Would you like to tell me about it?'

'No, I don't think so.' Billy was surprised at himself, he'd said it with a certainty that belied his own confusion.

Vince decided to try the second tactic. 'Look, Billy, you've broken your nose, you're upset, you've got two days here before you go to St Peters. Just give us the two days, then you can decide, eh?'

Billy shook his head slowly. 'I'm sorry, I can't.'

The program director decided to throw caution to the wind. He straightened up and leaned forward, pointing the biro at Billy. 'You won't achieve anything. If you go after the boy and can't find him right off, which is on the cards, you'll be on a downer and you'll go straight to the pub. In forty-eight hours you'll be back where you were five weeks ago! Billy, listen to me. You can't make it on your own out there, not at this stage of your rehabilitation, you're simply not ready, mate, you're too fragile. You'll be back on the sauce and then what good will that do the boy? The boy doesn't need another drunk in his life, does he?'

'He's in trouble, I have to find him, that's all. I have to take the chance.'

'Billy, you're not taking a chance, you're committing suicide! It's your duty to yourself to stay!'

Billy shook his head. 'No, you're wrong. If I stayed I'd be committing suicide. I'm not going to repeat what I did to Charlie.'

'Charlie? That the boy's name?'

Billy didn't answer, instead he took a deep breath. 'Vince, I have to leave. I'd like to think you'd allow me to come back if I needed to?'

Vince shrugged. 'This is the Salvation Army, they don't turn anyone away, mate.' Billy could sense that Vince Payne thought the request purely academic, that he'd just witnessed the opening of the last chapter in the final demise of Billy O'Shannessy. 'You'll have to stay here today and tonight, there's a fair bit to do, paperwork, your disability pension transfer, you'll have to have another medical.' He threw the biro down on the desk. 'You'll be allowed to go first thing tomorrow morning.'

'Oh, I was hoping simply to slip away unnoticed.'

'No, you can't, you see . . .'

Billy held up his hand. 'Please, Vince, I know you're hoping the group will bring pressure to bear collectively. It won't work. I'm not leaving the rehabilitation program because I'm tired of it and think I can manage my life back on the street. I'm leaving because I have something I have to do and if I don't try to do it, then remaining sober for the rest of my life would be pointless.'

Vince sighed. 'Righto, Billy, I'll make arrangements with the major for you to leave quietly after breakfast tomorrow. Just remember, it's never too late to change your mind.'

'Yes, thank you,' Billy said, rising from the chair. 'Thank you, Vince, for all your help, I'm sorry I've let you down.'

Vince Payne wasn't a happy loser. 'No, Billy, be sorry that you've let *yourself* down.'

At morning tea, when the mail was handed out, a very excited Davo came rushing up to Billy. 'Lookee here!' he said, flashing an envelope. 'Jeff Fenech, he's wrote to me!'

'Hey, that's great, Davo, what does he say?' Billy cried, pleased as punch for Davo.

'Read it for yerself,' Davo said, handing Billy the envelope.

Billy removed the letter and unfolded the single typed page. 'Look,' he pointed to the letterhead, '"Team Fenech", pretty posh, eh?'

'Fair dinkum, that what it says? "Team Fenech"?'

Billy had caught himself just in time. Davo, of course, was illiterate, and he'd guessed the letter was from Jeff Fenech because of a pair of boxing gloves drawn in the bottom left-hand corner of the envelope. The letter was typed.

Dear Davo,

*Thank you for your letter, I was really glad to get it.
You sound like you're in a spot of bother, mate. Don't
worry, we all have these bad things happen to us, you've
just got to fight your way out. Remember you're only out
for the count after the man has counted to ten. Don't take
that poison no more, mate, that way the bastards are
winning. If you going to do time, then do it clean, come
out with a clean record, give the shit the knockout
punch! Kapow! No more drugs! Pow-pow-pow!
No more grog!*

*You say you like to box, eh? Well, here's my
proposition. Stay clean, stay healthy, work out in the gym
where they send you, build up your body and keep your
nose clean, mate. Earn respect. If you can do this, then
here's my idea. When you get out, come and see me at
Team Fenech. I reckon we'll be able to sort something
out for you, mate. If you'd like to learn to fight then I'm
in your corner. That's my promise, I'll give you a fair
dinkum go, but only if you keep your side of the bargain.
Have we got a deal?*

See you in the ring, buddy,

*All the best,
Jeff Fenech*

'Jesus! Jesus Christ!' Davo said, shaking his head,
hardly able to believe what he'd just heard.

'Shhh! Language, Davo!' Billy cautioned, looking around.

'You reckon he's for real? I told you, didn't I? He's a top act, the champ of champs, best there ever was, best there ever will be!' Davo couldn't stop shaking his head.

Billy folded the letter, placed it back in the envelope, and held it out for Davo to take. 'Well then, Davo, what say you?'

'Bloody oath! Team Fenech, eh? Jeez, Billy, a man feels like cryin'.' Davo's eyes suddenly filled with tears. He grabbed the letter and took off down the passageway and into the shower block. Billy wondered how long it had been since the young bloke had had a good cry simply because he was happy. Despite his own anxieties, Billy smiled. Davo had found his motivation to go straight and Sydney's BMW owners could breathe a little easier.

After the evening meeting, when they were all together again in the room, Billy waited until Freddo, Morgan and Davo were settled before he made the announcement that he was leaving in the morning. What followed was complete silence from the three men.

It was Morgan who was the first to speak. 'Billy, don't go, mate, please.'

'Yeah, don't go, Billy,' Freddo echoed.

Davo said nothing, a look of incredulity on his face.

Morgan, like the others, had been lying on his bed and now he sat up, swinging his legs onto the floor. He sat on the edge of the bed, looking down at his feet. After a few moments he raised his eyes to look over at Billy. 'We need you, mate,' he said simply. 'I don't know about Freddo and Davo here, but I been tellin' myself all along, if the old bloke can hack it, then so can I.' The hint of a smile appeared at the corners of his mouth. 'You're a wise old bastard, it's like havin' a proper dad, someone you trust.'

Freddo nodded and Davo burst out, 'Billy, yiz me mate, look what yer done for me!'

'We loves yer, Billy,' Freddo said simply.

'Don't give it away, Billy, you've come this far, we've held each other together . . .' It was Morgan again.

'Billy, I want yiz to be there when I have me first fight, Team Fenech, mate. Like Morgan said, youse our dad.'

Billy was finding it difficult to contain his conflicting emotions. These were young men who had long learned not to trust, not to love, and now they were saying they trusted and loved him. It was almost too much for him to bear. He'd always been Mr Nice Guy, well-mannered, polite and even, in his younger days, gregarious. With sufficient liquid refreshment, he'd been the life of the party. Essentially he was a loner, unable to love, unable to trust anyone, and as a defence mechanism he'd developed an ability to fake his emotions. When it had come to the crunch in any relationship, he'd been careful always to keep it at arm's length. The way his father had treated him as a boy was how he had responded to his wife and daughter. There were times when he was so drunk he couldn't even remember his daughter's name. Then there was Charlie, it had been even worse between the two of them.

Now these young blokes, misfits like himself, the dregs, had crept in under his guard to reach out to him. Almost without being conscious that he was doing so, Billy had begun to open up, to say some of the things that lay buried deep, hidden in his subconscious.

'I guess we all know a bit about each other, a bit about our past lives, and when I hear the stories of your background, your childhood, I feel ashamed because my childhood was nothing like yours. My old man was a Supreme Court judge. I had the best education money could buy, a career in law that some people have said was spectacular, and, well, here I am, in a rehabilitation unit, an alcoholic trying to make amends.

'I'm not at all sure how I got here,' Billy said sadly. 'People would say I was headed for the bench, I'd be a judge like my father. They were right in a way. I did end up on the bench, the one beside the Mitchell Library.'

'Billy, yiz too good to be a judge, they's all bastards,' Davo interrupted.

Billy smiled at the young bloke. 'Anyway, when my boy Charlie died that finally tipped the scales for me. Now I could allow myself to have what everyone would say was a nervous breakdown and give myself permission to run away from the past. I could walk away from the mess I'd created and leave it to the people I was supposed to love, my wife and daughter, leave them to pick up the pieces and get on with their lives.'

It was Morgan, not able to resist a one-liner, who said, 'Yeah, mate, tough, someone's got to pick up the pieces. Big house, money, yacht, BMW, overseas travel, them's the breaks.'

'BMW!' Davo cried out. 'Shit, yiz didn't, did ya?' He was plainly shocked.

Billy was forced to laugh. 'There was a Mercedes and a Volvo. I think my daughter had a Honda, one of those Japanese models anyway.' Billy discovered to his surprise that he was telling them the story of his life in a completely dispassionate voice. As he dredged up the past, visiting his greatest fears, he was able to remain calm. He was facing up to the person who lived deep inside him and whom he'd been trying to avoid meeting all his adult life.

Freddo, who, in his own way, or as Morgan might have put it 'in his own fucked-up way', was the most serious-minded of the three of them, now spoke. 'It wasn't your fault your boy died, Billy, you don't have to take the blame for everything.'

Billy was silent for a few moments. He was grateful for the interruption, he was indulging himself, this wasn't the time to talk about himself. His own troubled background would seem inconsequential compared to what they'd been through. 'I guess you could say that, but it wouldn't be true, Freddo,' Billy answered, leaving it there.

Billy appeared to be thinking, but was trying to find a way to deflect the conversation away from his personal life. 'Do you know what came through for me in most of the lectures and the group discussions?' he began. Not waiting for a reply, he quickly continued, 'Almost every one of us at some time talked about our mothers or the women in our lives. We mostly associated them with whatever warmth and comfort and love we'd experienced as kids, even if, for some blokes, like Davo for instance, there wasn't a lot of that either.'

'Nah, that's wrong, Billy, I loved me mum 'til she gorn away and left me,' Davo protested.

'Well, there we are, even Davo has some good memories of his mother, but what I found of particular interest was that whenever the subject of a father came up, he turned out to be a bastard. He was always someone who beat us or abused us sexually, neglected us, or in my case ignored me on the one hand and demanded perfection on the other. The father figure in our lives was the bloke we were always trying to please and never could. So, as we grew a little older, we started to resent him, then hate him for what he did to our mums and to us. When we grew up, we became just like him, the grog or drugs took over. It was the same pattern all over again, we found we couldn't maintain a relationship with our wives or girlfriends or even our children. We started to abuse them physically or, with me, the mental torture my father put me through was what I was doing to my own children, in particular to my son Charlie.' Billy sighed. 'Freddo and Davo, you're not married and you haven't got kids yet so you don't know how you would have responded if you hadn't decided to go straight.' Billy turned to Morgan. 'How about you, Morgan? You once mentioned that you'd been married?'

'You've just written the script, buddy. I fucked up big time.'

'Okay, now let me ask you something. My father went to war and so did his father. Mine ended up a prisoner of the Japanese on the Burma railway and in Changi, his father went through Gallipoli and France. How about your fathers?'

'Right on,' Morgan said. 'Second World War, captured in Singapore. I was born ten years after the war.'

'Vietnam,' Freddo said, 'he died there when I was nine months old. But wait on! All them "uncles" me mum brought home, they were all Vietnam vets, every one o' the bastards. It was like she felt guilty or something, she could only screw a Vietnam vet. I gotta tell you, mate, some of those blokes, the ones she brought home, they were sick puppies, they was damaged huge, man. Don't nobody tell me that the Agent Orange they sprayed everywhere was harmless. Them blokes, their lives was blown away with that defoliant.'

'Dunno,' Davo replied. 'All I know is me old man was a drunk and a deadshit.'

'And your grandfather, his father?'

'Dunno, wouldn't 'ave a clue, mate. Me old man said he were an orphan, Dr Barnardo's.'

'It's curious, isn't it, we don't know about Davo, but all the rest of us had fathers who went into combat. We now know that many of the guys who went to Vietnam suffer from post-traumatic stress disorder and, although it wasn't diagnosed before Vietnam, there's no reason to suppose this hasn't occurred after every war. In fact, there is a lot of evidence to suggest that it did. There's been a war every generation this century, which means every war produced a great many men who were deeply traumatised by the experience. I now realise that my father was, and I'm quite sure his father was before him, and the one thing we know about this condition is that the wives and children often suffer the consequences. We grow up hating our old man but deny it to ourselves as long as we can. They grew up hating theirs and doing the same. Those of us with an addictive personality, well, we treat our children much the same as we were treated, and when it comes to talking about our fathers in the groups we can't, the hurt and the denial are too deep.'

'What are you saying? That you're an alcoholic and I'm a drug addict because of our fathers?' Morgan asked.

'No, I'm merely suggesting there's a definite pattern. As the saying goes, like father like son.' Billy was beginning to touch a deep truth within him, one he'd avoided facing since Charlie's death. His attempts to keep the conversation impersonal and speculative seemed to be working. He had managed to deflect the conversation from himself to avoid bringing Charlie up again. Now he could examine his denial slowly by himself, it wasn't necessary to share his shame with anyone else. The three weeks in the group discussions were paying off.

'Your son, what happened?' Davo asked ingenuously.

Davo's direct question caught Billy unawares and, because he'd just thought himself saved from a public confession, he was suddenly emotionally overwhelmed. He was a trained lawyer so he fought to keep his voice steady. 'I wasn't much of a father to both my children, too busy at the law, drinking, being a popular public figure, charity boards, anything to avoid going home. I was generally loaded when I got home and the kids were usually in bed or they'd learned to avoid me. The girl had her mother so it wasn't too bad for her, but a boy needs his father and I was never there for him. On a Saturday morning when he played sport at his school I had a hangover. I was the dad whose absence was noted by the other kids. Charlie learned to lie, he'd say I was away in America or some other excuse his little boy's mind could dream up.'

'You're breaking my heart,' Morgan suddenly interrupted.

'Shut up, Morgan, can't yer see Billy don't like saying all this?' Freddo cried.

'Yeah, mate, fair go,' Davo added.

'No, Morgan's right, it must all seem pretty harmless compared to what you've all been through.'

'No, Billy, I'm sorry, mate, I've got a big mouth, I shouldn't have said what I just did,' Morgan said, clearly regretting his words.

'Kids get hurt for lotsa reasons, just because we think we had it worse doesn't make Billy's kid less hurt and resentful,' Freddo said.

Billy could sense Freddo was being kind, that what he'd told them about Charlie was pretty tame stuff. Fathers who were workaholics and who were also hard drinkers were a dime a dozen and neglecting your kids for your vocation or work was practically the Australian middle-class way of life.

Billy tried to recover, get out of the mess he was making of his story. 'No, please, everyone, don't get me wrong, nine-year-old kids are pretty resilient and Charlie was a nice kid, full of life, and I don't think at that stage he'd lost faith in me. It's what I did to him later that sent me into complete denial and put me on the bench outside the library.' Billy looked up. 'I guess it's not that interesting, let's leave it at that.'

'Hey, wait on! I'm sorry about my big mouth, what I said was unfair, but you can't leave it there, mate. We've just been through three weeks of group-discussion therapy, what was that all about, man?' Morgan said accusingly. 'You can't leave it hangin' like that, mate.'

Billy had recovered sufficiently to keep his voice calm. 'When my son was nine he was going off to a school camp. It was summer and he was so excited he couldn't stop talking about it. My wife was to drop him off at school at five on the particular afternoon but my daughter, who is an asthmatic, had a bad attack and my wife phoned me to ask if I'd come home early and take Charlie. I'd had a liquid lunch and continued drinking all afternoon and was pretty pissed, so I told her to send him in a taxi. "Charlie wants to say goodbye to you. He's very excited. He'd like his father to take him," my wife said, so I relented and said I'd come home. I don't want to labour the point, but on the way to his school I guess I was speeding and I missed the red light at an intersection and collected a semitrailer.

'The truck hit Charlie's side of the car and had we not been in a Mercedes I dare say he would have been killed, but he received severe head wounds and suffered an intracerebral haemorrhage to the right side of his brain which affected the movement on the left side of his body. The specialists said that in time and with the right kind of exercise he would regain most of the movement. I was unhurt and when the police tested my alcohol level it was .19, nearly four times over the limit.

'Charlie spent two months in hospital but on his return home we soon realised that he had become deeply and chronically depressed. We put an exercise bicycle and gym equipment in his room and he'd sometimes do the exercises, but more often than not he'd refuse and lock himself in his room all day. Already guilty for what I'd done, I'd rage at him and then, just like my father, go into my study and get drunk. Two years later, although he'd regained enough movement in his left side to ride a proper bicycle, his depression if anything was worse.

'I came home one evening, half-tanked as usual. Charlie had locked himself again in his room all day and had missed school. I went upstairs and asked to be let in but he wouldn't respond, so I went down to the garage, got a jemmy, forced open the door and gave him hell. I can remember how he cowered in the corner, holding his precious cat, a big tabby known as Baby Grand. I called him a coward and told him he was useless, a failure, that he'd grow up to be a no-hoper, I think I used the words "useless little shit!" when all the time it was me who was the failure. I was doing exactly what my own father had done to me, humiliating him. I left him crying, holding the cat, and stormed downstairs into my study where I polished off a bottle of Johnnie Walker. Eventually I must have collapsed in a drunken state on the carpet because my wife woke me the next morning to say that Charlie wasn't in his room.'

Billy stopped talking, ashamed that he was losing control when he most needed it. In a voice not much above a whisper, he said, 'Charlie had ridden his bicycle to Watsons Bay and thrown himself off the Gap.'

Billy could feel the tears running down his cheeks. 'He left a note:

> Dad,
> *Please look after Baby Grand.*
> Love,
> *Charlie*

'That was all. A month later I took Baby Grand to Charlie's grave and took a picture of him sitting on the marble slab. I wanted Charlie to see he was in good shape, that I was looking after him.' Billy wiped away the tears with his hand. 'Stupid really, I suppose. I took the photo and then started to cry. When I looked up, Baby Grand had gone. I searched for him for three hours,' Billy stopped, sniffing. 'I even fucked that up,' he whispered. It was the first time any of them had heard him use an expletive.

The three men were silent and then Freddo gave a little cough, 'That's rough, mate, a real bastard.'

Billy leaned down and, using the edge of his sheet, wiped his eyes. 'I'm sorry to burden you with all of this but, you see, it's the only way I can tell you why I'm leaving tomorrow.'

'Billy, stay, mate. You've come this far, don't pull out now,' Morgan urged again.

Billy then told them the story of Ryan. They'd all heard Ryan sing and he'd been the subject of a great deal of conversation among the men. When they'd returned to their shared room the previous evening, Morgan had held up his Bible. 'Well, fellas, they gave us our Bibles and then the big bloke in the sky sent us a bloody angel to sing the last hymn.'

'I have no choice. This time I've got to get it right,' Billy said finally.

'How will you find him?' Freddo asked.

Billy shrugged. 'I don't know, I'll just keep looking, asking.'

Freddo thought for a while. 'Billy, you're in my territory, I done much the same, though I was twelve when me mum threw me out. I know the Cross, the kid's gunna find a squat if he's lucky or he'll go to the Wayside Chapel or one of Father Riley's people will find him and he'll turn up, young blokes don't stray far.' He paused. 'That's the best scenario, mate.' Freddo shook his head. 'I got to be honest with you, the chances of that happening are just about zero. If the kid thinks he's in trouble with the police, he's going to be frightened and he'll stay away from charity help or a refuge.' Freddo spread his hands. 'I seen him yesterday in chapel, he's beautiful, I'm tellin' you, he's got Buckley's.'

'What's that supposed to mean?' Davo asked.

'The paedophiles will be on to him like a pack o' hungry mongrels.'

Billy thought his heart would jump out of his chest. 'What do you mean?'

'She's got people out on the streets at the Cross and at Central Station looking for kids all the time, they'll snap him up, no risk.'

'She?'

'The Queenie, from The Sheba.'

'Eh, say again?'

'It's a sex club, a brothel, fully licensed, legit. It's on the main drag, The Queen o' Sheba, but it's just called The Sheba in the trade. The Queenie is, like, the madam who runs the joint.'

'You mean it's a brothel for kids, for children?' Billy asked.

'Nah, it's a legit brothel but it's a front for kiddy-sex. The Queenie is really running a club for paedophiles.'

'Eh? It's a brothel that's legit, but it isn't because there's kids, what's that supposed to mean?' Morgan asked. Freddo had a reputation for taking the longest possible way around to make a point. In a conversational sense, he could turn a visit to the bathroom into a fully blown marathon.

Freddo sighed. 'The Queen o' Sheba is a real sleazy joint, a sex club and a brothel. It caters mostly for young blokes who come in from the western suburbs, you know, big night out, six or seven mates pissed or high on eckies or whatever's the latest good thing to swallow, looking for some cheap action after midnight. Bucks' parties, young blokes celebrating a footy win, gang-initiation nights. You musta all seen 'em, the Lebbo or the big Maori at the door soliciting business, shoutin' out, picking their mark. "Twenty-five-dollar entrance fee per person. Hey, are you guys in a group? Celebrating, eh? I'm feelin' generous ternight, fifty bucks and you're all in, the lot of yiz! Come on in, boys, nude acts, exotic dancers!"' Freddo paused. 'It's the rough end of the trade. All the girls are on heroin, working to support their habits, and they solicit the audience while the show is going on, inviting them upstairs for a quickie, the house takes fifty per cent of what they make.'

'Audience? I thought you said it was a brothel?' Morgan said.

'Yeah, well, outside it says it's a strip club. Brothels are not allowed to advertise so that's where the exotic dancers come in, they're freelancers and they work five or six places a night like this around the Cross. They'll do a bit of dance, most are pretty crook sorts that can't no longer work the better-class strip clubs, but some of them ain't too bad. They'll remove some o' their gear and then offer to screw anyone in the audience in the buff for a hundred bucks. A dancer will make half a grand, more on a good night. If the Yank navy is in town, they can make a couple of grand.'

Billy thought immediately of Ryan's mother and it explained how she supported her habit and how she could give him a fifty-dollar note to spend.

'Yes, but what's this got to do with paedophiles and who's The Queenie?' Billy asked anxiously.

'Yeah, well, like I said before, The Queen o' Sheba is a cover, see. The Queenie is supposed to be the owner of the joint, the madam, only now she's called the manager, but it ain't really what she's on about. She leaves the brothel to one of the Arab Mafia, a Lebanese or Assyrian crim named Mohammed Suleman. There's four rooms at the back done up perfect, like a suite at the Regent, it's where the big-time and the overseas paedophiles come. The entrance is in the back lane, just a dirty, unmarked door, paint peelin', with a speaker to the side.' Freddo gave a little snort. 'Above the door it says "Back entrance". Back stairs is pretty crook but then you come to the first landing and it has marble tiles and walls, with a fuckin' crystal chandelier.'

'Why didn't you say so before?' Morgan said, exasperated. 'We didn't need to know all that shit about the brothel! How do you know all this anyway? Or shouldn't I ask?'

Freddo shrugged. 'It's where I learned to put a value on my arse, it was better than The Wall at Darlinghurst,' he said simply. 'The Sheba's not the only one, there's others. Costello's, The Pleasure Chest, they're both at the Cross, the Orchid Club, it's American but they're also here in a big way. The Queenie does a lot of travel business with them. The Children's Liberation Railway, that's in Glebe, there's the Blaze Group, they've even got their own kiddy-porn magazine, and the Rene Guyon Society, they got this motto, *Sex before eight or it's too late!* And the Rat Pack, not a very original name but their motto is: *Never rat, never tell.* They're mostly the rich and the famous, Australian, but they's now gone worldwide. The Queenie does big business with them as well.'

'Jesus!' Morgan exclaimed. 'Who'd want to bring kids into the world? I read somewhere that one in four under-age girls are sexually abused, though I think that's mostly at home, and one in seven boys. I mean, it happened to me, to Freddo.' He looked over at Davo. 'How about you, Davo?'

'Yup.'

'Why do you think I'm warning Billy about this boy?' Freddo said. 'Sydney is big time for overseas paedophiles. The rich ones who don't want to shit on their own doorstep. The Queenie specialises in them sex tourists from Europe, a lot from Germany, some from the Orchid Club in America, from everywhere. It's a bloody United Nations of perverts. She also caters for lots of the top local citizens, judges, lawyers, politicians, doctors, big business, they all know each other and she keeps it like a club. You can't just come off the street, no way, man.'

'Do you know this woman, this, er . . . The Queenie?'

'No. Not this one. She's new since my time in the kiddy-sex trade. The one who was there before, in my time, is now a prominent socialite in Surfers Paradise.'

'What she do? Sell the business to this one, The New Queenie?' Davo asked.

'Nah, it don't work like that. Like the old one, The Queenie is probably a partner in a syndicate, a paedophile ring. You see, you've got to have protection at the bottom and the top and from the police. You can put money on it, the Arab who runs The Sheba is the muscle, the standover man, then there's a politician at the top, maybe more than one, to see nobody rocks the boat. They'd be partners with The Queenie, some police would also be involved, though they're usually just on the take. You need them to leave the joint alone, but if the press or the Church gets a bit upset because they've heard a rumour, they'll raid the street front, find something like drugs, a few amphetamines or a coupla blocks o' hash on the premises, and the magistrate, who's in on the whole thing, will fine one of Mohammed's people, who'll fess up, two grand and a suspended sentence, so everyone can see it's a legit raid, then it's business as usual.

'The Sheba, they've even got their own travel agency where they book the overseas visitors into certain apartments, mostly in Bondi Junction. The sex tourists are picked up by limo at the airport, brought to the agency so their bona-fides can be checked and there they are shown a video of the kids available. The Sheba, the premises behind the brothel, is only used for interstate paedophiles staying in a hotel or for the local bigwigs to use for kiddy-sex.'

Billy shook his head sadly. 'I'm sure Ryan wouldn't let that happen to him, he's street-wise, he'd yell and scream and make a fuss. Surely all the children taken can't be compliant?'

Freddo looked directly at him. 'Billy, you may have been an important lawyer but you're an innocent, mate. Take my own case. I was twelve years old, frightened, hungry, and on the streets with nowhere to go, I'd run away from home so I reckoned the police were looking for me. That's a joke, by the way. They may be looking for Ryan, but it won't be because he's run away from home. Anyway, a bloke comes up to you in the street, "Hey, kid, you look hungry. Are you hungry?" You nod and he takes you to McDonald's for a hamburger, chips and a thickshake. He tells you he's a karate black belt and is training a whole heap of kids. "Would you like to learn karate, be able to defend yourself from scumbags?" he asks you. You're twelve years old, man! A helpless little kid and of course you say you would. "Where do you live?" he asks. You shrug or you mumble something. "Look, we've got some kids come to learn from interstate, we've got this nice pad, you can crash there if you like."'

Freddo sighed. 'After you've been raped the first time they've got you for keeps. You're too ashamed to talk, or they threaten to harm you or take you to the cops on a trumped-up charge. Some of them introduce the kids to addictive drugs, or they just brainwash them. Some o' the kids are under ten, they've had miserable lives. That royal commission that's been going on this year found only one per cent of paedophiles are ever convicted and only eight per cent of sexual abuse is ever reported. Those dirty bastards are safe as houses, man!'

'Yes, I've read something about it,' Billy said. He didn't know if he could listen to too much more, he wouldn't sleep tonight but one thing was certain, he'd find Ryan, or die in the attempt.

'How do you think I became a heroin addict?' Freddo continued. 'I got me first needle at thirteen! I know I'm not much, I've been floggin' me arse for drugs for thirteen years, but I don't go along with child sex abuse. That there royal commission says there's three thousand girls and eleven thousand boys flogged for sex every year. Imagine that, there's three thousand little girls and eleven thousand little Freddos out there, they're selling their bodies like I done for a place to stay, food to eat, grog, drugs, even for the clobber on their backs!'

'Freddo, I don't think I can take much more,' Billy said. 'Frankly, I'm terrified about what you've told me. But I thank you, at least I'm forewarned. I have to try and find Ryan. I must get to him. If he managed to get to chapel yesterday, surely that means he's still on the loose, doesn't it?'

'Yeah, maybe you're right,' Freddo conceded, though he didn't sound too hopeful. 'Go to the police, tell them you're a lawyer, threaten them, tell them they've *got* to find Ryan and when they do, to let you know. Then you go to the Kings Cross police station and the cops at Surry Hills every day and make a fuss. It's yer best chance, buddy.'

Billy nodded, though in his day the Kings Cross and Surry Hills stations mostly featured the likes of Sergeant Orr at Parliament House, the about-to-be-superannuated blokes who knew of him and his fall from grace. He doubted if they'd take the slightest notice of his request. They'd be more likely to escort him to the door via a stiff boot up the backside or threaten to charge him. Billy didn't tell Freddo that his influence, in terms of the law, no longer existed.

'If the police find him before I do, I don't suppose they'll give me custody,' Billy said.

'No way, you're not a relative and you're, er . . .'

'An alcoholic,' Billy completed the sentence for him.

'Yeah. They'll turn him over to DOCS, who'll then hand him over to the Salvos, who've got an early-intervention home for little kids at Hurstville. He'll stay there three months and then they'll try to find him a foster home,' said Freddo.

'No good,' Davo cried emphatically. 'I ran away from six o' them. Sometimes, if you're lucky, you get a good home, but mostly them that take you just want the money from the government. They don't want no twelve-year-old kid with behaviour problems. In one of them I was raped on the first night and I ran away the next day. Police charged me with being an intractable child and a disturbed adolescent, the magistrate at the Children's Court sent me to Osmond Hall.'

Billy was hating the process of asking. With each question or explanation his heart sank further and his anxiety increased, but he realised that Freddo and Davo could give him valuable insider information he might not otherwise be able to get. Information that might help him with Ryan. 'What if the child is in trouble with the police?' he asked.

'Children's Court,' Davo said, 'same as they done me. If you're dead unlucky, you get Osmond Hall.'

'I thought you said you could hack it there?' Morgan said.

'Yeah, as a big kid, no probs. It's the Wild West, man! Yer can do what you like, management don't care, kids run the joint, staff can't do nothin'. Management, the people from DOCS, don't even come near the joint. Little kid's got no bloody hope, most of them take to sniffin' petrol and aerosol cans soon after they come in. You can get alcohol and dope, all yer want. Paedophiles were waiting outside, they was called "tow-truck drivers", I dunno why, I suppose the tow-truck drivers were the first to get onto it.

They'd have sex with the girls after they got them to leave Osmond Hall. That's where I learned to drink. Sometimes I'd wake up outside in the yard in the mornin' lying on the bricks after I'd gone walkabout the night before to get grog and I'd be lying in me own vomit. I were fourteen years old, man! The staff, they done nothin'. Kids from thirteen were having sex with each other. I got me first dose from a fourteen-year-old girl when I was the same age as her. By the time a kid who come in at twelve gets to sixteen, some o' them have iced their brain from petrol sniffin'.'

'Surely it can't be that bad?' Morgan asked doubtfully.

'You better believe it, buddy. I'll swear it on a stack of Bibles,' Davo said, reaching for the Bible he'd been given at chapel.

'So all that about sewing on buttons, that was bullshit?' Morgan asked again.

'Nah, that was before they changed it. When I first come in I was twelve, it were a secure unit then, like a kids' gaol. You had like cells and dormitories, you was locked in at night, bars on the windas and the place were bloody strict and you did yer time, it was bloody hard yakka. Then two years later they changed all that and they had this open-door policy and they's called it "a therapeutic environment". That was when it become the Wild West. That place is real sicko, mate, they should burn it down.'

Billy hardly slept that night, his nose was hurting and his left eye had closed completely and all he could think of was Ryan out there on his own, trying to survive with nowhere to go. At one stage he cheered himself up a bit by thinking that Ryan might go to Mr Cesco. After all, the coffee-bar owner was a relation. Then he thought he might contact Dr Goldstein at St Vincent's. But then again, he told himself, if Ryan thought he was wanted by the police he might not go to either for help. Billy simply couldn't imagine what Ryan might have done for the police to be involved. It was probably something quite innocent and the boy had panicked, although the letter from his principal said he had been absent from school and had left before the ambulance arrived.

At breakfast on the day of his departure, Billy was feeling bleary-eyed and miserable when Morgan came to sit beside him. 'We were pretty rough on you last night, Billy. I'm sorry.'

'Good morning, Morgan. No, I needed to know all that stuff. I've been a street drunk for four, four and half years, but that's not my world. It will help me with Ryan, help me find him.'

'I hope so, mate, I really do.'

They were both silent for a few moments then Morgan said, 'I haven't told you a lot about myself, Billy.'

'No, you haven't, but that's up to you, I guess.'

'I hope we'll meet again, Billy.'

'Yes, of course, that would be nice.' Billy sensed Morgan wanted to say something so he waited.

'When you get out, I mean if you have a bit of time, could you go and see my girlfriend, Billy?'

'I don't see why not. Yes, of course.'

'You see, I'm an actor. Well, that was my profession until I discovered heroin.'

Billy now understood why Morgan's reading at yesterday's chapel had sounded so professional. 'So your addiction wasn't something from your teens, like Freddo and Davo?'

'No, I came from a pretty rough family and I *was* abused, but I have no excuses. I was fostered out at eight into a pretty good home, my foster parents were very kind to me and treated me like one of the family. I did pretty well at school and then went on to NIDA, the National Institute of Dramatic Art, where I was nominated in my diploma year as outstanding student. My career, as they say, blossomed. I got married early to an actress of the bums-and-tits variety which my ego at the time demanded. From the very start it was a disaster, and I admit mostly my fault. I was drinking heavily, we quarrelled constantly and we divorced three years later. I was still doing well in television and there was talk of a prime-time show of my own. It didn't eventuate but I won a Mike Walsh Fellowship and went to Britain for a year to study documentary drama at the BBC.'

'Kids?'

'Thank God, no! My wife wasn't exactly Mensa material but she was bright enough to stay on the pill. Then I returned from England and met the love of my life, a blues singer, part-Aborigine. I wouldn't say that normally but you'd never tell from looking at her. She's a beautiful woman.'

Billy looked at him. He still wasn't sure about Morgan and this last remark didn't help.

Morgan continued, 'I was crazy about her, still am. What I didn't know at the time was that she was a heroin addict, though I don't suppose it would have mattered, I worshipped her anyway. Well, no need to go into the whole sordid mess, but pretty soon I was also winding a tourniquet around my arm and sharing a needle with her. That was two years ago. Now I'm in here and she's out there, still using. I know she wants to kick the habit, to get clean, but she doesn't have the courage yet. She said if I could do it, she would.' He stopped for a minute. 'Mate, I love her with every breath in my body, she's my Higher Power. If you could see her, tell her it *can* be done, that I'm surviving and you're pretty sure I'm going to make it, she might just have the courage to take the plunge and go into rehab.'

Billy turned to face him. 'Morgan, of course I'll see her, but you know as well as I do, she's got to have a reason to give up. Your reason is her, is hers the same, you?'

'I think so, I hope so.'

'You don't sound too sure?'

'No, no, I am, we're devoted. They say heroin destroys love but that hasn't happened. Please, Billy, can you just talk to her? I know she loves me and wants to get back into singing.'

'Where can I find her?' Billy asked.

'She's moved into one of the casino apartments at Darling Harbour with two other girls.' Morgan hesitated. 'She's working as a high-class whore at the casino, it's how she supports her habit.'

'Let me have her address, I'll try. What's her name, by the way? What if she won't see me?'

'I've written to her, telling her about you. She'll see you, I promise.' Morgan handed Billy a scrap of paper. 'Thanks, mate, we're going to miss you heaps. She calls herself Kartanya. She's from the Kaura people from the Adelaide plains, though her mother is a white woman.' He patted Billy on the arm and left abruptly. Billy wasn't a man who judged others but he sometimes wondered about Morgan's sincerity.

Billy was waiting outside Vince Payne's office for the program director to arrive. On the way he'd stopped at reception and handed them a note to give to Ryan on the off-chance that he might return. Billy was conscious that the police might come around and make inquiries, that Ryan's principal might have told them of his connection with the boy, so the note simply read:

Dear Ryan,

I'll be at Trim's window,

Billy

Vince Payne came waddling into the building carrying his usual styrofoam cup of coffee from Rocco's. 'Come in, come in,' he said, unlocking the deadlocked door to his office. He'd been around sufficiently to know that while some addicts are honest, others don't bring a set of newly reformed morals into rehabilitation.

Billy sat down on the now familiar straight-backed kitchen chair.

Vince was all business, 'We've fixed up your pension so it will go to the bank,' he said. Then, looking steadily at Billy, he said sternly, 'You haven't changed your mind?'

'No, Vince, I haven't. I have to leave.'

The program director sighed. He was a good sigher and Billy suspected he practised squeezing the utmost disappointment out of a sigh. 'I must be honest with you, Billy. Like I said yesterday, your chances out there on your own are not good. On the other hand, you have a mission to find the boy and that's something at least.' He reached for an envelope on his desk. 'In here is the address of an AA group who meet every morning at the G'day Cafe Coffee House at the Rocks and at three or four other venues, none too inconvenient, in the late afternoon or evenings. I beg you to join them and to attend *twice* a day. Do you hear me, Billy? Not once. Twice. They'll do the Twelve Steps you would have continued on with at St Peters. It's not quite the same, the rigid discipline is missing and, of course, you'll be constantly open to temptation. But if you're determined, you can do it. You'll get a lot of support from these guys. In here is a note to the fellow alcoholic who runs it. There are several of your type there, successful businessmen, professionals, you'll probably be quite comfortable in their company.' He stopped and picked up the biro. He's going to start tapping, Billy thought. He does it when he wants to make a significant point. '*Don't, don't, don't* go near a pub, Billy! You're *not* cured, you *never* will be! One drink and you're gone, back where you were when you went into detox.'

'Thank you. Yes, I understand,' Billy replied. The biro was going tap, tap, tap, tap. He'd been told the same thing maybe a thousand times since he'd arrived. Maybe if they said it less often, it might have more meaning, he thought.

'Okay, let's go upstairs and get your things,' Vince said briskly, throwing down the biro and rising from his chair.

Having signed for and collected his possessions, Billy stood at the front door with his briefcase handcuffed back around his left wrist. After being absent for three weeks the briefcase felt strange, no longer the essential friend it had been. So much had happened in such a short period, though he imagined he'd soon grow accustomed to the briefcase again being his constant companion and security blanket.

Several of the men had come to his table at breakfast to say goodbye and to wish him luck. They were a strange fraternity. After three weeks of being locked into a small space they had become almost a family, exposing their emotions and sharing their innermost secrets. Billy couldn't remember ever having been closer to his fellow humans.

Now, as he stood waiting to be released, only Freddo and Davo were present in the foyer. Freddo held Billy's hand. 'I'm gunna miss you a lot, Billy. I know you gunna make it, mate. You gunna make it for all of us. I hope you find the kid. I don't write so good, but I've wrote down all the places you should look. Wait outside and watch who comes and goes.' He handed Billy a carefully folded note.

'Freddo, I am grateful to you and it's important that good people like you get clean. Remember, I'll be out there cheering you on.'

Freddo's froggy face beamed. 'Nobody's never called me good people before, Billy.'

Davo stood awkwardly, kicking his right trainer against the side of the left one. He extended his hand, squinting slightly, glancing sideways at Billy. 'I'm gunna make Team Fenech, Billy, you'll see, mate.'

'I know you will, Davo. I'll come and see you fight.' Billy gripped his hand. 'It's been good knowing you, son. I'll be ringside watching on the big night.'

Billy glanced towards reception and caught the receptionist's eye, then heard the buzz as the electric door opened. 'Goodbye, Freddo, goodbye, Davo. Good luck.' He turned quickly and pushed open the door.

'Billy!' Davo called out suddenly.

Billy turned back, hoping the purple bruises and his one bunged-up eye hid his nascent tears.

'You and Jeff Fenech, you're the champ of champs, the best that ever was, mate . . . The best there ever will be!' Davo called, his voice trembling.

Then Billy stepped out into the frightening sunlight.

CHAPTER TWELVE

Although he had been outside the William Booth Institute on several occasions when the men were taken for a short walk after breakfast, they had kept close together, a tight little group which, in their own minds, was marking time and so stood apart from the outside world. Now, as he walked away towards Oxford Street, despite the grubby and cluttered confines of Darlinghurst, Billy had a feeling of too much space, with the air surrounding him seeming to contain a tincture of malevolence.

Billy was about to enter a recidivous and duplicitous world inhabited by male predators in thousand-dollar suits, silk ties and polished black shoes who knew their wine and groomed their sons and daughters to replace them in the better-paying professions. It was also a world of weirdos and deadbeats, tinkers, tailors and candlestick makers. Paedophiles are not a class of men but a malignancy in humankind, a suppurating mental sore carefully concealed behind a bandage of respectability. It was also a world, as Freddo had explained, where someone called The Queenie sent her honey-tongued scouts out onto the street to gather a harvest of hungry, frightened runaway children for the carnal appetites of powerful and outwardly sanctimonious men who laughed quietly amongst themselves over slogans such as *Sex before eight or it's too late!*

He decided that one of his first tasks was to visit the Pring Street school and introduce himself to the principal, Ms Flanagan. Ryan might just conceivably turn up there and Billy wanted to cover every eventuality. Besides, she had shown courage in telling Ryan of his whereabouts when she'd been specifically instructed not to do so and he wanted to assure her that he wasn't a danger to the child. She might also have further information on why Ryan had chosen to run away and why the police were involved.

But first he had an urgent need to visit the Botanic Gardens, which he'd greatly missed. It was nearly spring and while most of the native shrubs and trees wouldn't be flowering at this time of year, many of the acacia varietals would be out and a number of exotic plants from Asia and Africa would be blooming. He thought particularly of a magnificent magnolia tree he would visit. He would sit quietly on his favourite bench, where he would have an opportunity to think, away from the confines of the William Booth Institute.

Billy sat in the sunshine, listening to the fall of water over rock. The air around him had none of the malevolence he'd felt earlier in the day and it hummed with the sound of bees and other small pollen-collecting insects. A dragonfly, its wings trembling, hovered above the water in the small pond beside his bench. He could hear the distinctive *chewee, chewee, chewee* of a Restless Flycatcher coming from the direction of the great old Moreton Bay fig he so dearly loved. The tiny native figs would be ripening, the sticky fruit attracting insects and bringing the Satin Flycatchers into the Gardens.

For the first time, he felt the unaccustomed effect of no alcohol in his bloodstream, and he realised he was beginning to imagine a life where he was not constantly preoccupied by the need for a drink. While he had been clean for more than a month, he had also been incarcerated with other addicts in the process of recovery and it hadn't allowed him to see his life beyond the next twenty-four hours. One day at a time was the mantra of recovery and he had been warned not to abandon it lightly, each hour was a milestone and a day could feel like an eternity. Billy quickly shut out the thought that he might need to organise a permanent life where the need for alcohol no longer dominated every moment. He knew that such speculation would only cause him to panic, he was still too vulnerable to make plans and there were a great many questions to which he didn't have the answers.

The one great advantage of being a drunk was the freedom from any outside obligation and the knowledge that you had been cast aside by a society who largely didn't care if you lived or died, as long as you didn't invade their neighbourhood or interrupt their lives. Like sex workers on suburban streets, the chic weren't supposed to mix with the shab. Living on the street, the decisions you needed to make were singular and uncomplicated and not necessarily chaotic. Billy's life as a homeless person still consisted of an established routine, which was important to him. As an alcoholic in abeyance, his existence would need to be entirely different and he would need to think it out carefully. This was an unfamiliar dish he would have to taste one tiny portion at a time.

For this reason he decided to remain sleeping on the bench outside the library, though of course the primary purpose for doing so was that Ryan might locate him. Billy unshackled the briefcase, took out his notepad and made a note to visit the the Wayside Chapel to obtain a blanket and a large plastic bag. The weather was still cold and, with his internal combustion no longer fuelled by a bottle of scotch, he would be cold sleeping on the bench at night.

Billy replaced the pad and biro and opened the envelope Vince Payne had given him. It contained, as the program director had mentioned, a list of the morning and evening Alcoholics Anonymous meetings in the inner-city and Kings Cross environs. The AA meeting that evening, Tuesday, was at the Wayside Chapel in Kings Cross, which was only a couple of minutes' walk from the main drag where he would begin his vigil in the lane behind The Queen of Sheba. Freddo had given him the locations of the three places in the Cross he claimed were frequented by paedophiles. He had also told Billy not to take up his observation post during the day, which was when most of the clubs were closed and when kiddy-sex took place in the various apartments rented by sex tourists. 'Do it after eight and establish yerself as a derro who comes to the same place every night to drink and sleep, that way they get used to you being there,' Freddo had advised. 'There's nothin' more invisible around the Cross than an old derro.' Billy would take the blanket along with him so that it appeared he was tucked up for the night and if anyone passed by he'd pretend he was either drunk or in an alcoholic stupor.

His principal concern was how he would conduct his day without its customary alcohol content. He'd basically solved the mornings. The AA meeting would start the day and it would occupy the time when he used to cadge a cup of coffee from Con. After the meeting he would visit The Station just in time for breakfast, after which he'd shave and shower, a habit he'd resumed with some personal satisfaction at William Booth. It was a funny thing. Almost more than anything else, a wash and shave suggested to him that he was making progress. It was a habit he must be careful to continue now he was back on the street. After The Station, he'd visit the Botanic Gardens and continue his usual routine until it was time for Operation Mynah Bird. In his absence, the birds had probably replaced the numbers he'd systematically culled from their ranks.

Similarly, the evenings would involve a meal in Martin Place at the Just Enough Faith van and then he'd attend the other AA meeting. This would take care of the first part of the evening and the remainder would be taken up by his surveillance outside one or another of the addresses Freddo had given him.

With the mornings and the evenings taken care of, Billy realised that the long afternoons were going to create a problem for him. With nothing to distract him, the craving for a drink would become overpowering. Billy knew that his life depended on using his time well, filling every available moment, or he was almost certain to crash. It was then that he hit on the idea of spending the afternoons in the Mitchell Library, where he would research and write the final part of Trim's story. This would also help keep his hopes alive of finding Ryan, who, he told himself, would be the ultimate benefactor of his two new Trim stories. Having his mind occupied elsewhere might prevent his constant, gnawing urge to visit a bottle shop. It would also keep him in touch with Trim, his designated Higher Power for the AA Twelve Step meetings.

Billy crossed the Domain, walked down past the back of the Art Gallery and crossed Crown and Bourke Streets in order to give the Flag Hotel on Cowper Wharf Road a wide berth, finally working his way through several small streets to Pring Street Public School. He'd timed it well and the children were out of their classrooms enjoying recess. To his delight, the playground was being supervised by the music teacher, Ms Sypkins, who, to his further surprise, recognised him immediately.

'Hello,' she said, smiling. 'You're back? Goodness, what have you done to your nose?'

'Oh, you remember me? Billy O'Shannessy,' Billy said, in case she'd forgotten his name. 'I really did run into a door.'

'Remember you? How could I forget?' she laughed. 'I hardly slept a wink the night we met.'

'Oh, I'm sorry, it was very kind of you to act as my courier.'

A troubled look came over her face. 'Mr O'Shannessy, if you're looking for Ryan, he isn't here. We're all terribly worried, we haven't seen him for weeks.'

'Yes, I know,' Billy replied.

Sylvia Sypkins looked surprised. 'Do you know where he is then?'

'No, your principal wrote to me to tell me what happened. That's why I've come.' Billy paused a moment before asking, 'Would it be possible to see Ms Flanagan?'

The music teacher hesitated just sufficiently for Billy to sense that she didn't know whether the principal would welcome a visit from him. 'If you'll wait here, I'll ask her.'

Billy waited, watching the children playing. Kids, it seemed, never really changed, the boys rushing around chasing each other, yelling, quarrelling, pushing, arguing, laughing, mocking and, in the process, burning up enormous amounts of energy. As always, the little girls were wiser and more sophisticated, either paired off or in small private groups, sharing secrets or sandwiches, skipping or playing hopscotch. Ms Sypkins returned to say that the principal would see him.

After taking Billy to the principal's office, Ms Sypkins said, 'I need to get back to the playground; just knock and enter, you're expected.' She extended her hand, 'Nice to see you again, Mr O'Shannessy.'

Billy took her hand. 'Thank you, and next time we meet, will you please call me Billy?'

'Of course, Billy, I'm glad you've returned, you made quite an impact the first time we met.'

Billy knocked on the open door of the principal's office. 'Come in, please,' a voice called. Billy entered to see a pleasant-looking, grey-haired woman whom he judged to be the same age as himself. She was seated behind a desk and still had her fountain pen poised where she'd been writing. She capped the pen and placed it down. 'Mr O'Shannessy, is it?'

'Yes,' Billy said, entering.

Dorothy Flanagan smiled. It was a nice smile and Billy relaxed a little. She indicated one of two smallish green easychairs in front of her desk. 'Won't you sit down, Mr O'Shannessy?'

'Please call me Billy,' Billy said, sitting down.

'I don't think I could do that,' Dorothy Flanagan replied.

Billy looked up, surprised. 'Oh, I do apologise, I didn't mean to be familiar, Ms Flanagan. It's just . . . well, you see I used to be Mr O'Shannessy, but that was an entirely different person. Once you're on the street you're only known by your first name. I've just spent a month in a detox and rehabilitation unit where only first names are ever used.' Billy sensed that he was talking too much and that Dorothy Flanagan was from the old school and didn't have the easy attitude of her much younger music teacher.

'Nevertheless, I shall continue to call you Mr O'Shannessy,' the principal said firmly. 'Now, what is it we can do for you?' Then to Billy's surprise, she added, 'Is it about the money you left for Ryan?'

'Good Lord, no!' Billy exclaimed. 'I came to inquire about the boy himself.'

'Did you not get my letter?'

'Yes, thank you, it was very kind of you to write on all three occasions.'

'Well, I'm not sure there is a lot more to add, Mr O'Shannessy, though we still have all the money you left, which I shall arrange to have returned to you.'

Billy put up his hand to restrain her. 'No, please, that's not why I'm here.' Billy began to sense that he might have a slightly hostile witness on his hands. 'The money was intended to help Ryan. His grandmother was terminally ill at the time and expected to die; I simply thought the money would be useful with funeral expenses, that sort of thing.'

'That was kind of you, but like so many of her generation, she'd already paid for her plot and her funeral. We sent a wreath but that was from a collection taken up here in the school.'

'I had hoped there might be more news of Ryan since your last letter, for instance the specific reason the police wished to see the boy.'

'I really can't say, Mr O'Shannessy.'

'Can't say, or won't say? There is a distinction.'

'I am aware of that,' said Dorothy Flanagan, a little tetchily.

'Well, which is it?' Billy said, surprised at the quiet yet insistent tone of his voice. He was back in court, ferreting out the truth. 'May I put it to you this way, Ms Flanagan, did you personally talk to Ryan at any time in the three-week period prior to his mother's death?'

'Are you asking me if he attended school?'

'Well, yes, that would be a part of it, unless you saw him after school hours.'

'Yes, he attended briefly on two occasions.'

'I see, and did you talk to him on one or both occasions?'

'Look here, Mr O'Shannessy, I'm not at all sure that it is any of your business. You are not a relative and I have already been advised by the Department of Community Services that you are to report to them before any further commitment in the interest of Ryan can take place.'

Billy spread his hands, trying not to show his impatience. He liked her careful and precise phrasing, she would be a good witness in a court of law, but now he needed to rough her up a bit. 'Ms Flanagan, Ryan is a little boy who has recently turned eleven, he has run away from home and I'm sure you don't need to be told that he is in moral danger. If he is on the streets of Kings Cross, anything can happen. He'll be hungry and frightened and, with the fear that he is wanted by the police, will not go to any of the refuges for help.' Billy sighed, 'We can decide later whether I am a fit person to be with him, but first we have to find him and that's why I'm here. Is there anything you can tell me? Anything! No matter how small or insignificant it may seem. Something he said, his attitude at the time, his reason for attending school, albeit for only a short period of the day on each occasion?'

'I have done all I can. I advised him, against my instructions, of your whereabouts. I begin to see that may have been a mistake.'

Billy ignored this last remark. 'You would have told him that on the first visit. What did you say to him on the second?'

'Really, Mr O'Shannessy, I don't think I am prepared to say anything further.'

Billy suddenly changed tack. 'Did you let him know that I had left money for him?'

'Yes. But I told you, his grandmother had already paid for her funeral.'

'So the second time he came he asked you for the money, didn't he?'

Dorothy Flanagan remained silent.

'Didn't he?' Billy insisted.

'Yes.'

'Did you give it to him?'

'No.'

'And why not?'

Ryan's principal was beginning to realise that she was trapped. 'I just couldn't, that's all!' She sighed. 'It's no use, Mr O'Shannessy, I'm not going to say any more. I'm afraid I must ask you to leave now, I have a great deal to do.'

'Just one more question, Ms Flanagan, and then you may kick me out. I gave you sole discretion to decide how the money I left for Ryan was to be used and now you tell me when he asked for it, you refused. So, you used your discretion not to give him the money. Why? I think I have a right to know at least that much.'

'He wanted it for drugs.'

'Drugs? He came up to you and said, "Please, Ms Flanagan, I need the money Billy left to buy drugs." Is that it?'

'No, of course not. He said his mother was ill with an asthma attack and they needed the money for the doctor.'

'You knew he was lying?'

'Of course. We know he takes her to St Vincent's, Dr Goldstein is well known to the school.'

'And knowing his mother was a heroin addict, you guessed it was for drugs?'

'Ryan is street smart, Mr O'Shannessy, but he's still a child. I've run a school for his kind of child long enough to know how to get to the truth.'

'So, of course, you refused to give him the money?'

'Yes, it would have been a dereliction of my duty if I had suspected why he wanted it and then allowed him to have your money, *any* money.'

'Quite right, of course. You couldn't have acted in any other way.'

'Thank you,' Dorothy Flanagan said primly.

Billy was silent, then he said quietly, 'And we both now know why Ryan ran away after his mother's death and why the police want to speak to him, don't we?'

Dorothy Flanagan started to cry softly. 'What was I supposed to do? I couldn't give him the money, could I?

I feel so terribly guilty, so terribly, terribly guilty,' she sobbed.

'Have you told all this to the police?'

'Yes, I had no choice,' she said in a small voice.

'Did they tell you anything, why they were looking for him?'

'Yes, Ryan had taken his skateboard and a gold wedding band and locket, I imagine they were his grandmother's, and tried to borrow money on them from a cash converter.'

Dorothy Flanagan reached into a drawer and produced a tissue and, first wiping her eyes, she blew her nose. 'He was under-age and the merchant refused but was obliged to notify the police in case the child had stolen the ring and the locket.'

Billy shook his head slowly. 'No, that's not sufficient reason for Ryan to run away. He would have faced up to the police, told them the ring and the locket belonged to his grandmother and that his mother was ill and they had no money to eat and she'd sent him to the cash converter. Tell me, did he come to you *before* he attempted to sell his skateboard and grandmother's jewellery, or after?'

'I've checked on that, it was after.'

'I see. So you would have told the police about the death of the grandmother and suggested where the ring and the locket had come from, that there was no reason to be concerned?'

'Yes, of course.'

'But Ryan had already run away so he couldn't be told that the police were no longer after him?'

Ryan's principal sniffed. 'Yes, but the point is they're still looking for him.'

'What, as a missing child?'

'Yes, that also, the school made that notification.'

'I see. So what you seem to be suggesting is that there is something else the police told you?'

Dorothy Flanagan burst into tears. 'They said he had stolen money from a club in Kings Cross and used it to buy heroin!' she wailed, no longer able to control her distress. 'What have I done? What have I done to the child?'

If Billy had ever known how to comfort a woman in distress, he'd long since forgotten. All he could do was keep repeating, 'You haven't done anything you can be blamed for, Ms Flanagan.'

'I called the Department of Community Services after Ryan's visit,' she said. 'The case worker they allocated arrived three days after the mother's death. I should have gone to his house myself. I could see Ryan was distraught. I only have myself to blame, I've failed the child miserably!'

'Please don't fret,' Billy said, aware that it was quite the wrong word to use and entirely inappropriate to the situation. As a good lawyer he'd broken her down methodically to get to the truth but now he had no idea how he might calm her and restore her to some sort of equilibrium. So he simply waited until she'd grown calmer, awkward that he could do no more to comfort her.

Eventually Dorothy Flanagan dried her eyes. 'I feel both a fool and ashamed,' she said at last.

'You are not a fool and you did what you could at the

time,' Billy replied, thankful that she had stopped weeping. 'Now I need to know one more detail.'

'What is it?' Dorothy Flanagan asked, still a little tearful.

'Did the police tell you the name of the club from where Ryan is alleged to have stolen the money to buy heroin for his mother?'

'No, I didn't ask,' Dorothy Flanagan admitted. She hesitated. 'I'm glad you came, Mr O'Shannessy. I have had sleepless nights over this whole thing. This is not the first time I've cried over what appears to have happened to Ryan. I'm terribly frightened for him. We see lots of distressing things in this school: children who are abused and neglected, and we do what we can for them, which frankly is never quite enough. They're all special, I know, but Ryan Sanfrancesco is a brilliant boy, not just a musical one. When a boy or a girl like that comes under your guidance, and it doesn't happen very often, they are the reason you teach in schools like this one.' She stopped, tears brimming, 'And now I've lost him,' she said, her voice just above a whisper.

Billy took his leave of the principal of Pring Street Public School after being assured that he was most welcome to return at any time. 'We have a mutual interest in Ryan, Mr O'Shannessy, and I would be most grateful if you will let me know if you make contact. Anything we can do to help, you may take for granted.' Dorothy Flanagan had also given him her after-hours number, telling him that he could call if he had news or needed help at any time. 'I don't want to lose him, this child is special,' were her parting words.

Billy found a nice blanket at the Wayside Chapel. He was tempted by a big thick Onkaparinga still in excellent condition but realised it would be too heavy to carry so settled for a well-used and much lighter blanket and, while he was there, found a blue shirt not dissimilar to the one he'd bloodied when he'd damaged his nose. Afterwards, he purchased a packet of mynah-bird bullets, as he referred in his mind to the rat-poison pellets. After doing the avian deed and reciting his poem on the library steps, he bought a sandwich and a cup of coffee, something he hadn't done in all the years he'd been on the street, where alcohol had been his food and drink. It was yet another tiny step forward into a normal life.

Billy was well enough known at the library for the senior librarian on duty, Marcia Trengrove, to comment, 'Haven't seen you in quite a while, Billy, been away, have you?' She had known Billy since his legal days when he had been a member of the State Library Board.

'Surfers Paradise,' Billy said, not explaining any further.

'Some people have all the luck,' she said, smiling. 'Let me know if you need anything.'

What Billy would have liked to have said was 'Ms Trengrove, if I make any attempt to leave these premises before six o'clock, will you kindly render me senseless.' But, instead, he merely thanked her and added, 'I'd like to research Matthew Flinders.'

'Oh, how fortunate for you!' Marcia Trengrove exclaimed. 'We're just beginning to curate an exhibition to celebrate the bicentenary in 2001 of his epic voyage and there's a lot of material coming in. Is there any special area of interest?'

Billy hesitated, rubbing his chin. 'Well, yes, his cat, Trim.'

Marcia Trengrove looked surprised. 'His cat?'

'Yes. And his capture by the French.'

She looked dubious. 'The cat's or Matthew Flinders'?'

Billy was forced to conclude that the librarian wasn't a cat person or she'd be sympathetic, knowing as she must of the statue of Trim on the window ledge near where he slept. 'Well, Matthew Flinders, of course, but I understand the cat was captured with him. I thought it might be useful to er . . . write from the cat's perspective.'

'Hmm, I see,' the librarian said, thinking no doubt that Billy was beginning to lose his marbles, and, lost for further words on the subject, she handed him his allocated number. 'I must say, you look very well after your holiday in Surfers Paradise, Billy.'

'Could you please call me at five minutes to six, Marcia, I have an appointment I must keep elsewhere,' Billy said, hoping that he could last the remainder of the afternoon without attempting an escape.

I shall resume the story of Matthew Flinders' departure from the sandbank. Trim was sad at not accompanying his master and deeply concerned for his welfare in an open boat that seemed ill-equipped for such a journey. Master Flinders had pointed out to him that the great Captain Bligh had sailed nearly two thousand miles to the island of Timor in a very similar boat after the dastardly Fletcher Christian and his cohorts had mutinied on the *Bounty*.

'Trim, think on this, lad. Mr Bligh's boat was no bigger than ours and we sail no more than two hundred and fifty leagues to Port Jackson. We are stout-hearted and still well-nourished and the men I have chosen will row their hearts out when we are unable to hoist our sail.' Then he chided him gently, 'Thou art of little faith, Trim, dost thou not remember that it was the great Captain Bligh himself who taught yours truly the rudiments of navigation?'

Trim, of course, knew all this but he told himself they'd struck a sandbank in the much bigger *Porpoise*, that there was a strong wind at this time of the year prevailing from the shore, and that the Indians they might encounter if they went ashore for water or to shelter from a high sea or storm could not always be counted on to be friendly.

'Trim, you must take care of my brother, young Lieutenant Flinders,' Matthew Flinders instructed and then explained, 'He is far too phlegmatic for my liking, he is determined to be the calm and wise one well beyond his years and I should like him, with your help, to be more animated of spirit.' He went on to explain further, 'Men prefer calmness in a man who must lead them, but he must also show them, at the very least, a kindling of fire in the belly. My young brother is not yet sufficiently experienced to denote only calm in his character and it will be seen by the men under his command as a masquerade for uncertainty and inexperience.'

But the young Lieutenant Flinders, so very much in awe of his older brother, did not share his brother's affection for the ship's cat. At best he was ambivalent, relegating Master Trim to the status of just another member of the two shipwrecked crews. Although this may have been his deliberate intention, a part of his carefully contrived calm, Trim found it most disconcerting. The young naval lieutenant took scant notice of Trim's presence and completely ignored him when, endeavouring to follow his master's orders, Trim rubbed his fur against his ankles. On two separate occasions the young lieutenant had brushed him impatiently from his lap after Trim thought to bring him some softness and comfort. Trim was forced to conclude that while 'fire in the belly' was not to be found in his master's brother, the even stronger emotion of affection was also missing. A lack of imagination was indeed the true nature of the man and there was nothing much Trim could do to alter his disposition.

Trim soon realised that his time was better spent among the men who needed his cheerfulness and who responded as they always had with their affection returned. They would later tell how Trim kept their spirits up and how his antics at chasing seagulls and catching soldier crabs (a lively variation of his famous cockroach act on board ship) kept them all entertained. 'Aye, it were Master Trim who kept us all together and saved our minds from sinking into despondency and despair during them weeks wrecked upon the desert island,' they would say in later years, having transferred, for the better entertainment of the story, the sandbank to the status of a desert island. 'Though only a ship's cat, he were a true leader of men,' they would conclude. Although Trim was sad that he couldn't follow his master's orders and enliven the bland nature of his younger brother, he was a ship's cat, a master mariner and, above all, a pragmatist. He knew to get on with life when things didn't work out as planned.

We shall skip here the first part of the rescue journey of Matthew Flinders in the newly rigged six-oared cutter. Most of this time was spent out at sea and, though hard work in the extreme which required great character and resourcefulness against the elements, it was nevertheless uneventful. We take up the story when the little cutter was only fifty miles from Port Jackson, in the proximity of Port Hunter. The seas were high and the weather squally and it was decided to go ashore for the night, being already four in the afternoon. The crew spent an uncomfortable night in the rain, sheltering under the sails of the ship, and in the morning, with some difficulty, they got a fire going. They were out of ship's biscuits but what flour remained they baked into small cakes for the rest of their journey. At eleven o'clock, having filled the ship's water barrel and with the rain finally ceased, they sailed, staying as close to the coastline as possible.

This last effort to reach their destination was not easy sailing and for a great deal of the time they manned the oars. By the following morning the north head of Broken Bay was in sight. They were fortunate that a sea breeze blowing E.N.E. finally enabled them to hoist all the sail they had and by two o'clock in the afternoon they entered the heads and sailed up the harbour to Sydney Town, arriving in the early evening nearly two weeks after they had departed Wreck Reef.

Matthew Flinders, having sailed two hundred and fifty leagues from the sandbank in an open boat, was in great need of a razor for his chin, and a pair of scissors would have made hard work of his matted hair. His clothes were rank-smelling and his boots still soaked from the constant rain when he stepped ashore with Captain Park. Rather than first seeking the services of a barber and purchasing a change of linen, they made directly for Government House, where Governor King was found at dinner with his family. The surprise of the governor could not be contained when he was presented with two thoroughly bedraggled gentlemen whom he supposed to be many hundred leagues away on their journey to England.

'My dear Flinders,' he cried, embracing Matthew Flinders despite his hirsute and ragged appearance, 'what circumstance brings you back to us?' When he heard the melancholy tale, an involuntary tear ran down his cheek for he was a good man who could well imagine the effort it had taken to return in an open boat along a strange coast inhabited by savages.

Matthew Flinders and Captain Park were made to sit down at once and partake of a fine meal of stew and boiled potatoes after Governor King, not without kindness, asked his family if they might complete their meal in the kitchen while he listened to the report by the two honourable seagoing gentlemen. At the conclusion of their story, the governor promised his every endeavour and all the aid possible in the task of rescuing the men on Wreck Reef.

'You must stay a few days before we get this task under way, Mr Flinders,' he suggested.

'With the greatest respect, Your Excellency, I shall only rest when I am back at Wreck Reef. I should like to leave tomorrow if this were possible.'

'It will take a few days to prepare such an operation so that you will all return safely here.'

Matthew Flinders paused sufficiently for the governor to look up. 'Sir, it is my earnest desire to sail on from the sandbank to England.'

'Oh, but I don't think that is possible, Captain Flinders,' the governor said, not concealing his surprise. 'I have no vessel that can sail you safely to England.' He thought for a moment. 'Of course, if you must be homeward bound, there is the *Rolla*, lying at present in port and bound for China. She is under the command of Mr Robert

Cumming and I dare say, being an Englishman, he will readily agree to sail via Wreck Reef and take on board those of the men who wish to sail with him to China and thereafter to England. For the remainder, I have two schooners which can make the voyage to rescue those men who wish to return here. I am sure Mr Cumming will agree to have you on board as well.'

'Your Excellency, I cannot afford the time to take the long route back to England by way of China. Is there no other way you might accommodate me?' Flinders asked.

The governor sucked on his tobacco pipe, thinking. Finally he said, 'No, my dear Flinders, I think not, unless of course you take one of the schooners?'

It was not an offer to be leapt at, a schooner is a small vessel and by no means ideal for sailing such a distance. But Matthew Flinders did not reject the offer outright and asked to see the better of the two vessels. When the schooner was examined the following day, the *Cumberland* proved to be something less than a Gravesend passage boat, Gravesend being the English port used on the Channel crossing to the French port of Calais.

However, it wasn't the unsuitable nature of the ship for such a long voyage that concerned Matthew Flinders but rather its size. So small a vessel would create a good deal of turbulence when she sailed. Flinders would have a great amount of work to do on board. He needed to replace some of the charts he had lost when the *Porpoise* had been wrecked and had others to complete. He also needed to prepare his journal from the volumes of notes he had kept. The lack of suitable accommodation and the quick, frenetic movements of the ship would make these tasks difficult to accomplish.

As his superior officer, Governor King would discuss the voyage and the route Matthew Flinders proposed to take to reach England. While King knew better than to interfere with a navigator of Flinders' reputation, of one thing he was certain in his orders, they were not to call in at Mauritius.

This was decided on two counts, it was hurricane time for that neighbourhood and the island was a French colony. With England poised for war with France, it was not considered judicious to make contact, especially with Port Jackson undefended and Sydney Town a small and vulnerable settlement should the French decide to act as the aggressor in the Antipodes.

Thirteen days after Matthew Flinders had arrived in Sydney Town, the three ships set out on the return rescue mission. The news of the rescue attempt had spread throughout the community, with many of the citizens of Sydney Town and Parramatta coming down to the harbour to wish them well. They brought with them gifts of produce from their gardens and small farms, squealing pigs, ducks and hens, some brought wine and others fresh vegetables, which they offered with a generosity of spirit for the delectation of the poor starving souls wrecked on the reef.

Sydney, with its large convict population, was not known to be a generous town, more a taker than a giver and with no reason to be concerned with the affairs of government or navy, so Governor King was quick to express his gratitude and to congratulate them for their kindness, never having witnessed anything to approximate such open-hearted generosity in the colony.

On the day of sailing, the governor once again expressed his concern as to the seaworthiness of the *Cumberland*, 'Mr Flinders, will you not reconsider? The *Cumberland* is not built for such a voyage whereas the *Rolla* will see you safely home via China and not more than three months later.' In a final plea he added, 'Your navigational charts are of the utmost importance to the realm, it would be a tragedy should they be lost at sea.'

Matthew Flinders possessed all the qualities that had allowed him to succeed as a great explorer and navigator. Courage, determination and perseverance were an abundant part of his character but so too was stubbornness and he thanked the governor for his concern while declining passage on the *Rolla*.

Later, on his return to Wreck Reef, he privately confessed to Trim, 'Though she (the *Cumberland*) is too small and as frisky as a well-bred pony and not suitable to our purpose, I confess I was finally tempted to accept her for the most vainglorious and unworthy reasons.' Matthew Flinders paused and stroked Trim's back, finally pulling gently at his tail. 'You see, I like the idea that I will be the first to undertake so long a voyage in so small a vessel, it will serve my reputation well.'

As a Master Mariner Cat, Trim thought this a ridiculous and foolhardy vanity. 'Had they not been wrecked once already?' he asked himself.

'You see, Trim, I am at the mercy of the Admiralty who prepare for war with France. If we should arrive in England by means of the generosity of Mr Cumming, master of the *Rolla*, we would be mere passengers on his trading vessel. Can you not see how this would seem to my masters? I have already wrecked one of His Majesty's precious men o' war and have returned to England to lick my wounds. Ha, I see it clearly! They would regard me in a singularly dispassionate manner and, with war approaching and the realm in danger, they'd rule me quite unworthy to command another precious ship for the unimportant reasons of exploration.'

'That's a joke, sir!' Trim meowingly protested. 'The *Porpoise* was an old tub and no part of the British fleet. She would have served as cannon fodder should the Admiralty have been stupid enough to take her against the French!'

'Be that as it may, she is no longer a fighting ship on their manifest and I am the disgraced one who must vindicate myself. Now, if we should arrive in a Gravesend schooner, a vessel built and plainly intended for short passage and, at the same time, I have completely charted the Torres Strait, I shall be regarded as somewhat less than a hero and something better than a nautical vagabond.'

'If we arrive!' Trim meowed. 'Dead, drowned, it will not matter if you are prince or vagabond or I a humble ship's cat or related to the cat that visited the Queen in the company of Dick Whittington!'

Matthew Flinders ignored this feline outburst. 'With the *Cumberland* safely sailed across the treacherous seas, my seamanship will not be in question and, with a quicker passage to England discovered through the Strait, my credentials for the task of exploration will remain intact. Furthermore, when I have related the perfidious tale of the notorious Captain Palmer of the *Bridgewater*, they will be further obliged to grant me a ship so that we might continue our important work. Fairness, my dear Trim, is at the heart and soul of Englishmen of good breeding.'

Aye, and stupidity owns a fair portion of their nature as well, Trim thought to himself. 'You have told me when you'd not yet reached Port Stephens in this tub and were not much more than spitting distance from Port Jackson, how in a sudden squall and rising sea you were set to man the pumps as water poured into the hold of the *Cumberland*. The pumps proved all but useless and you might well have sunk had you not entered the safety of a small coastal bight.

Moreover, you admit that the *Cumberland* can scarcely bear a close-reefed mainsail and jib without threatening to overset. How then, sir, do you propose to reach England?'

Matthew Flinders gave the anxious Trim a patronising smile. 'My dear Master Trim, she is not as bad as you make her sound and although she promises hard sailing we shall endure, and this voyage will be a small hardship compared to the one in the open boat from Wreck Reef to Port Jackson.'

All this speculation by Trim was purely academic. The decision had been made by his master, and the *Cumberland* had arrived together with the *Rolla* and the second schooner, *Francis*, at Wreck Reef. There was no turning back, commonsense having long since been thrown out of the porthole. Trim flicked his tail with annoyance at his master's stubborn and romantic nature and thought to himself that a little of his younger brother's pessimism would not have gone amiss in the elder.

As might be expected, there was great joy among the shipwrecked crews when Flinders returned, and the men on the sandbank immediately fired a salute of eleven guns from the cannonades salvaged from the wreck of the *Porpoise*. On seeing his master return, Trim was overjoyed, though also somewhat concerned at the prospect of telling him that he had failed miserably in the task of enlivening the emotions of his younger brother.

However, Trim was completely vindicated by the following incident. The *Rolla*'s topgallant was first seen by a seaman when they were out at sea testing the new boat they had built to effect their rescue should Matthew Flinders fail to return. 'Damn my blood, what's that?' the man shouted, seeing the topgallant and at first mistaking it for a bird, but, moments after confirming it as a sail, they saw the *Rolla* and the two accompanying schooners moving towards them. Overjoyed, they hastily returned to inform Lieutenant Flinders of their imminent rescue. At the time he was in his tent, calculating some lunar distances, and even though he must have heard the clear sounds of excitement as the men rushed to give him the news, he didn't look up from his work.

'Sir, sir, a ship and two schooners in sight!' the senior man among them shouted, his eyes bright with the joy of being the first to tell of the good news.

Silence followed as the younger Flinders thought for some time. 'I suppose it must be my brother returning,' he said in a dispassionate voice. 'Please inform me when they anchor.' Whereupon he dismissed them and calmly resumed his calculations.

Once out of sight, Trim saw one of the men grunt, then spit to the sand at his feet and say, 'He be a cold sod, that one. He hath no joy in him.'

There is just one more thing of interest to talk about before Trim and his master sailed for England. In Matthew Flinders' absence, the men, not knowing how long they might be stranded on the reef, planted oats, maize and pumpkin seeds. Men who go to sea are not of an agricultural mind so they planted seed in the sand where the salt spray was prevalent. The seeds did come up, especially in the inlet where the soil was of a more nourishing nature, but ultimately all were doomed to die well before harvest time.

Seeing the attempts to grow sustenance in such poor conditions, Matthew Flinders made a promise to himself: If he should return to the Great Ocean and Indian Sea, he would take aboard ten thousand coconuts and these he would distribute amongst the numerous sandbanks of the two oceans.

'This will be my gift to all the maritime nations and to every sailor, no matter whether friend or foe or what his colour or creed, whether Malacca captain or Chinee boatman,' he told Trim, looking up from his journal. 'If there had been a stand of the coconut on the sandbank we would not have struck Wreck Reef; they are an excellent beacon, the mariner's guide and friend in these treacherous seas. Moreover, if there is a shipwreck, they will provide a nourishment which will keep a man alive and healthy as a supplement to his fish catch.'

There remained a final task before they sailed. The *Cumberland* moved to the eastern extremity of the reef to collect seabird eggs and hopefully a turtle for its succulent meat. Such fine fare was rare while in the process of a voyage and it seemed a good omen when they caught a large specimen for the ship's larder and, with Trim's help, discovered all the nests they needed to fill a great cabbage-tree basket with eggs.

At noon on the 20th of October, with the breakers in sight, they fixed their latitude to check their position with respect to Murray's Islands before entering the Torres Strait on their voyage to England.

The next thirteen days at sea were without mishap but it was becoming apparent that the indifferent sailing of the schooner was against making a quick passage and Trim had not resolved his apprehension concerning the little vessel. By the time they had sailed through the Timor Strait and reached the Dutch settlement at Coepang Bay, it was clear that the schooner was in trouble. She was leaking badly when the wind caused her to lie over on her side and one of the pumps was by now near useless. Matthew Flinders was hopeful that the pumps might be re-bored and fitted and that pitch could be procured to pay the seams in the upper works after they were caulked. But neither was available in the tiny settlement and he had to settle for fresh water and provisions. The only compensation was that they managed to stop a leak in the bow and were warned that the Malay pirates had become the scourge of the straits between Java and Timor so the *Cumberland* was fitted with netting to prevent the pirates from boarding.

Matthew Flinders decided to sail south of the Sundra Islands to make it to the Cape of Good Hope, where he knew they could effect the repairs the tiny schooner badly needed. The monsoon weather was already threatening and the winds were changeable, with squalls prevalent, so that several days out of Coepang, the jumble caused by the different movement in the water made the little schooner labour exceedingly. The starboard pump, the only one still effective, was made to work continuously day and night. Flinders' greatest fear was that it too would soon fall into disrepair from overuse. They sailed on towards the Cape, the little vessel becoming more and more unseaworthy, so that by the 4th of December Flinders knew that they would not make their immediate destination and his only chance was to make for Mauritius, the island he had been expressly forbidden to visit by Governor King.

Matthew Flinders found himself in a great pickle. He was not aware that England was now again at war with France and, as he held a passport from the French government, he hoped for a cordial welcome to the island. His hopes were to be severely dashed and his life and that of Trim forever changed.

Marcia Trengrove tapped Billy on the shoulder. 'Time for you to leave, Billy,' she said quietly. 'It's nearly six o'clock.'

Billy couldn't believe the time had passed so quickly and

that not once during the afternoon had he thought of slipping out for a drink, though straight after the librarian had alerted him to the time the craving returned, such was the insidious nature of his addiction. Still, despite having had a sandwich for lunch, he was hungry so decided to walk down Martin Place where the Just Enough Faith food van would be waiting.

Billy decided to visit each of the food vans progressively in the hope that Ryan might be spotted. He intended asking everyone coming in for their evening meal if they had seen him, describing his looks and, in particular, his black Independent T-shirt, Vans trainers and skateboard. There were always street kids at the vans and one of them might have seen Ryan.

Billy told himself that, with the police looking for him, Ryan would be careful not to show himself too openly in public but he still had to eat. He had no money and, short of scavenging in the bins in the back lanes of restaurants, a food van was the most likely place for him to come.

Jeff Gambin greeted him like a long-lost friend. 'Haven't seen you in ages, Billy. What happened? Got yourself arrested, did you? Warm cell for the winter?'

It was an old joke. 'No, I've been to Surfers Paradise, a place in the sun for shady people.' This was an even older joke.

Gambin laughed. 'I can offer you an excellent lamb chop, mashed potato whipped to a frenzy, with rich brown gravy, what say you, Billy?'

Billy had not yet reached the point in his rehabilitation

where he thought to choose his food according to his mood and he nodded. While he waited for Jeff Gambin to prepare his plate, he asked him if he'd seen Ryan.

'We know Ryan well, Billy, he's a regular customer, has been for a couple of years, though we haven't seen him for . . .' He stopped to think, holding Billy's paper plate, which now contained three lamb chops and a small mountain of mashed potato, although the gravy had not yet been added. 'Three weeks, maybe more, not since his grandmother died.'

'You know about his grandmother?' Billy asked, surprised.

'Oh yes, Ryan would always take a plate of food back for the old woman, almost always mince and mash. She also loved sausages and fried onions. We'd put it in a plastic container for him to keep it warm. When he stopped coming we asked around and someone, I forget who, said the old girl had passed on. Haven't seen the boy since.'

'If you do, could you tell him he'll find me with Trim?' Billy asked.

'Find you with Trim? That all?'

'Yes, thank you, Jeff.' Billy took the plate and sat on a bench, surprised at just how hungry he was.

Billy completed his meal with a paper mug of sweet, milky tea, into which he put only two teaspoons of sugar. It was yet another tiny step forward. He had just sufficient time to walk up William Street to the Cross and the Wayside Chapel.

Carrying his briefcase in the usual way and his Wayside Chapel blanket wrapped in the plastic bag under his right arm, he appeared the derelict more than ever. His knee was playing up from all the walking he'd done but he was sober and hanging on grimly. At this moment in his life he was as far from the famous barrister as he had ever been, yet he sensed that he was slowly closing in on the human being he might some day become if he could stay off the grog.

The thought of everything changing, and the prospect of entering a life of sobriety, frightened Billy. He knew how to conduct himself in the world of drunks but he didn't know how to live in that same world as a sober person. On his first night out of William Booth and still sober, he was planning to spend some of it in a dark alley behind The Sheba, acting out the accustomed role of an alcoholic, and after midnight on the bench underneath Trim's window ledge as a homeless person accommodated in the Starlight Hotel. He was back on the street and sleeping rough, but this time without the warmth and comfort and final oblivion provided by Mr Johnnie Walker. He was going to need the affirmation he hoped the AA meeting he was about to attend would give him.

Billy arrived at the Wayside Chapel just after seven o'clock with the AA meeting due to begin at seven-thirty, so he waited outside, not sure he wanted to enter until the last possible moment. It was getting cold and he was annoyed with himself that he hadn't thought to pick up a sweater when he'd gone for his blanket that morning. There seemed to be a lot of young people around, most of them with bits and pieces thrust through their various facial orifices, rings through their noses, eyelids, ears and tongues, not to mention the multi-ringed ear lobes. Billy wondered what it was in human beings that required this kind of self-mutilation in the name of fashion or originality. If it was a need to stand out as a different caste, what was the particular defiance they wished to articulate? A loop through the tongue seemed to him to be a very inconvenient implementation, so what was such an obvious impediment trying to say?

Men and women somewhat older than the youngsters started to arrive, some dressed much as he was, though the majority wore business suits and ties and had obviously come straight from work. Billy didn't carry a watch, another habit he would have to take up again, but after several of the men had entered, he followed.

The meeting, which took place in a back room, was largely unstructured and it became at once obvious that its central purpose was to offer mutual support to those attending. As at William Booth, only first names were offered and no other details followed unless these were volunteered. The men sat around, talking one to one or in groups, and almost immediately a man in a suit and tie who seemed in his fifties came over to Billy and offered his hand.

'Hi, I'm Don, welcome to AA.'

'Thank you, my name is Billy.'

'This is your first visit, Billy?' Don asked.

Billy nodded. 'I've just come out of William Booth, my first day as a matter of fact.'

'Good on ya!' Don cried, immediately gripping Billy's

shoulder. 'You've come straight in, that's bloody marvellous, mate.'

Billy could sense the sincerity of Don's response and felt a lot more comfortable. 'I'm not sure what I'm supposed to do,' he ventured.

Don grinned. 'What you've asked sounds like a simple question but it isn't. AA meetings are not very structured unless you want to do the Twelve Steps, we call those "step meetings" and they take place in a separate room. Otherwise we are all here for mutual support. If I'm chairing the meeting, I'll bring it to order and we'll say a short prayer and then ask if there's anyone who wants to share. Someone will stand up and tell of his experience as an alcoholic and when he's finished we'll give him a lot of vocal support. You will find there is a very strong bond between everyone here.' He smiled. 'It's a bit like a secret society, someone can only enter if they've had the experience of addiction. Your paid-up membership is because we all share the same experience. We're all alcoholics and we're all here for each other.' He touched Billy on the shoulder. 'Come and let me introduce you to a few of the blokes.'

After a while, as he told Billy he would, Don called the meeting to order and said a short prayer. Then he asked if anyone wanted to share. A man stood up and introduced himself as Bryan, whereupon there was some clapping and calls of 'Gidday, Bryan' and other expressions of encouragement and welcoming sounds. Bryan told his story and some of the problems he was having to confront, at the end of which he sat down to the applause of the rest of the men and women. This happened on three more occasions and afterwards the meeting moved back to one-on-one and group discussions, with everyone included.

By the end of the evening, Billy had met and listened to almost everyone. He was surprised at the frankness of many of the discussions and the willingness of the members to participate. It wasn't as much the wisdom of their thoughts, after all they shared the one experience in common, but their warmth and sincerity and their genuine need to be with each other, even though it was obvious they didn't all belong to the same social environment outside. Billy said very little himself and nobody tried to push him into joining in, but nevertheless he felt included. Over tea and biscuits he met more of the people, all of whom encouraged him to keep attending, promising their support.

By the end of his first AA meeting, Billy felt reasonably comfortable. This was something he would need to do twice a day for a long time to come and he was vastly relieved to find that he could accommodate himself without a feeling of apprehension or alienation. He would most definitely attend the meeting the following morning to be held at the G'day Cafe at the Rocks.

Billy was happy that the first part of his day wouldn't differ too greatly from his previous existence. The difference was that he would swap a hangover for a craving, and eventually his Higher Power, Master Mariner Trim Flinders, might take him to the point when the craving ceased, when only the warning that he would always be an alcoholic would persist.

At the conclusion of the meeting, Don came over and explained that he was the voluntary chairman and did Billy mind if he asked him one or two questions. Billy told him to go ahead.

'Your anonymity will always be respected, Billy, but if you'd like me to go through the Twelve Steps and explain the step meetings, I'd be happy to do that. Also, are you familiar with the idea of a sponsor?'

'Is that someone I can have access to at such times as things get rugged?' Billy replied.

'Yes, someone who is always available to talk with you, whether face-to-face or on the phone. Most of us have such a person and I commend the idea to you.' He grinned. 'You know how it is, the spirit is willing but the flesh is weak. We all reach that certain point when we think we can't continue and that's the time to call your sponsor. It sounds crazy but it works, in fact it is one of the basic platforms of AA.'

'May I think about it?' Billy replied. 'In my present circumstances I don't have a phone or even a reliable address. The public telephones are usually in disrepair in my sleeping locality.' In fact, Billy wanted time to get to know the men around him so that he could pick a sponsor among them whom he liked and respected.

'Sure, just shout when you're ready,' Don said. 'Will I see you at the G'day Cafe tomorrow morning? I'll shout you a coffee and a sticky bun.'

It was no more than five minutes' walk from the Wayside Chapel to the lane behind The Queen of Sheba and Billy soon found a doorway not quite opposite the back entrance Freddo had described to him. He rummaged around in a bin until he found an empty wine bottle, which he wrapped in newspaper, and then he settled down, the blanket wrapped around him and the bottle lying on its side beside him. If anyone approached, he would pretend to be in the usual alcohol-induced coma or, if he had to, he'd simply act as if he was very drunk.

The hours passed slowly and even though Billy had washed out the wine bottle at the Fitzroy fountain, he was convinced he could still smell the residual alcohol. The bottle was intended as a prop, the usual accompaniment to be found with a drunk, but its presence was beginning to disturb him. Twice he moved the bottle away, placing it two doorways along, and both times he lasted no more than half an hour before retrieving it.

During the evening four men approached the door, all of them well dressed, and Billy soon became aware of the routine. The bell, it must have been an internal buzzer because it made no outside sound, was situated on the lintel above the door and would not be visible to anyone not knowing it was there. A few moments after the bell had been pressed, a light above the doorway suddenly came on and moments later went out again. At first Billy was puzzled, then he realised that there must be a camera focused on the doorway and the light was needed so that the observer inside could identify the caller. Even then the door didn't open, the caller was required to insert a card into a slot beside the door and had to wait some twenty seconds for the soft buzz of the electronically-controlled door opening. The card inserted into the slot was obviously not a key but a further means of identifying the visitor.

Close to midnight, Billy could bear the imagined fumes coming from the bottle no longer. He had to have a drink and he rose. Leaving his blanket in the doorway, he started down the lane. He had hardly taken two steps when he heard footsteps approaching. Darting back into the doorway, he hurriedly wrapped himself in the blanket and waited, pretending to be asleep, though in the darkness of the doorway his eyes were open. The bottle had rolled away and had come to rest in the gutter.

Billy watched as a large man approached Freddo's door. He stood in front of it for a moment before he went through the usual routine but, as the light went on, Billy got a clear view of his face and of the brightly coloured tie he was wearing. He'd seen that face before and he clearly remembered the tie, it was of pink silk emblazoned with purple rats. The man was the one he had seen at Marion's Bar at the Flag Hotel.

Then, like a bolt from the blue, Billy made another connection that had been scratching around in his mind ever since the morning Sergeant Orr had stopped him outside Parliament House in Macquarie Street on the day he'd first met Ryan. The man standing at the door was the politician who'd had the fight with the television reporter over an accusation that he was concealing the name of a prominent judge who was a paedophile. Orr had been a witness for the politician in the case where Billy had appeared for the television station. He now recalled how the politician had subsequently lost his seat in the next election and had been given a cushy job in the Department of Community Services by the incoming Liberal government. His name was Petersen, Alf Petersen, and he was Marion's so-called boyfriend.

CHAPTER THIRTEEN

Billy awoke to the usual raucous laughter of the two kookaburras. He felt stiff and sore, a month sleeping on a mattress had made his body soft. It was several minutes before he could stand upright without holding on to the back of the bench. There was one good piece of news, in his absence the drinking fountain some six metres from the bench had been repaired. Unshackling his briefcase and handcuffing it to the leg of the bench, he moved over to the fountain and rinsed his mouth, drank again, then washed his face.

As Billy drank from the fountain, he realised that he'd made yet another tiny step in his rehabilitation, he hadn't woken to find his mouth bone-dry and his tongue sticking to its roof as it would have been had he been drinking. Along with a clear head, this was another small victory in the fragile world he now lived in. His heart skipped a beat as he recalled the previous night when he'd left his blanket and was about to go and find a drink. Had Alf Petersen not chosen that very moment to walk into the alley, Billy knew he would have been a goner. Life works in mysterious ways, the evil bastard had inadvertently saved him from personal disaster.

The repair of the drinking fountain was for Billy the equivalent of having running water brought into his home for the first time. He was considerably cheered by the wonderful convenience, knowing he didn't have to go all the way down to Martin Place Station for fresh water. On his way to the AA morning meeting at the Rocks at seven, he'd use the toilet at Circular Quay. He folded his blanket and placed it into the plastic bag, then walked over to the clump of palms and tree ferns at the extreme perimeter of his sleeping quarters. The city council had spread a deep layer of woodchips on the ground under the foliage in order to retain moisture in the soil. Billy scratched a hollow among the chips and placed his blanket within it, then covered it over. Except for a slight bump on one part of the surface, the blanket was completely concealed and unlikely to be discovered. Retrieving his briefcase, Billy started out for the Quay.

After finishing his ablutions, Billy decided he'd shave and shower at The Station after the AA meeting. He also hoped a letter might be waiting from Trevor Williams at the daytime retreat for the homeless. The G'day Cafe was only a couple of hundred metres from the Quay in Lower George Street so he would have sufficient time to buy several slices of bread and make up his day's supply of mynah-bird bullets before the meeting.

Walking down the concourse, Billy was about to cross the road to avoid Con Poleondakis at the New Hellas Cafe when he stopped abruptly. On the spur of the moment he decided to attempt a reconciliation. If the Greek cafe owner rejected him, Billy felt he was strong enough to accept it. The sudden and unexpected conniption between them over Ryan had been so abrupt that Billy felt he'd not been able to reason with the irascible Greek. Just by attempting a reconciliation, even if it should fail, he would be making a statement to himself that he was no longer a derelict and wasn't obliged to accept the scorn of others without the right to protest.

Billy took a deep breath and, squaring his shoulders, walked over to the New Hellas. To his astonishment, the first thing he noticed was a carton of coffee, a finger bun and the better part of a loaf of bread placed at the end of the counter. A thin lick of steam emerged from the opening in the plastic lid that covered the coffee container.

Con had his back to Billy but now he turned and met his eyes. 'Jesus Christos!' he yelled. 'Billy, Billy, my good friends, thank Gods you is come back!' Con's broad face was wreathed in a huge smile though Billy could see the sudden tears in his eyes. He pointed to the coffee and bread. 'You look, Billy. Always, every days I puts the coffee. Every bloody days, myte! Fingers buns also. Every bloody days!' He emerged from behind the counter and embraced Billy, giving him a great bear hug. 'Billy, Billy, where you gone, myte?' Con Poleondakis sobbed.

'Con, I thought we should try to clear up the misunderstanding that occurred with the boy,' Billy said, pleased and relieved at Con's effusive welcome.

Con pulled away from Billy and lowered his eyes, shaking his head slowly. 'Billy, you no clears nothings up, me, I clear, I am stupid Greek man and I am bloody ashame, myte. My wife she says, "Constantine, you find Billy, he help you, you find him, he good man. I want to thanks him for my life to come to Astraalie."'

'Wife? She's arrived?' Billy cried, delighted at the news.

Con beamed. 'She's a beautifuls, myte, like a Goddess!'

'Young and beautiful, what more could you want, eh, Con?'

Con pursed his lips. 'Maybe not so youngs, Billy, but Goddess for cookings. *Halva, loukoumathes, stafithopitta, tiropitta, spanakopitta, pasticcio.*' He reeled the names off as he pointed to a display case under the counter, 'Everythings she is makings.' He patted his stomach. 'Also she is Goddess for the house and the bed, first class in da cot, myte, fair dinkums, put down your glass!'

'That's great, Con, I'm glad it turned out well.'

'Tonight you come. She's cookings what you like, Greek lambs? Maria, she's cooking Greek lambs and rice, *arni a la hasapa*, you come tonight, Billy! Firsts class tucker, myte.'

'I thought her name was Sophia!'

'No, no, Sophia that her sister, she dead now, but she sends photograph of her sister because also she look like dat one, only she don't have photograph for herselfs.'

'But that was a picture of a young girl?'

Con shrugged. 'That photographs they takes nineteen sixty-eight, myte.'

Billy laughed. 'As long as you're happy, that's all that matters, Con.'

Con spread his hands and Billy thought he was going to embrace him once again. 'Happy like Larries, myte. In two day she makes dat coffee machine nearly good like me. You come tonight, we have Greek wine, we all happy like pig in shits.'

'I'm on the wagon, Con. I don't drink now,' Billy said quietly. It was the first time he'd admitted it aloud to someone he'd known and he could feel his heart beating faster.

Before Billy could escape, Con had embraced him again, hugging him to his large chest. 'Bloody beauties, myte, congratulations! We drink grapes juice, Greek grapes juice.' He pulled away and kissed the tips of his fingers. 'Beautifuls, bloody oaths!'

'Thank you, Con, I can't come before half-past eight. I have to go to a meeting to help me get better.' Billy was running out of time and it was the only way he could think to explain AA without having to go into a lot of detail.

'Here, you take your coffee, Billy. I see you tonight, half-pasts eight o'clock, I meets you this place, New Hellas Cafe. Black Mercedes, okay?'

Billy took the coffee, bread and the finger bun. He would have just enough time to consume both before the AA meeting and he'd have to make his ammunition later. 'Thanks, Con, I'm glad we're friends again.'

Con was silent for a moment. 'Billy, tonight, you brings dat boy, no worries, myte.'

'Thank you, Con, but I can't. I'll talk to you about him tonight.' Billy started to walk away.

'Billy!' Con called after him. Billy turned. 'You my fren, fair dinkums, myte.' He thought Con was going to cry again.

The breakfast meeting was much the same as the one the previous night though there were several new faces. Billy also asked Don if he might have some literature on the Twelve Steps before he decided to attend a step meeting. He realised that he should probably embrace the program, which was the same as the one he would have completed on a compulsory basis over seven months if he'd gone to the Salvation Army hostel at St Peters. Don had greeted Billy with sincerity and Billy was beginning to realise that a missing face at a meeting was a potential tragedy and an attendant one a small victory for everyone. All these men and women shared both their hopes and fears, and the collective will and close bonding was an important factor in staying sober. He told himself he dare not miss a meeting.

It was another bright morning and the walk up to The Station, the day refuge for the homeless, after the meeting was pleasant. The sky was a perfect wash of blue. Alas, when he arrived at The Station, Sally Blue wasn't at the desk and he was greeted by a pleasant-looking woman who appeared to be in her forties. Allowing the blue-eyed Sally to be the first to sign his plastered arm must have had the desired effect because when he inquired after her, the new woman said she'd left to join a computer company. Billy recalled how guilty he'd felt at breaking his promise to Ryan.

'May I inquire if there is any mail for me? It's Billy, Billy O'Shannessy.'

'Oh, yes, a letter for O'Shannessy,' the new receptionist replied. 'It's been here a while, I remember it clearly because of the beautiful copperplate handwriting on the envelope.' She started to sort through a pile of letters. 'Here we are,' she said finally, handing Billy an envelope. She was right. The address on the envelope looked like something out of an early nineteenth-century legal document. Billy turned to look at the flip side of the envelope, on which was written:

Trevor Williams
Lot 36
Murtee
Via Wilcannia, NSW, 2836

Trevor Williams was full of surprises. There was no question that the writing was that of an educated hand. The receptionist, who'd introduced herself as Toni Frazer, said, 'There's also a parcel for you, Billy, hang on and I'll get it.' She left reception and returned a minute or so later, holding an ordinary plastic bag to which was pinned an envelope with his name typed on it.

Billy looked into the bag to see that it was the old dressing-gown Sally Blue had brought for him from home.

He opened the envelope smiling. Except for her signature, the words were typed.

> Dear Billy,
> I got the job. Thanks for bringing me
> luck. This is your old dressing-gown,
> I just didn't want anyone else to have it.
> All the best,
> Love,
>
> *Sally Blue*
>
> Computer Guru

Billy asked if he might have a towel and then went through to the bathroom where he shaved and showered. His clothes were rather grubby from sitting in the alley the previous night so he put them through the washing machine and the drier, ironing and then changing into the spare khaki pants he'd acquired at William Booth and the blue shirt he'd found at the Wayside Chapel. Somehow he'd managed to cram both garments into the remaining space in his briefcase. Brushing what he laughingly referred to as his hair, he felt finally ready to open the letter from Trevor Williams.

> *Dear Billy,*
> *I am writing on behalf of my husband Trevor Williams*
> *who does not count letter writing among his many skills as*
> *a bushman.*

On the other hand, I am a trained school teacher and jolly well should know how to compose a letter. As a girl in Ireland my pater always said, 'Girl, the Irish are a people to whom words come naturally. To write a sound letter is the first requirement of a good mind.'

Well, I don't know so much about that, but we were overjoyed to get your letter and to know that you would help to find our daughter.

When you asked for details of her appearance, I asked Trevor what he had told you and he scratched his head and mumbled that he couldn't rightly recall.

'Did you give Billy her name?' I asked.

'Buggered if I can remember,' he replied. 'Maybe not, eh?'

I suspected as much. He always refers to her as 'my little daughter'. I often wonder if he remembers her name, which is Caroline.

Caroline has dark hair, though it is perfectly straight like my own. I am sometimes referred to as Black Irish. During Sir Francis Drake's victory over the Spanish Armada, a great many Spanish ships were wrecked on the coast of Ireland. The fair-haired Irish women took rather a fancy to the dark handsome sailors and, as the saying goes, one thing led to another and today some Irish are of a dark complexion, myself among them. Although Caroline has fair skin, she has dark eyes. They're beautiful eyes and, like her father's people, seem to see everything.

It is a difficult task trying to describe someone you love, even one's own daughter. We, of course, think she's pretty and

I enclose a photograph, though it was taken when she graduated from the Conservatorium of Music in Adelaide some eight years ago and I don't think it will help much in an attempt to identify her. Oh dear, so very much has changed.

If it helps, people have always thought of her as very attractive, some say beautiful. She is slim and is, I think, about five feet six inches tall (she's been taller than Trevor and myself since she was fifteen). Oh yes, I almost forgot, she has a mouth that seems at first bigger than it should be, very much like the actress Julia Roberts. As Trevor will have told you, she once used it to sing rather well.

As to identity marks, it probably doesn't help much to know she has a small birthmark on her right buttock about the size of a ten-cent piece and it looks remarkably like the head of a man, maybe a Roman emperor, because there is even the suggestion of a laurel wreath upon his head. I don't suppose she'd happily bare her bottom for you, though.

There is only one other thing that will identify her without question. When Caroline was eight she was bitten by a brown snake (King Brown) directly on the Achilles tendon and Trevor sliced the bite open and sucked out the poison. Caroline recovered but limped about for months and Trevor was sick for nearly three weeks, but what remains of this experience is a thin, white, slightly jagged line where Trevor's pocketknife sliced down the Achilles. If you find her and she will bare her heel for you, this would be positive identification.

Billy, we are so very grateful to you for even agreeing to try to locate Caroline. These last five years have been very sad for both Trevor and myself, we love her very much and only wish that she will come back to us. If my tears could bring her back, then she would be washed home on the crest of a tidal wave.

Trevor and I will, of course, travel to Sydney on a moment's notice should you have any success. We quite understand that the chances of finding Caroline are very slim and that Trevor's travelling to Sydney on the last attempt to find her wasn't very well-advised. But he's a bushie and stubborn as hell and you can't tell him anything, even if it's for his own good. I'm pleased to say that he's well and completely recovered.

Trevor tells me that you are a great man, the finest whitefella he has ever met. If he says so, then I am happy to agree with him. Trevor doesn't hand out too many bouquets, black or white. The last person who got one from him was Eddie Mabo. Trevor reckons his mob on Murray Island stuck to their guns on Aboriginal land rights and 'they're fair dinkum heroes'. When he told me about you returning his money I can understand why he feels the way he does. You must have an extraordinarily generous and loving nature.

I apologise for this rather rambling letter. I know I haven't been very specific even though Caroline is my daughter. You think you know every inch of your child's body, which you've held and cherished since she was clutched to your breast as an infant. Suddenly you realise she is a stranger. The soft, innocent parts you kissed and pampered have long since gone away, turned into muscle and sinew.

Unfortunately we're not on the phone or fax out here as this is only a shearing camp, but a letter will eventually reach us.

We both send our sincerest good wishes to you and thank you from the bottom of our hearts. Whether you find Caroline or not, the fact that you are willing to try fills our hearts with goodwill towards you.

We remain your friends whatever happens,

Trevor and Bridgit Williams

P.S. Trevor says to tell you he's started on 'The Ballad of Billy O'Shannessy' and it's coming along 'real nice'.

B.W.

P.P.S. Careless. I forgot to tell you that Caroline is twenty-eight years old.

Billy smiled as he completed reading the letter. Trevor, he thought, despite the terrible tragedy of his daughter, was a lucky man. Bridgit Williams seemed a strong woman and he could feel her affection for Trevor in her letter. He examined the photograph of Caroline. It showed a very attractive young girl in cap and gown, though it was a full shot and taken at some distance. It would be difficult to make a match if she'd changed a fair bit since it had been taken, as Bridgit Williams had suggested.

He thought of Morgan asking him to visit his de facto

and, from his description, it just might be a fortunate coincidence. Although the names were not the same, Morgan's partner calling herself Kartanya, the fact that she was part-Aborigine and also a singer seemed to fit and Billy told himself that she may well have used an Aboriginal name, which was common enough among many of the younger liberated indigenous women.

Morgan had said that Kartanya's forebears came from the Kaura tribe on the Adelaide plains. Caroline had been educated at the Adelaide Conservatorium and Trevor may well have originated from the Kaura tribe. Wilcannia and Broken Hill, the area he now lived in, were closer to the Adelaide plains than they were to Sydney.

While Billy knew he must make the search for Ryan his immediate priority, Morgan had left him his girlfriend's phone number and address and he decided he would visit her as soon as he could possibly arrange a time.

In fact, Billy was finding himself with little disposable time, which was a good thing, he supposed. It meant he didn't have too many idle moments to think about his craving for drink. One thing he told himself he must persist with, under all circumstances, was his routine. He must only substitute the time he would have normally taken up drinking with something else.

Billy knew that he was a creature of habit, that he was apt to panic when his routine altered. It was a strange contradiction in his personality. As a lawyer his mind had been famously agile, constantly capable of speculation that more often than not proved to be accurate. He had been known for his ability to remorselessly follow a convoluted argument, setting mental traps on the way and exploring the dark corners in the minds of others, discovering the secrets they hoped to conceal.

But, paradoxically, in the physical world, he craved order without complication. It was the reason he had wanted the button sewn back onto his shirt when Davo had come to his rescue. It was unlikely that any of the other alcoholics at William Booth would have even noticed it missing from a garment they were wearing. Billy would only be able to attempt to track Morgan's partner in what he considered the time previously occupied with grog.

Perhaps this was selfish, an allocation of time that best suited him, but Billy knew that unless he was very careful he could easily lose the plot. Rigid adherence to a plan was required. He reasoned that to aimlessly wander around the Cross, hoping that he might run into Ryan, wasn't a sensible way to behave. He felt sure sooner or later Ryan would find him. That he had only to stick to his routine and the boy would eventually sniff him out. That was, of course, if he wanted to do so.

He'd do all the sensible things, leave Ryan's name and description at all the food vans and refuges, such as Father Riley's group. He would also maintain his vigil in the lane at night. The Sheba sex club was the only connection he had to the boy's mother. Freddo's description of what happened to kids of Ryan's age who suddenly found themselves on the street was the gloomiest of all possible speculations, but the sex club and what lay concealed behind it was the one very fragile and tenuous connection he possessed and he was obliged to maintain his observation.

Billy's speculative mind had put together a scenario which, for once in his life, he hoped from the bottom of his heart, was incorrect. If Ryan's mother had been ill with Hepatitis C, as had been the case, and if she had desperately needed heroin and was too weak to get out of bed to make a connection with her supplier, as had also been the case, then she may have begged Ryan to procure it for her. Assuming that Ryan was initially successful, her need for heroin would soon have left him without any money. With no money to buy heroin, Ryan had gone to Dorothy Flanagan for some of Billy's funds. He had failed and thereafter had tried to flog his grandmother's wedding ring and locket and his own skateboard. Billy further reasoned that Ryan couldn't have needed the money for food, he'd get that easily enough from the Just Enough Faith van. There could only be one possible reason why he needed the money. Dorothy Flanagan's instinct had been correct, it was to feed his mother's addiction.

Billy now attempted to think out the rest of the scenario. Based on what Freddo had told him, Ryan's mother would tell the boy where to go, where they might give him heroin. Freddo had said that most addicts get their shit away from home, he'd suggested Ryan's mother probably got it at the place where she worked. As an exotic dancer, she was a freelancer at The Queen of Sheba, among other places. It was just possible that her dealer came from there, the heroin supplied to her by the proprietor or one of his henchmen, a doorman, someone like that.

Billy was aware that he was drawing a long bow, that a small boy trying to obtain heroin for his mother was an unusual circumstance. But he also knew heroin addicts had no conscience, all that mattered was that they fed their habit. They'd steal, lie and betray and it was even possible that a mother might use, even sacrifice, her son to satisfy her craving.

Billy hated himself for his next hypothesis but his legal mind was forced to make it. Ryan goes to The Queen of Sheba and Mohammed Suleman, the Assyrian proprietor, sees this tender little boy. Ryan was a beautiful-looking child and, with 'the club' out back, the notorious crim might agree that heroin could be supplied 'under certain conditions'. Billy winced inwardly, ashamed for even thinking in such a way. He prayed that it was merely his febrile imagination that was taking him to places he didn't want to go. His fervent hope was that Ryan had simply panicked when he heard the police were after him and was hiding in a squat somewhere, hungry and miserable, but safe from such vile predators.

To confirm either his fears or his hopes, Billy first had to find out why the police were looking for the boy. His next task was to visit the police at Kings Cross. He was even willing to break his precious routine and skip his usual visit to the Gardens as well as his mynah-bird duties. But he knew of old that mornings are chaos in a busy police station, that it was much better to call in during the afternoon if you hoped to speak to the patrol commander or one of the detectives. He would spend the early part of the afternoon in the library and then arrive at the police station about three o'clock. A cop with a bit of lunch in his belly was always in a better mood and easier to talk to.

Billy entered the Kings Cross Police Station just after three and asked if he could see the patrol commander.

'Can you tell me why you want to see him, sir?' the young policewoman at the counter asked.

Billy smiled, then said politely, 'Yes, of course, I'm a lawyer and I wish to inquire about a client.'

The young woman looked a little bemused. 'You're a lawyer?' she asked doubtfully.

'That's right and I wish to see the patrol commander, please,' Billy repeated calmly.

'Just one moment, sir,' she said and left the front desk.

Billy was tired from the walk so took the opportunity to sit down. After perhaps another ten minutes the young policewoman returned accompanied by the patrol commander. He appeared to be in his mid-thirties, the new breed, sharp, intelligent and businesslike. 'Yes, sir, what can I do for you?'

'My name is O'Shannessy, I'm a barrister and I wish to inquire about a client, a juvenile whom I believe you wish to question in relation to a drug-related incident.'

'Oh, I see. His name, Mr O'Shannessy?'

'Ryan Sanfrancesco, like the city, only with an *e* where the *i* is usually found.'

The policeman smiled, 'Thank you, bound to have typed that incorrectly.' He moved over to a computer and tapped in Ryan's name. 'Yes, here we are, Ryan Sanfrancesco. You will need to speak to a detective, if you can wait a moment.' He turned to the younger policewoman, 'Constable, will you see if Detective Barker is in.' Turning back to Billy, he said, 'Will you excuse me please, sir?' Without waiting for Billy's reply, he turned and left the reception area.

A couple of minutes later a detective in his fifties, almost a dead ringer and of the same vintage as the dreaded Sergeant Orr, Billy's Parliament House nemisis, came into the reception area. Billy thought to himself that men like Orr and Barker were probably a dying breed, too stout, too tired and too long in a police force that had long since passed them by.

He heard the older cop say to the younger policewoman in a voice intended for him to overhear, 'That him?' He stepped up to the desk some two metres from where Billy stood and leaned both his elbows upon it, sticking his chin out, his overlarge gut dented by the edge of the counter. 'Over here, please, sir!' he commanded.

Billy had seen it all before, belligerence, impatience and intimidation all implied with body language and a short, sharp, commanding opening statement that ended with the obligatory and deprecating 'Sir.'

Billy rose slowly and walked over to the detective, showing he wasn't to be bullied. 'Good afternoon, detective, my name is William O'Shannessy, I'm a barrister-at-law, and yours is?'

The older policeman was caught momentarily off guard. 'Barker, Detective Sergeant Barker.'

'Pleased to meet you, detective, I would like to inquire

about a missing juvenile whom I believe the police are looking for in connection to some matters and I would prefer the discussion to take place somewhere other than at the front desk.'

Billy could see that the policeman was responding to the authority in his voice. Only politicians and senior lawyers talked to policemen with such polite firmness and, despite Billy's appearance, Barker's years in the force had given him a finely tuned ear, so that he usually knew when to bite and when to keep his mouth shut. He gave an obligatory sigh. 'I knock off at three-thirty, sir.'

Billy glanced at the station clock. 'Good, that gives us twenty minutes detective.'

He followed the detective through a door to the left of the counter and along a small corridor and then down a set of steps into a downstairs corridor, past an open-plan area and into a small interviewing office.

The room was only just big enough to contain the usual table and three chairs. On the table sat what looked like a black box with a snorkel sticking out of it. It pointed directly to where Barker asked Billy to sit. The box, Billy was to learn, was called an ERISP (Electronic Recording Interview Statement Provider) and contained three tape decks and various knobs. The snorkel turned out to be a video camera focused on Billy. The policeman reached over and switched on one of the tape decks. Then, leaning back in his chair and still remaining silent, he scratched delicately at the corner of his nose. He appeared to be thinking. 'Don't I know you from somewhere, sir?' he finally asked.

It was yet another ploy but Billy didn't fall for it. 'You may do, detective. After all, I'm a lawyer and you're a policeman, although I don't remember meeting you and I have a very good memory for such things.' Billy was telling him in unspoken terms not to play funny buggers.

'What is it you want to see me about, sir?' Barker asked, his demeanour a study in lack of interest.

'My client's name is Sanfrancesco, Ryan Sanfrancesco, I'm sure you'll agree it's not an easy name to forget. I believe you are looking for him to aid you in your inquiries?'

'Right, Ryan Sanfrancesco, juvenile offender, age eleven, address 15 Nicholson Street, Woolloomooloo, that him?' the detective said right off.

'Thank you, yes.'

'I'm happy to say this isn't my case although I'm well briefed with the facts. The detective in charge is off duty.' He tapped the desk with his forefinger. 'He's wanted for procuring.'

'Procuring! An eleven-year-old pimp? Don't be ridiculous.'

Barker shook his head. 'Heroin. He may also be guilty of manslaughter, his mother died of an overdose from heroin, which was allegedly supplied by your client. I don't have to tell you, Mr O'Shannessy, it's a serious charge. I've got grandchildren nearly as old as him.'

'And it's also a preposterous one!' Billy cried. 'Children don't kill their mothers by giving them an overdose.'

'I said it was manslaughter, *suspected* manslaughter,' the policeman replied, without changing the tone of his voice.

'It seems that a supply of high-quality South East Asian heroin, sixty-five to seventy-five per cent pure, came onto the market for the price of heroin of lower purity and came to the Kings Cross area at the same time your client was alleged to have procured it. The autopsy reports that the heroin was too pure,' the cop shrugged, 'and, well, apparently she overdosed.'

Billy knew better than to argue, this wasn't a court of law after all. Trying hard to stay calm, he said, 'This looks very much like a set-up, detective.'

Barker sighed. 'I told you this is not my case, sir.' He tapped the table again. 'I just acquainted you with the charge and some of the details. I must remind you that this is on tape and video, and what you have just said may have been careless but could be taken as a serious accusation against the police.' It was obvious to Billy that Barker believed he had the upper hand. 'Now I must ask *you* a question, do you know the whereabouts of your client?'

Billy noted that he'd dispensed with the formality of 'sir' or even his name. 'No, I don't, Detective Sergeant Barker,' Billy said, his voice even.

Barker sighed and wiped his hand across his face. Like Vince Payne at William Booth, he was a champion sigher. 'I must warn you, sir, that concealing information from the police is an offence.'

Billy ignored the warning. 'May I see what evidence you have to make the charge, please?'

Barker grinned. 'You know better than that, sir. Besides, there is no formal charge, you also know that. Your client is simply wanted for questioning.' He suddenly slapped his palm against his forehead. 'Christ! Of course! You're Billy O'Shannessy, the fallen hero.' He leaned back in his chair, a big grin spread across his face. 'From barrister to barfly in a hundred thousand easy gargles. Is it true that the distillers of Johnnie Walker pay you a pension?' He switched off the tape and leaned forward. 'Now bugger off, Billy, I'm busy!'

Billy remained calm. 'I should remind you, Detective Sergeant Barker, that whatever you think of my present position in life, I am still two things. I am sober and I am a lawyer. If it doesn't seem too great a presumption on my part, I believe I am still a good lawyer. I can and I will be representing Ryan Sanfrancesco!'

But Barker wasn't listening any longer. Even angry, Billy wasn't a very prepossessing presence, and Barker obviously knew enough about Billy's sustained career as a derelict to call what he now regarded as nothing but bravado on Billy's part. He rose and Billy thought the cop was going to evict him, but instead he took three steps towards the door and closed it, clicking the latch on the old-fashioned Yale lock.

'Jesus!' Billy thought, 'He's going to have a go at me!'

But Barker returned to his chair and leaned forward on the table, his big frame dominating the small room. 'Billy, do yourself a favour, will ya? You don't want any part of this. This isn't about some poor little kid trying to get heroin for his sick mum. There's other things here that both you *and* me don't want to know about. If you don't want your loved ones to find you dead in the gutter with multiple knife wounds, you'll stay well away.' He pointed a hairy forefinger at Billy, 'And don't think it's an idle threat neither, mate.' He leaned back slightly, a small smile on his face. 'Who's gunna worry about an old derro found dead in the gutter, eh? Sure, someone will find out who you once were, that won't cut any ice neither, you're a nothing now, less than a nobody, a drunken derro, a homeless person.' Barker was pushing the envelope. 'As a policeman, I'd wrap up your case and have it filed away in the Coroner's Court in less than a morning. We'd assume the usual, some addict rolled you when you were pissed. You tried to resist and he slipped you a blade. You know yourself it happens all the time. Drunks get set alight, stabbed, murdered for a few lousy bucks, sometimes even for fun. Let me tell you something for nothing, even in your former glory you'd be bloody stupid to take this case on. Billy, you're pissing against a force nine gale, mate!'

Billy held up his hand. 'What are you saying, detective, that this is too big for the law? That the child is disposable, a sacrifice? For what? Drug trafficking? What?' Billy was hoping like hell Barker would come out with the word he needed to hear the most, 'paedophile'.

Barker looked at his watch. 'Look, you're wasting my time, Billy. I've said more than you need to know. I'm warnin' you now, I mean it. If I see you trying to interfere again, I'm going to have you arrested. Charging you with something won't be too difficult. I'm gunna arrest you, *not* to cover my own arse but to protect you from *yourself*. Leave this alone, you hear me, Billy? There's powerful people involved, people you can't get at. Go and get pissed, drown yer sorrows, and stay away from the boy! He's dangerous.'

'Thank you for that advice, detective, I hear what you say,' Billy replied. His heart was beating rapidly but he appeared outwardly calm, he was back in a business he understood and his brain hadn't gone on him.

'Oh, one more thing, Billy. If you're seen with the boy, you'll be arrested and charged with sexually molesting a juvenile.' He paused for effect. 'Believe you me, the people involved will make the paedophile charge stick, big time, you'll be a very old man when you get out of Long Bay.' He spread his hands and sighed, 'Now be a good boy and bugger off, stop trying to be a hero, stickin' your nose in where it don't rightly belong.'

Detective Sergeant Barker had said it, the magic word Billy wanted to hear. Whatever had happened to Ryan, he was now free of the immediate clutches of a paedophile ring. Barker had as good as told him that this wasn't routine police business; the mother, an addict dead from an overdose, the child missing, the usual desultory public-don't-much-care police inquiry. It was something that involved powerful people. It had to be paedophilia. Billy reasoned that powerful and influential people in society don't run drug cartels. They, whoever *they* were, wanted Ryan apprehended and put away because he had escaped their clutches and knew too much. They wanted Ryan convicted and, as a minor, placed in Osmond Hall where Davo had been and where they would effectively keep him out of the way while, at the same time, contributing to his ultimate corruption. With a bit of luck he might even take up petrol sniffing or aerosol cans and by the age of fifteen have a brain turned into mush.

Billy returned to the library and worked on Trim's story until it was time to walk to his AA meeting at the Rocks. The meeting would end at eight-thirty and he would only have a three-minute walk to the New Hellas Cafe, where Con would be waiting for him. Con's business closed at ten o'clock and, because there wasn't a huge demand for coffee at night, it was run at that time by any two of the various young women in his six-female family.

Con was already waiting for him, illegally parked in a gleaming Mercedes. 'Come, Billy, we go!' he yelled excitedly, lowering the electric window of the big black car.

Billy climbed into the passenger seat. 'I thought only buses and taxis were allowed to park in this part of the Quay,' he remarked.

'Coffee!' Con replied, laughing. 'Coffee for parkings inspector, no probs, myte!'

Maria, Con's new wife, wasn't exactly ugly but neither was she pretty nor even attractive, she was dead plain and slightly plump. She was dressed in a purple silk shantung suit with the jacket tucked and flared at the waist and it seemed to be two sizes too small, with the tight mini-skirt fifteen centimetres above her knees. Wearing high-heeled shoes dyed to match her outfit, she was forced to walk in small, mincing steps. It was obvious that she'd dressed in her best for the occasion.

Con touched Billy on the shoulder and whispered into his ear. 'Very sexy that dresses, eh, Billy.'

Billy guessed that Goddesses must come in all flavours and, while beauty faded, a good cook lasted the distance.

Shy at first, Maria soon turned out to be very gregarious and, all things considered, spoke surprisingly good English. She was also not in the least afraid to remonstrate with Con and was by no means the grateful migrant bride. She laughed a lot and cried in anguish when Billy refused a dish, of which there were numerous and in sufficient quantity to feed ten people. None of the girls seemed to be around and when Billy remarked on this, Con explained, 'Tonights, Billy, Goddess time, for meetings my wife, myte.'

At one point during the evening Maria asked, 'The boy, why you not bring that boys?' She looked over at Con. 'That boy's not bad one, *ise vlakas Kosta!*'

Con shrugged. 'Maria, she is right, I am stupids Greek man.'

After Con's invitation that morning, Billy had anticipated her question. He had intended avoiding a long explanation by saying Ryan was away and he hadn't seen him since his return from Queensland, ignoring Ryan's visit to the chapel at William Booth. But he could sense that Maria was not the sort of woman to whom you gave truncated explanations. Moreover, he couldn't remember when he'd felt so warmly embraced and he started to tell Con and Maria the whole story of Ryan and Trim, ending with the visit to the police station that afternoon.

He hadn't needed to explain the notion of a predatory

paedophile ring to Maria, who seemed to understand immediately. At the end of the story, Con simply looked up at Billy with tears in his eyes. 'Sorry, Billy, I ashame, myte,' he said softly.

Maria's eyes blazed at the conclusion of the story. 'You find, Billy, that boy, he come Maria!' she cried, her forefinger stabbing her chest. Then she looked defiantly at Con. 'Many girls, no boy! No good, Billy. He come stay here! To cook only girls not so good.'

Con looked at Billy and shrugged. 'Bloody oaths, Billy, no problems, myte.'

Con tried to insist that Billy stay the night, though Billy declined. He couldn't help wondering how they might accommodate him with seven people in what was not an overlarge terrace house tucked somewhere in a back street in Newtown.

'Thank you, Con, that's very kind of you both but I must be back at my bench in case Ryan turns up in the morning.'

Clutching two large plastic cartons containing an assortment of Greek sweetmeats with unpronounceable names, which threatened to keep Billy munching for several days, they drove back to the library. Con seemed reluctant to go, even though Billy knew he had an early start down at the Quay. Finally he took Billy's hand in both of his large, hairy ones, making Billy's freckled paw disappear in their embrace. 'Billy, you my fren, myte. You find that boys, we take a him to Maria, soon he be fat like pigs, fair dinkums.'

Billy retrieved his blanket from among the woodchips

and settled down on Trim's bench for the night. He didn't know what to do with the food Maria had given him so he tucked it under the bench, reasoning that even city rats couldn't chew through a vacuum-sealed plastic container without waking him up.

He was dog-tired. It had been a long and emotional day and not without the usual craving. It was close to midnight when Con had dropped him off and he reasoned it didn't make much sense to drag himself all the way back to the Cross to take up his vigil. Alf Petersen had turned up just on midnight and there had been no other visitor when he'd packed it in about two a.m. Petersen had left at about one, accompanied by a woman, but this time the light hadn't come on over the door when they'd emerged. Although he could make out the bulk of the ex-politician, the woman had been partially protected by Petersen's size. He could only tell that the other person was female by the tap-tap of her high-heeled shoes. The other visitors he'd seen arrive earlier in the evening had all left after an hour or so. Billy concluded that the woman must be The Queenie, which immediately raised an interesting question in his mind.

Now, as he lay on the bench wrapped in his blanket, he thought of the interview with Barker, the detective sergeant at Kings Cross Police Station. Over the years he'd met dozens, no probably hundreds, of his kind. Some lawyers referred to them as the salt of the earth, men who knew the limitations of the law and were good practical cops. Working on the principle that what the eye doesn't see the law needn't grieve over, they got the job done. They kept their districts reasonably quiet and they knew where to find the troublemakers when the shit hit the fan. There was even a name for it in law circles, they were referred to as 'Bumper Farrell Cops', meaning that men such as the notorious Bumper Farrell saved the courts a lot of trouble by accidentally falling on the so-called perpetrators of crime. Farrell's two hundred and ten pound frame had proved amazingly effective in breaking bones and teaching crims to behave themselves.

The only trouble with old-timers like Barker was that they eventually grew cynical and disillusioned with the law. The bad guys seemed to escape punishment too often and the good guys, conscientious policemen, seldom received the credit due to them. It was an altogether shit job, shit pay, shit working conditions, shit promotional opportunities and the public and the media constantly heaped shit on them. It was difficult for a policeman of Barker's seniority and position not to conclude that the big crims were winning. If a cop stayed in one precinct too long, eventually the bad guy and the good guy made some sort of compromise. This inevitably meant that the good guy was materially a lot better off and a lot less conscientious.

Billy wasn't sure that Barker was corrupt. Even if he was on the take, that didn't mean he was involved with protecting paedophiles. The mention of his grandchildren suggested that he wasn't, though you could never tell, humans have an amazing capacity to rationalise evil and to compartmentalise their lives. Maybe that was true of Barker, yet Billy thought not. His instinct told him the man was a traditional policeman, almost certainly with compromised values but only those he could live with. A paedophile club would be unlikely to be one of the contributors to his welfare.

On the other hand, a code existed among his kind that you never dobbed your mates in, what you saw or knew about them stayed in the district. Billy couldn't help observing to himself that the paradox was that cops and paedophiles followed the same no-talkies-no-ratting code. A bent policeman was, in effect, a brother-in-arms with the evildoers. Moreover, an honest cop contributed to the welfare of both by keeping his eyes closed and his mouth shut because to be a whistleblower was considered to be the worst crime a cop could commit.

Gazing through the canopy of leaves above his bench and catching a glimpse of an occasional star that managed to penetrate the blaze of the city skyline, Billy concluded that what had happened with Barker was this quid pro quo among older policemen. Each had something on the other and thus an unspoken agreement to say nothing. He reasoned that Barker wasn't helping to protect kiddy-sex or why would he have taken the trouble to warn Billy as explicitly as he had? He was by no means a fool, yet he'd pretended that Billy wasn't worth a pinch of shit any more as a lawyer, despite Billy warning him that he was still a member of the legal profession. If he'd been involved with the paedophiles he'd have said very little and fingered Billy for a quiet demise, just another homeless person ending up dead, albeit one who'd once been a famous barrister. Tut-tut, such is life, evil will always be amongst us.

Billy fell asleep reasonably certain that he would need to be careful but that his life wasn't yet in danger. He speculated briefly on the change that had come over him. As a drunk, the merest suggestion by Marion that he might be thought of as a paedophile had sent him scurrying in a blind panic to Queensland. Now sober, he had faced up to a direct warning from an influential policeman and was about to fall asleep under the glorious stars, prepared to take his chances. Though he'd still kill for a drink, he'd taken a small leap forward on his second day out of captivity. 'Well done, Billy,' he said to himself as sleep closed him down for the night.

Billy woke to the usual raucous laughter of his two feathered friends but then, his eyes still closed, he distinctly heard Ryan's voice. 'Jeez, where'd yiz get this cake and stuff, Billy?'

Billy thought he must be dreaming, but the noise of Ryan's mastication forced him to open his eyes. 'That you, Ryan?' he asked tentatively.

'Yeah, hi, Billy,' Ryan replied, his mouth crammed with a Maria delicacy.

Billy sat up slowly, his second night hadn't been much better than the first and he hurt in a dozen different places. Groaning, he was forced to grab hold of the back of the bench to pull himself up.

'Me mum's died of an overdose and me nana's also dead and I'm in the shit,' Ryan said in a matter-of-fact voice that, even in his bleary state, surprised Billy.

'Yes, I know. I'm sorry.'

'Nah, me nana told me she was gunna die and it was me who killed me mum,' Ryan said.

Billy couldn't believe what he'd just heard the boy say. 'Hey, wait a minute, lad, I don't believe that.'

'It was in the newspaper. It was them Vietnamese from Cabramatta, they brought in this heroin, see, it was not like the other stuff, more pure or something, they's called the 5T gang. They gimme some for me mum and they told me that was what killed her. It were in all the newspapers.'

'Who is *they*? The Vietnamese? They told you?'

'Nah, the woman, The Queenie, she said I'd killed me mum and if I ran away or told someone they'd tell the police.' Ryan's bravado suddenly collapsed and he started to howl. Billy reached out and grabbed him, pulling him against his chest. Ryan sobbed and sobbed, clinging to Billy, who was soon bawling himself. 'They gunna catch me and put me in gaol and throw away the key,' Ryan said.

'No, mate, they're not going to do that.'

'That's what they said!' Ryan protested, sniffing and knuckling away his tears.

'I'm not going to let that happen, Ryan,' Billy said. 'You'll see, it will be all right.'

The boy's mouth was sticky from the *baklava* he'd been eating. He looked thin and pale and very frightened. He started to cry again. 'They said I couldn't tell anyone because I was a poofter. I'm not a poofter, am I, Billy?' he asked.

Billy put his arm around Ryan. 'No, mate, you're not,' he said, trying to smile and make light of the matter, but he

531

could feel the tears running down his own cheeks. 'Come along now, you have a bit more of that cake, then you can tell me your story and I'll tell you our plan. Okay?'

Ryan looked at him doubtfully. 'We've got a plan?'

'Yes, son, we've got a plan.'

'But yiz don't know what happened.'

'I know a fair bit and I hope you're going to tell me the rest. That's if you want to,' Billy added gently. 'You don't have to say anything if you don't want to.'

'Billy, why did you leave?' Ryan asked suddenly. 'You just went away and wrote me that letter, then me nana died and me mum.'

Billy tried hard to contain his emotions but, despite his efforts, Ryan could see that his chest was heaving as he fought to control his sobs. 'Because I was a coward,' he managed to stammer at last. 'I ran away because I'm a coward, Ryan.'

'No, you're not, Billy. Did somethin' happen?'

Billy explained as best he could. 'Ryan, I am terribly sorry, I told myself at the time that I was doing it, going to Queensland, for both of our sakes, but I was lying to myself. I was frightened and wanted to save my own skin. I was a coward. If I'd stayed, then perhaps things might have turned out differently for you.'

Ryan didn't reply and after a few moments, in order to cover the silence between them, Billy pointed to the plastic cartons on the ground, 'If you don't tuck into that, it will get stale.'

Ryan helped himself to a honey puff and bit into it,

chewing slowly. With his mouth still half full, he said, 'Nah, it wouldn't have changed nothin', me nana was gunna die, she told me herself. She made me phone the funeral people and the cemetery to make sure they didn't forget she'd paid them already.'

'But what about your mother, perhaps I might have been able to help?'

Ryan shook his head and Billy could see that the boy was trying to get him off the hook. 'No way, me mum was crook and she wouldn't have let you in, addicts don't like straights to come near when they need a fix.'

'Ryan, you do understand that if I'd been here we would have found another way to manage things?'

But Ryan was stubborn. 'Ain't no other way, Billy.'

Billy didn't think he should take it any further, it was water under the bridge anyway. He'd failed Ryan and now it was up to him to make amends in any way he possibly could. 'Perhaps you'd like to tell me what happened?' he asked.

Ryan thought for a few moments before he took a deep breath. 'You know how I told you me mum had asthma?'

'Yes, and you'd take her to St Vincent's.'

'Yeah, well, it was true, but I didn't tell you the other thing.'

'You mean that she was a heroin addict?'

'Yeah, that.'

'I imagined you thought it was none of my business. Every family has things they like to keep private.'

'It was just me and her and me nana, see. I knew what me mum done was wrong, but I done it also.'

Billy looked surprised. 'Did what?'

'I helped her with the smack, like preparing it. She'd get the shakes and start vomiting and she'd panic like it's an attack. She can't do nothin' about it, sweat pourin' off her, and sometimes she got the cramps and she'd beg me to help her to do the stuff. You know, get it ready.' Ryan was plainly upset as he began to explain.

Billy held up his hand. 'Ryan, you don't have to tell me, lad.'

But Ryan seemed not to hear. Billy was almost certainly the first person, the *only* person he could talk to, whom he could trust. 'I was seven when I done it first. Do you want to know how you do it, Billy?'

Billy wasn't sure how to answer. Plainly Ryan wanted to talk, the poor little bloke was carrying a terrible burden of guilt and Billy didn't want to stop him talking. 'I'd like to hear everything you have to say, lad.'

'Well, a chunk, that's fifty bucks worth, you place it on a spoon, like a spoon for eating puddin'?' Billy nodded. 'Then you take up so much water in the syringe,' Ryan indicated the first joint of his pinkie, 'and you squirt it into the spoon with the smack already in it. Then you get a lighter and you heat up the bottom of the spoon. You got to hold it real steady because the stuff melts and you can't afford to spill it, see.'

Billy was inwardly amused at Ryan's caution that 'you can't *afford* to spill it', which had obviously been a past injunction from his mother and had stuck in his small boy's mind.

'Oh, yes, I forgot. Before you start all that, you take this cotton wool and you roll a little ball about this size,' Ryan indicated the nail of his forefinger. 'When it's melted, you drop the little ball in and it, you know, fluffs up like. Oh yes, and also you have to have this cotton bud, that's to stir it when you're warming it with the lighter so it melts quickly. After you've dropped the little ball in and it's fluffed up, like I said, you push the tip o' the syringe into the smack and you suck it up through the fluffed-up cotton wool.' Ryan looked up, 'You see, there's impurities in heroin when they cut it with somethin' else and this is the filter, see, so she don't get stuff in her veins that shouldn't go in, that's bad for her.'

Billy wanted to cry at the innocence. Again he was forced to admire Ryan's ability to tell the process sequentially, or so it appeared, as Billy had no previous experience of how heroin was administered. If asked, he could probably have said that it involved a syringe together with a spoon and a tourniquet. Like everyone else in his generation, this information had come via Frank Sinatra's part in the film *The Man with the Golden Arm*.

'Now you done all that and there's the torniket, that's this, like, leather belt that you pull real tight around the top of yer arm and then keep makin' a fist.' Ryan demonstrated by opening and closing his fist. 'It's to pump up the vein so the needle will go in easy. You stick it in here,' he pointed to the bend in his arm, 'that's the best place, see. You place the needle flat to the skin so it don't wiggle too much and you push it in the vein. You must be careful you go up the vein and not through the side.' Ryan paused. 'Do yiz know what happens when you inject and you ain't got it in proper?'

Billy shook his head.

'It will make this blister that burns like hell and it takes hours for the smack to get into the body.' Ryan laughed. 'I done it a few times and me mum wanted to kill me. But sometimes you can't help it, she's shaking and sweating and stuff and you get nervous and fuck it up.'

'Did you have to do it for her all the time?' Billy asked, trying not to show his horror at what Ryan had just told him.

'Nah, only sometimes when she was real crook. She done it herself mostly.'

Billy put his hand on Ryan's shoulder. 'I'm so sorry about your mother, lad. A boy should always have his mother to love him.' Billy was conscious that it was an insensitive thing to say, but it had come out spontaneously.

To his surprise Ryan didn't start crying again but silently helped himself to an almond biscuit. With his mouth full, he said, 'It's orright, Billy, me nana said me mum wasn't gunna make no old bones. I cried a lot about that before, when you're a little kid you don't want yer mum to die. I once asked her not to. I told her what nana said and she gave this laugh and said not to worry, she was gunna be around a fair while yet, but that she didn't want to be like the old cow and wanted to have a bit of fun and be a good-lookin' corpse.'

Billy thought his heart would break at Ryan's ingenuous

retelling of the incident. 'Ryan, you were a good son and grandson, you can always be proud of that. I wish I had been as caring and loving with my own mother and I hardly knew my grandmother.'

Ryan grinned. 'It's easy, you just got to listen all the time and nod yer head and don't interrupt and think of other things.'

Billy laughed. 'I've got two new Trim stories to tell you, Ryan.'

'Cool!' Ryan exclaimed, obviously excited. 'When I was with them, I tried to think what Trim would've done but I don't suppose cats know about them things.'

'Ryan, would you like to tell me what happened?' Billy asked tentatively, not wishing to push the boy.

Ryan looked down at his feet, he had gone to sit on his skateboard at Billy's feet with Maria's two containers in front of him, one was already empty and now he started on the other. There was a long silence before he looked up slowly. 'They made me do a bad thing, Billy.'

'Tell me about it, lad. When you're forced into doing a bad thing it's not the same as doing a bad thing on your own.'

'Yes it is! They said if you're a poofter then it don't never go away. If you do it once, it's the same as a hundred times.' Ryan began to weep again, softly, sniffing, trying to control his misery. 'I ain't a poofter, Billy, I know I ain't.'

'No, of course you're not, lad.'

'But they said.'

'It doesn't matter what they said, Ryan. It's what's in your heart. But who are *they*?'

'The Queenie.'

'Just The Queenie?'

'No, and some of the men there.'

'Why don't you start at the beginning, lad?' Billy said.

'Didn't you say you had a plan?' Ryan asked.

'Yes, I did.'

'Am I in it?' Ryan asked anxiously.

'Of course, and you'll be safe, I promise.'

Ryan sniffed and wiped his snotty nose on the back of his hand, his face sticky with biscuit crumbs and honey. 'It was two days after we buried my nana, and me mum woke up and said she felt crook. I asked her if I should call the ambulance, like you know, go to St Vinnie's because of her asthma. But she said it weren't bad asthma, just the flu or somethin' like that. But she stayed in bed and that night when she was supposed to go to work she couldn't. The next day she was the same, she tried to get up but she fell down and it took me ages to get her back in bed because she were too weak and couldn't help me. She was sweatin' and shiverin' and then she threw up in the towel I brought to wipe her sweat. I seen it before – it's the withdrawals. I know where she keeps her smack so I did it for her and she's a bit better but next mornin' she's still crook and can't get up.'

Ryan explained that there was no more heroin in the house and his mother started to withdraw again. He went to St Vincent's to see Dr Goldstein but was told that the doctor was on nights that week. The registrar saw him and Ryan explained that his mother was ill but he didn't tell him she was a drug addict, and they hadn't looked up her records as casualty was very busy at the time. The registrar told him if she got worse to call the ambulance or to see her GP in the morning. Ryan told him that Dr Goldstein was their GP, that he'd come in the past to see his nana and once before to see his mum when Ryan had asked him. The registrar said he'd leave a message.

Ryan returned home and found his mother on the kitchen floor having a withdrawal. She'd managed to get out of bed and crawl through to the phone in the kitchen to call someone about heroin but the phone had been cut off for the last week because she'd neglected to pay the bill. She was too weak to stand or to crawl back to her bed and Ryan had dragged her to the sitting room and fetched the blankets from her bed and covered her up.

'I shoulda called the ambulance like that doctor said,' Ryan said, 'but she told me that it was just that she needed a fix. She said to take a hundred dollars out of her bag and to go to this place in the Cross and see this bloke, to take a photo we had of me and her when we'd gone to Luna Park, so as he'd know I was, like, her son. She said to give him the hundred bucks and ask him for two caps of smack.' Ryan looked up, 'I didn't want to do it but she begged and cried and then she done a vomit on the carpet and she'd et nothin' and it was just this green stuff come up. She said she'd be fine, she only needed the fix.'

'This place she sent you to. The man you had to see. Where was that and did he give you his name?'

'Nah, me mum did, it was Mr Suleman, it was where she worked of a night.'

'Mohammed Suleman, at The Queen of Sheba?'

Ryan nodded, 'I showed him the photo and give him the money and he give me two caps. He was real nice and gimme a Coke and told one of the Lebbo blokes at the door to take me to McDonald's across the road for a hamburger. I told him nah, I had to get back to me mum. Mr Suleman said I was a good boy lookin' after me mum and if I needed some more smack to come back. He said to tell her she could come back to her job when she was better.'

Dr Goldstein turned up in the morning after his shift at St Vincent's that night. He examined Ryan's mother and took a blood sample. When he saw that she was too weak to get out of bed, he said he was pretty sure it was Hepatitis C, which accounted for her chronic fatigue, and that he was going to put her into hospital. She only agreed after he promised they'd give her morphine. She spent two days in hospital on a drip, getting Interferon by means of a subcutaneous injection, then signed herself out, saying that she couldn't leave Ryan on his own and that she didn't want 'none of them bastards from DOCS taking her son away from her'.

It seemed that she tried to go back to work but collapsed and they sent her home in a taxi. She had no money and she needed a fix. It was at that time that Ryan had called on Dorothy Flanagan to get some of Billy's money and when she'd refused, tried to pawn his grandmother's ring and locket along with his skateboard.

'It were just the same as the last time, she was real crook, but we had no money, so me mum said to go and see

Mr Suleman again.' Ryan paused. 'You see, I'd told her about the Coke and McDonald's and how he'd said I could come back any time if I wanted. I went to see him that night and I told him what me mum said, that we'd pay him when she got better. He was real nice, but he said he didn't have any smack though he knew someone who'd give me some for nothing. One of the girls there then took me round the block to the back lane and we come to this door and she pressed this button and a light come on and she said our business and the door opened and we went up these stairs that was just ordinary and suddenly we're in, like this palace. There's flowers and a fish pond and these leather couches and marble and pitchiz on the wall and this girl who brung me told me to wait and left. Then this lady come into the room.

'"Hello, Ryan," she says.

'"Hello," I say to her, but I don't know how she knows me name.

'"How's your mother?" she says. She's got perfume on and you can smell it. "Oh, Mr Suleman told me she's not well," she says. I still don't say nothing. "Would you like a Coke?" she says. I don't really want one, but I say, "Okay, cool."

'"Monkey!" she shouts out. This bloke come out and he's dressed like a waiter in one of them black suits and bow ties and he has a Coke with a straw on a silver tray. "Monkey's a dancer," she says as he puts down the Coke.

'"Hello," I say. You can see he's a poofter.

'Monkey smiles and looks at The Queenie. "Hmm,

lovely," he says to her. I don't know if he's talkin' about the Coke or him being a dancer or he thinks she's pretty, so I say nothing, except I think Monkey is a real crook name.'

Ryan looked up at Billy and then down at the second container of Maria's delicacies, which was now half empty. 'I can't eat no more, Billy.'

'Good, I'm glad you enjoyed them.' Billy pointed to the fountain. 'The drinking fountain's working again. Why don't you go and wash your face, lad?'

When Ryan returned and seated himself back on the skateboard, Billy hoped that he might continue, but now he said, 'You said you had two more Trim stories, when will you tell them to me?'

'Any time you like, lad, but I had rather hoped you might tell me what happened next. You see,' Billy explained, 'I have a plan I'll tell you about later, but I think it might help if I knew a bit more.' Billy marvelled at the ability of the young to live in the present, though he knew that Ryan would be deeply affected for the rest of his life.

Ryan started right off where he'd left his story. 'She said she could give me what I wanted but she hoped I could do something for her. "What can you do, Ryan?" she asked me.

'I don't know what she means. "I can't do nuthink," I say, "I'm only eleven."

'She smiles at me. "A little dickie bird told me you can sing," she says. I don't know how she knows but I tell her I can a little bit. "Well then, perhaps you'll sing for us?"

'There's only her and me and I say "I dunno."

'She holds up a cap, "Come now." She kind of laughs,

like it's just us two havin' fun. "One good turn deserves another, Ryan."

'"I don't know lots of stuff to sing," I tell her.

'"'Ave Maria', you know that," she says. I dunno how she knows this, but then she says, "The school concert."'

Ryan glanced at Billy. 'We done this concert at school last year and she must've come or something. Lots of people came from all over, it was a big success.

'She's holding up the cap o' smack. I stand up. "No, no, we have an audience!" She takes my hand and we go into this room that's like marble, white everywhere, and there a big spa and there's four blokes sitting in it in all these bubbles. "What have we got here, The Queenie?" one of them shouts out 'cause the spa is making a noise with all the water and the bubbles.

'Now I know her name. So Queenie walks over and switches off the spa. "This is Ryan, gentlemen, he has a voice like an angel," she says.

'The blokes clap. "Good on ya, Ryan," one o' them shouts.

'So I sing "Ave Maria" and one of the blokes is crying when I done it and one of the others says, "I'll give you fifty bucks if you'll sing another song."

'That's cool. If he pays me fifty bucks I can give it to the lady and then we don't owe her no favours like. So I sing, "We are One but We are Many", it's a song we done at school. And they clap again and he gives me the fifty bucks which is exactly what a cap costs.

'The lady takes me back where we come in and she gives me the cap. "I hope your mother is better soon," she says to me. I hand her the fifty dollars. "No, no, that's yours, Ryan, you've earned it, you have a beautiful voice."

'"It's fifty dollars for a cap, Queenie," I say, 'cause now I know her name.

'"This one's on the house, Ryan." She smiles at me. "But I tell you what, if you need more I'll pay you fifty dollars to sing any night you want. Have we got a deal?" We go to the stairs so I can go home and she says, "By the way, it's The Queenie, that's my name." She says it again, like it's very important, "*The* Queenie."'

Billy again marvelled at Ryan's ability at his age to capture the detail and the atmosphere of his surroundings. He'd make an excellent lawyer, he thought. And then instantly he remembered what Davo had said about Osmond Hall and what could happen to this bright little boy.

Ryan told Billy how his mother had remained in bed, too weak to move. Dr Goldstein had visited her again and given her another injection of Interferon. He had tried to persuade her to return to hospital but she'd been paranoid about leaving Ryan and the prospect of DOCS placing him in an institution until she recovered. At one stage Dr Goldstein had arranged for the Salvation Army Early Intervention House at Hurstville to take him, but she wouldn't hear of it. She'd even tried to con him into believing she was off heroin because of the Hep C, although he probably wouldn't have believed her. Anyway, Ryan sang for his supper for the next eight days. He also managed to turn up at school for some of that time, which had stopped Dorothy Flanagan initially calling in DOCS.

On the evening of the eighth day of Ryan getting a cap of heroin in lieu of his fifty dollars, The Queenie had said to him, 'Ryan, there is a man who's come all the way from Germany who wants to hear you sing, he'll pay you two hundred dollars.'

Ryan had grown accustomed by now to 'the club' and, besides, no one had laid a hand on him, but nevertheless he was no fool. 'Why, The Queenie? I can't sing no better for two hundred dollars.'

The Queenie had laughed. 'No, of course, but he can't come here, it's in the afternoon, you have to go to the apartment he's rented in Bondi Junction.' The Queenie shrugged. 'It's good money, Ryan, and Monkey will drive you in the limo.'

'What's a limo?' Ryan asked.

'It's like a taxi, only it's a Mercedes or BMW,' The Queenie had said. 'It's all right, Monkey will take you,' she said again.'

'Did you tell your mother all this?' Billy asked.

'Nah, she just thought I was getting it from Mr Suleman.'

'But why didn't you tell her? After all, apart from procuring heroin, you hadn't been compromised.'

'What's that mean, "compromised"?'

'It means you weren't coming to any harm.'

Ryan shrugged. 'I dunno, she didn't ask, so I didn't say nothin'.' He looked up at Billy and then, as if explaining the obvious, said, 'Addicts just want a fix, they don't care where it comes from, Billy.'

In some things, Billy thought, Ryan was already too old for his years.

Ryan went on to tell Billy how he'd arrived at the apartment block in Bondi Junction and Monkey had pushed a button in the foyer from a whole row of buttons with names on them. 'But the one he pushed didn't have a name, only a number.

'"Ja?" a voice says through a grid thing on the wall.

'"The Boys' Boutique, sir," Monkey says.

'"Okay, I press the lift, tenth floor," the voice says.

'"What's that mean, The Boys' Boutique?" I ask Monkey.

'"It's like a password," he says. "They don't like people they don't know coming into these exclusive apartments."

'The lift stops on the tenth floor and Monkey presses the bell on number 111 and a very tall man comes to the door. Then Monkey says to the man to call him on his mobile when he wants him to return and he give him this card with his number on it. I asked him why he wasn't stayin' and he said he'd be waitin' downstairs in the car, that this was a private aud . . . aud . . .'

'Audition?' Billy suggested.

'Yeah, that. So this German bloke says to me, "Hello, Ryan, my name is Karl. You can sing very well, I am told?"

'He's very big and he puts his hand on my shoulder. "I dunno, suppose," I tell him.

'"Have you heard of the Vienna Boys' Choir maybe?" he asks me.

'We had this CD at school which Miss Sypkins played sometimes. "Yeah, they sing a Mozart Mass. It's called

'Benedictus'," I say, because that's what was on the CD we learned it from.

'"You can sing Mozart, a song?" he says. "Mozart is a great Austrian composer."

'"We learned one song," I say. "But I don't know what the words mean."

'"You will sing this song, please," he says.

'I done that and he clapped and then he says, "*Wunderbar!* You know what means that, Ryan?"

'I didn't know, so he says, "*Wunderbar*, it means wonderful."

'I tell him I don't know any more German songs and he says if I come to Germany he'll teach me some. "Now you will sing more, but first I change my clothes, it is very hot. In Germany it is winter and I only come today, there is snow on my house. You like to ski, Ryan?"

'"I dunno," I say. "I never done any. I never seen the snow."

'"In Bavaria, in the mountains, the snow is very beautiful, you will come to my lodge, we will go in the forest to shoot a deer."

'He goes out of the room and I'm sitting waiting, it's a big room and I can see he must be very rich, it's got the biggest television you've ever seen and there's this swimming pool that's half in the room and half outside on a terrace. I've never seen a swimming pool that come inside a house. He comes back and he's wearing only a white dressing-gown, one like me mum's got, that's made out of towels.

'"Now I am much more comfortable, we have a swimming pool. You like to swim, Ryan?"

'I tell him I didn't bring my bathers.

'"*Ach*, it don't matter bathers here, we are all men, nobody can see where we are swimming."

'But I tell him no, I didn't want to.

'"So now you sing again, you have a good voice, Ryan."

'I ask him what he wanted me to sing. "Ave Maria", or what?

'"That is *gut*, 'Ave Maria', that is very *gut*, Ryan."

'When I finished he's lying on the couch, "*Mein schöner Liebling*," he says over and over again.'

Ryan was now talking from memory and without emotion, not looking up, simply telling what had happened, his voice even.

'Then Karl pats the couch next to him. "Come and sit here, Ryan, we will have a nice talk now, ja?"

'I didn't want to, but he held up a hundred dollars. "Extra, for singing Mozart. Come, we talk now or maybe you sing some more."

'So I go and sit next to him, but it was creepy, I don't know what to do.'

'"Sing, *Liebling*, you sing for Uncle Karl."'

Ryan looks up at Billy. 'There's this song, it's not really a song, it's in Latin, it's called "Soli Deo Gloria" and it's a part of saying Mass at St Mary's. I dunno why, maybe I was frightened and if I sang to God it could help. Anyway, that's what I sing and he's crying and stroking me and I want to run away, but where to? He's saying "*Wunderbar*" and "*Mein kleiner Liebling*" and all that stuff, then he asks me to kiss him.

548

'"Just for friends, you understand," he says. "A little kiss for your Uncle Karl, who gives you hundred dollars."

'But my nana told me when I was little you don't kiss men never, only if you're gay and they are also. So I jumped up, so's I could get away from him.

'"I'm sorry, so sorry," he says, "It was the 'Gloria', so beautiful."

'He hands me another hundred dollars and gets up. "Maybe you like to rest now, *Liebling*? You can sing more later. There is a nice bedroom here with a television."'

Ryan looks up at Billy again. 'I ain't an idjit and I'm scared. "I want to go now, please, sir," I says to him.

'"Go? You don't want to sing for me?"

'"I done all the songs I know," I tell him. It's a lie 'cause I know lots, but I wanna get out of the joint,' Ryan says, enjoying the tough phrasing in retrospect.

'"Okay, Ryan, you go now. I am very disappointed," he says.

'I take the money, the two hundred dollars he give me, out of me pocket, "Here, you can have it back," I tell him.

'"No, no, we make a deal," he says. "You can keep it." He takes a card from the pocket of the gown, I think it must be the one Monkey give him because he goes to the phone and he says for him to come up and fetch me. But the dressing-gown, the belt, it's come loose and fallen on the floor and I can see he's got this enormous hard-on.

'"Your chauffeur is coming now, boy," he says. He's real cranky and has got his back turned so I can't see his front no more, but he ain't picked up the belt what's fell to the floor.

549

'I go to stand on the terrace 'cause I don't want to be near him because of what I just seen. I hear a buzzer go and then Karl's voice, "Ja, you come now, please, the boy is ready!" he says to Monkey. Then a bit later the doorbell rings and I run to it and open it so I can escape, but it's not Monkey! There's these two men in black suits and T-shirts and all their hair is shaved off and they grab me. This German bloke is now lying back on the couch and he's took off his gown and they drag me over and make me bend down on the carpet in front of him. One of them's got the back o' me head in his hand and he's pushing me down. "Suck him, you little cocksucker!" he says. "Suck the man's cock or I'll break yer fuckin' neck!"'

Ryan looked up at Billy. 'Afterwards they made me bend over the end of the couch and he, the German bloke, done it to me up the back.' Ryan started to sob. 'He kept shouting, *"Mein schöner Liebling!"* It hurt, Billy, it hurt a lot!' Ryan whimpered. 'I don't wanna be no poofter, Billy!'

And then Ryan began to sob uncontrollably, sitting on his skateboard, hiccupping, gasping for breath, his mouth wide open and bawling like a small child.

Billy's gammy knee wouldn't allow him to crouch next to Ryan. He leaned forward and put his hand on Ryan's shoulder. 'It's all right, lad, it's all right.' Billy felt a love for the boy that was greater than the sum of his entire life, more than Charlie, more than anything he had ever felt before. He would happily kill to protect this child.

Suddenly Billy sensed that with his sudden and total commitment to Ryan, the fighting lawyer was back and that

Billy the human being, with a love greater than his addiction, was emerging. His rehabilitation had taken a hop, step and great leap forward. Billy O'Shannessy was crying his heart out for the kid, for himself, for a world that did such things to children, for the whole of human existence.

CHAPTER FOURTEEN

It had taken some time to comfort Ryan sufficiently to suggest they move. Billy was afraid that Sergeant Orr, the sergeant-at-arms coming off his shift from Parliament House next door, might spot them. Although he mightn't know anything that would place Ryan in danger, it was just as well to get moving. Orr, like Barker, could sniff trouble and Billy reminded himself again that Orr had been a witness for Alf Petersen. Policemen like Orr were like old bull elephants, constantly suspicious and with a prodigious memory.

'Ryan, we have a fair bit to talk about, but I think we should make a move. There's a way of getting into the Botanic Gardens before they open the gates, I think that's where we should go, don't you?'

Ryan nodded, rising from his skateboard. Billy realised how small and frail he looked and how much the poor little boy had been through. 'I have to bury my blanket, then let's get going.' Billy made no mention of Sergeant Orr, the child was already traumatised to the point of shaking all over, his teeth were chattering.

Billy took Ryan to his private bench beside the rock pool. The sun was just coming up and, catching half of the bench, was sufficient for them both to share in its warmth. Ryan was still shivering, his eyes were red and swollen from crying, and Billy could see that he was still thoroughly miserable. More than anything in the world he wanted to comfort Ryan, to give him the assurance that he was safe, but he knew this wasn't true and Ryan was far too intelligent to buy such a notion. When he'd been a child and miserable, his nanny would sing a little nonsense song and now Billy put his arm around Ryan and started to sing softly:

> *Never mind the weather*
> *as long as we're together.*
> *The elephant and*
> *the kangarooooo!*
> *Never mind the weather*
> *as long as we're together.*
> *We're off to see*
> *the Wild West Show!*

'They said I was gunna go to Osmond House,' Ryan suddenly cried, unable to respond to Billy's feeble attempt to cheer him up.

'Ryan, I told you, I have a plan. We'll sort this out, lad, you'll have to trust me.'

Ryan looked tearfully at Billy. 'But you said you was a coward and you're a derro.'

Billy knew he had it coming to him, that Ryan hadn't said it to hurt him. Despite his misery, the child was still thinking correctly and it was a fair enough question under the circumstances.

'Sometimes being a coward helps you think things out, fearful men look at consequences far more closely than brave ones.'

'What's that supposed to mean?'

'It means if you can see all the bad things that could happen, you can do something to avoid them, that's if you don't simply run away.'

'You won't run away again, will yiz, Billy?'

'No, lad, I'm tired of running away, I've been doing it all my life.'

'And you've got a plan so I don't have to go to Osmond House?'

'Yes, I think so.'

'What is it?'

Billy hesitated, not quite sure how to go about telling Ryan about Con's offer. 'It may mean you've got to go into a foster home. They won't let someone like me be a foster parent, but I've got that more or less arranged, Con Poleondakis and his wife Maria are happy to take you.'

'Who are they?'

Ryan was shocked when Billy explained. 'But he said yiz was a poofter! I don't like Greeks, that's a shit plan,' Ryan shouted, upset.

It took Billy some time to calm him down again. 'Ryan, listen to me, for the next little time we're going to have to hide you until we've got things sorted out. It'll be like a trial run for you with Con and Maria. See how you go and if you like it, you'll see me every day anyway. I'll even take a room around the corner so I'll always be near.'

'I can hide in a squat like I done before,' Ryan protested, though Billy could sense that was exactly what the child didn't want to do. He was worn out, frightened and lonely. Without money, there was only one way for him to survive on the streets.

'Ryan, I'm a lawyer and once I was a very good one. I still know a few people and I know how to open this thing up. Justice Wood is setting up a royal commission, it's just getting under way. It's an examination of police corruption in society and there is reference in it to paedophilia and organised paedophile networks. So, you see, this is the perfect time for us to strike, to get sufficient evidence on Mohammed Suleman, The Queenie, Alf Petersen, their clients and the corrupt policemen involved. It's an opportunity to expose the whole sordid business.'

'But they'll catch me also 'cause I'm a poofter now,' Ryan said.

'Ryan, you're not now and you never will be!' Billy said sternly. 'You must get such nonsense out of your head. You're a child who's been abused and those bastards are going to pay for that.'

'Monkey said once it's done to you, yiz one forever!' Ryan cried.

'Well, Monkey's lying, Ryan. He's trying to make sure you don't tell anyone what happened. Now listen to me, Ryan, and I'll try to explain the situation. When the royal commission gets under way, everyone's going to duck for cover and somebody's going to squeal. It always happens, someone makes a deal with the inquiry in order to get protection. Now, when that happens, the rest of the mongrels try to destroy the evidence. That's when we're both going to be in danger, but especially you. You've escaped their clutches and they can't afford to have that happen. We know that, because they've already set you up for drug procurement and a possible manslaughter charge.'

'You mean for killing me mum?'

'Ryan, you did not kill your mother!' Billy shouted angrily. It was the first time he'd raised his voice. 'The manslaughter charge is purely technical, you can't possibly be blamed for that. That's just a way to bring you to the Children's Court, part of the indictment. On the other hand, as a child handling drugs, a children's magistrate could have a strong case for putting you into a juvenile correction centre, and that could mean Osmond House. These are powerful people and, with corrupt police in their pay, it's quite possible they'll succeed. I've been to see the police and they know that I intend to represent you if you get caught. In hindsight it may not have been the best thing to do, but I needed to know exactly why they were looking for you.'

Billy now explained his interview with Detective Sergeant Barker. 'I don't think Detective Barker took me too seriously or that he is involved with paedophilia, but if push comes to shove, the cops who are on the take will hear about my visit to the Kings Cross Police Station. Barker has what I said on tape. The Queenie and the rest of them who gave you drugs and sent you to the German will know they're in trouble and the search for you is going to hot up. Not just you, Ryan, we're both in this together, lad. The idea of "just another derelict", as Barker put it, being found dead will seem a very attractive and easy solution. After all, it happens every day.'

Billy paused to let what he'd said sink in with the distraught child. He was aware that what he was saying would further frighten Ryan, but it was of the utmost importance that the boy understood what was happening and accepted the need for him to hide.

'So, you see, we have to get this right the first time, there isn't going to be a second time for either of us. What's more, we're going to have to stay away from DOCS. Alf Petersen is a very senior public servant in the Department of Community Services and if he thinks he's in trouble there's nothing he won't do to cover himself. If you go back to a squat the police will find you, and Petersen will make damned sure there's a strong case against you and you'll be committed to the Children's Court as an intractable juvenile. With that happening and the right magistrate, there's every chance you'll end up in Osmond House.'

'So that's why you want me to go to the Greek bloke?'

'Ryan, I can trust Con and Maria. You see, by harbouring you, I'm breaking the law. Because of your mother's death leaving you with no relatives, DOCS are already looking for you. The legal procedure here, even if you're not in trouble, would be for them to place you in a foster home. DOCS is not the only foster-care agency and when the time comes we can have Con and Maria apply to one of the others, but in the meantime if we can break this paedophile ring wide open, you will be a key witness at the royal commission. I dare say, even though I've broken the law by harbouring you, when the reasons for doing so are understood they will get me off the hook. When it is seen that I've placed you with responsible people, who took good care of you, then we'll both be in the clear.'

'What's being a key witness mean?' Ryan asked, a little fearfully.

'It usually means that you have information to give to the court, or in this case the commission, that will be vital to the outcome of their inquiries. Without your evidence, the case would not be as strong.'

'Do I have to tell everything that happened, like with the German?'

'No, not to the court or the inquiry directly. As a child witness you are protected, but as your lawyer, I'm going to have to write everything down, every word, just the way you told it to me. I will submit it as evidence, and a qualified case worker or probably a child psychiatrist appointed by the court will see you to determine whether the evidence you've given me came from you in the first instance and is a reliable and accurate version of what you claim happened.' Billy knew it was difficult to get the testimony of a child witness accepted in court and he'd have to get it exactly right.

'They'll just say I'm lying,' Ryan protested. 'Me mum said never to tell them trick-cyclists from DOCS nothin' because they'll make it mean something different and I'll be taken away.'

'Don't worry, Ryan, you're as good a witness as I've ever presented before a judge or an inquiry, that's simply not going to happen.' Billy paused, reluctant to do what he knew he should do next. 'Ryan, if you're up to it, is there anything else that you can remember and want to tell me, either before you were taken to the German, or afterwards?'

'You mean after he done *it* to me?'

'Yes, or before.'

Ryan thought for a moment and then began talking. 'The German must have gone in his bedroom 'cause I hear the door slam. I'm crying and I'm pullin' up me pants and one of the big blokes gimme a slap. It ain't too hard and he's laughing and he says, "Don't cry, mate, you'll soon get to love it." I try to stop cryin' but I can't and me bum hurts and later, when I get home, there's blood on me underpants.

'In the car Monkey says to me, "Well, now you're one of us, darling."

'I'm still sniffing and I say, "No, I ain't."

'"Oh yes, you are, The Queenie's got you now, you're a member of The Boys' Boutique."

'"You said that didn't mean nothing, that it was a password," I tell him.'

Billy suddenly remembered where he had heard of The Boys' Boutique before. He put it aside, he'd think about it later.

'"It certainly is, darling. It's a passport to money, lovely, lovely money. You're very pretty, sweetie, you're going to command a premium price. The Kraut got his virgin, I'd love to know what she got for you. Bloody sight more than two hundred bucks, I can tell ya." He laughed. "The bitch will sell your video to the Kraut as a keepsake, a little thousand-dollar keepsake. She'll also sell you as a virgin for as long as she can."

'"I ain't going back!" I shout at him. "Lemme get out!"

'But he keeps drivin' and he laughs, "We all say that, sweetie. When you're homeless, no food, no place to sleep, no place to hide and you need drugs and a warm place to kip, you'll come crawling back on your hands and knees and that's the position she wants you in."

'"I ain't homeless and I don't do drugs," I tell him.

'"Get real, sweetie. Your mum's an addict who's whacked most of the time. Now she's got Hep C, she won't have the energy to be a dancer. It will be up to you, darling. You won't sing for your supper any more, from now on you'll earn it bending over frontwards." He looks at me and takes both hands off the steering wheel. "It's nearly show time, darling!"

'I didn't say nothin' 'cause I don't know what to say. He's right, me mum's still got no energy. Instead I say, "Why does they call you Monkey?"

'He laughs. "Because when I was fourteen and in 'the ring' I used to get up to all sorts of tricks."

'"What sort of tricks?"

'"Well, if you're a good boy, I'll teach you some. You can make a lot of money with tips in kiddy-sex. You have to be careful, the bitch wants her cut of everything. I hate her." Then he says, "Oh, by the way, do you want cash or caps for the audition today?"

'I've already got two hundred bucks the German bloke give me, so I say caps. Maybe with four caps, me mum will get better. It's four days I don't have to find smack. He hands me the caps. "Be careful, Ryan, this shit is new on the street, it's from the slopes in Cabramatta and it's very pure, tell your mum it's her lucky day, she can get three hits out of every two caps."

'We get back to the Cross and Monkey stops the car. I want to get out but he grabs me arm and he says, "Ryan, don't tell anyone what's happened, you hear? There's witnesses that will inform the police that you've been buying heroin, that you stole the money from The Sheba. That's a crime. You're a juvenile, they'll put you in Osmond House. You heard about Osmond House?"

'All the kids at school know about Osmond House, so I say, "Yeah, I heard about it before."

'"Well, whatever you heard, it's worse! I was there when I was fifteen, I got raped and beaten up and nobody paid me for the privilege."'

Billy immediately thought of Davo and wondered how many children this evil place had destroyed.

'"You just shut your trap, you hear?" Monkey says. He smiles at me, "You're one of us now, Ryan. You're lucky, you're prime meat and beautiful, darling. The Queenie will use you, but she'll also take care of you until the pimples kick in. She and Alf only trade with the best. Stick with me and I'll teach you the tricks and you can have anything you want. I'm not a paedophile so you'll be safe." He's got this sort of smile on his face. "Well, safe until you're seventeen anyway." Then he gives me a card with his phone number on it. "You'll be back, sweetie, call me when the time comes," he says.

'"I ain't comin' back," I tell him again.

'But he just laughs, and he pats me on me knee. "Don't worry, angel, you'll soon be bending over and thinking of the new set of wheels you want for your skateboard. There are worse ways to make a living, darl. This ain't the worst thing that can happen to a kid, the Darlo Wall is the worst. That's where you pick up the clap and lots of other nasties like AIDS. Be grateful that you're with the best in the biz." Then he lets me out. "See you soon, precious!" he shouts after me, "Tell your mum she's got a sweet boy!"'

'We'll add Monkey to our list of mongrels,' Billy said to Ryan. 'Do you have the card?'

Ryan fished into his pocket and produced a card, which he'd folded into four, and handed it to Billy.

Billy simply dropped it into his briefcase. 'Can you tell me what happened next?'

'I come home and me mum's a little better. She's out of bed and says she's a bit hungry but we've got nothin' to eat, she ain't et for five days. I give her the four caps and tell her about them being too pure, what Monkey told me, to make three hits out of two caps. She says that's real cool and she loves me a lot. She's okay to do her own needle so I go to the Just Enough Faith van and get something to eat and I bring her back some sticky date puddin' 'cause that's her favourite. When I come back she's drinking some brandy I didn't know she had and she eats a bit of puddin' and says she's going to bed. I'm pretty whacked meself and hurtin' so I go to bed also where I do a bit of cryin' 'cause I wish my nana was still there and I could talk to her.

'In the mornin' I looked at me mum but she were still asleep so I left and went to school.'

'You went to school, that was the day your mother died, wasn't it?' Billy asked.

'Yeah, that was later when I come back home.'

'But you spent the day at school? Are you sure?' Billy was concerned with Ryan's answer because Dorothy Flanagan had said she hadn't seen him since he'd tried to get some of Billy's money.

'Nah, I only went, but I couldn't go in, I was frightened they'd see that I was now a poofter.'

Billy thought his heart would break, but he managed to say, 'What did you do that morning?'

'I come here,' he pointed to the giant Moreton Bay. 'Remember how you left me the book and buried it under some leaves? I come and sat under the tree but it was too dark and cold so I come here.'

'Here, on this bench?'

Ryan nodded, unaware that Billy couldn't quite believe that of all the dozens of benches in the Gardens Ryan had selected this particular one beside the rock pool. 'Then I went home,' Ryan concluded.

'Approximately what time was that?'

'It were one o'clock 'cause I heard the gun go at Pinchgut.'

'So you got home, what, five minutes later?'

'Yeah, I went to me mum's room and the door was shut and I opened it real quiet and she was still asleep. When she ate some of the puddin' I brung her from the van, it was half-past six and she went in her room with the brandy bottle. I didn't worry because she's a dancer, see, and she come back very late at night and she always sleeps 'til it's arvo, I reckoned she'd wake up soon. So I put on the TV. At two o'clock I went to her bedroom again, she's never slept this long even when she's working. The brandy bottle was lying on the floor and I could see the syringe on the table and the lighter and the spoon, but then I seen there's three caps left.' Ryan looked to see if Billy understood the implication before he explained it. 'You see, if she'd broke two caps to make three hits she'd 'ave wrapped the spare smack in silver foil, there shoulda only been two full caps on the table.'

'You mean she took a full cap, that she didn't split two to make three?'

'Yeah, she musta got drunk and forgot or somethin'. When I touched her to wake her up she don't move and she were cold. I shook her and shook her and put me hand on her heart, but she were dead like me nana said she would be.'

'And so you decided to run away?'

'She'd overdosed. The police always come when that happens. Monkey said if I didn't come back, The Queenie and Mr Suleman would tell them about how I got the smack and they'd think I murdered me mum. But I didn't, Billy, I told her it were too pure, she said that was cool, I was a good boy and she loved me.' Ryan had started to tremble but he didn't cry, Billy guessed he had just about used up all his tears.

Ryan told Billy how he'd found some kids who said he could share their squat if he stayed in at night and minded their gear. 'That was good, because the police and DOCS look for missing kids at night. I had the two hundred bucks the German gimme and I buried it the same place you done with me book under that big tree. I'd come every day and take enough so I could get something to eat 'cause I couldn't go to the food vans, there's always plainclothes there and also DOCS, they's lookin' for kids, but two days ago there wasn't no money left.'

'You hadn't eaten for two days?'

'This Abo woman, she was drunk, she gimme a hamburger and half a packet o' Smith's chips.'

'If you hadn't found me, Ryan, what were you going to do?'

Ryan shrugged. 'Like Monkey said, I was already a poofter, I was allowed ter go back to them.'

'Ryan, why did you come to William Booth to see me and then run away?'

He was silent for a while. 'I dunno. I just got scared. I wanted to tell you everything, about me nana and me mum and what happened, but then I thought you wouldn't like me no more now I was a poofter and maybe you didn't like me anyway 'cause you went away.' He shrugged. 'So I ran away and cried a bit.'

'You know they all talked about your singing in the chapel, it was beautiful.'

'It's no big deal,' Ryan said. 'Singing's just somethin' some kids can do.'

'What's the time, lad?' Billy asked.

Ryan looked at his oversized rubber-encased watch. 'Ten minutes to seven.'

'Heavens! Time to go.'

'Where we goin'?' Ryan asked.

'Ryan, you have to go into hiding. I'm taking you down to the Quay, to Con at the New Hellas.'

Ryan still looked doubtful. 'Billy, you ain't gunna leave me again, are you?'

Billy was silent for a moment. 'No, lad, I won't do that, ever again, but I need to see some people today about the plan.'

They made their way down to Circular Quay, where Con seemed overjoyed to see them and wanted to make Ryan a milkshake.

When Ryan declined, he seemed upset, until Billy told him how he'd polished off all of Maria's delicacies. 'My wife, she like to cooks, all Greek women they likes to cooks. He patted his stomach. 'She make you everything you wants, Ryan. You ask, she makes, fair dinkums, put down your glass.'

Con turned to prepare a takeaway coffee for an early commuter and Ryan, giggling, turned to Billy. 'Me nana used ta say that, it's "put down your *glasses*!" ' Billy could see that he was beginning to warm to the Greek cafe owner.

Con made a phone call home and announced that one

of his daughters working in the back of the cafe would take Ryan to his Newtown house in a taxi. 'Maria, she's waitings at the gates.'

'Can't you come with me, Billy?' Ryan asked plaintively.

'Ryan, I'm sorry, mate. I have an AA meeting. I'm already five minutes late. It's about staying off the grog. I have to go, lad, it's part of my recovery. I'll be back to pick you up at four o'clock.' Billy placed his hands on Ryan's shoulders. 'Please, Ryan, don't leave Con's house on your own, it's terribly important. Will you promise me?'

Ryan nodded. 'Yiz'll fetch me this arvo, Billy?'

'I promise, around four o'clock, it's part of the plan.'

'You haven't told me the Trim story,' Ryan said, desperate to delay their departure.

'Two stories! I'll start one when we see each other this afternoon,' Billy promised.

The AA meeting had already started when Billy entered the G'day Cafe but several of the men smiled and lifted their hands in recognition when he entered the room. Don did a silent little clap and then indicated a spare chair. After only three meetings Billy realised how important the fellowship was becoming. There was a genuine look of relief in the faces of the men who had seen him entering the room. The victory of his attendance was almost as much a confirmation for them as it was for him. It reinforced in their minds that the whole was greater than the sum of the parts and that they shared both triumph and disaster.

Despite the joy of reuniting with Ryan, the boy's terrible

distress could easily have tipped him over the edge. Billy needed the constant affirmation of AA to stay sober. He was about to tackle something that he'd have had serious doubts about doing on his own when he'd been at the height of his legal career. If he weakened for one moment and had a drink, he would be responsible for ruining a small boy's life. He would be repeating what he'd done to Charlie, and Billy knew he didn't want to live if that should happen. If only the craving would go away, he thought, just for a little while, so that he could cram everything he needed to know and do into his head without being constantly distracted by the need for a drink. But he knew it wouldn't. The odds he was taking on were enormous and, without the support of AA, he had no chance.

It was pension day so after he'd shaved and showered at The Station he visited the bank at Martin Place and obtained five dollars worth of twenty-cent pieces for the phone. From a phone booth, he dialled a number.

The phone rang a couple of times before it was picked up. 'Good morning, Justice Eisenstein's phone, Doha Jebara speaking.'

'Yes, good morning, may I speak to Marcus, please. It's Billy O'Shannessy here, I'm a barrister.' Billy hoped by using the chief justice's first name he would avoid the usual runaround.

There was a moment's hesitation on the phone and then the woman said, 'He may have left for court. Just a moment, I'll see if I can catch him.'

It was the standard response, she wasn't falling for the

first-name ploy. Billy knew what was to come. She'd return to the phone in a minute or so with the usual regrets that she'd missed him, he'd be in court all day, did Billy wish to leave a message? If she was any good, she'd do a bit of research on Billy and she'd call him back later in the day to say that Justice Eisenstein had asked her to get more details. Billy would say he couldn't discuss the matter on the phone and she would ask him whether what he had to say pertained to any ongoing matter in the courts or public inquiries. Billy would be forced to admit that this was the case. She would tell him, again politely, that the chief justice could not receive such information and that he should take it either to the police or to the ombudsman.

Billy was relying heavily on a schoolboy friendship and the many years he and Marcus Eisenstein had practised together. It had always been thought in chambers that, of the two of them, it would be Billy O'Shannessy who would be the first to sit on the bench.

To Billy's surprise, the woman returned and said, 'Just one moment, Mr O'Shannessy, I'm putting you through now.'

'Billy! How nice to hear from you. Marcus here. How are you keeping?'

Now that he was through to Marcus Eisenstein he wasn't quite sure what to say. The judge knew of his circumstances and it showed some courage on his part that he had answered the phone. 'Not too bad, thanks, Marcus. Thank you for taking my call, I'm sure you are busy.'

'Got a bit on today, but how can I help you, Billy?'

'Marcus, our worlds are very different now and I wouldn't think of calling you if it wasn't a matter of some urgency. May I see you privately?'

Billy waited for the pause but none came. 'Of course, how long will it take and how private?' Marcus Eisenstein, as usual, cut to the thrust.

'About an hour and very confidential.'

'Tonight, six o'clock at my home. Will you be alone?'

'No, I'd like to bring an eleven-year-old boy with me.'

'In some sort of trouble, is he?'

'It's rather bigger than that, I wouldn't bother you otherwise.'

'Good. I look forward to meeting you, Billy. It's been some considerable time.'

'Yes, thank you, Marcus, I appreciate your help.'

'Haven't done anything yet. Six o'clock tonight. Cheerio, Billy.'

Marcus Eisenstein hadn't changed, he still seemed to calculate the allocation of his time by the seconds. He was notorious for cutting short extraneous verbiage from over-loquacious barristers; on the other hand, he would take infinite pains with a witness who wasn't articulate or who needed help. Marcus Eisenstein was known to be a no-fear-or-favour judge who put justice ahead of any other consideration. He was a constant thorn in the side of self-seeking and ambitious politicians and big business who thought they knew what was best for society.

Billy was hugely relieved at the prospect of meeting the judge privately and, in particular, at six o'clock, which meant he would still have time to get to the AA meeting that night. The gods were smiling on him. If his preoccupation with AA in the light of what was happening around him seemed to verge on the obsessive, it was because Billy knew that he was capable of backsliding, that alcohol still had a tremendous psychological hold on him. He had always been obsessive about maintaining a set routine, but now it was critical.

It was the first time since he'd fallen from grace that he had called a fellow member of the legal profession and he'd expected to be rejected. Even though Marcus Eisenstein had been a boyhood friend and close colleague, Billy had always accepted that friendship, professional or personal, needed to be nourished, and as he'd been the one to cut all his past ties, he had therefore no right to expect a favour or even recognition. If his wife and daughter were unwilling to speak to him, the judge had every right to refuse to take his call.

Billy purchased half a loaf of bread and, seated on his bench in the Botanic Gardens, made up the day's ammunition. Attempting to remember exactly what Ryan had told him, he began to write up his notes so he could present them to Marcus Eisenstein that evening.

It was Billy's obsession with order and detail that had made him such an outstanding lawyer, it was also the quality his peers thought would eventually take him onto the bench. His ability to replicate verbal evidence or an interview almost exactly as it had occurred was well known in legal circles at the time. Even though alcohol had partially destroyed his prodigious recall so that it wasn't always spontaneous, it was still very effective. These days it would sometimes take a little longer, such as remembering where he'd first heard the name The Boys' Boutique, but he knew that eventually it would come to him. Billy, despite everything, still trusted his mind to deliver the goods.

Marcus Eisenstein would be able to read his notes and then, if he wished, cross-examine Ryan. Billy also knew that the judge would do so in the kindest, gentlest way. He knew Ryan sufficiently well to realise that the boy had done his crying and possessed a great deal of personal pride, so would answer the questions he was asked with honesty and courage and would hold back his tears in front of a stranger. This wasn't necessarily a good thing, the tears of abused children, even in front of a judge, were always heart-wrenching and, in a lawyer's book, generally useful.

Billy spent the rest of the day as usual, except that he left the library at half-past three and took a taxi to fetch Ryan. They returned to the bench in the Gardens and Billy went over his morning's notes carefully with the boy. Then he started telling the story of Trim and the wreck of the *Porpoise*.

At a quarter to five they walked down to Cowper's Wharf Road and found a concealed position where they could watch the entrance to the Flag Hotel.

'Now watch very carefully, Ryan,' Billy cautioned. 'I want you to identify anyone who comes out that you recognise.'

'There's lotsa people round here I know,' Ryan answered.

'Yes, that's possible, but we're looking for someone you haven't known for that long.'

'Who?' Ryan asked.

'No, Ryan, I can't tell you, you have to tell me, it's part of the plan.'

They hadn't been waiting long when a taxi pulled up outside the pub and the driver sounded his horn. 'Now watch carefully, Ryan,' Billy urged, his hand on Ryan's shoulder.

A few moments later Marion came out of the pub and Billy felt Ryan start. 'It's her, it's The Queenie!' he said in a frightened voice.

'It all begins to make sense,' Billy said, half to himself.

They watched the taxi move away and Billy took Ryan to sit on the edge of the Finger Wharf, where he continued the story of Trim on Wreck Reef. Later, they caught a taxi to Bellevue Hill, where Justice Eisenstein lived, Billy explaining on the way where they were going.

'It's very important that you try to answer the questions you are asked. Just tell the judge what you told me, Ryan. Don't be frightened. Marcus Eisenstein and I went to kindergarten together and then to Sydney Grammar and university, and for years we were lawyers together. He's an old mate and a very nice man.'

'Can he put me in gaol?' Ryan asked.

Billy laughed. 'No, not tonight anyway. I told you he's a friend, who I hope is going to help us.'

The taxi stopped outside a large and rather clumsy-looking red brick mansion in Victoria Road where Billy had played so often as a child. He didn't mention to Ryan that his own family home was only three doors down and an even more imposing edifice.

Marcus Eisenstein welcomed them personally at the

front door and led them directly into his study. Shortly afterwards, a maid brought in tea and cake and a bottle of lemonade for Ryan. Ryan was strictly a Coca-Cola man and Billy wondered for a moment if he would reject the lemonade. While he was a very nice child, he hadn't acquired any of the social niceties and had a tendency to speak his mind. But Ryan accepted the drink without a word, though he declined the offer of cake. No doubt Maria had been plying him with her pastries all day.

The judge's study was lined with books, half of them covered in green or red leather, their titles and volumes stamped in gold. There was a library ladder in one corner of the room, and the parquet floor was covered by three large colourful Persian rugs. Each of the deep leather club chairs had a small table to match, and in an area on its own there was a grand old desk with a green leather top and, behind it, a modern typist's chair. It was the kind of study you might see in an English movie, and all it lacked was the ancestral portraits on the wall.

'Well now, why are we here?' Marcus Eisenstein asked, pouring Billy a cup of tea. 'Though I must say it's nice to see you, Billy. Help yourself to milk and sugar.'

Billy, who was down to two teaspoons of sugar, thanked him again for seeing them. 'I thought it might be best if you read my notes and then perhaps we can talk.' The briefcase was still handcuffed to his wrist so he reached for the key around his neck, opened the handcuff and retrieved his notebook. Marcus Eisenstein didn't remark on the shackled briefcase and accepted the notepad, which Billy had opened on the appropriate page. He read for a good ten minutes, occasionally grunting and glancing up at Ryan, finally returning it to Billy.

'I'm glad to see you haven't lost any of your skills, Billy, these notes are excellent.' He started to question Ryan, asking him to elaborate on various aspects. It soon became obvious that he was impressed with the child's intelligence and recall.

Ryan had also managed to answer him with only an occasional tremor in his voice and only once had tears run silently down his cheeks.

'Well done, Ryan,' Marcus Eisenstein said at the conclusion of his questions. Turning to Billy, he said, 'If you will come to my chambers tomorrow afternoon, I will have arranged for Ryan to be placed in safe custody with Mr and Mrs Poleondakis as a protected witness. As we have no case yet, I will get the necessary papers from Justice Wood. Unfortunately, the royal commission's terms of reference only include the police and public servants and not members of the public. But I see from your notes that a Mr Alfred Petersen, a senior public servant in the Department of Community Services, may be involved. He would, I imagine, fall within the scope of the inquiry so Justice Wood will be able to justify Ryan's protected witness status.'

'Thank you, Marcus, do you think the papers can be dated as of six this morning?' Billy asked. 'Otherwise I'm breaking the law by harbouring someone wanted by the police for questioning.'

'Good point, I'm sure that can be arranged.' Marcus Eisenstein turned to Ryan. 'Ryan, I need to talk to Billy about some legal matters. How would you like to go into the lounge and watch television?'

After Ryan left, the judge turned to Billy. 'Poor little blighter and so bright, how easily the lives of the disadvantaged young can be ruined.' He was silent for a moment. 'Have you thought how we might go about the apprehension of these people, this network, Billy?'

'Yes, certainly, Marcus. Your mention of the inquiry into police corruption is one of the things I wanted to raise with you. We certainly know one, possibly two, locations where this activity takes place, so we know from Ryan's testimony and my own observation the *where* and some of the *how*. We also know *who*, in terms of at least the principals in the operation. My fear is that we cannot trust a police force already under investigation for protecting paedophiles to launch an operation against such a network.'

'My sentiments exactly. We have a problem here, mate. Ryan's experience with the German, Karl, may or may not suggest that he is a sex tourist and while under the Crimes Act the definition of sex tourism allows for the arrest of Australians who engage in sexual intercourse with a child abroad, it does *not* cover foreigners entering Australia for the purposes of utilising Australian children for the same purpose. In other words, the first example falls under the authority of the Federal Police and Federal Court while the latter comes under the authority of the state police and local jurisprudence.'

'Yes, but can we trust the locals?' Billy replied.

Eisenstein laughed. 'In part you're asking if I can be trusted? I'm not sure I know the answer. One of my senior judges has already been made to stand down pending an inquiry. We are going to have to be very careful how we go about this whole matter.' Marcus Eisenstein sighed. 'There's one thing we do know, paedophile networks have *not* been the subject of proactive law enforcement. The excuse is that there is a lack of resources, though privately I think there may also be a lack of will. We know that large profits are involved and that these networks are highly organised. You may rest assured that where such covert criminal operations take place with so little police intervention, there is corruption present on a considerable scale. This is not simply a question of mounting a police raid and bringing these people before the courts. First, we have to find men in the force who can be depended on to mount such an operation without leaking it, then we have to ensure a legal system that can effectively prosecute the offenders. So far, our record on both counts is abysmal.'

Marcus Eisenstein rose from his chair, went over to a bookshelf and returned with a file. 'Here are some of the current statistics, Billy. One in four girls and one in seven boys have been sexually abused before the age of sixteen. Available evidence shows that many of the so-called rings or networks are either run by economically advantaged, high-profile individuals, or their clients. In other words, important people in the community. We have absolute proof of the cynical and self-serving nature of these paedophiles who introduce children to addictive drugs and cult-like brainwashing so their under-age victims are too afraid, substance-dependent, or too ashamed to tell or to appear as witnesses. This manipulation of minors has become a legal trick of the trade.'

The judge looked up from the file he was reading. 'As the chief justice of this state, I am ashamed of our record. Less than one per cent of perpetrators are ever convicted. If it helps, and it doesn't, the statistics are the same for the rest of Australia.' Marcus Eisenstein was visibly upset. 'Imagine a society, any society, with one-quarter of its daughters and one-seventh of its sons struck down by a plague, a virus that isn't immediately fatal but which has an incipient result that leads to suicide, persistent lifelong nightmares, intractable psychiatric disorders, drug and alcohol abuse, anorexia and depression, all of which require lifelong treatment. What do you suppose that society's response should be? Yet that's what we have here and nothing is done about it.'

The chief justice was now totally wound up. 'Sexual abuse of children probably accounts for more misery and suffering than any of the great plagues of history, if for no other reason than that it lasts a lifetime. That, my dear old friend, is what we are up against. That is truly why the law is an ass! A massive public-health problem like child sexual abuse demands a massive social response, yet there is no shout or even a whimper of indignation. There is no National AIDS Council equivalent, no National Heart Foundation, no National Quit Smoking program, no Anti-Cancer Council! Despite the glaringly obvious evidence in front of us, we do nothing! And evil men are allowed to trample the young seedlings of our nation underfoot!'

Billy was truly confounded by the judge's response. He'd expected a reasoned and sanguine reaction. Marcus Eisenstein was a man who cherished the rule of law, yet here he was decrying the very institution he was responsible for, and privately despairing at what had been his life's work.

'Marcus, you don't sound very hopeful. Are you saying that there is nothing we can do about child abuse, specifically about Ryan?'

'No, Billy, I am in a very small way exultant. I thank you for bringing this matter to me. This child has not been corrupted as a witness, he is bright and believable. While it may only be one small hammer blow where a thunderbolt is needed, we are going to make damn sure this one sticks. We will not rely on the Wood Royal Commission. Its terms of reference are too restrictive, too limited.' Marcus Eisenstein covered his face with both hands and appeared to be thinking. When he looked up at Billy again, he said, 'I'm going to need some time.'

'How much time?' Billy asked anxiously.

'I don't know. If we can get the Federal Police involved it could solve a lot of problems, but I don't know if that's possible. I dare say the German is back in Bavaria by now so that's not an excuse we can use, though I'll have the Department of Customs and Immigration check. We may be forced to rely on the locals, it's a question of finding the right police personnel. Not all policemen are corrupt.'

'Marcus, I have an idea.'

'What is it, Billy?'

'Well, when you think about it, who in the community would be most opposed to paedophiles?'

'Their victims, I imagine,' the judge replied.

'Yes, sure, but what about their mothers?'

'I'm not sure I understand.'

'Policewomen. I'm sure there are several senior enough to head up a strike team.'

Marcus Eisenstein hesitated briefly. 'Billy, that is bloody inspired! You always were someone who could think outside the square, the legal profession has missed you.'

'How do you think the police commissioner will react? Will he agree to an all-female operation?'

Eisenstein thought for a moment. 'James Bullmore is new, an Englishman, he just might buy it. No harm in trying.'

Billy had followed the brouhaha that had occurred with the appointment of what the police union referred to as an unknown, untested foreigner. Bullmore's appointment had unleashed a bitter controversy from senior police officers, politicians and the media and there had been a sustained effort to reverse the decision, the argument being that only a local would be able to do the job.

Marcus Eisenstein laughed. 'He's got his job cut out, poor bugger. I recall being invited to a Police Officers' Association dinner at Rosehill Racecourse in August to meet Bullmore. It was his first official social function. I sat at the same table with him and Tony Miller, the Police Minister. When Bullmore rose to speak to the three hundred and fifty or so officers present, there was barely a ripple of applause, truly the sound of one hand clapping. It wasn't hard to tell he wasn't being made welcome. When Jim O'Reilly, the recently retired commissioner, followed him, the applause rose to a veritable crescendo with foot-stomping and cheering. The Police Minister, next to me, leaned over and said to Bullmore, 'Bastards! See what you've let yourself in for, James?' Though I must say, I liked the Pommie and now I see he's appointed a woman to be his senior assistant commissioner.' He leaned back. 'He may just be our man, Billy.'

Marcus Eisenstein was in court when Billy picked up the papers for Ryan's protected-witness status the following afternoon. He'd left a handwritten note for Billy to say that he would be seeing the police commissioner the following morning and for Billy to phone him at his chambers before lunch.

Billy called him the following afternoon, having to go through the same routine as before with the protective and ever suspicious Doha Jebara, the judge's personal assistant. Billy knew her name was Lebanese, although he wasn't sure if it was Maronite Christian or Muslim, but thought it typical of the Jewish judge, who wouldn't be concerned in the least about the ethnic origins of his assistant.

'Hello, Billy, good news about the matter we discussed, I've seen the man. He's agreed to the operation the way we discussed. It's going to take a little time to organise. Call me in a week. I trust you are well?'

'Yes, thank you, I'm still hanging in there,' Billy replied.

'Good man, cheerio,' the judge said and Billy heard the receiver at the other end click back in its cradle. Marcus Eisenstein was back to a few well-chosen words.

Ryan seemed to have enjoyed his first days with Maria, although he felt a little restricted not being able to leave the house, being accustomed to coming and going as he wished. But he soon settled down, even, Billy suspected, enjoying all the attention. One of Con's daughters, a local hairdresser, had come up with a possible solution that would allow him a little more freedom. He was going to spend the afternoon of his third day as a protected witness at the hair salon where she worked, having his hair and eyebrows dyed blond. After which he was being taken to Kmart to get new gear. This second suggestion wasn't as much to his liking, he was a skateboarder and his white-on-black 'Independent' T-shirt, his Vans shoes and his suspended dog chain were important to his perception of himself. He nevertheless agreed, understanding the necessity to alter his appearance. Maria hadn't left it at that, she'd persuaded Voula, the oldest of Con's nieces, who was conceivably old enough to have an eleven-year-old child, to have her hair blonded as well. Ryan's Italian skin tone matched her own Greek ancestry almost exactly and later Billy would coach them both into developing a cover story if they were ever questioned.

Billy found a room in a boarding house at the back of the Rocks so that he could be close to the G'day Cafe and his AA meetings. He'd decided against living in Newtown but, instead, Con brought Ryan into the New Hellas at five-thirty every morning and Billy would meet him there and they'd slip into the Botanic Gardens for an hour and a bit when Billy would tell him the ongoing saga of Master Mariner Trim before Billy attended his morning meeting. Con would then send Ryan home in a taxi.

That week, waiting for further news from Marcus Eisenstein, Billy spent much the same as usual, sticking to his routine, the afternoons at his disposal to spend at the library researching Matthew Flinders and writing Trim's story. Each morning he would tell Ryan about Trim and, as he was rapidly getting to the end of his second tale, he now had to finish the story of Trim's capture on the Ile de France in a hurry.

Billy enjoyed this time spent in the library and he almost resented the fact that he had promised to contact Morgan's partner, even though he thought she might be Caroline, Trevor Williams' daughter. On the third day after the meeting with the judge, he called her from a public telephone just before doing mynah-bird duty.

A female voice answered and he asked if he could speak to Kartanya.

'She's still asleep, call after two o'clock,' the voice said, whereupon the woman abruptly hung up.

Billy called again at two o'clock, and this time a different female voice answered. 'May I speak to Kartanya, please?' he asked.

'Who's speaking?' the voice asked.

'My name is Billy O'Shannessy and I have a message from Morgan for Kartanya.'

The voice asked him to hold on and he was almost at the point of hanging up when he heard a woman say, 'Kartanya speaking.'

Billy explained why he was calling and asked if they could meet for a cup of coffee. There was a moment's hesitation before Kartanya agreed that they could meet at the coffee lounge at the Darling Harbour casino at four o'clock that afternoon. 'It's the one at the top of the escalator with the waterfall,' she directed. 'I must go now.'

Billy sensed that she was anxious to get off the phone. 'How will I know you, Kartanya?' he asked hurriedly.

There was another slight hesitation. 'I'm wearing jeans and a blue shirt, I have dark hair down to my shoulders, thank you for calling.' This was all said in a single breath before she put down the receiver. Billy thought she must have been taking word-miser lessons from Marcus Eisenstein.

Billy arrived at the coffee shop on time and positioned himself at the table nearest the door and then waited a further half an hour. He was on his second flat white when Kartanya appeared at the top of the escalators. Billy had no problem recognising her and stood as she entered. 'Kartanya?' he asked.

The woman in front of him was very attractive though painfully thin, which Billy put down to her addiction. She looked older than twenty-eight, more like her mid-thirties, though this again could have been because of the heroin. She wore no make-up apart from a little lipstick, and he wondered if she had a cold as the base of her nostrils seemed a little inflamed. Her mother had been right, her mouth did seem a little large for her face but, if anything, it added to her unusual looks.

'Hi, you must be Billy,' she said, extending her hand. In the flesh she sounded quite different from the anxious voice he'd heard on the phone. As though reading his thoughts, she said, 'I apologise if I sounded abrupt on the phone, I take a whole heap of time to wake up.'

They had hardly been seated when the waiter, without taking her order, placed a short black in front of her. 'Thank you, Carlo,' she said and, not waiting, took a long sip from the small glass. 'That's better,' she said, 'my first coffee hit of the day.' She opened her bag, took out a packet of cigarettes, then put it back again. 'Damn, I forgot, you can smoke in the casino but not here.'

'Do you work nights, Kartanya?' Billy asked.

Kartanya shrugged. 'I'm sure Morgan told you, I'm a prostitute here at the casino. He's a big mouth, he'd have told you I'm also a heroin addict,' she added. 'It's an easy way to feed an expensive habit and the boys bring in cocaine as well.' She shrugged again. 'You sleep with the high rollers, they tip well. Smack and cocaine are always available.' She said it all in a matter-of-fact voice, not caring if he took it or left it. Billy could see that under her soft-looking exterior she was tough, perhaps 'hard' might be a better word. 'Well, how is Morgan?' she asked, though not with a great deal of interest.

'He's doing really well and seems determined to make it,' Billy replied.

Kartanya gave a short little laugh. 'That's our Morgan,

he can't stand being out of the limelight, he'll clean up his act just to get his ego reinflated.'

Billy wasn't quite sure what she meant but, taking a punt, said, 'Well, I guess he's an actor.'

'And a good one when he isn't showing off,' Kartanya said. 'I'm glad he's getting clean, I'm to blame for his addiction. He wanted me and I came with a habit. If he comes out clean, I won't let him back into my life.' She paused. 'I'm bad news, mate.'

Billy didn't try to comfort her. 'All addicts are, Kartanya. We share that in common and I understand what you're saying.' Billy changed the subject. 'Morgan tells me you're a singer, a very good one.'

'Was.'

'Do you still sing?'

'Sometimes, when I'm high or pissed, but professionally, no, I gave it away, the junk was too important.'

'That seems a pity,' Billy replied.

Kartanya sighed. 'It was all a long time ago, about a thousand hits ago, mate.' She suddenly sounded a little impatient or perhaps she expected a lecture and didn't want any of the usual bullshit.

Billy didn't quite know how to broach the subject of her family but finally decided that as she'd answered his questions directly, there seemed no point in trying to be overly tactful. Besides, he felt she was getting close to the edge and could easily walk away. 'Kartanya, what about your parents?'

Kartanya was silent and Billy thought she was about to

rise, but she remained sitting. 'That's not a question you ask someone like me, Billy. Addicts don't have parents!' Suddenly she lost her cool. 'What is this? The fuckin' Salvation Army?'

Billy thought he'd blown it, but persisted anyway. 'You don't think you're causing them a lot of pain by staying away from them?'

'I'm not sure that's any of your business,' Kartanya said, starting to rise.

Before she could do so, Billy said, 'Do you have a scar, from a snake bite, a King Brown, on your left Achilles, Caroline?'

Kartanya looked startled. 'How do you know my name, my old name?' She added quickly, 'And the scar, the bite?'

Billy told her the story of Trevor Williams, then he handed her the letter he'd received from Bridgit Williams.

Kartanya had hardly begun to read before she started to sob. Reaching for a tissue in her bag, she continued reading and by the end of the letter could no longer contain herself. She buried her face in her hands and wept. Somehow the letter had managed to penetrate the hard exterior. There was still some softness there, Billy decided.

He wanted to comfort her but was afraid. He hadn't physically touched a woman for so long that he thought it might be seen as obscene if he placed his hand on her shoulder, though he ached to do so. 'They both love you very much, Kartanya, they'll take you any way you are.'

After a while Kartanya stopped crying and looked at Billy and, almost in front of his eyes, he saw the hardness return and a defiant look in her dark eyes. 'So what do you expect me to do?' she asked.

'Do you think you could write to them, just a short note?'

'Yeah, okay, I've got to go. I'll write, I promise,' she said. Taking the pack of cigarettes out of her handbag, she added, 'I need a fag.'

Billy smiled. 'Kartanya, I'm an alcoholic and addict like you and I simply don't believe you. Perhaps you think you'll write, but you'll leave me and go home and tell yourself you're upset and need a hit and you'll snort a line of cocaine and you'll convince yourself that what you're doing is the best for everyone.' Billy paused. 'But it isn't, my dear. Your father and mother love you. By not seeing them, you're breaking their hearts.'

'No, you're wrong! They won't want me back the way I am, I'm bad news.'

Again Billy didn't offer any sympathy. 'You may be right, addicts have an ability to use up affection very fast, even from their parents. But *they* have the right to make that decision, *not* you. Your father wants his daughter back, that's all. There are no reservations, no conditions. They simply love you, always have and, I dare say, always will.' Billy added, 'Will you give them another chance, Caroline?'

Again Billy saw a glimpse of softness return. 'Yes. Yes, I promise. I'll get in touch.'

Billy withdrew a brand-new notepad and a biro from his briefcase and placed both on the table in front of Kartanya. 'Write!' he commanded.

'What, now? Here?' Kartanya cried in alarm. 'Christ, no.'

Billy nodded his head.

It was touch and go for a moment, then she grabbed the pen. 'Jesus!' Without further protest Kartanya began to write, at first hesitantly and then faster and faster, her tears dropping onto the page. Soon she'd filled two pages and finally completed the letter halfway down the third page.

Billy reached into his briefcase and produced a stamped, addressed envelope. 'Fold it and put it in the envelope, seal it and I'll post it,' he said, not quite believing what he'd achieved.

Kartanya Williams folded the letter, sealed it and handed it to Billy. 'Thank you, Billy,' she said quietly. 'I'm glad you're my daddy's friend.' She smiled, her eyes red from crying. Then she rose and walked away. Billy watched as she walked towards the escalators and disappeared in sections as the moving steps lowered her, bit by bit, out of sight.

Billy turned up at Marcus Eisenstein's chambers on the appointed day. This time Ms Jebara met him with a smile. She was an attractive young woman, rather too thin and pale, and the conservative black business suit she wore didn't help her complexion. 'The chief justice is waiting for you, Mr O'Shannessy,' she said, leading him to the judge's chambers.

'Hello, Billy, still on the straight and narrow, I hope,' Marcus Eisenstein said, tact not being among his major talents.

'Hanging on like grim death,' Billy replied, laughing, although it was closer to the truth than even he dared admit.

'Billy I don't have to tell you that what I have to say can be shared with no one, not even the boy,' he began.

Billy nodded. 'Yes, of course,' though he thought it a bit patronising.

'The new bloke took a little convincing, but finally agreed.'

'What was he was worried about? Using women?'

'No, as a matter of fact, he was delighted with the idea. But he's new in the job and already up against the establishment in the Force and in Parliament. An all-women police bust (pardon the pun) has never been done before in New South Wales.' Marcus laughed. 'We'll be making history.'

Billy grinned. 'Only if it succeeds.'

'That's what he said, it's great publicity if it succeeds, a disaster if it fails.'

'Properly done, it has every chance. These people believe they're protected and if anything is going to happen they'll be warned in good time by the police in their pay. From my observation, they're not exactly paranoid,' Billy said.

'Well, let's hope you're right, but that's not the only concern.' Marcus Eisenstein scratched the tip of his nose. 'There isn't a charge for paedophilia, we'd have to get them on carnal knowledge and that's never easy. We're not dealing with the usual criminal here, they'll have the best silks in the business defending them. The German, by the way, is well gone, it's the word of an eleven-year-old boy against a powerful group of men.'

'What are you saying, Marcus? That the odds are against us?'

'Yes.'

'And you're reluctant to go ahead?'

'No, but we have to get it right first time. We don't know what we'll find at The Queen of Sheba or at the Flag Hotel. We could end up with egg on our faces.'

'But this is a covert operation. It could be made to look like a routine raid, nothing special, police got a tip-off that there's an illegitimate business being run in a pub and the other is simply a raid on a strip joint looking for drugs. Two separate operations.'

'Sure, with a history-making all-female squad in charge of both. The police, that is the male police, will be the first to call the media. All hell will break loose.'

'And you'll be in the eye of the storm?' Billy said.

'You're not wrong there, mate,' Marcus said. 'The premier wouldn't be too happy, I assure you.'

'So what are we going to do?'

'We're going ahead but it's tricky, according to Nora Watman, the assistant commissioner who's putting the team together. Ideally we need an insider with a video camera.'

Billy laughed. 'Do me a favour, Marcus. A video camera!'

'I know it sounds absurd, but evidently filming sex scenes with children is all part of the action. It's the trophy.'

'What? Well-known people, pillars of the establishment, collect videotapes of themselves in action?'

'Evidently.'

'With the greatest respect, Marcus, that's hard to believe.' But as he said it, Billy remembered something Ryan had said. 'Hey, wait a minute!'

'What is it?' the judge asked.

'Something Ryan said Monkey told him. I neglected to put it into my notes. Bloody careless. He said they'd have filmed the German raping him and it would be sent to him as a keepsake, a little thousand-dollar keepsake. Blackmail, I guess, or perhaps, as you say, paedophiles like to keep records of their conquests. If I recall correctly, Monkey said that he hated The Queenie.'

'Billy, I think you'd better see Nora Watman,' Marcus said. 'Monkey sounds promising.'

'I have his telephone number, he was confident enough to give it to Ryan.' Billy dug into his briefcase and after some time found the card Ryan had given him. 'I've never looked at it,' he said, opening it. He handed it to the judge.

Marcus Eisenstein arranged for Billy to meet the assistant police commissioner out of uniform and in an unmarked car outside the parking lot at Central Station. In the course of the conversation, he learned that she was no Constable Plod but held a Masters degree in public policy, a Bachelor of Arts and a Diploma of Education.

'Mr O'Shannessy, I've studied your career in the past few days; you have an enviable record as a barrister,' she began.

'That was some time ago, Commissioner Watman. In the past few years I've earned an unenviable record as a drunk.'

'Thank you for saying that, Mr O'Shannessy, it means I

can come right to the point. With only Ryan's testimony we've got very little. The German who raped him is out of the country, the two standover men who held him down are probably in Mohammed Suleman's employ, so they won't talk. Frankly, we need a lot more to go ahead with any confidence.'

'The chief justice mentioned video evidence?'

'Ideally, yes. Someone from the inside, your Mr Monkey.'

Billy grinned. 'I think it's just Monkey and I don't know him, I can't imagine why I left the bit about him giving his card and telephone number to Ryan out of my notes. It was very careless.'

'Mr O'Shannessy, your notes are exemplary, but thank God you remembered it. Do you think you could persuade Ryan to call this Monkey and arrange a meeting?'

'Will he be safe?'

'Yes, of course, there will be a plain-clothes policewoman standing close by.'

'What if Monkey doesn't cooperate?' Billy asked.

'He will, if we frighten him enough and promise him indemnity from prosecution. Mr O'Shannessy, we've had a psychiatrist go over your notes, and we're glad you wrote them quasi-verbatim. Even allowing for Ryan's verbal translation, we believe this Monkey has a deep antipathy to The Queenie. He may just be willing to co-operate.'

'I repeat my question. What if he doesn't?'

'Well, then he'll be tidied away until the operation is over. It's not unusual for such people to disappear from their jobs, especially if they're also drug addicts.'

'Here's hoping,' Billy said.

'Mr O'Shannessy, after Ryan has identified Monkey you won't hear from any of us. This is a covert police operation, we will not be sharing the details with you or the chief justice. You do understand?'

'Yes, of course, commissioner.'

Two days later Ryan called Monkey, who arranged to meet him outside the Wayside Chapel later that afternoon. Billy was not permitted to accompany him but he was waiting at Con's house at five o'clock that afternoon when an unmarked police car dropped Ryan off.

'What happened, Ryan?' Billy asked him.

Ryan shrugged. 'It was cool. Monkey came up to me and he said, "Hi, Ryan, what took you so long, sweetie?" Then the policewoman come up and arrested him. "Bitch!" he said ter me. "You'll keep, Ryan."'

Billy continued his daily routine without knowing when the police raid would take place. Every morning he opened the newspaper anxiously. He wasn't expecting to read something in a banner headline, not necessarily even a leading article, but certainly as news deserving a column on the front page of the *Sydney Morning Herald* and perhaps even a larger headline in the *Telegraph*. A week passed and then another and he was becoming worried that by telling him they would not make any further contact with him, they had decided to abort the raid. He called Marcus Eisenstein, who expressed himself equally concerned, although he too had been told that he would not be privy to police plans. In the meantime, Billy spent his afternoons writing in the Mitchell Library.

Almost three weeks after he'd talked with Assistant Commissioner Nora Watman, he opened the *Sydney Morning Herald*. At first he didn't see it, then in the left-hand bottom corner, in a single-column report, he read:

Police Raid Sex Tourist Office in Woolloomooloo

Police last night raided the premises of a Woolloomooloo hotel where they found a three-roomed complex in an unused upstairs section of the hotel that appeared to be retail premises. Later inquiries revealed that it was involved in selling imported lingerie to transvestites and cross-dressers. Trading under the name Kings Cross Dressers, the business was operating illegally on premises licensed only to sell beer and spirits, but this was not given as the reason for the raid.

Police were forced to break in when the proprietor of the Flag Hotel, Mr Sam Snatchall, an ex-waterfront union organiser, told them he was unaware of the nature of the business and did not have a key to the premises he had rented out, believing it was being used as accommodation in line with hotel licensing requirements. Police removed several hundred videotapes, a computer and files containing photographs of young children believed to be in sexually compromising poses. Later, a spokesperson for the NSW Police, Asst Commissioner Nora Watman, said, 'We believe the premises were being used as a travel bureau for paedophiles visiting Australia from overseas as well as Australians travelling to foreign destinations. We also believe it is an organisation used for the purposes of importing juveniles of both sexes from Thailand and the Philippines.'

No arrests were made.

In a separate operation in Kings Cross last night, police raided The Queen of Sheba, a notorious strip joint owned by Mr Mohammed Suleman, a well-known criminal identity gaoled in the past for drug-dealing. Several people are believed to have been arrested in premises to the rear of the club, though no names have been released to the press. It is not known if the two raids are connected.

Both raids were conducted by an all-female task force, believed to be a first in the history of policing in the State. New English Police Commissioner James Bullmore, when questioned by the *SMH* on the make-up of the two teams, stated, 'In my police force we will not be gender specific, they were police personnel selected for the tasks because they were available and adequately trained.'

The *Telegraph* reported the facts in more dramatic language, though giving essentially the same information. The marked difference was the headline. Spread all the way across the front page, it read:

Girls Raid Kiddy-Sex Trade!

EPILOGUE

Billy continued his daily routine, which included writing Trim's story at the Mitchell Library every afternoon.

The grand saga continues, the leaky bucket known as the *Cumberland* carrying Matthew Flinders and Master Trim sailed into Port Louis at four in the afternoon flying the Union Jack. She was such a small ship that onlookers thought she must be from the nearby coast of Africa, or the island of Madagascar, though the colours she flew made no sense for there was no English colony in that part of the Indian Ocean. She was so obviously constructed in the manner of a coastal trading vessel that it would not have occurred to them that she might have sailed the treacherous seas from the British convict settlement in Port Jackson. As she hove to, they could see that she was an old tub in poor condition and they were even more surprised to see that she purported to be a British naval vessel that had sailed into a French harbour in broad daylight in a time of war.

Unbeknownst to Matthew Flinders, the fragile peace between Britain and France had collapsed and war between the two nations had broken out again. The *Cumberland* was sailing into the very jaws of the enemy. Trim was not in the least impressed by the scowls from the inhabitants as he performed his usual trick of tight-roping the main hawser to be the first ashore. Sweaty black slaves looked at him hungrily, and white and indifferently coloured men pointed to him and jabbered in some strange language. The moment the gangplank was lowered, he scampered back on board to report the obvious lack of cordiality he had observed from the locals.

Matthew Flinders was aware from Trim's meowing that he was cautioning his master to be most careful in how he approached the locals. 'Trim, do not vex yourself, lad, I have a passport from the French which was given to me when we were on the *Investigator*. I am sure the authorities will validate it and give us a most cordial welcome. I shall ask to see Governor de Caen at once.'

The ship's master, Mr Aken, had gone ashore and returned presently to tell Matthew Flinders that Britain was once again at war with the French. 'This could be a nasty business, sir,' he suggested.

'Not at all, Mr Aken. Like us, the French are a civilised nation, they will soon enough know who I am and that we come in peace.'

It was to be a severe miscalculation, for the French were considered by their very nature suspicious of other nations and in particular of the perfidious English. Matthew Flinders was once again allowing his optimism to rule over his commonsense. Here was a situation to be approached with great diplomacy and the utmost caution. 'We shall soon sort the matter out,' he said to Trim, 'Mr Aken is ever the pessimist.'

However, it had always struck Trim that Aken was a very down-to-earth and sensible man and his heart sank at his master's overweening confidence which, he was forced to admit, bordered on arrogance.

English men of the naval officer class, while always gentlemen, did not see other seagoing nations as quite the equal of the ships of His Britannic Majesty and were apt to presume rather too much for Trim's liking. Napoleon may have conquered Europe and Egypt but he had yet to set foot on British soil and they were there to see that it never happened. Trim was a cautious, good-mannered cat, sensible to the feelings of foreigners, and what this situation called for was a little humility, though quite plainly this was not going to be forthcoming from M. Flinders Esq.

Matthew Flinders, sensing Trim's disapproval, defended himself by saying, 'Do you not recall that on the previous occasion we were at war with France, Captain Baudin of the French expedition of discovery arrived in Port Jackson. When was that, now?' He appeared to be thinking, though Trim knew his prodigious memory would soon bring the date to the surface of his mind, 'Ah, yes, 20th of June last year, but three days short of eighteen months ago. Only twelve of his crew of a hundred and seventy men were in a fit state to work, the others being laid low with scurvy. On that occasion Governor King provided most handsomely for them, slaughtering some of the precious government stock so that they might have fresh meat when no convict or citizen or even the governor himself had the same at their disposal. You will remember we entertained Captain Baudin and the naturalist fellow, François Peron, on board the *Investigator*. Such civility comes naturally to us English, and

I expect the French, who do not care to be in the debt of an Englishman and who consider themselves the more civilised nation, will be anxious to repay that kindness in order that the chart of equal charity is all squared up.'

But, alas, the French thought no such thing and when Matthew Flinders, changing into his best uniform, which had been recently boiled to get rid of the lice, asked to be granted an interview immediately with Governor de Caen, the courier returned to say that the governor was unable to see him. This was stated without the courtesy of an apology for not doing so because of some other unavoidable task. The signs were ominous and Trim, observing his master's pride so dented, cautioned him to be calm. 'A little purring is called for here, sir, a brushing of the soft fur of diplomacy.'

'Trim, I am a sailor and navigator, not a smooth-tongued diplomat! We have been insulted, our flag and our navy are dishonoured, this man is a veritable poltroon!'

And we will be prisoners of war if we are not very careful, Trim thought to himself, though he knew not to argue with his master when his mind was made up. It was the very stubbornness of nature that made M.F. who he was.

Several French officers arrived and asked Matthew Flinders to accompany them to the port offices. Trim, of course, was not permitted to go along and would later only hear his master's version of what had occurred. As the Frenchmen spoke very little English and Matthew Flinders not even a smidgin of French, even having trouble getting his tongue around the word 'monsieur', Trim expected that there might be some misunderstanding.

'They kept asking me if I knew of the voyage of some Englishman named Monsieur Flinedare and I answered them earnestly and honestly that I did not. They seemed most agitated with my denial,' he later told Trim.

'Oh dear,' Trim thought and even though his French was no better than his master's, he was not in the cantankerous frame of mind that allowed Mr Flinders' intuition to miss the obvious, that Flinedare was the French pronunciation of Flinders. By denying his own existence, the French immediately smelled a rat. By travelling incognito, Captain Flinders was trying to pass himself off as someone else. Furthermore he refused to show his passport to anyone but the captain general, who was also the governor. The French knew that Flinders commanded a British warship named the *Investigator* but now he arrived in a leaky tub named the *Cumberland*. Matthew Flinders must think them fools and it was easy enough, in the climate of war where sensible conclusion is in very short supply, to erroneously deduce that the English captain must be a spy.

Trim worked all this out in a matter of a few seconds, though his master, despite his acknowledged intelligence, had got hold of quite the wrong end of the stick. Trim was in a state of despair and realised they were in a great deal of trouble. Trying to make fools of the French was a serious miscalculation and he knew they would not forgive the arrogant English captain in a hurry.

Finally a message was sent that Governor de Caen would grant him an interview. 'About time!' Matthew Flinders said, buckling on his sword, 'I had begun to think that the French must be quite devoid of sensibility, Master Trim.'

'Do be careful, sir,' Trim meowed. 'Tread softly with a cat's paws, do not put your big, clumsy seaman's boot in it, I smell a rat.'

Once again, Trim proved to be right. When Matthew Flinders was finally admitted to an interview, Governor de Caen demanded through an interpreter that the great navigator and explorer show him his French passport and also the articles of his commission as an officer in the British navy.

Matthew Flinders, who had already adopted a somewhat recalcitrant attitude, was now incensed, for he held his honour precious. After a terse exchange the Frenchman lost his temper and shouted, 'You are imposing on me, sir!'

Matthew Flinders was led away. The ship's master, Mr Aken, and Trim were fetched from the ship and it was supposed that they would be taken to the gaol. Trim's master was quite unrepentant, boldly declaring on the way to their incarceration, 'The captain general's conduct must alter very much before I should pay him a second visit.' It seemed to Trim that de Caen was in the box seat and not the other way around. While Trim gave his master tribute as a man who loved charts and instruments and the lay of land, depths and sightings, he was forced to conclude that he was not always of sound judgement when it came to mankind.

Gaol turned out to be the Café Morengo, a lodging house that was a fair exchange for the *Cumberland* as it too abounded in bugs, lice and mosquitoes, whereas the food proved to be even worse than that served on the vessel. They were now under constant guard with no recourse to help, although, much to Trim's joy, an occasion did arise when everything could conceivably be put to rights.

The following day Governor de Caen's aide-de-camp, a certain Monsieur Monistral, paid them a visit at the Café Morengo and asked Matthew Flinders for his orders from Governor King and extended an invitation to dine with the governor. It seemed an opportunity for a reconciliation had occurred.

Trim could not contain his delight and did two spectacular

somersaults, landing on Matthew Flinders' lap to the consternation and surprise of the very dignified aide-de-camp. 'Bravo!' Trim meowed, 'We may now undo this net of intrigue.'

'Whatever has got into you, Master Trim, can you not see I am busy?' Matthew Flinders scolded. Then, to his utter consternation, his master turned to Monsieur Monistral and hotly declined. 'You may tell your governor I shall accept his offer only when set at liberty!'

The aide-de-camp, who was a pleasant and conciliatory man, urged Trim's master to reconsider. Trim, his patience worn thin, scratched at his ankle and meowed, 'Monsieur Monistral is right, do not turn this offer down!'

'Trim, you are being impertinent, whatever has got into you!' Turning to the Frenchman, he repeated, 'Until I am at liberty, sir!'

The governor, hearing Matthew Flinders' hot-headed response, replied, 'No, sir! My next invitation will come only after you are liberated!'

And so the lines were drawn and the English and the French, in the guise of the governor of a small, inconsequential island in the Indian Ocean and the great British navigator, were at war. As Trim observed, the odds were heavily stacked against the two Englishmen and a British cat, who were taking a considerable pounding from the French big gun and would continue to do so for the next six and a half years.

Matthew Flinders was not always an easy man to live with and now, as his depression increased, Trim became more and more concerned. Flinders became engrossed in writing letters, most of which were aimed at the villainous and duplicitous French governor, who continued to command his compliance and punished the lack of it by confiscating Flinders' precious papers and the ship's stores. Flinders' imprisonment, which under other circumstances might have been only for a few days, was now indefinite. Finally, to Matthew Flinders' humiliation, de Caen made him surrender his sword, making him officially a prisoner of war. Things were not good and Trim found himself increasingly popping through a window to avoid the guards and going for a quiet stroll just to be by himself, though at the same time feeling guilty that he was leaving his beloved master on his own.

In April 1805 the governor, relenting a little, moved the three prisoners, Matthew Flinders, Mr Aken and Master Trim, to new quarters away from the awful Café Morengo to the Maison Despeaux, which was set in a lovely garden and was much more salubrious accommodation. It was here that he met a young gardener with the improbable name of Paul Etienne Laurent le Juge de Segrais, who took an immediate liking to Trim, who consequently introduced him to his master. To forgo the impossibility of remembering or even pronouncing his name, Flinders dubbed him Monsieur Seagrass and the two men spent many hours together discussing the plants from Terra Australis and the Far East.

Monsieur Seagrass was to become a renowned botanist and was instrumental in establishing the splendour of the magnificent botanical gardens in the north of the island named Le Jardin de Pamplemousse, which contains a grove of palm trees brought from the Far East that flower only once in a hundred years. As they were previously unknown to European botanists, the young botanist named them Flinders' Palm in honour of the great navigator. Matthew Flinders was never to return to plant his coconut trees as beacons to sailors in treacherous waters but Monsieur Seagrass honoured him with a tall and wonderful palm of his own.

Trim, in his increasingly frequent adventures outside the garden prison, was not simply indulging himself but was learning the lie of the land. If Matthew Flinders refused to soften his stance towards the

French governor, Trim, a far more practical thinker, decided he should take the matter into his own hands. It took him several weeks to find the governor's residence and then a great many more to ingratiate himself with the servants in the slave quarters. From there, over many weeks, he made his way through the kitchen, the first requirement if ever he was to make it deeper into the governor's mansion. He'd won the admiration of the African cook, Eloise du Preez, a large and fearsome black lady, by emerging from the pantry on four consecutive days with a large rat in his mouth and depositing it at her feet. Needless to say, he'd caught the rats in the grain store situated in the expansive grounds and brought them into the house, emerging with great dignity from the pantry at precisely the right moment, his eyes blazing with the sincerity of a duty well done.

Trim did not consider this reprehensible, his master was at war with a foreign nation and he saw himself as a spy behind the front lines. His ultimate aim was to win the affection of Governor de Caen's staff and family with his tricks and his charm so that he would become a favourite with the household and eventually be brought to the attention of the governor himself. Trim was not yet sure how he would bring about the reconciliation between his master and the governor, but his rough plan was to attend the governor's residence at certain hours and ingratiate himself to such an extent that he would provoke a curiosity as to where he went when not present. Eventually, or so Trim's speculation went, they would send a slave to follow him, whereupon he would lead him back to his master in the Maison Despeaux. With the two men bitterly opposed to each other, but having a cat they loved common to each, it was Trim's earnest hope that he might bring the two together. It was a ploy he had engineered often on board ship between two men who, angry with each other over some small incident, had been brought to agreement by Trim's showing spontaneous affection for them both. Trim had yet to find a human being who, once they knew him, did not feel immediate affection for him. He was confident that Governor de Caen could be made to feel the same way.

It must be remembered that Trim was a ship's cat brought up in the inherent nature of the British seaman, simple and straightforward, a stranger to the ways of duplicity or cunning. In his world, men lived in close proximity and had few secrets to share. Life on board ship was a simple business and the sailors' problems were usually of a similar nature. Therefore Trim had no knowledge of the outside world and, in particular, of a man who possessed grand ambition and illusions of greatness in the era of the all-conquering Napoleon Bonaparte, yet found himself in charge of a small and insignificant island in the Indian Ocean. A dollop of earth that in the affairs of La Belle France had less purpose than a wash of foam on its distant and forgotten shore.

Trim knew that his master was also an ambitious man who longed to be possessed of sufficient means to live a gentleman's life. But Matthew Flinders was prepared to work for the honours that might be bestowed upon him and expected to earn the rewards due to him by venturing further and daring more than any other man had done before him. Governor de Caen was not such a man, but rather one of great self-importance, who felt that greatness was his entitlement. The two men had nothing but ambition in common.

And so Trim made the greatest mistake of his life when, after several months, he managed to find himself alone in the library with de Caen. Trim was quite unaware that he was already a well-known cat among the island's better families. The fact that the famous English prisoner possessed a great affection for a cat was the subject of dinner conversation whenever the matter of the stubborn

Englishman was brought up. Trim had been oft seen and described, a large black cat with a white star blaze on his chest and a similar dab of snow to his chin, with gloves to match on all four paws. The slaves at the governor's residence also knew of the Englishman's cat and he became affectionately known as La Treem. No other cat on the island possessed similar markings, most being of the tabby variety, so that even the governor was well aware of the existence of Trim Flinders.

On the particular night that Trim appeared, as if an apparition, licking a snowy paw and seated on the Afghan carpet not five feet from where the governor sat alone, the Frenchman was very drunk. He had consumed two bottles of wine at dinner and was now on his fourth cognac of the night and was feeling maudlin and sorry for himself, slumped in his armchair, in appearance half asleep.

Trim had often observed his master in a vacant and pensive mood and knew that he preferred nothing better than his leaping quietly on to his master's lap so that he might feel the comfort of his presence without disruption of his quietude. Seeing the governor in what seemed a very similar mood, Trim thought to act in the same manner. With great dignity he had ceased cleaning his paws and with a soft meow walked three steps towards the governor before he leapt into his lap, landing so softly that it was as if a feather had fallen from the ceiling.

But this was not how the Frenchman saw it. By nature a dangerously vindictive man, and now drunk, he observed Matthew Flinders, the hated Englishman who refused to bow to his authority, seated on the carpet not far from where he sat. He had taken the form of a cat and, in the nature of an Englishman, was calmly licking his paws before he attacked. He watched, mesmerised, as Matthew Flinders came towards him and, with a great leap that seemed to set fire to the air, landed on his lap. De Caen screamed, though the drink had muted his voice and nobody in the sleeping house heard him. He grabbed Matthew Flinders about the throat and squeezed as hard as he could, the brandy and the wine inuring him against the pain as he felt his waistcoat ripped apart and the linen of his shirt torn asunder as the devil Englishman tore at his very heart. But he was a big man and enormously strong and he held his grip on the great navigator's neck until at last he felt the resistance gone.

In the morning, Eloise du Preez, the black cook, found him snoring, his chest splattered with blood and his hands still around her precious rat-bringing cat, La Treem, who lay silent as if asleep in her hated master's lap, his snowy front paws stained red and touching as if in prayer.

Vale Trim Flinders.

Trim was buried by one of the slaves beside a small stream where the water bubbled over rock and where slave women went to wash their clothes. Slowly the story of La Treem, the Englishman's cat who had decided to assassinate the hated Governor de Caen when England had been at war with France, became a part of the folklore among the blacks of the island. When the now famous Paul Etienne Laurent le Juge de Segrais, or Monsieur Seagrass, now a famous botanist, was tending his marvellous botanical garden, Le Jardin de Pamplemousse, he heard the story told by one of the black gardeners and asked to be taken to the grave of the redoubtable La Treem. Here he planted the grove of Flinders' Palms, which die after flowering and throw seedlings that will flower again in a hundred years. This year, 2002, will be the second blossoming of the clump of palms originally planted over Trim's grave. Vale La Treem.

2002

The Queenie, Marion Bentson, proprietor of Kings Cross Dressers Pty Ltd, a registered travel agency, and secretary and part-owner of The Boys' Boutique, a men's social club in Kings Cross, and Alf Petersen, public servant and owner of the Flag Hotel, joint owner with Bentson of the travel agency and social club, were charged with importing and exporting pornography, videotaping sexual acts between adults and children and, along with Mohammed Suleman, with supplying prohibited drugs to a juvenile. They were also charged on fifteen other counts, for which a jury found there was not sufficient evidence for a conviction.

Marion Bentson received four years' imprisonment with a non-parole period of three years, Petersen received six years for the same offences as Bentson but additionally for carnal knowledge of juveniles while in the employ of the Department of Community Services.

Of the six men found on the premises of The Boys' Boutique on the night of the raid, four were charged with aggravated indecent assault of a child on the evidence given by Mr John 'Monkey' Burns and supported with a videotape taken by Mr Burns on the premises, showing them indecently assaulting three under-age girls and one boy. They each received eighteen months. The other two were not charged. The six children found on the premises on the night of the raid were eventually placed in foster homes. As Marcus Eisenstein had once said to Billy, 'That is why the law is an ass, we do not even have a legal definition for a paedophile.'

This year Ryan Sanfrancesco turned seventeen and entered the Sydney Conservatorium of Music on a scholarship. He also moved out of the home of Con and Maria Poleondakis where he had spent the past five years and nine months thoroughly indulged by the six women in Con's entourage.

Billy and Dorothy Flanagan were married last year in a civil ceremony and Ryan chose of his own accord to move in with them. Billy is again practising as a barrister-at-law, specialising in sexual abuse cases and the defence of juvenile offenders. He is also chairman of the newly formed Committee on Children and Young People. He hasn't touched a drop of alcohol in six years, two months and six days and he's given up gritting his teeth because the Indian mynah birds have won and the flying shit factories are even more prolific than ever.

In Monday's paper, Billy's eye caught a seven-centimetre column in the sports pages of the *Telegraph*.

Davo Davies wins Lightweight Title!

Last night, Davo 'The Beamer Boy' Davies won the New South Wales lightweight title from Trevor 'Bulldog' Wright in a fourth round knockout at the Bankstown RSL. Davies fights out of Team Fenech. Jeff Fenech claims his fighter is ready, and is the No. 1 contender, for the vacant national title to be fought in November.

The sun is setting over Sydney Harbour and Trevor Williams and his wife Bridgit are standing on the balcony of the O'Shannessy two-bedroom apartment in Elizabeth Bay with Ryan, Billy and Dorothy. From where they are, they can see Billy's beloved Royal Botanic Gardens, and the first of the fruit bats taking to the air. They have just returned from Rookwood Cemetery after attending the burial service held for Kartanya Williams, who died of a heroin overdose three days ago. They are drinking to Caroline's memory with Con's special Greek grape juice.

It is a lovely early spring evening and, with the light just beginning to fade, Trevor takes his harmonica from his pocket and begins to play. Ryan, listening to the first few bars, starts to sing to his accompaniment in a beautiful light tenor voice:

Southern trees bear a strange fruit,
Blood on the leaves and blood at the root,
Black body swinging in the Southern breeze,
Strange fruit hanging from the poplar trees.

Pastoral scene of the gallant South,
The bulging eyes and the twisted mouth,
Scent of magnolia sweet and fresh,
And the sudden smell of burning flesh!

Here is a fruit for the crows to pluck,
For the rain to gather, for the wind to suck,
For the sun to rot, for a tree to drop,
Here is a strange and bitter crop.